Shadow Rising

A Novel of the Shadow World

Dianne Sylvan

ISBN: 1979234507
ISBN-13: 978-1979234504

ALSO BY DIANNE SYLVAN

The Shadow World Novels:
Queen of Shadows
Shadowflame
Shadow's Fall
Of Shadow Born
Shadowbound
Shadowstorm

The Agency Series, Volumes 1-5

Nonfiction Books:
The Circle Within: Creating a Wiccan Spiritual Practice
The Body Sacred

Part One

The Raven's Blade

Chapter One

Silence in Avilon.

For hours, as the night deepened and the cold grew bitter, not a leaf stirred in the woods that ringed the fallen Sanctuary.

At first the noise was deafening. Screams of panic and then pain; the guttural shouts of the human men, the strange rapid percussion of their weapons; fire roaring, buildings collapsing.

Gradually the human sounds faded, and eventually so did the conflagration. Every half hour or so another wall or roof would cave in somewhere.

Only the occasional wail of a child, quickly shushed by whatever adult had grabbed her to run into the forest, gave any sign that anyone still lived at all.

They wouldn't survive out here much longer. It was midwinter, and though their dwellings had been warm, the forest was not. They had all been driven out of bed by the chaos and hadn't had time to even grab a cloak or shoes. Eventually they would have to leave the relative safety of the underbrush and venture back toward the fires…toward the bodies…their families, friends, lovers…piled up and burned like cordwood, many while still alive.

Neali had not seen the pyres. She was grateful for at least that small grace. Her dwelling had stood on the edge of the Sanctuary and the fires had been lit close to the center, near the Temple. The buildings there were closer together and the fire spread happily with plenty of fuel--animate and inanimate--to devour. She had been on her way home from a Bardic performance and didn't have as far to run for cover.

Inaliel fussed quietly on her hip. She shifted the babe from left to right, trying to find a comfortable position for them both.

Where was Aila? Neali had heard the infant crying and found her hidden among the roots of a tree, but Inaliel's mother was nowhere to be found. Aila must have run back toward danger, the way Healers always did, willing to give her own life but not her daughter's. If the humans had caught her with Inaliel the child would have been thrown on the pyre for certain.

Were any of the Enclave still alive? Was there anyone left to lead what was left of Avilon?

What were they going to do? The Veil had been breached. It could be again. How could they stay here and rebuild when the humans knew how to find them?

And that was, of course, assuming they survived the night.

Her eyes burned with tears and with smoke. She tried not to think about the ashes that were floating through the air. Someone she knew could be coating her face right now. The mere thought made her so nauseated she nearly dropped the baby.

She didn't understand. None of them did. She could see the utter bewilderment on the faces of those hiding nearby. Filthy, frozen, exhausted, grief-stricken, one and all, their centuries-long dream of peace murdered in front of them. Why would anyone do this? Humans were barbaric and evil, but...what purpose did this serve?

It might not serve any. Humans could invent reasons to hate with hardly any effort. The Elentheia had been made to help their human cousins, but humanity had turned on them. Now it seemed they were doing it all over again.

Suddenly weak, she turned her back against the tree where she and Inaliel were hiding and slid down to the cold, hard ground, holding the baby to her chest almost desperately.

Little Inaliel seemed unconcerned now that things were quiet again. Elflings were often tended to by adults other than their parents, and often ran in packs around the Sanctuary having a meal at one house, games at another, sleep at a third. Neali had never liked children much but she wasn't about to leave the babe alone and frightened.

Inaliel looked up at her, lavender eyes – her mother's shade, light and almost heathered--wide and worried in the darkness. She patted Neali's face with both her chubby hands, apparently trying to comfort her. Neali had to smile at that--Healing instinct always bred true.

Not far away she heard the rustle of leaves and the snap of a branch. Someone was going out. Neali pushed herself back up so she could peer through the brush and see who had been so brave, so desperate, or so mad.

The woman who stepped out of the woods and hesitantly walked toward the main path into the Sanctuary wore a blue cloak, marking her as a Weaver. After a moment Neali recognized her: Kalea. It made sense she would be one of the first; Kalea was known for her fearlessness.

Kalea moved like a deer, testing the air, every sense on alert. Gradually, though, her posture straightened, her breathing deepened.

Then there was a sound behind her, and Kalea spun toward it, eyes going wide and face ghostly white. She seemed suddenly paralyzed as she stared down the path, and Neali saw why.

The air was shimmering. It began to turn to water, that water to expand.

A portal. They were coming back. *Oh Theia--save us--*

She wanted to yell to Kalea to run, but she too was unable to move. She could feel the fear all around her rising, closing in on panic, everyone getting ready to try and escape again, deeper into the forest perhaps...but they were all exhausted, many injured. How could they keep running? And where was there to go?

The portal grew large enough for an adult to pass through, and she saw it opening. Moonlight poured through, along with a blast of cold, damp wind that smelled of mud and something vaguely mechanical.

There was a burst of light, and then the portal disappeared.

Neali's mind was running in circles: Surely not many humans could have traversed the Veil in that much time. The portal had only been open long enough for a handful of people to pass. Could the remaining Elves perhaps mount some kind of defense? Or was the thought so ludicrous it would be better to simply surrender?

A scream grew in her throat. Fear and shock and horror clawed through her. She wanted to flee but she couldn't. They were all going to die.

She heard a gasp.

Kalea's paralysis broke, as did her composure, and she clapped her hands over her mouth in astonishment as she stared at the two figures who had walked out of the portal.

It only took Neali a moment to realize why, mere seconds before Kalea said in a harsh whisper, "My son."

There were two of them, one considerably taller than the other, both in human dress--but their semblance to mortals ended abruptly right there. The taller had the slender grace of their own, though his hair was oddly short. Even without strong Sight Neali could see the fathomless well of power within him. He was being fed, it seemed, from somewhere she couldn't make sense of--but also from his companion.

For his part, he had an aura uncannily like an Elf's, but the shining moonlight of their blood ran deep below the surface. If he'd been human, she would have pinned a young age on him, but the youth of his features was belied by his eyes. He was old, she realized...very old...and very powerful...and very dangerous. He held himself regally, yet was at ease in his own skin the way dancers often were. She saw several flashes of silver in his face, and another much larger at his hip.

A sword? What use were swords when there were weapons such as the humans had?

Her eyes fell on what the second figure wore at his throat, and she stared into the stone for a long minute, trying to understand what she was seeing. In fact they both wore the amulets, with identical green stones that glowed softly in the night.

Kalea came forward and embraced the first visitor fiercely. "At last you have come home."

Neali knew whom she was looking at, of course. She hadn't known him personally, but there was no one in Avilon unfamiliar with the twins. They had both been the center of controversy and gossip for decades...even more so in the last few years.

"Nico," Kalea said, her voice uncharacteristically close to hysteria, "Where is your brother? And Lesela? What has happened to everyone? And why did this happen?" She swept her arm back toward the smoldering remains of their home.

Nicolanai Araceith held her tightly for a second before kissing the top of her head and drawing back a little. "There is little time," he said. "I will tell you everything, but we must get everyone out of here before the humans come back."

"We're being watched," his companion said quietly, eyes on the woods.

"Human?" Nico asked, hands tensing on his mother's arms.

"No. There are no humans left here."

Nico nodded. He stepped away from the others and faced the trees, speaking calmly and not loudly, but Neali knew everyone would hear.

"You are not safe here," he said. "We've come to offer you asylum at our Haven. Everyone is welcome. You will be well protected under the watchful eye of the Signet of the South, and there is warmth and food and clean clothes. Once we can be sure the humans will not return, we can help you rebuild. Of course you are free to stay here in the woods where it's cold and wait for them to come back…but if you wish to follow me, make yourselves known here on the path in the next twenty minutes."

He bowed, then turned away, letting those riveted to his words make their decisions in semi-private. "Do you think there are many alive in the Sanctuary?" he asked Kalea.

She looked doubtful. "There may be some trapped in the houses, or who found hiding places. I would guess many are injured."

Nico's companion spoke up. "As soon as we have the majority through the portal we'll come back with a group of Healers--we'll save as many as we can."

Kalea seemed to realize he was there for the first time, and stared at him, her mind probably about as awhirl as Neali's. Nico saw her expression and actually laughed.

"I know, he's a little confusing," Nico said. His companion shot him a look that only made him laugh more. "I suppose now's as good a time as any for introductions. Weaver Kalea Ithdirriali, meet Prime Deven Burke."

Kalea nodded slowly, still looking him over critically. "I see," she said. "So you are my son's Ghost. I have heard quite a lot about you."

The Prime bowed. "I am certain you already dislike me, Lady Weaver." he told her with a faint smile. "I have been the cause of much of your son's suffering. But I am trying to make up for it. Since we're immortal I may even have time."

The Weaver gave one last nod--a bit curt, but not unkind. Then her expression changed. "You are Lesela's grandchild," she said.

"I am."

Kalea looked around--Elves had started to emerge from the forest, in twos and threes at first, gathering on the path, huddled in the cold. "Where is Aila? Has anyone seen her?"

A new, male voice said, "I saw her in the thick of it, helping Berren free himself from wreckage. That was the last time."

He walked up to the head of the column, and Neali sighed. Of course it was Thestel. The next surviving member of the Enclave had to be the Elf who had lobbied so hard for Nico's banishment. He was glaring daggers at Nico and strode right up to him, practically in his face.

There was cold fury in his voice. "As far as I am concerned this is your fault--you were the only Weaver in the mortal realm, and only a Weaver or a Gatestone made by a Weaver could have created that portal. You brought your blood and darkness here to our Sanctuary and now look at the consequences. What reason have we to trust you with our lives? You are nothing more than a monster, and not one of us."

Prime Deven took a single step forward, his hand lifting to rest on the hilt of his sword. Neali couldn't be sure because of the lack of light, but it looked for all the world like his already-pale eyes went almost silver.

"You will take a step back," he hissed. "Of he and I only one of us is a monster, and you don't want to find out which."

To his credit, Thestel went pale and moved back. He couldn't seem to stop staring at this dark, inhuman creature standing in Avilon threatening him bodily harm.

Nico held a hand out toward the Prime, and the other toward Thestel. "That's enough out of both of you," he said firmly. "There's been enough violence tonight. Thestel, you're welcome to hate me--or fear me, rather--all you want, but everyone here will either die or be taken captive if you stay, and trust me, death would be better."

Kalea let out a breath that sent a cloud into the air. "I ask again--has anyone seen Aila? Or Inaliel? I assume Aila didn't have the child with her."

Finally, Neali took a deep breath of her own and, lifting the baby up higher, left the cover of the trees and joined the growing throng on the path. She swallowed hard as she got close to the front. "Here, Lady Weaver. I have Inaliel."

"Thank Theia," Kalea said. "And thank you, Neali, for taking charge of her. Did Aila hand her off?"

"No. I came upon the wee one in the woods beside a tree. Aila was nowhere to be found."

Kalea held out her arms, and Neali gratefully gave up the baby. Her arms hurt from holding the child so tightly for so long.

Kalea turned back to her son and his...person. "Not long after you left Avilon, Lesela introduced me to one of the Healers I had not yet met, though I had heard of her by reputation. As soon as I saw them together I knew what I was seeing: Lesela and her daughter."

"Elendala Seara," Deven said softly.

She nodded. "She had lived quietly for all these years, devoted to her work but mostly solitary. Lesela helped her stay out of the Enclave's view until enough time had passed that her human traits had faded and she was indistinguishable from the rest of us. Not long ago Aila took up with a Bard, and little Inaliel was born only eight months ago."

Deven's eyes had gone wide and he shifted back away from Kalea.

Nico, however, was smiling. "How about that," he said. "You have a sister, Dev. And look...she's even got your eyes."

"I..."

Nico saw the look on his face and put his arms around him quickly. "I'm sure Aila's alive, and even if she isn't we won't have any trouble finding someone to take care of the baby. One thing at a time."

Finally Deven nodded. "Right. Let's get everyone organized." He walked off to the side a bit, gaze sweeping over the assembly--counting, Neali realized.

Kalea and Nico were exchanging a look. "Lesela is dead, isn't she," Kalea said quietly.

Nico looked at the ground, then shut his eyes. "Yes. I'm sorry."

"You needn't be sorry, my child…unless of course you killed her."

The last part was clearly meant as a halfhearted jest, but Nico looked so stricken that Kalea turned scarlet, tears forming in her eyes. She turned away, hand over her mouth again.

"I'll tell you everything as soon as we're settled," Nico said. His voice was shaky.

Her child's distress broke through her shock--Kalea immediately looked at him again and took his hand, squeezing it. He looked relieved, and was about to say something when Deven returned.

"Ninety-six," he said. "Eighty adults, six babies, and ten older children."

"Less than a third of the population," Kalea said, tears finally spilling. "Dear Goddess."

"Nico, we need to move," Deven said, returning to his side. "We've already been here too long. Not to mention every finger and toe here is going to end up frostbitten if it's not already."

"All right," Nico said. "Mother, if you and Thestel could get everyone into a double line--once the portal is open start sending them through in twos."

Kalea frowned. "Do you not want my assistance? It will take you hours to build a portal without help, let alone keep it open that long. We can gather the remaining Weavers."

Nico blinked at her, then grinned. "Don't worry. I've got all I need."

Clearly unconvinced but too worried about the others to argue, Kalea turned to Thestel and gestured for him to go with her.

Neali stayed where she was near the front of the line, close enough to watch what happened while the others got organized. She started to offer her help several times, but she couldn't help it…she was afraid of him. She was afraid of both of them, but not just because they were vampires.

It was the power. She could sense it even more clearly now that she was nearby. It was black and deep and terrible, though she knew it didn't mean them any harm. She had no way to understand such power; she had lived her whole life, a comparatively short one of 70 years, here in Avilon where power arose from the moon and stars and trees, from the river, the stone; this seemed to come from dark dreams and shadows, both death and rebirth from the same source. And as she watched Nico lift his hands to begin the portal, and Deven moved up behind him and placed a hand on his back, she could see that power as it rose up, expanded...and looked for all the world like great black wings.

She watched with her Sight, mad with curiosity to see him work. He raised the Web and spun it around so the air in front of him was aligned with the threads. Neali's eyes widened; she'd never seen anyone bring up the vision so quickly or move through it with so little exertion.

He then took hold of two strands of the Web and gently but firmly pulled them apart. In front of him, the air began to shimmer.

Neali was speechless. No, he didn't need any other Weavers. Compared to the amount of power he was using, apparently without effort, the entire corps of Weavers in Avilon – before tonight, anyway--could have pooled their strength and barely touched him.

He was drawing energy from Deven, and because of the latter's Elven blood...and whatever their connection was...they worked together like a single being in two bodies.

The portal grew large enough for three or four people to walk through abreast in less than five minutes. As it opened, she smelled the same air and earth as when they had arrived, felt the wet cold of wherever it was they were going. After a moment the portal cleared and she could see it, as well: a vast garden draped opulently in moonlight, with the heads of night-blooming flowers nodding somnolently in the breeze.

And there, waiting for them on the far side, was a woman in black, a tumble of curly red hair falling over her shoulders, authority and calm written in every inch of her countenance. Another glowing stone, this one red, shone from her neck; she, too, bore a sword. Framed by the portal and seeming to emerge from the night in a cloak of shadow and mist, she stood with the queenly strength of Theia Herself, wit and intelligence in her green eyes, moonlight in her hair.

Everyone was staring at the woman, but it was obvious to anyone with any degree of Sight that she was no threat, and something about the way she anchored the world they were walking into was reassuring even as it was frightening. In the end it didn't matter anyway--they had nowhere else to go but toward her.

Kalea and Thestel began to usher the Elves through. The first pair held each other's hands tightly and steeled themselves. Neali watched with her heart in her throat as they stepped through the portal.

Once they were through, after two seconds or so, they appeared again on the far side of the portal. The woman there smiled at them and spoke quietly, gesturing down the path for them to keep walking.

Satisfied, Kalea nudged the next pair in. Before long the Elves were passing through in a steady stream.

Neali took a deep breath as her turn came up. She glanced over at Kalea, who was still holding Inaliel. The baby was laughing, clapping her hands and then grabbing at the air, eager to touch the magic she could no doubt See before her.

The last thing Neali saw before Avilon disappeared was Deven, who still stood behind Nico. She saw him look over at the child, and saw him smile.

*****

As large as the Haven was, it wasn't quite big enough to house a horde of Elves without a bit of rearranging. Most of the Elite already shared their quarters, but the upper tier had private rooms; they were temporarily doubled up to free up some space, hopefully just for a night or two. With cots and sofas four adults could easily sleep in a single suite in the main house, and the children would hardly take up any space at all. Once they got a final count and figured out who belonged to what family group, they could work on better arrangements.

Miranda worried, waiting for the portal to open, that the refugees were going to panic when she was the first thing they saw, but there wasn't much choice. Only the Tetrad spoke fluent Elvish, and Nico and Dev would be last through the gate, possibly even later if they needed to stay and search for survivors. Stella had a decent command of basic conversation, so she was inside the house with David helping the Elite direct traffic.

The Queen also fretted about her own linguistic acumen--she'd only had the language in her head for a day. Nico had made sure to transfer it to her before he and Deven left; she was the only one who didn't already speak it. She had practiced a little, but it was so weird to hear a whole different language come out of her own mouth that she stumbled over the words. As long as she took it slowly and enunciated carefully it should be okay, but...

She stood in the garden where the boys had left, trying to stay grounded. She had no idea what to expect from all this--everything had happened so fast. Thank God she was married to the king of logistics; in the last few hours David had gotten the whole thing organized as if putting together a trip to the movies.

Miranda felt the air start to change. *Here we go.*

To their credit the first Elves through the gate didn't freak out when they saw her, or at least they didn't freak any farther out than they'd already freaked. They both drew up short, gripping each other's hands.

Miranda stepped forward and bowed. "Welcome," she said. "Please go to the door that stands open, where the woman in black is waiting. She will send you to the next place."

They looked at each other, nodded at her, and followed her extended right arm toward the Haven. The paved path led straight to the side door where one of the Elite lieutenants was waiting to pass them to the next Elite, and so on, until they reached the first set of empty rooms--and on to the infirmary if necessary where Mo was ready. Up until they got where they were going the Elves didn't really need to talk, and if something came up the Elite were ready to call for a translation.

She had intended to look as imposing as she could, not to scare them, but to reassure them; they needed to feel safe, and even if they knew nothing about the Shadow World they would know they were looking at someone more powerful than the humans who had attacked them. But once they started arriving, filthy and bruised and bloody, some with infants in their arms or children passed out from exhaustion over their shoulders, her resolve cracked, and she extended her empathy to let them know everything would be all right. They were already remarkably calm but she saw a few visibly relax once she'd touched them with her gift, and several of the children stopped crying.

Meanwhile she tried not to stare. It was damn near impossible. She'd never seen anything like it--even injured and in shock the Elves' unbelievable grace was breathtaking. She could only imagine how beautiful they all were on a normal day.

"How is it going, beloved?"

Miranda smiled and surreptitiously tapped on her com. "I feel like I'm in a really weird Pantene commercial."

She heard David laugh. *"Do you need me out there?"*

"I don't think so. So far they're in a bad enough state that they just do what I say without paying much attention to me."

"Good. I think the two of us together might give them all coronaries."

"How are things in there?"

"Well, first they come around the corner staring at everything. Then they see me and turn white, or whiter. Then they take a second to decide if they're going to bolt. Once I start talking they decide I'm either not the devil or the devil has clean sheets and is their new favorite person. Overall they're just relieved. Stella is apparently giving lessons on human-world plumbing."

"What, they don't have flush toilets in Avilon?"

"Oh, they do, they just work differently. And they don't really have showers, just hot springs and strategically managed waterfalls. We're going to be out a fortune in hair dryers."

Miranda held back a giggle. "Okay, there's another group coming. Back to work."

It took nearly half an hour to get them all through. Miranda hoped Nico was okay--she didn't feel him flagging, but Deven was drawing a huge amount of power from her and David to funnel into his Consort.

This was the first time they'd really tested the bond this way; in the weeks since they'd gotten Nico back they'd been working with it systematically, learning how energy flowed among them, and moreover how they connected back to the rest of the Circle. They knew the others could feed them--they'd seen that the night Miranda had her near-disastrous second stab at Weaving. But it was time they got serious about the Circle's dynamics, now that Avi had joined them, and David was being as scientific as he really could be considering they were talking about magic.

It was only three weeks to the Winter Solstice, when they'd attempt the summoning ritual in the Codex. Luckily there didn't seem to be much prep involved aside from painting some symbols on the floor--they needed time to figure out what they were going to do with their new houseguests.

Finally, the last couple of Elves came through--an imposing woman in a blue cloak and a man who looked like he might faint dead away at the sight of Miranda. The woman was carrying an infant.

The woman looked familiar. It took a second to place her, but once she did it was obvious. This had to be Nico and Kai's mother. Miranda didn't remember Nico mentioning a little sister, but the baby might not be hers. It looked like everyone had grabbed any kid nearby regardless of kinship and run like hell.

Miranda bowed to her and asked, "Are you Nicolanai's mother Kalea?"

She froze, caught off guard. "I am," she said cautiously. "And you are?"

"I am Miranda Grey-Solomon, Queen of this Haven. You are most welcome. Is this your daughter?"

"No. She is the child of a friend, and apparently is kin to my son's Ghost."

The baby chose that moment to open her eyes, and Miranda's mouth fell open.

Kalea half-smiled at her astonishment. Before she could say anything, however, the portal behind her began to collapse. Miranda's veins ran cold with fear for a moment--had something gone wrong? She didn't feel anything wrong. But would she this far away?

Kalea noticed her distress. "They stayed behind to have a quick look around the Sanctuary for survivors but said they would be back well before sunup."

"Yes, of course. Um...if you'll follow this path to the open door, my people will guide you the rest of the way to a room and medical attention if you need it."

Kalea bowed slightly to avoid jostling the baby, and she and her companion, who had stood there staring at Miranda the whole time, headed toward the Haven.

She wasn't sure if she should follow or wait here for the boys. She was too anxious for them, however, to leave, so she sat down on the stone bench a few yards away and let David know what was going on.

"All through," she said. "The portal's closed but the boys are having a last sweep of the place before they come back. And you'll never guess who I just met."

"Someone from Keebler?"

"No, even better: Nico's mom…and Deven's sister."

A pause. *"Sister?"*

"Half-sister, anyway. She's maybe six months old, so unless they somehow turned Dev's dad into an Elf she has a different father. I can't wait to hear what he thinks."

"Does that mean they found his mother?"

"I don't know. I'll ask when they get back. Do you need me? If not I'm going to wait here."

"Not at present. We've got almost everyone settled. If something changes I'll call."

Miranda pulled her coat more tightly around her. It was a cold night; just in the last hour frost had begun to form on the plants.

She took out her phone and looked over the network and her email, trying to fill the time without sitting there fretting. This had to be a nightmare for Nico…after what had happened with Lesela, and Kai's hijacking by that bastard Prophet, seeing his home destroyed could very well destroy him. But every time she thought he was broken beyond the point of no return, he somehow made it…and this time was very different. This time he had Deven.

Actually they all had Deven. She smiled.

The Pair had worked a miracle on each other. No, everything wasn't magically all better, but the balance they'd found had done wonders for them both. She knew they both had nightmares, and Nico was dreading the coming New Moon in three days, but he had shed so much fear in the last few weeks, just as Deven had shed years and years of despair. It was amazing to watch. So was their partnership; she'd never seen two people share energy so seamlessly.

It was strange, but ever since the Tetrad had formed Miranda had been…happy. She wasn't delirious with joy or anything, especially given everything looming over their heads, but something about this crazy new reality of theirs was giving her a sense of contentment she'd never had before. Being with David had always felt like exactly where she belonged, and it had been wonderful even when it was awful, but now it felt like some circuit she hadn't known existed in her had been completed. She was sure she'd lost her mind until she took a chance and mentioned it to David, who had, to her surprise, said he felt the same way.

They'd been a magnificent Pair, and still were. But now they were all so much more than that. Wherever all this went, whatever their eventual fates, she was thankful to have had this for however long it lasted.

Miranda frowned. Hopefully she hadn't just damned her luck.

*****

"My home," Nico said softly.

Deven turned back to him, the loss in the Elf's voice almost unbearable. "You can stay back near the portal," he told the Consort gently. "We can handle this."

Nico shook his head. "No, I need to see. And I want to know if my house or Mother's is still standing."

Nodding, Deven started along the path again, glancing over at their companion, a Healer named Ethelin. She had volunteered to stay behind and help them search the ruins for anyone still alive. They'd needed at least one person with them who would calm anyone they found--God only knew what the Elves thought of Deven, and the difference in Nico from his life here was so profound it would upset them. This way they could have Ethelin do the talking.

It became readily apparent, however, that there weren't going to be many survivors...if any. Deven wasn't surprised. The only hope the Elves had had was to reach the trees and hide.

Part of the Sanctuary was still burning, and the smoke choked them even before they'd reached the first orderly row of houses. The dwellings on the outer rim were the least damaged; if nothing further befell Avilon in the next few days their owners would be able to salvage many of their belongings. The closer they drew to the center, however, the worse it got.

When they came to the first bodies Deven had to keep Nico from collapsing. Ethelin gave a wail of anguish and turned away, unable to take another step.

According to Kalea most of the dead had been burned. But some had been left where they'd fallen, like broken dolls discarded by a distracted child. Deven moved closer and bent, closing violet eyes fixed on the night sky.

They'd all been killed the same way: Bullets. Morningstar had come here and opened fire the way they couldn't on vampires. Elves could survive a lot, and one gunshot even to a vital area probably wouldn't kill them before they could get help, but a burst from a machine gun would, especially if there were no Healers near. Some had been so disfigured by blood and bullets they were barely recognizable as Elves.

"Don't come closer," Deven said sharply when he heard Ethelin creeping up next to him. "You don't need to see this. It won't do any good."

"He's right," Nico agreed, voice hoarse, no doubt from mourning cries he couldn't let out. "You don't want to remember them like this. Just keep walking. Look for the living."

It went on like that until they'd reached the town center, where almost nothing remained but giant piles of ash and scorched wood...and bodies. Most of the dead who had burned here were already dust, but here and there half a corpse protruded from a pile of blackened timbers, or part of an arm remained in a burnt-out pyre. The stench was incredible, and Deven hoped against hope that at least Ethelin wouldn't realize what she was smelling; according to Nico Elves normally didn't eat meat so it was unlikely most of them had any frame of reference for burning flesh.

"Mother's house was over here," Nico murmured, deviating from the main path.

Deven waited behind for a moment, breathing deeply, fighting down violent tremors of his own.

Don't think about it. Don't think about it.

Everywhere he looked were fallen buildings and scorched earth. Roofs had fallen on people, trapping them...trapped in the dark, bleeding out, and so scared...no comfort in those last moments, only torment...

You can't fall apart now--he needs you. Lock it away until later.

"Look," Nico called, voice tight with pain.

Dev joined him in front of a pile of burnt out wood and stone, where Nico was moving quietly among the debris, looking for anything salvageable. His eyes were wet when they met Deven's.

"I was born right here where I'm standing," Nico said. "Only a few minutes after Kai. We grew up in this house."

Deven reached out to him, lay a hand on his shoulder. "I'm sorry, Nico."

The Elf only nodded, giving the ruin one last look before he walked away, expression bleak and bewildered.

They picked through the ruins for several hours, until it grew close enough to sunrise that the air had taken on that feeling of wrongness that only vampires ever experienced. By then they'd made it to the far side, where Nico's house had been; he'd lived on the fringes of his own world, solitary and quiet, until he followed the call of prophecy and compassion and his life had cantered merrily into hell.

"There," Nico said. "It's still there."

It was a little house, just big enough for one, unassuming yet lovely. All the structures in Avilon had been painted and carved intricately with vines and flowers and forest creatures, or scenes from their folklore and mythology. Nico's house was no exception, but unlike most of the others his still stood and was mostly unharmed. The front door had been ripped from its hinges, probably so the humans could search inside for its occupants; they had dragged every Elf who didn't make it to the trees into the town center, chosen a couple dozen to take back to Earth, and murdered all those who didn't make the cut.

The inside was a shambles, but not everything had been destroyed. Nico had lived here as he did at the Haven: surrounded by books and plants. Even wrecked the place had the lingering trace of Nico's presence, and Deven touched a wall or shelf here and there, almost smiling. He wished he could stay here for a while, in a place so much a part of the Elf, one that meant so much to him he never spoke of it. Perhaps if the Elves rebuilt the Sanctuary he could help Nico restore this place.

"I brought everything with me that really mattered," Nico was saying as he stepped over broken furniture and gathered up a few last belongings. "But there have been a couple of things I've found myself wishing for, and one or two I think Mother would like to have. Give me just a minute..."

Deven stayed out of the way; they still had time. Nico emerged from another room--the only other, it looked like--with a bag in which he'd stowed his treasures. He slung it on his shoulder and gave the little house a long, searching look.

When he turned back to Deven his eyes were damp again. "Okay…let's go."

Ethelin was standing on the path, staring back at the Sanctuary, which they could see almost in its entirety from here. It wasn't a large town, its main section branching off the central circle, a web-like arrangement of houses, shops, and schools. The whole thing was about half the size of the Haven property in Austin. The view here must have been breathtaking before tonight. Now, it revealed only a wasteland…and a graveyard.

"We didn't find anyone," Ethelin said, heartsick. "I thought surely there would be a few."

"Where are the rest of the bodies?" Nico asked. "As many as there were in the Commons it wasn't enough--and if they only took twenty alive there should be dozens more."

Deven sighed. "They piled them inside the houses," he replied, "then set fire to the walls. Even if the bodies weren't reduced to ash there will be debris covering them."

He coaxed the two Elves back down the path the way they'd come; Nico could have built a new portal here but there was always the possibility that a straggler or two had appeared in the meantime where they'd started.

"Do you want to check your house?" Nico asked Ethelin.

She shook her head and resolutely didn't look at the destruction as they passed. "I saw it already, on the way in, or what was left of it. Only the chimney still stands."

"I'm sorry."

She looked at Nico keenly. "Is it true what they're saying? That this happened because of you?"

Deven watched Nico's face, unsure what the answer would be--he expected Nico to claim guilt, but instead the Weaver said, "I made the Gatestone for Kai, and the humans stole it. And the only reason he came to Earth in the first place was to help me. But I think perhaps it would be more productive to place the blame on those who burned this place to the ground and murdered all our friends. No matter what hand I had in it, their leader chose to do this. And it is he who will pay for it."

Nico didn't add that first they had to find a way to get the Prophet out of Kai's body. Best not to drop that particular bomb on just anyone.

They made the rest of the trek in silence, pausing here and there to double check an empty house or pile of rubble that caught their attention.

Now and then he saw a look of despair or panic cross Nico's face, and reached out to him both with a hand and with energy, keeping him steady. There would be time to weep later, at home in the safety and quiet of one of their suites, either in each other's arms or with the whole Tetrad. Just a little longer, and Nico could exhale again.

Finally, they reached the part of the path where the survivors had departed, and with a heavy sigh Nico got ready to open another portal.

As soon as the gateway stood open Ethelin darted through as if the horror she'd seen here was snapping at her heels. Deven, still holding his palm against Nico's back, slid his hand around to take the Weaver's and lead him through. Once Nico took his attention from keeping it open the portal would fall shut in about thirty seconds, long enough for them to pass.

Their eyes met. Then Nico lowered his head to rest on Deven's shoulder, and they held on to each other tightly a moment before taking that last step through the portal and leaving Avilon behind.

*****

As soon as they were back at the Haven Nico went looking for his mother, and found her at the infirmary where Mo was giving the baby a looking-over. All the children had been brought for a quick examination even if they weren't obviously injured, as the smoke inhalation was worse for them. Two others sat in the clinic with oxygen masks over their fair little faces.

Kalea and Nico embraced, and she even had a smile for Deven, who again hung back so none of the other Elves around would be distracted or made anxious by his presence. He stood near the door, arms crossed, fighting two strange urges: one to go get a closer look at the baby and another to run screaming into the night.

"If you'd like, Mother, you can stay in my suite," Nico said. "You and Inaliel will have more space and privacy and you might find the atmosphere in here more soothing."

Kalea looked at him, dubious. "I have no desire to intrude."

"You wouldn't be. I spend most days with my Lord anyway." Nico glanced over at Deven inquisitively--up to now they had never made assumptions about who would sleep where on the days they were alone together, but ended up wherever they ended up.

Deven nodded.

Kalea visibly relaxed once they had her in Nico's suite, and Deven could understand why; of all the places in the Haven where she could stay, this one was the closest thing to Avilon she would find. The bedroom was full of the gentle, verdant feel of Nico's energy.

They settled Inaliel, who'd been given a clean bill of health from a bemused Mo, in a sort of corral made of pillows on the bed, and Kalea went to shower and change into the robe Nico gave her. She'd be one of the few Elves sleeping in familiar clothing. The rest would have to make do with the mountain of clothes the Elite had donated or lent. A preliminary shipment of food and supplies had already arrived but tomorrow would bring the first big delivery to a Signet-owned warehouse in town where the Elite would bring it the rest of the way to the Haven.

Once they had the Weaver and the baby settled, the Pair left for the Signet Suite, where David and Miranda were waiting for a debriefing on the night's events.

Miranda got up from her chair and came over to embrace Nico. "How are you holding up?" she asked.

Nico didn't know how to answer that, but managed, "Better than most of the others." He still hadn't been able to let his grief show, and probably wouldn't for a few more hours. Deven had seen many, many people endure too many calamities over the years and knew the general timeline.

They quickly went over the numbers and a rundown of how many Elves were sheltered where in the building. It turned out relocating the Elite hadn't been necessary--there were far fewer survivors than they'd hoped. The displaced Elite had already returned to their quarters.

"We've got a truck coming this afternoon that's just supplies for the babies," Miranda told them. "It didn't even occur to me to think about stuff like cribs and diapers. They only have to get by for a few more hours, though."

"Most of the injuries Mo reported were superficial," David added. "There were a handful of broken bones and lacerations that needed stitches but mostly it was bruises and smoke inhalation--not to mention traumatic stress. We're going to need to keep an eye on everyone's mental health as much as physical."

Miranda looked over at Dev. "How are you?" she asked. "That can't have been easy...all those fallen buildings."

He had to smile. Of course she would think about that, even when Nico hadn't. "I'm all right."

Nico looked dismayed and embarrassed. "I'm sorry," he said. "It never even occurred to me..."

"Nor should it have," he replied. "You had enough to worry about. I can handle it."

"Not to call bullshit on your resiliency, Dev," David said, "but I call bullshit. After the last two years we're not taking anything for granted with either of you. Now, do you two want to stay here tonight?"

He and Nico exchanged a look. "No, that's all right," Nico told David. "I think I'd prefer to stay in Dev's room, if he doesn't mind."

Deven smiled. "Of course I don't, silly Elf."

Miranda nodded. "I figured as much--but if you decide you need more support, we're here."

She reached over and squeezed the Elf's hand. He smiled at her. "Thank you, my Lady."

"You said there's no way to break the spell that makes a Gatestone," David said. "So basically it will never be safe for them to go home."

"It cannot be broken," Nico affirmed, "but it will wear off. Even if it were never used the spell upon it would fade within three years at most, and factoring in the number of trips Kai had already taken I imagine they have a half-dozen more portals or six months' time, whichever runs out first. But we cannot predict how they will use it."

"Then we'll need to come up with a more long-term solution." David frowned, thoughtful. "Obviously we can't relocate them all to the city; they'll need something as close to nature as we can provide. It will have to be secure, or at least someplace we can *make* secure."

Deven lowered his eyes to the fireplace, just listening.

"Is anyplace really secure?" Miranda asked. "Can't Morningstar go anywhere they want with the Stone?"

"No," Nico replied. "The Stone is made using Kai's memories; they can only use it to go places he himself has set foot upon. Until coming here he had never left Avilon."

"But they could come here," she said worriedly. "They could be here now."

"In theory, yes, but I would feel it if a portal opened near me. Now that I know they have the Stone I can block any attempt they make. In fact if they try I can latch onto its energy and drain it. The problem isn't really *this* Stone, it's the fact that they have taken Weavers captive; there is always a chance they could force one of them to make a new Stone that will go to Avilon. One or two of those taken have even visited the other Sanctuaries, so they are now in danger too, but I have no way of reaching them to warn them. We may end up with refugees from all three by the end."

He paused, then added, "There is far too much we don't know to say for certain what Morningstar intends or is capable of; I think our best course is to find the refugees a new permanent home. If they can return to Avilon eventually, so be it, but we cannot rely on that hope. Between the Signet forces and my own abilities, we can make a new Sanctuary safer than Avilon ever was. I can seal it completely against the presence or awareness of any human. We just need a location, somewhere the Elves will be comfortable that is defensible, and someplace neither Kai nor any of the other refugees has ever seen."

Deven didn't really intend to make a noise, but apparently they all heard one, and looked at him inquisitively.

He lifted his gaze to Nico and smiled softly. "I think I know the very place."

Chapter Two

Sleep and Nico met only briefly that afternoon, and their encounter was strained. Not only did he lay awake most of the day with his mind running in exhausting circles about Avilon, Kai, and the bleak future of his...well, what had once been his people...there was another problem, one that had been building for weeks, finally growing too intense to ignore in the two days since the refugees had arrived.

It was finally the New Moon. He'd been feeling it inch closer and closer for over a week, and with it a dread like nothing he'd ever known. They'd been given a reprieve after the Tetrad formed--the energy among the four of them had been so overwhelmingly strong it had effectively shielded them all from the worst of the death-lust. They'd all fed normally up until a few days ago when the dust had finally settled and the pull of their Thirdborn nature began to rear its dark, intoxicating head.

He was terrified, yet at the same time craved that hunt so badly he could think of little else, and that terrified him even more. Every second that his mind wasn't occupied with the Elves or his brother or Morningstar, the thought crept into his mind again: *In a few days I will murder a human. After that, I will never stop.*

The others had some kind of coordinated plan to take care of him that night, to keep him calm and safe, as if there truly were a way to ease him into what could be hundreds of years of killing.

He couldn't help but smile at that, as he stood in the bathroom that afternoon washing his face. They were dedicated to his well-being, and the love in their efforts touched him deeply.

Miranda in particular worried over his welfare--she knew what he was feeling, knew what he was facing. She hated it, and hated it for him, but she was determined to make sure his first time was as gentle as it could be. He loved her for it--loved all of them for it.

Thinking of the Queen, and of how good they had all been to him, gave him his first moment of something like acceptance. Yes, it was horrible, what they had to do. But if he must become this creature at least he would return home with these incredible people who had taken him in, given him their love and support when even those whose blood he shared had rejected him. These remarkable beings, his three, lovers and friends and heroes, one and all.

He smiled faintly and reached for a towel. He doubted whatever human he killed would find it a fair trade…but if this was what he had to do to earn the life he had stumbled into, the arms he was about to climb back into…so be it.

His smile grew.

I get to walk through that door and…he'll be there. Right there, next to me, and he'll grab hold of me in his sleep and pull me close, muttering something in Gaelic and winding around me like a climbing vine.

Even as he had the thought, however, he heard a cry of fear in the bedroom, and his own heart clenched.

Nico left the bathroom in time to see blankets erupt in a storm of flailing arms. There was panic, pure and mad and heartrending, in the sound Deven made as he fought himself awake.

Nico was beside him in a heartbeat. "Hey there," he said gently, taking hold of the Prime's arms and shaking him slightly to jostle him the rest of the way awake. "It's all right…you're safe, *l'lyren*. You're safe."

Wide, frightened eyes met his, almost without recognition for a moment. Deven's voice was young and hoarse, though Nico hadn't heard any screaming this time. "The walls are falling," he all but sobbed, clenching Nico's forearms painfully hard. "They're falling…there's no light…I mean there wasn't…and I woke up and you weren't here…"

"I'm here now. I'm here with you." Nico drew him close, letting Deven's hands clutch and pat where they needed to to convince himself Nico was alive.

Even after only a few weeks they had their routines. Deven dreamed about the Haven falling down on him, and of trying to dig Nico out of the wreckage. Nico dreamed of being torn apart and of the cruel humiliating laughter of the Prophet standing over his dismembered but still-living body. Sometimes Dev's nightmare was of Miranda being crushed, or David, and often it started out as Jonathan and cycled through everyone he loved before he ended up dying himself, trapped in the dark in agony. Sometimes Nico looked up to see Kai's face watching the humans carve Nico open and stomp on his internal organs or sew explosives or even living creatures up inside his body cavity. They both woke screaming at least twice a week, usually more. So far they'd managed not to do it on the same night.

Gradually the nightmare faded and Deven grew still, his tremors subsiding, breath deepening. He vacillated between freezing and burning up for a while until the dream lost its power over him.

"Sorry," Nico felt him mutter shakily against the Elf's neck. "I promise I won't always lose my damn mind when you go to the bathroom."

Nico smiled. "No apologies necessary. We both have our monsters in the dark."

Deven burrowed in as closely as he could, and Nico took a moment to bring up the Sight and take a quick look at the energetic matrix he'd built what felt like a lifetime ago to keep the Prime reasonably sane. It rarely needed attention these days, but he didn't want to take that for granted. Just after the Tetrad had formed he'd made a few adjustments to accommodate the increased power moving through it.

As David would say, situation normal. The strands he had Woven around Deven's mind were holding steady without a glitch. It had taken several disasters but the version that he'd come up with the last time was practically a citadel. It wasn't a shield against grief or loss but it kept the foundation of the Prime's mind intact in spite of seven centuries' worth of debilitating pain. It was, Nico thought privately, the most beautiful thing he'd ever Woven.

"Everything okay in there?" Deven asked drowsily.

Nico chuckled. "I didn't think you knew I was looking."

"Mmm." Nico felt a hand sliding around his hip, then up along his back. "I almost always notice you touching me, especially from the inside."

The low purr in the words, and their intimacy, sent a shiver through the Elf.

He recalled Jonathan saying once that for most of their Pairhood Deven had had a fairly low sex drive--he'd happily participate upon request, but didn't often initiate. In the last few years of their relationship that had started to change, to the Consort's delight. David had mentioned something similar; the Prime's need for physical contact waxed and waned.

Nico seemed to have caught Deven on an upswing--whether it was the newness of their relationship, the added energy of the rest of their foursome, or just a returned enthusiasm for being alive, Deven had a tendency to pin him against walls or drag him off to empty rooms without warning.

Honestly Nico didn't care much about the why. He was far too busy enjoying the how.

Case in point.

Then their coms beeped, and they both groaned.

"I know you're awake," came David's voice, terse. *"I need you both in the Batcave."*

Deven rolled his eyes and said, "You have reached the bedroom of two people about to shag like mad rabbits. Unless you plan to participate, please leave a message after the--"

"Tanaka is dead."

The change in Dev's expression was disconcerting to say the least. "What?"

"Mameha isn't."

Taking a deep breath, holding Nico's eyes, Deven said, "Five minutes."

*****

The office echoed with the silence that hung over the conference line. The entire Circle was present, but no one seemed to know what to say; as everyone joined in Pair by Pair, the quiet waiting turned into a vigil.

Miranda sat gripping David's hand, and he hers, tightly; the Prime looked as shocked as she'd ever seen him. So did Dev, for that matter, who mirrored her position on the other side of the desk, fingers laced with Nico's.

Finally, Jacob cleared his throat and said quietly, *"We have her."*

Another pause before he went on, *"The Red Shadow Operatives in Tokyo got to her before Morningstar could, and they got her someplace secure--Tanaka's surviving Elite and mine are coordinating to keep her under guard. Does anyone...how long does she have?"*

Miranda realized she was crying--tears were running down her face even though she hadn't even felt them start. All she could think of was Mameha, the towering woman she'd met only twice and been terrified of both times...a stately, elegant pillar of absolute strength in her midnight-black kimono, gold and silver glistening from the crests around the bottom, her face impassive but her eyes bright with wit. Miranda imagined that woman torn apart by screaming grief, her soul rent to shreds, all the dignity and intelligence in her face giving way to madness before she finally burnt out from the inside and fell dead as her Prime had.

No one was sure exactly what had happened--Tanaka had been attacked while out on business in downtown Tokyo, and Mameha had been home at the Haven, miles away. The Morningstar attackers hadn't tried to kidnap Tanaka to use his Signet for blood magic; but they hadn't just killed him, either, or Mameha would have died instantly. For some reason they'd shattered Tanaka's Signet, leaving Mameha to die slowly. The Order of Elysium's Awakening ritual had used a Bondbreaking to free Persephone...what had Morningstar done?

"Kill her," Miranda said softly.

All eyes turned to her.

"Don't make her go on. Open the door and let her walk out into the daylight if she wants to. Don't make her live like this. Just..."

David immediately pushed his chair back from the desk and turned to her, and she fled into his arms, shaking. She stayed as quiet as she could, not wanting to make the situation even worse with hysterics, but she couldn't keep it all clamped down like he could.

She tried to ground enough to listen to the others, who politely went on around her.

"Maybe a week," Deven said, and though his attention was on the call she felt him offering strength, which she took, as well as more from Nico, then Cora, and all around the Circle--the eight of them were on different continents and some had never met, but they held her, and each other, as closely as they could.

"She'll fade quickly assuming she doesn't find a way to kill herself. She'll either lapse into catatonia or go feral--whatever you do don't let that happen. That's not how she would want to go out."

Jacob took a long, slow breath. *"I don't know if I can kill her,"* he said. *"What if..."*

"Don't, Jacob."

Silence again as it registered that, for the first time since taking her Signet, Cora spoke up in a conference call. She was almost always present for them but stayed out of the spotlight; often she had insights to offer later, once she'd thought it over, but she tended to keep quiet and take everything in first.

Cora sounded a bit surprised at herself, but her voice was firm. *"We have had our miraculous resurrections and the cheating of death,"* she said. *"You know, as do we all, that there will not be one for Queen Mameha. We must let her go if she will go."*

The Prime sighed. *"I know."*

Miranda looked up at David, and to her surprise his eyes were bright with tears; she knew he was thinking about his old friend, and the Queen, but also about Miranda--he'd only seen a moment of what her life had been like after the Bondbreaking but he remembered the pain as well as she did.

Still, he was calm as always as he said, "We have to deal with Japan. Were there any contenders?"

"Not that I know of," Jacob replied. *"My intel suggests there were a few extremely minor warlords with eventual designs on the Signet but none of them were considered a real threat. Tanaka had that territory for a century. He might have been the Council's peacemaker but in his own reign he was about as Zen as a stake to the heart. Not one challenger ever made it close enough to face down his Second in Command."*

"What about Zang?" David asked. "Did they take him out too?"

"Yes. Him and the entire top tier of lieutenants. The battle was, to use the American idiom, epic. Even if the Signet wanted

Zang, it can't have him. Right now there's just a massive power vacuum, and you know what that means."

Miranda watched the acknowledgment settle over David; she'd seen that look before. Her eyes lifted to the glass case where a growing collection of empty Signets hung; so far they were only from North American territories David could manage without stretching his resources too thinly.

Everyone had expected challengers--surely there would be upstarts trying to lay claim to those Signets. But there had not been a single one. David insisted he was only keeping the Primeless territories from falling into chaos, but something very different was happening. As soon as he had his hands on a Signet, took over and reorganized the Elite, absorbing them into his own forces and imposing his temporary rule, that territory was no longer contested. The wars stopped before they could start. No one wanted to take a run at the Signet anymore.

He refused to admit it out loud but they all knew what was really happening. Those unclaimed Signets would never be claimed again...because they already had been. The territories hadn't been placed under protection. They had been annexed. The oldest and most powerful governing body of the Shadow World had been unable to stop David Solomon from reaching out and taking control...no vampire with anything but a death wish would try to do what the Council couldn't.

The Council had claimed that regardless of his intentions that much power was dangerous, and what was there to stop him from taking any territory he wanted from whomever happened to have it if this went on? At the time Miranda had laughed at their paranoia.

She looked up at the Signet map to the vacant territories across the ocean. India was still clawing itself to pieces. Japan had gone dark. David hadn't tried to grab anything outside the US because of the logistical insanity involved...but Tanaka had been his friend. The thought of letting Tanaka's legacy be one of war and bloodshed after all he'd done for the Shadow World was unacceptable.

Her eyes met her husband's. He lifted an eyebrow.

She nodded.

"All right," David said. "Here's what's going to happen."

*****

In her dreams, she heard screaming. Why did she always dream in screaming?

She stood in the center of an inferno, watching helplessly as people--men, women, from all parts of the world--ran in fear, the way she knew the Elves of Avilon had run, fighting blind panic to escape into the forest...a different forest...even though the sounds and the stench of burning were eerily similar.

Where was this? She turned in a circle, feeling strangely disconnected from the carnage, watching the ranks of humans advance on the little cluster of stone buildings so lovingly hidden among the trees. There were two other Avilons out there somewhere, with different names and different customs, but these were no Elves. In fact...

She fixed her gaze on one of the women and followed her as she sprinted for the treeline. Her body moved preternaturally fast, and for just a second Miranda saw it: silver eyes.

Vampires. Vampires? Living out here, like this? This was no Shadow District, it was more like...

...a monastery.

Quickly, she turned back toward the fires and tried to memorize everything she could. What did the trees look like? What kind of weather could she smell in the air? What accents clung to the voices of the vampires trying desperately to escape? The humans were growing closer, but unlike those who had destroyed Avilon these did not have guns. They had crossbows, swords, and it turned out flame throwers. Efficient.

Burn it all down. Bring me the Stone. Kill them all. Only the Stone matters.

Stone? She reached down out of reflex and felt the metal disc attached the back of her Signet. They'd called it a Stone, even though it wasn't one. It had once been in the safekeeping of people like these--creatures of darkness living in quiet, shadow-robed peace.

What did they eat out here in the middle of nowhere? She wondered, unbidden. Deer?

She knew she'd be awake soon--she should have been afraid, or angry, or upset in any way, but apparently this wasn't that kind of vision. All she could do was watch and try to remember.

She needed to know where they were, if there was still time to avert fate. Had this already happened? Was it happening now?

Suddenly a dark-skinned woman running past where she stood froze and turned to her, eyes wide.

The woman was covered in sweat and soot, and all of hell was snapping at her heels, but she stopped and fell to her knees, her hands extending past her head to offer something she was carrying.

"Please, my Lady," she cried. "Please take it--only the Stone matters. Take it and save us all."

Miranda tried to speak, but the woman had already scrambled to her feet and raced away, leaving the thing she'd held out in the grass.

Amid the cacophony and the sound of dozens of bows firing, she stood over the object and bent toward it, wondering what it really was.

To her surprise, it really was a stone...and that wasn't all.

There, in the grass, shining softly in the dark, was an oval-shaped labradorite in a heavy silver setting. The stone was glowing even without a neck to adorn. Her heart froze in her chest. She knew what it was...and to whom...to Whom...it belonged.

A Signet.

The Signet.

She reached toward it, but before she could touch its cool surface, her hold over the dream--if a dream it was--was shaken loose, and she tumbled upward, toward the feeling of someone gently shaking her shoulder.

"Miranda...wake up, beloved. Wake up. It's only a dream."

She laughed as she woke. Only a dream?

No such thing.

*****

"The woman you saw...you said she was black. Was she short, curvy, maybe wearing a dark robe with red trim?"

Miranda let out her breath. "Sounds right."

Deven, too, sighed. She could hear him moving around--getting dressed, probably, for their hunt. The sun would be fully set in an hour. *"It had to have been Xara. She was next in line to take over for Eladra. The amulet you saw wasn't a Signet exactly, though it had the same essential function--they call it the Moriastelethia."*

"Gesundheit," she heard David mutter from his desk.

"What does that mean?" she asked.

"I don't know…it's not Elysian Greek. Back in the day every time I asked Eladra what it meant she said it wasn't ready to be known yet. She loved her damned riddles. But--"

"It's ancient Elvish," Nico said, sounding half asleep. None of them had gotten much rest today. *"Sounds like the archaic dialect from the Codex. I have most of it translated now, and if I'm right, that name would mean…something like, the Hallowed Star, but…no, more specific than that, a Darkened Star. The suffix 'thia' would indicate it's a holy relic, but it wouldn't need to be said in so many words. Darkened Star. That sounds right."*

"So this Darkened Star was the High Priestess's Signet?" Miranda concluded. "More or less, I mean."

"I'm pretty sure it has powers ours don't, but of course I wasn't privy to what they were. Another five years and I would have been. Too bad."

"But where are they? Is there time to save them? And why would Morningstar want it?"

"Forgive me, beloved, but that's a pretty silly question," David said around a yawn. "If it's anything like a Signet God knows what they *could* use it for, but blood magic is a certainty. And if it's got that kind of symbolic value…it's exactly the sort of thing they'd want. We may not know exactly what the Prophet's endgame is but it involves destroying Persephone, and that amulet is as close as we have to Persephone's own Signet."

"Yeah." Miranda rubbed her forehead with both hands. "We need to get our hands on that Stone before Morningstar can, assuming it's not already too late. You know their location, right, Dev?"

A pause. *"Based on your description, I'm afraid not. Both Cloisters I knew have been destroyed, and even if they rebuilt Eladra's the buildings wouldn't be as old as the ones in your vision. The trees you said were most prominent weren't right for that area. It's almost certainly in the US, though--after the Inquisition most of the Order moved Westward."*

Nico was starting to sound a little more alert. *"As soon as we get home tonight I'll talk to Stella about locating them--finding things and people seems to be one of her particular talents. Any details you can remember to help us narrow the search would be useful, my Lady."*

She waved a pad of paper in the air even though they couldn't see it. "Wrote it all down as soon as I woke up. We can get on it tonight, like you said. Meantime, you guys meet us at the car in half an hour--let's get this show on the road."

"See you there."

David was still working--hadn't stopped, in fact, since the conference call. He'd contacted the surviving upper-echelon Elite in Japan that he could track down and had them organizing those who remained at the Tokyo Haven; Dev's operatives and Jacob's Elite had the place secured already and were keeping watch over Mameha. The Queen wasn't being confined--if she wanted to kill herself, the guards were not to stop her. But right now she was unresponsive, and they'd decided to just keep her safe for the moment to see if she became lucid long enough to make her desires known. Miranda doubted they'd have to wait more than another day.

Meanwhile David had deployed teams of his own Elite from the Midwest, where things were quiet and could spare the swords, to Japan to help secure the city. Where Tokyo went the rest of Japan would follow; keeping the city stable was key to holding the whole country.

"We should probably go," Miranda said, hating to interrupt him. Tanaka's death had been rather inconveniently timed--especially for Tanaka, she supposed--given what they had ahead of them tonight.

"Right," David said, sighing. He had never been back to sleep so he was already dressed and just had to arm himself. She joined him by the door where all their gear was waiting.

He was quiet, thoughtful--not a new phenomenon, but she knew the trouble weighing down his mind. Still it was something of a surprise when he said, hands resting on the Oncoming Storm, "The Council was right about me, weren't they."

"That you're a tyrant in the making who wants to subjugate the entire Shadow World? Hardly. You've been responding to the situation as it unfolds--it's not like you had some master plan for world domination."

"But I did," he said. "I do."

She looked at him. "Say again?"

"When I designed the version of the sensor network that I licensed out to the other Signets I left a backdoor in the code so I could get in and slave them all to my original network. I told myself it was programming access in case a problem arose that their admins couldn't handle. It's barely even a backdoor--it's more like flipping a switch. A few commands and ownership of the whole thing transfers back to me. My original plan, or so I told myself, was to close the gap later on once they'd gotten everything up and running for themselves…but I didn't. I left it wide open. Why?"

She didn't know how to answer, but he went on. "And as soon as I had California, even though I hoped it was only temporary, I started thinking bigger and long-term. How would I manage far-flung territories in the corners of the world if something went wrong? It was an intellectual exercise at first but before I knew it I had an entire drive full of plans and data on half the territories in the world…just in case. What did I think was going to happen? Apparently I thought this exact scenario was coming."

She hadn't been aware of all that. "David, you always make plans for crazy scenarios. World-conquering strategies are like Sudoku for you. Don't read so much into it."

"I'm not saying I have any intention of changing my mind," he replied. "Not as long as you're on board. But there are times I worry myself, Miranda. I'm not comfortable with how comfortable all of this is."

She leaned over and kissed his forehead. "Well, quit it," she said, aiming for at least some semblance of a good mood to help lighten his. "I don't like it when you're insecure about things. It screws with my notion of universal order."

He made a squinchy face at her that contrasted quite amusingly with all the leather and edged weapons. "Just let me know if you catch me monologuing or saying things like 'death is too good for my enemies.' Then we'll know I've lost it completely."

"Deal." She slid her arm through his as they left the suite. "For now…let's try and act like we've got it together. We need to present a stable front for Nico. Tonight's going to be hard enough on him without us being all weird."

"True." A different sort of uncertainty touched his expression. "It's not too late to--"

"We talked about this," she said firmly. "I know you wanted to do the whole thing somewhere safe and indoors, but it was Nico's decision and we have to honor it."

"But we should all be together, then. I don't like the idea of him going off--"

"With his Prime? They'll be fine, baby. We won't be far away--within easy Misting distance, remember? He just didn't want to call too much attention to himself, and I don't blame him."

David signed, dissatisfied and a little irritated--he hated not being in charge. "He says he doesn't want to be coddled, but that's exactly what he needs. We have no idea what this will do to him. Just this once, this first time, he should let us..." He trailed off, shaking his head. "I don't like it."

"There will be guards all around the area. We'll be a block or less out of earshot. The second anything looks wrong Dev will call us. And we'll all have the whole rest of the night together to help him deal with whatever comes up. It'll be fine."

She had to wonder, falling into step beside him on the way to the garage, if his agitated mood was due to Japan, Nico, or the Moon itself--they'd both learned to manage the hunger more skillfully over the months, but it still left them both pretty miserable and stressed out. He'd been handed an extra helping of worry he hadn't really needed...but still, there was something she didn't like in his behavior. He was too edgy, even bad-tempered, which wasn't like him at all. He was practically glowering by the time they reached the car.

Nico and Dev were already there, looking gorgeous as always, though Nico's face betrayed no little anxiety of his own. Deven was staying close to him, keeping a hand on his arm, holding him steady both inside and out. Really, David had nothing to worry about; Nico had come a long way in the last few weeks, and as long as he had his Prime he'd be fine.

The ride into town was mostly silent. Dev looked from David to Miranda, raising an eyebrow; she shrugged very slightly.

"Have you spoken to your mother tonight?" Miranda finally asked to break the tension.

Nico looked at her; he, too, had been watching David with narrowed eyes. "Not tonight. As of yesterday she was doing well--they are trying to organize a new Enclave, of sorts, and want me to be the liaison between them and the vampires, which I suppose is progress."

"They should ask you to lead it," David muttered, eyes on his phone. "They owe you that much."

Nico smiled. "I am not like you, my Lord--I have no desire to lead and certainly not the talent. I was never good at working in the spotlight."

"I'll bet you would be better at it than you think," Deven told him.

"Perhaps. But I think I shall leave it to my mother to keep the refugees organized. She says everyone is coping surprisingly well; there have been a few emotional breakdowns, as you might expect, but the remaining Healers are watching over everyone and attending to whomever needs their help as quickly as they can. As I understand it they have been enjoying an amiable information exchange with Mo down in the clinic."

Miranda grinned at the mental image. "How about the babies? And your baby, Dev?"

"She's not my baby," Deven said shortly--almost a snap but not quite. At her expression, he looked out the window for a second before saying, "Sorry. Just…I want to know that she's being taken care of, of course, but I think it would be best if no one knew we were kin."

"Why not?" She squeezed his knee. "You love kids--I've seen it. You don't have to be her dad or anything, but you could at least have a relationship of some kind. Every kid deserves a freaky aunt or uncle."

"I don't think so." He wouldn't look at her, but she didn't need to see his face to know what was there.

Instead she met Nico's gaze. He half-smiled--he agreed with her. If their suspicions were correct and Deven's mother had been taken by Morningstar to be used in some kind of blood ritual, he might never have a chance to know her; Inaliel might be all the blood kin he had left, and while he could pretend that meant nothing to him, centuries of longing to know more about where he had come from and what his life had meant to the family that had given him away were hard to shake. At least if he got to know the little one he might have a chance to do better by family than they'd done by him; it might help him gain some kind of closure, since fate clearly wasn't interested in helping him otherwise.

She smiled back at the Elf. Let fate be a jackass; Miranda and Nico were far more stubborn.

"Here we are, my Lady," Harlan said. "The address you asked for."

"Thank you, Harlan," she replied. "Okay, boys, let's go."

She expected Nico to grow tenser once they'd gotten out of the car, and she was right; he grew visibly more rigid and shrank back a little against the side of the car despite Deven's arm trying to draw him forward.

Miranda wanted to stay with them, but they had a plan, and as she'd told David, Nico's wishes had to be honored--if it turned out he couldn't cope with his way and wanted all of them, he'd say so, and they had to respect that he wanted to come to an understanding of this himself.

"Come on, baby," she said to David. "Why don't you head east and I'll head north, and these two can go west like we talked about."

He basically grunted in assent and disappeared.

"What the hell is his deal tonight?" Deven asked as soon as the Prime was gone.

"I don't know," she answered. "I've been wondering that all evening. Stress, maybe? But that's a little out of character. It might just be a combination of everything. He did just lose one of his oldest friends, after all."

"He's not the only one," Deven pointed out. "Jacob in particular was really tight with Tanaka. You don't see him acting like an asshole."

Nico finally spared a smile though he was watching the city. "I doubt anything could make Jacob act like an asshole. Even if he transformed into a literal asshole."

Miranda couldn't help it--she burst out laughing. Nico came off as such a serious person most of the time, but he could crack her up with the most unexpected comment...a lot like his brother.

Sudden sadness stabbed her in the chest. She swallowed the lump in her throat. "Okay...um...I'll be right around the corner looking for mine. You know where to go--if there's trouble just think it and I'll be here."

She started to walk away, but a hand grabbed her arm, and surprised, she turned around and met Nico's anguished face.

"Wait," he said. "Wait, don't..."

She folded her hand over his. "What do you need?"

He looked helplessly from her to Deven and back. "Don't leave," he said. "I know I said...but would you come with us? Just this once? I think you might...you understand."

She hugged him tightly. "Of course I will."

She decided not to worry about whether David would be upset that he hadn't been asked to stay--he was an adult, surely once he was in his usual mood again he'd understand. It wasn't that Nico didn't want him there; he didn't want any of them there, to be honest. But he knew he couldn't do it without Deven, and Miranda shared his feelings about the killing--not to mention her empathy would be a grounding force and a nurturing one.

She kept a little distance, though, behind them as they left the car and headed down the street. They had a very particular set of targets in mind for tonight; David had decided that the only way to manage four murders was if they knew in advance who to hit, so he had partnered with Detective Maguire to get a list of known offenders--violent, if possible--who had slipped through the cracks of Austin's justice system. The list was surprisingly long, and even if they made it through the whole thing, there were always more criminals wriggling out of the dark...and Texas was a death penalty state with a long backup on Death Row, another possible source of prey for the Thirdborn. Even Maguire had a hard time arguing with that idea given what a quagmire of corruption and wasted taxpayer money the prison system had become.

"Over here," Deven said. They gathered at the corner of a building just out of sight; Miranda hung back and waited to be needed.

"Do you want me to call her over?" the Prime asked. "Or are you ready to try it?"

Nico swallowed, nodded. "I'll try. Just...walk me through it."

"It's easy. Just fix your gaze on her...good...and then do the same with your mind. Don't bother with the Sight--the Web is no use to you here, this is all pure vampire instinct. Imagine you're touching her on the shoulder, getting her attention...good."

Miranda leaned back against the alley wall, listening, her eyes darting around to check for cameras even though they'd picked this spot because there wouldn't be any. She'd gotten understandably paranoid about the idea.

A moment later a woman's figure entered the alley, and Deven guided her into the shadows, one hand on her shoulder and the other on Nico's arm. The Elf looked like he desperately wanted to bolt, but his hold over the human remained firm. Her face was pleasantly blank with no resistance whatsoever.

Miranda drew closer to provide an extra visual shield between Nico and the rest of the city. "It's okay," she told the Elf. "She won't know what's happening."

Nico took a deep breath. "Why is this one on the list?"

Deven moved up next to him, putting one hand on Nico's back to hold him steady. "She's involved in a human trafficking ring," he said.

"Don't you want to stop all of them, then, not just one woman?"

Miranda nodded. "We're working on it. The police have been watching her and several others--they can't get enough evidence to arrest her. Stella's dad gave David all the information they had, and he's going to hunt the rest of the group down. We'll get food, and they can free potentially dozens of girls from slavery. We're doing what we can to make all this worthwhile."

Nico nodded, swallowed hard again, and stepped toward the woman. Miranda could feel his hunger as much as her own--they were all starving. No doubt their own need was feeding off each other's, which made the prospect of doing this every month even more daunting. It was already hard enough...how were they supposed to deal with four times the hunger?

Miranda pulled the human's head to the side, baring her throat. "Go on," she urged Nico, keeping the desperation out of her voice. She'd have plenty of time for her own hunt once this was taken care of and they got the Elf back in the car where he'd feel safe again.

She'd always hated to admit how attractive it was to watch David feed--and now she had two more insanely hot boys to gaze upon. Seeing the predator's razor-sharp senses come over Nico made her entire body feel like it was turning to liquid. She glanced over and met Deven's eyes--he clearly felt the same way. She could just imagine both of them after they'd fed on a normal night, that lazy satisfaction, the intense relief. It often sent her and David to the nearest hidden alcove they could find for a hard, fast shag against the wall.

Imagining Nico and Deven doing the same was almost more than she could take.

She caught Dev's grin. Of course he knew what she was thinking. Nico probably would have too if he hadn't been so absorbed by the matter at hand.

He leaned in and inhaled the woman's scent. There really wasn't time for him to put off the bite--every minute they were here was a minute closer to being discovered by the humans--but she didn't want to rush this one. It was too important that Nico's first experience was, if not positive, at least not traumatic.

Finally, closing his eyes, he drew a hissing breath that was a telltale sign of canines lengthening, and struck.

She and Dev both moved up close enough to touch him, her hand on his shoulder and Deven's still on his back. "Slow down, my love," Deven said softly in his ear. "You'll make yourself sick, and you don't want to have to do this again."

Nodding, Nico slowed down his frantic swallows and Miranda felt him try, mostly in vain, to relax. She had to smile at that--even in his fear of this moment, he was trying to accept what he was, a far cry from the Nico of the last two years. The reason why was standing next to him, murmuring something encouraging in his ear.

Deven, too, had changed in the wake of their long-denied union. He'd taken up his old wardrobe and piercings, and the tips of his hair were dark purple--a shade chosen, she imagined, to match his Consort's eyes. The old confidence had returned, though not without a subtle difference, some of the hard edges ever so slightly gentled. She knew that all these months of mourning would never entirely leave him--even Nico's presence couldn't make up for Jonathan's absence. Miranda had worried about that, and asked Nico if it upset him knowing there was part of Deven that would be unreachable, and he'd looked at her like she was insane.

"Of course not," he'd said. *"I never wanted, or intended, to replace Jonathan--I want to be something new. Such a loss as his will leave an empty place that cannot be filled. My hope is to help make that place less one of grief than one of beloved memory. But that place is not mine to claim."*

She'd shaken her head. Elves.

The moment had come...Miranda could hear the human's heartbeat coming into synch with her killer's. He had perhaps ten seconds to choose. Miranda willed him to remember that this woman was not good, was complicit in horrible crimes and would never stop. Normally they preyed on the innocent, or mostly, but not this time, not on nights like this. This time he'd be the hand of justice when human law was hamstrung by its own--vital to the survival of society--fairness. It might not be a *good* thing to do, but it was necessary. She wanted him to understand that at a level that all the talking in the world couldn't touch.

To her immense pride, she felt him make the choice and draw harder from the wound in the woman's neck.
Five...four...three....

Suddenly Nico lurched backward, dropping the human on the ground and startling Miranda so badly she didn't have time to grab him. Luckily Deven was faster and had an arm around Nico with lightning speed.

"I can't," the Elf panted. "I don't understand..."

"You were doing so well," Miranda lamented, snatching the discarded scarf from the human's neck off the ground and using it to wipe the blood from Nico's face, trying to hide her disappointment. "Just a couple more seconds, and--"

"No," he breathed, looking dizzy and confused. "I did not change my mind. I was ready. But something isn't right. Can't you feel it?"

Miranda and Deven exchanged a glance and, both frowning, sought after the part of the Web that would show the Pair's new and black-threaded hunger.

She realized then that in the last minute or so her own need had faded, though she'd been too focused on Nico to notice...and now it was gone. So was Deven's, and Nico's.

"Where did it go?" Deven asked. "It hasn't disappeared, it's...it's been sated. How is that possible when none of us killed?"

Miranda shook her head, having no answer for him, and said to her com, "Star-One."

There was no reply. That was strange. "Star-One, this is Star-Two...David, are you there? Something weird's going on."

Nothing. Heart starting to pound, she tried his phone. It went straight to voice mail.

Her hands were shaking with foreboding as she pulled up the sensor grid on her phone and said, "Locate Star-One."

The grid zoomed in, turned east, and showed the dot that represented David, just like normal.

"Vitals," she said.

Elevated heart rate. Elevated temperature.

"Come on," she said urgently. "We have to find him."

No argument from the boys. They followed her out of the alley and down the street--as per the plan, he hadn't been far away. She wasn't sure what the environment would be like--most likely a hidden alcove like their own--but without knowing what it looked like she couldn't Mist there.

The feeling of dread increased the closer they got. Nico, too, was pale and fearful; she'd forgotten that as a Consort he'd have precog now, even more than what he'd had as a Weaver. Clearly it had kicked in.

"Wait," Deven said as they reached the dark space between the backs of two restaurants. It wasn't quite big enough to consider an alley, but she had no idea what else to call it. "Let me go first. Is there anyone else in there?"

Miranda looked at the grid again, but nothing had changed. "No. One set of life signs."

Dev drew a knife from...somewhere...and gestured for them to stay put. Even if there were no other signs, they didn't know if the Prophet would show up as an Elf would, and there was no way to rule out some other kind of creature--at this point, who the hell knew what was out there?

She heard him quietly call David's name, and announce his own. She could see his little dot on the grid moving into the alley as she saw him swallowed by the darkness.

Then she heard him gasp. "Jesus Christ."

There was something way too close to genuine fear in Deven's voice. That was all Miranda could take. She charged into the alley, ready to draw Shadowflame but unsure whether there'd be space or having a sword out would be a liability.

Deven grabbed her arm and pulled her back before she could pass him. She started to protest but he inclined his head toward the back of the alley and said softly, "Look."

She turned and did as he'd said, and shock hit her so hard she could not make sense of anything she was seeing.

There were bodies everywhere.

Dead humans, all with gaping eyes and blood all over their necks and torsos, all looking abjectly horrified at whatever they'd seen last.

And there, up against the wall, was David. He was curled up in a ball on the ground, and the hand she could see was wet with blood.

She heard Nico swear in Elvish, then whisper, "There are four."

She stepped over the humans and dropped to her knees beside her Prime, not sure where to touch him--there was blood all over him but he hadn't shown any signs of injury on the grid.

"David," she said, and to hell with the blood; she eased one hand in to help uncurl him. A moment later Deven and Nico joined her, each on one side, all six of their hands touching him, offering comfort even if none of them really understood what had happened here.

When she saw David's face she shrank back unconsciously.

His eyes were black, yes, but there was blood all over his mouth like he'd completely lost control of himself. How was that even possible? He was the one who'd taught her that only monsters and animals left their prey gory and themselves bloody. Civilized vampires left only two fading holes as evidence they'd been there.

She leaned back in and carefully turned his head to face her. There was no recognition in his eyes at all.

"David," she repeated, more firmly, then snapped, "Prime, focus."

The tone made him literally twitch, then blink. She started to see her husband in the wild-eyed, almost feral face she'd never seen before.

The others kept their hands on him to help shore him up and offer comfort. Whatever this was, they knew he would never have done it willingly. That just wasn't the David Solomon any of them knew.

Finally recognition began to return to his expression and his eyes began to fade back through silver and into blue. He started shaking.

"What happened?" she asked barely above a whisper. She was afraid to scare him lest she lose him again.

He leaned his head sideways to look past her shoulder and confirm what he had apparently been hoping was a hallucination.

Then he returned his gaze to her, and there was so much fear and bewilderment there she had no idea how to react except she wanted to get him home, clean, and in bed before this could hurt him anymore.

He swallowed. His voice was strange, almost childlike, when he said, "I was so hungry." A violent tremor ran through him and his eyes filled with tears. "I couldn't stop. Why couldn't I stop?"

She had no answer.

Deven, however, did. "Because there are four of us," he replied, stroking David's head. "A moment ago our hunger disappeared. You got all of it somehow."

"What do you remember?" Miranda asked. They were all whispering, trying to shield the Prime from the gruesome scene behind them. He'd seen it, but they didn't want him staring at it and losing his hold again.

"I couldn't stop," he repeated. "I killed one, and it wasn't enough. It usually goes away after that, but...it didn't. I needed another, and another, and another...and...when it was finally gone and I looked around..."

He started to curl up again. They all tightened their grip to stop him.

"It's okay," she said.

He looked at her as if she had gone mad. "No it's not."

She sighed. "Okay, well, it's not. But we'll figure it out. Let's get you home and get this taken care of. Boys, would you..."

They didn't need instruction. Both rose, bringing David with them, holding onto his arms like he was an invalid. Deven told him not to look down, just to follow their lead. He didn't argue.

Miranda could feel anguish building in her heart, but there was no time for that. "Dispatch, I need a body disposal team--we have a multiple Alpha Seven at these coordinates. Four victims. All need level three containment. This is priority--pull as many swords off patrol as you need to."

"As you will it, my Lady. ETA four minutes."

Good enough. "Harlan, I need you to bring the car to where we're at as fast as you can. The Prime is in a...well, he needs help, and we need to get him out of here."

"Two minutes, my Lady."

The Elite team exceeded her expectations--they were there before Harlan. She directed them into the alley, thankful that they knew better than to question her; if there was something to know, they'd hear it, or at least hear it through the Elite grapevine in the next few days. She was well aware that they talked; in fact it was something the Pair counted on, to get manufactured rumors and information into the Shadow District.

Harlan, too, would not ask, though usually he ended up finding out what was going on out of necessity. She'd trust him with her life and trusted his discretion. That was part of why he'd served in his post as long as David had held the Signet.

He didn't say "Holy shit" when he saw David, but she could see it in his face. He simply opened the door so they could coax David into the SUV.

There were emergency supplies in all Signet vehicles--some weapons, usually a bag of blood kept on ice, a change of clothes for the Pair, and first aid supplies to keep bleeding or broken bones at bay on the way to the Hausmann. There were also towels and enzyme-based wipes for removing blood without leaving a stain. Vampires were, by necessity, good at getting blood out of things, and a couple of months back Hunter Development had sold a version of that same formula to a human cleaning products company, so now mothers all over the USA were using it to get grass stains out of their kids' jeans, making Hunter's owner--David Solomon--another passive fortune.

Nico went around to the back to grab what they needed while she and Deven tried to get David comfortable. He was still shaking, of his mind with shock...and when Nico started to touch him to work on the blood on his face, David snarled and nearly attacked him before sinking back into a daze.

Deven had him pinned to the seat before he could even touch the Elf. He put a hand on David's neck. "Should I..."

"No, not yet," Miranda said, picking up a box from the med kit and taking out a pre-loaded disposable syringe. "Let's try this first." She clicked the safety off and thrust the needle into David's thigh.

Seconds later, his muscles went slack and he passed out.

It was the same tranquilizer they'd given Nico when he went feral, though the Elf had become immune to it quickly. She knew David had never had it, so it would still work for him, at least long enough to get him home. She could sense from the bond that once he was safe in bed he'd pull out of this…for now.

They all looked at each other. "What the hell is happening?" Deven asked. "Has either of you ever taken the hunger from the other?"

"No," she answered. "Never. It would have been nice, in a way. He could have killed for both of us. I know he would have done it willingly if it meant I didn't have to. But this…"

"I've never seen him like this," Deven said. "And I think I've seen just about everything he's capable of…or I thought I had."

"Me neither." She started stripping off his coat and shirt; the coat would survive but the shirt was probably ruined. No great loss; it was a nondescript black button-down, not one of his beloved collection.

It was cramped in the seat but the three of them worked in silent concert to clean David up and make him more comfortable. Miranda wiped the blood off his face while Nico did one hand and Deven the other. By the time they were out of the city, he looked almost like himself again.

The Queen hoped he wouldn't wake until they were home, and she got her wish.

"Here," Dev said. "I'll take him--let's just Mist to the suite so the Elite don't see. He'd be mortified if he thought he'd looked weak to them."

She and Nico agreed, and in a breath they'd all disappeared; Miranda took a second to psych herself up. She considered just walking, but she didn't want to be away from David any longer than she had to, and shut her eyes, determined not to be sick.

She stumbled out of the Mist a second later and into the safe familiarity of the Signet Suite. She joined the boys at the bed, where they'd lowered David into the pillows, and all three of them hovered for a moment unsure what to do next.

Thankfully there was another Prime in the room willing to take charge.

"I think this is a Tetrad sort of night," Deven said. "Nico, you take the first shower--I'll fetch us clothes, and Miranda can keep an eye on him. Sound good?"

He vanished before they could argue, but Miranda hadn't planned to anyway. Nico reached over and touched her shoulder. "Would you rather I waited with you?"

"It's okay. It's just for a minute."

The Elf left her reluctantly. She sat down on the side of the bed and yanked off her boots.

What the hell was happening? On the one hand, the thought that they could divide the burden of the New Moon made her heart leap--if he had a choice in the matter, David wouldn't shrink from killing, and neither would Deven. It might be the only way to keep Nico stable--she worried, though she didn't want to let him know, that the violence of killing even in the most nonviolent way possible might break him again, and the monster Morningstar had unleashed could return. The thought of protecting him from that, and no longer having to do it herself either, left her almost weak-kneed with hope.

It was the loss of control that worried her. Not once in the years she'd known him had David ever done anything like this. He didn't lose his calm, even when enraged; it was that steely-eyed composure that scared the hell out of his enemies. He was a quick and efficient hunter and never spilled so much as a drop.

She heard a groan and turned around. David's eyes fluttered open, and thank God, they were the right color, and not glazed with confusion or fear.

"My head is killing me," he muttered, shutting his eyes tightly.

"Are you okay?"

He frowned and opened his eyes again. "Of course. Why wouldn't I be?"

"Well...don't you remember what happened tonight?"

The frown deepened. "I..." He groped after the memory for a second, and she saw it returning: Slowly-dawning horror came over his face, and he sat up, staring down at his hands. "I don't...I don't..."

"Whoa," she said, sensing he was about to lose it again. She grabbed his shoulders and sent as much soothing energy along the bond as she could; she felt Nico do the same, and Deven, until their combined reassurance and love had wrapped the Prime like a cocoon and shielded him from his own mind.

Deven reappeared with an armload of clothes just in time for Nico to emerge from the bathroom in a towel. Miranda returned her attention to David while they divided outfits and Dev took the shower. They were deliberately acting like nothing awful had happened; she was glad of that.

"Did the Elite...the...bodies," David managed, head in his hands.

"All dealt with," she told him. "Can you tell me if they were on the list?"

David shook his head. "The first one was. The others...I don't know. I didn't read them, didn't care, I just...they were there. Walking by. I didn't care."

That was alarming too. Even when feeding off the innocent on an average night, they all took a minute to evaluate their prey, finding those healthy enough not to be seriously weakened or injured by the blood loss. The fewer humans who wound up in the ER with fang marks the better.

One by one they showered and joined the Prime in bed; when Miranda went into the bathroom for her turn she noticed a bag of blood and wine glass on the counter--Deven had left it there for her, and it looked like he'd had one himself. Only Nico and David had actually gotten any blood tonight, and though the death-lust was gone, she still had good old-fashioned hunger to deal with. She had a long drink while she waited for the water to heat up to the thermonuclear level she preferred, grateful Deven had thought of it.

By the time she returned to the bedroom David was dozing off, held securely between Prime and Consort; he'd visibly relaxed, and looked completely like himself again, just more tired than usual.

She climbed in with them. Deven swapped places with her so she was next to David and Deven was against her back. She touched David's sleeping face gently, checking for a fever she knew wouldn't be there. He didn't stir.

"What do you think?" she asked, not even sure what she was asking.

"I think that's another on a long list of questions Persephone will need to answer on the Winter Solstice," Nico replied, looking ashamed. "I admit the thought of escaping the killing sentence upon us makes my heart leap, but...not if the cost is David's sanity."

"I know," Miranda agreed. "I feel awful that my first reaction was relief. But I couldn't help it either."

Deven was smiling in spite of the situation, and shook his head. "You two. You act like this was your idea--he knows, as do we all, that you'd never ask him to do this even if it was a viable option. Perhaps you should hold off on guilt until we know what this actually was and if it's going to happen again." He reached over and flicked Nico's ear lightly, earning a quiet chuckle. "Now, let's all sleep...after what happened this afternoon nobody got much rest, and now we need it even worse. We'll deal with the fallout when there's fallout."

"Wise words as always," she murmured, burrowing down. Whatever was going on, the simple act of snuggling up with her husband had always lifted even the greatest burden for a little while, and now she could greedily drink in even more comfort, offered without hesitation, as if they'd all been together like this for decades instead of mere weeks.

"Life is weird," she said tiredly, letting sleep pull her toward the earth.

Dev nipped lightly at her neck just below her ear. "None of us would have it any other way."

"Good," she replied with a yawn. "Because I think it's about to get a lot weirder."

Chapter Three

The door to Nico's suite--currently Kalea and Inaliel's guest quarters--stood ajar, with flickering candlelight beyond. Dev paused and asked the guard, "Are they in?"

"The lady Kalea is at a meeting of the refugee leaders, my Lord," she replied. "She left the baby asleep." At his raised eyebrow she added, "She asked me to contact her immediately if I hear the baby stirring."

He nodded and eased the door open, no longer able to deny his curiosity about the strange little creature asleep in his Consort's bed. He wasn't sure what he wanted to know...just that he wanted a better look at her, to learn...something.

It turned out the shipment of baby things had arrived--he hadn't been paying much attention to what supplies were coming when. There was a crib in the room now, under the window where the moonless, starlit night streamed in through the open shutters.

The sense of "Elf" in the room had redoubled, as had the scent, but these Elves had a different quality to their energy from Nico's, something brighter he couldn't really describe. There were also the empathic echoes of heart-weariness, uncertainty, and grief he was sure saturated every room that currently housed a refugee of Avilon.

He moved to stand by the crib and rested a hand on the rail, peering in at the bundle of blankets that rose and fell steadily in the puddle of starlight. The baby slept in periwinkle, including a little cap to keep her head warm on these cold Winter nights and ridiculously tiny socks on her ridiculously tiny feet. She was as fat as a human infant, and would have been adorable enough already to anyone who liked babies, but the way her little ears pointed at their tips was almost too much.

"Aren't you a marvel," he said softly, unable to help a smile.

As if agreeing, the baby's fingers twitched against the blanket, and her eyes blinked open; she looked up at him calmly through her pale lavender eyes and, after a moment, rolled over and sat up.

That surprised him. She seemed awfully small for that kind of coordination...but then again he knew absolutely nothing about Elven babies. She didn't make a sound, just looked at him, the same way he'd been looking at her, evaluating, making up her mind.

Not entirely comfortable under her gaze, he reached down to the foot of the crib and picked up a stuffed purple bear, presenting it to her. She held out both hands for it and immediately set to sucking on its ear.

The quietly-cleared throat behind him didn't startle him; he hadn't been listening for footsteps but he'd been expecting Kalea to return any moment. He didn't acknowledge her arrival until she'd come to stand next to him.

"You could pick her up if you like," Kalea said in careful English. "I sense you know how to manage an infant."

He shook his head and replied in Elvish. "No thank you."

She was silent in the awkward way that meant she was trying to figure out how to say something. He might have thought she didn't want him near Inaliel, but she'd already given her tacit approval.

"I feel I should tell you..."

Deven waited, unmoving, eyes still on the baby, whose eyes were still on him.

"Your mother had no idea you survived until she had already come to Avilon and the way was sealed behind her. She regretted abandoning you...deeply, though not as deeply as she regretted sending you away as a child instead of here with Lesela. But I think, perhaps, it was best that you did not meet."

Now, he looked up. "Why not?"

"Elendala never lost the shame and self-hatred that plagued her when she lived as a human--and she was never the most...pleasant...person to be around. I only knew her for a short time, and I must admit I did not like her. She was bitter and angry; even reclaiming her Healing power was done out of shame, not out of a true desire to help others. She was atoning, she claimed, for..."

Kalea trailed off a moment--Deven had a feeling she wasn't the sort of person who often lacked for words, let alone twice in one conversation. He waited.

The Weaver took a breath and went on. "She said she was atoning for all the lives you had taken."

"What the fuck does that mean?" he burst out, to his dismay, and even the baby seemed surprised--she started and stared up at him with her wide, too-smart eyes. "What did she know about my life?"

"Oh, a great deal. Lesela was a Prophet, after all. Apparently Elendala had her scry for knowledge of you--that's how Lesela discovered you were alive. Elendala wanted to know if you died in the monastery or elsewhere, and to their mutual surprise, you had not--and moreover you were a...how did Nico put it? A gay vampire murder pimp."

He normally would have laughed at that particular set of words coming out of an Elf's mouth, but he was still too flabbergasted. "She was ashamed of me."

"I am afraid so. Lesela of course knew better--her Prophet's talent gave her insight far beyond just appearances. She knew the good you had done, and the pain you were in, but your mother...she lived so long among humans, their fear and prejudice never fully left her. And you know well the kind of judgment the Elves have heaped upon Nicolanai--she had those feelings as well, having seen firsthand the devastation vampires caused our people. But the truth is, she was never truly happy--though she made great strides once she met her beloved and even more when the little one was born. It made her rethink a lot of things, I believe. But if you had met her, I am afraid the reunion would not have been reconciliatory."

Now he did laugh, though it was a hollow and humorless sound. "Perfect."

"I think you would have enjoyed knowing your grandmother, however. She certainly wanted to know you."

"So much for that," he muttered, turning away from the crib, not sure whether to keep laughing until he wept or just weep. "But at least I don't have to spend the next few months or however long wasting my hope on Elendala."

Kalea shrugged fluidly. She really did remind him uncannily of both her sons--they all had the same gestures, the same head tilt. It was oddly comforting.

"I don't suppose you know what happened to my father," he forced himself to ask.

She took another breath. "If I recall correctly he died long before the Burning began--some sort of accident on the farm. She was alone for a long time before the Inquisition came. I think that made things worse."

"But how did he know what she was? And for how long? He knew her name."

"That I could not say."

They were both silent now, staring at Inaliel, who was back to gnawing on her bear. She was a quiet little thing, but obviously happy; every now and then she would break into a wide toothless grin and her little ears would wiggle.

"What's going to happen to her?" he asked.

"As her only blood relative, you would be entitled to take her in--or, as would be my recommendation, to choose a foster home for her. There will be plenty of offers, I daresay, given all the losses we have suffered."

"Can you help me? I don't know your people--you can tell me where she would fit best."

"Of course," she replied, sounding pleased that he'd asked. "I am happy to continue watching over her while we look--it gives me something to concern myself with besides our situation and...Kai."

He looked down at the floor. "I'm sorry."

He could practically hear the frown in her voice, and the lack of condemnation made him look back up at her. "You must not continue to blame yourself. My sons both made their own choices--prophecy or no, they took the paths they each felt drawn toward. No one forced this Prophet to start this war, or murder your Consort, or any other act of evil that has led us here. And as for Nico...well...he has suffered more than I can bear to think of, but when I see him watching you, and smiling at you, I believe that pain might truly be worth it in the end. He was never happy either...content, yes, but what good is contentment to a heart with so much more to give?"

He smiled at her tiredly. "I think I'd rather you hated me."

"I am sure you would rather everyone hated you. Pity, then, that no one does."

"I will bring Kai home," he said. "I can't promise he'll be the same, or even alive--you and I both know what we're facing. But I won't abandon him to whatever fate the Prophet has planned. I give you my word."

Kalea regarded him gravely for a moment before nodding. "I believe you."

Taking a deep breath, he looked over at the crib one more time and tried to change the subject. "Does she ever make any noise?"

The Elf chuckled. "Our guard outside asked something similar--am I to assume human children are very noisy? Ours, less so, though she does cry at times, and laughs with equal fervor. She speaks quite a few words--they usually start with the names of their guardians, or demands like 'up!' but she understands a good deal more than that already."

"It sounds like Elflings are smarter than human babies."

"I know little of the latter, but I think the circumstances are different for each. There is so much telepathy and empathy among our people that we are able to intuit communication from a very young age--just as Nico can learn and teach languages telepathically in some cases. It also makes verbal communication less important in the early years. Often our little ones are nearly silent for most of the first year and then one day start speaking in full sentences."

"Does that mean she knows what's happened to her mother?"

"That I do not know. She has asked for her, and cried for her, but accepts the comfort I offer without hesitation. I will try to explain it to her in simple terms as time goes on."

"What words do Elflings use for their kin? I'm sure she's not outright saying *Mother* or *Father*."

"Usually something like *Metha* and *Adde*," Kalea replied, abbreviating the Elvish *methere* and *addeneth*. "And instead of Sister or Brother, they often--"

"Veli!"

They both started and looked at the baby.

She was grinning. *"Veli,"* she repeated very clearly, gesturing emphatically at Deven with her bear.

Kalea's eyebrows shot up nearly high enough to disappear into her hairline.

The Elvish word for sister was *venithi*; for brother, *velinith*.

Inaliel nodded--actually nodded--to herself. She seemed inordinately pleased with herself for coming up with the word, and even more pleased at the looks on their faces.

Elf and Prime looked at each other.

"I imagine you'll want to run off now," Kalea said kindly.

Deven nodded, and disappeared.

*****

"She changes everything she touches
and everything she touches changes..."

Stella paused just inside the door to Revelry, listening to the merry jingle of the doorbell, letting the smell of years' worth of incense and herbs settle around her like a blanket against the Winter's night. The stereo system greeted her with a chorus of chanting that was mostly on-key, a recording she remembered from countless Wicca 101 classes and Pagan Student Alliance meetings.

"Stella! Babe! I never thought you'd set foot in here again!"

She grinned as Lark bounded out from behind the counter and all but tackled her with a hug. The handful of other customers looked up from the bookshelves and racks for a moment, didn't recognize the newcomer, and went back to shopping.

She did feel like a stranger. She hadn't been to the store in months--Miranda's people could order any Witchy things Stella needed and refused to let her pay for anything herself, so she hadn't really had reason to visit. Lark had said people asked about her once she stopped appearing at the store, but the people here tonight were unfamiliar--a new set of regulars, maybe, in the grand cyclical turn of retail patronage.

Behind her the door jingled again, and Nico stepped into the store, tall and dark and gorgeous as always...him, they noticed. Every eye in the place was suddenly on the Elf who had appeared in their midst like a swan dropped into a lake full of geese.

Lark grinned conspiratorially. "Look at you," she said, hugging Nico fiercely. "Out in public and everything."

Nico smiled and shrugged. "There are half a dozen guards with us...and I'm a bit more confident these days."

An even bigger grin. "Getting laid left right and sideways will do that to you."

Nico blushed, and Stella got the giggles--all the more so because of how awed people were just *looking* at him. They had no idea what he really was, or what it meant, but these were Witches, after all, and even the most head-blind ordinary human would feel something Very Very Different about the Elf...even if they couldn't see his ears, or his Signet.

Lark looked around and said, "Okay guys, back to your herbs. The hottie's oh so very taken." She squeezed them each around the middle with one arm and asked, "What brings you to our non-filthy-rich neck of the woods?"

"There's actually something I need," Stella told her. "We need to do a communication spell, and we have a Speaking Stone like the one I told you about before. But it works best if you're looking for a blood relative, and we're not, so we need something to boost the signal."

"Something like French white dittany," Lark said, nodding.

"I knew the shop carries it and that it's from a good supplier--I'd rather not wait for shipping from some random place."

Lark headed behind the register to the cabinet where the rare and expensive items--dangerous herbs, handmade grimoires, and the like--were kept with the special orders and anything else Foxglove didn't want the public touching. "Do you need the herb or a tincture?"

Stella glanced at Nico, who shook his head. "This is your territory, Mistresses Witch. We use herbs for medicinal purposes on occasion but our magic isn't nearly as elemental."

"So why not just Weave yourself a spell?" Lark asked. "Seems easier."

"The way the Stones are set up it's much easier to play with the ingredients than to...how would you put it, Nico?" Stella asked.

"Hack the operating system," he replied as if Elves talked about programming all the time.

Stella had to bite back another giggle. "Right. The first thing to try is to add something to the blood we use to activate it. If that doesn't work we move on to fiddling with the spell itself."

"Sounds like a good strategy. Well, if you're working with blood as your primary ingredient, I'd recommend adding tincture to it rather than whole herb, unless you want to make your own tincture...but that would take a lot longer."

Stella agreed, and she watched while Lark measured out a small vial's worth of the alcohol-based infusion; the stuff smelled dreadful, but thankfully they didn't have to take it internally like people usually did with tinctures. If they added a few drops to Miranda's blood and charged it with extra energy, it could overcome the fact that they had no idea who they were trying to contact.

She glanced over at Nico, who had drifted toward the shelves to examine some of the books, but noticed he had an odd, preoccupied look on his face. "Everything okay?" she asked.

The Elf frowned. "I'm not sure. Something seems off."

Her heart skipped. "Off, like precognitively off?"

Nico made an indefinite motion with his head. "I don't know." He tapped on his com and said, "Elite-32, what's your status?"

"Situation quiet, my Lord. No signs of movement out front or in the alley. Is something wrong?"

"I don't know. Just stay alert, please, just in case."

"Of course, my Lord."

Shaking his head again, he said, "Star-One."

"Yes, my darling?"

David's tone wasn't particularly intimate--he sounded a bit distracted, in fact--but something about the com line always added an extra layer of sexy to his already libido-shaking voice, and at the term of endearment, Nico turned a little pink at the ears. "Can you check the grid for this block?" he asked. "I have a weird feeling."

Any hint of distraction vanished. *"Checking it now."* A few seconds lapsed, and he said, *"I don't see anything out of the ordinary--all the vampire signatures are accounted for, and there are seven humans in the building - Stella and six others. Not much traffic outside. Let me widen the scope a bit, hang on..."*

Outside the store, Stella heard tires squealing. "Does the grid track cars?"

The Prime heard her, and replied quickly, *"No, but there are four humans coming in fast--Nico, don't--get down!"*

Stella felt her entire body freeze to the spot, panic overtaking her before she could even move, but vampire reflexes weren't screwing around. She felt hands gripping her upper arms, and she was flung hard to the side, dragged downward behind a body. All around her the quiet shop erupted into screams and the sounds of shattering glass as bullets blew out the entire front of the store and punched holes in everything they could reach.

She hit the ground with a cry, everything lurching into slow motion and back out again; she felt repeated impacts against her, but not into her body, and sound was muffled by the coat that surrounded her protectively against flying glass.

Though she was too panicked to focus her Sight, she could still sense a massive wall of energy erupting from all around her--she had no idea what it was, but it blew outward from the building on a tide of blood-red, black-edged *rage*. She shrank back from it, but it wasn't aimed at her--it struck its target so hard it felt like the ground beneath her shook, though it was probably just the Web, vibrating and shifting to accommodate the intense wave of magic.

Then she lost hold on the world, and everything went silent.

*****

The next few hours were a blur of noise and madness: sirens and screams gave way to the purposeful chatter of nurses and surgeons and the beep-beep of machinery; the sense-assaulting combination of incense and herbs and blood turned into the stink of hospital food and antiseptic.

Miranda arrived in time to help lift Nico off of Stella's unconscious body. He was covered in blood, his back punctured with a dozen bullets that were already starting to push their way out, and cried out in pain every time he moved...but the Witch beneath him was unharmed.

She was the only human who made it out alive.

Miranda held her tightly as the Witch fought to get free then screamed, sobbed, and threatened to find Morningstar and kill them all bare-handed. Stella's eyes were fixed in anguish on the ER bay where the hospital staff fought for over an hour to save Lark.

Finally, when all was calm, the elder Witch lay covered in a sheet, her blood in smears and puddles all over the operating room floor. She had been protected partially by the cash register, but bullets had entered her chest, and by the time paramedics arrived Miranda knew it was too late.

None of the other shop patrons survived long enough to reach the ER.

Six dead. Gang violence, according to the police.

Maguire arrived and took charge of his daughter, holding her while she wept.

Miranda knew he wanted an explanation...but he also knew, as did they all, that none was necessary. Whatever role Stella had in the fight against Morningstar, Morningstar knew more about it than they did, and at some point they'd decided she must be eliminated. If the target had been Nico they wouldn't have used bullets. They must have been watching any place Stella was known to visit.

Freed of her friend's grief-stricken embrace, Miranda wandered into the nearby bay where Deven had Nico facedown on a gurney, pushing the healing through. The Elf had passed out, presumably from the pain, but one look at Deven's face and she began to doubt that assessment.

"Is he okay?" she asked quietly.

Dev looked up at her. To her surprise, he was pale and shaky, and when he lifted his hands from Nico's back he nearly stumbled backwards. She grabbed the Prime by his arms and pushed him into a chair.

At her incredulous look Deven said, "He's fine. A couple of the bullets hit organs, but they're all out now. He'll be weak until he gets blood. One of the Elite is fetching some."

"Then why do you look like that?"

"It wasn't the bullets that were the problem. I don't know what he did, but right after I felt him shot, I felt...I don't know what. He did some kind of magic after he grabbed Stella, and it drained us both--I tried to block him pulling from the two of you, but I'm surprised you didn't feel it. Something huge and angry and...really, really violent."

Miranda looked at the unconscious Elf. No, she hadn't felt anything beyond the blind panic of knowing one of them was hurt. "Violent?"

Before Deven could answer, David poked his head in the curtain. "Is he awake?"

"Not yet." Dev leaned over and touched Nico's head, gently stroking his hair as he looked back up at David. "Did you bring in the shooters for interrogation?"

"Well I would love to have," David said, shaking his head, "but first I'd have to scrape them off the car windows."

"What do you mean?" Miranda asked.

"I mean that before the Elite could even take a step toward the car, every human inside it exploded."

"Exploded," Deven repeated.

David mimed an explosion with his hands and made a "poof!" noise. "People-jam all over the inside of the car. Quite possibly the most disgusting thing I've ever seen in my life." He held up his phone. "Want to see?"

"No!" Miranda waved him away, but her eyes fell on the Elf. "Are we assuming Nico did that? He just...blew them up? Surely he knew we'd want to catch them alive?"

"This wasn't an intent to apprehend," Deven told her. "It was pure, mindless rage. Bloodlust and revenge. Right before he passed out, he asked if we caught them--I don't think he realizes what he did."

"Jesus," Miranda muttered. She looked at David. "We were afraid something like this might happen."

He nodded. "After what Morningstar did to him, the way he snapped, there's no way that just suddenly got better. That kind of trauma doesn't up and vanish."

The Queen leaned against the edge of the gurney, hands on her forehead, thinking of an alley full of dead humans and her husband's black, black eyes. *What's happening to us?* "There has to be a way to help him."

Suddenly the curtain was jerked aside, and Detective Maguire demanded, "What's the--" He saw Nico and froze, sheepish...but gestured with his head out into the hallway.

David and Miranda followed him. The Detective was practically pacing, face red. "Do you mind telling me what happened tonight? Why my daughter's best friend is dead and she's been attacked again? You assured me she'd be safe--"

"I assured you she'd be as safe as she can be," David snapped.

Maguire paled and backed up a step--Miranda knew he'd never get used to the eye thing.

"Need I remind you your daughter--an adult--is involved in a war," David went on. "These people will do everything they can to defeat us, up to and including attacking Stella. She remains involved purely by her own will and is aware of the danger. Now then: the shooters have been dealt with. We were unable to apprehend one for questioning but I really don't think it's necessary. It's obvious they were staking out anywhere they thought she would go and came after her the first chance they got. They failed."

Maguire glared at him for just a second longer, then sagged back into himself, defeated. "So they're all dead? Good," he muttered. "What are you people doing to me? I used to believe in due process."

"Human justice is useless here," David said, tone a little chilly. Paradoxically Miranda had observed over the years that the coldness he affected in times like these tended to comfort those in distress.

"How did you miss those people coming in on the grid?" Maguire wanted to know, at least a little more calmly. "I thought you could track these enhanced humans."

"I can. But last time I checked vampires don't usually have to worry about a goddamned drive-by. The system isn't programmed to respond to people traveling at vehicular speeds."

The anger leaking out around the edges of David's voice made the Detective think better about any more questions for the moment.

A moment later Nico emerged stiffly from the curtained bay, with Deven holding him up. Deven had had the presence of mind to bring a change of clothes from the car when they arrived, so at least the Elf didn't have to leave the hospital in a coat cut to ribbons by bullets or a set of scrubs.

Maguire regarded the Elf. "You saved my daughter," he said, and offered his hand. "Thank you."

Nico shook his hand wordlessly, just nodding.

Stella returned from the ladies' room; she'd washed her face but her eyes were still red. "Nico, are you okay?" she asked tearfully. "You were shot--"

"I am fine," he told her gently. "I'm sorry…about Lark."

Stella moved away from Maguire and into Nico's arms, crying again, and Nico held onto her for a while, tears trailing from his eyes as he murmured comfort to the Witch.

"We need to go," David said quietly to the Queen, "before the press gets wind that you're here. I know at least one of the ER techs recognized you. The last thing Stella needs is cameras in her face."

"Yeah." Miranda turned to Maguire. "Mike, come stay with us for the day, maybe longer--you're probably not in danger but Stella needs you."

For once, the Detective didn't argue, and didn't try to protest Stella returning to the Haven. He knew it was the safest place for her, but that didn't mean he thought it was *safe*; she knew he was torn between wanting to end Morningstar and wanting to drag his only child as far from Austin as he could.

For the millionth time, Miranda was thankful she didn't have kids. Having her own family, thousands of vampires, and by extension the entire human population to worry about was more than enough worry and heartache and she had a feeling it was way easier than being an actual parent.

Nico rode back with Stella and Maguire; Deven joined her and David in the front car to talk strategy with the Prime.

David rubbed his face with one hand, sounding deflated. "Whatever it is we're waiting for from this Solstice thing had better be worth being stuck in a holding pattern this long. I don't know how Morningstar knows so much but I'm done being in the dark."

"I hope Stella can still do the ritual." Miranda watched the city turn to countryside out the window.

"Oh, she will," Deven told her. "She can't fight with a sword. She isn't preternaturally fast or strong. But she's got magic, and she'll marshal every iota of power she can to get back at those bastards no matter what the cost. You can see it in her eyes."

"It's the cost that worries me," Miranda replied. She leaned sideways into David's shoulder, reaching over to thread her fingers through Dev's, and let out a long breath. They both gave her a squeeze.

She closed her eyes for a minute listening to them discuss alterations to the sensor network that could compensate for acceleration and velocity; mostly David wanted a sounding board, but while he wasn't a programmer, Deven knew a surprising amount about physics, and he had a few insights. Really at this point nothing either of them spouted off with should ever surprise her; between Dev's age and David's brain they knew practically everything in the universe...except perhaps what to do about Morningstar itself.

As she drifted off, parts of the talk seeped into her waking dreams, and thoughts about the way things moved and the math behind it all gave way to the Web behind her closed eyes; without any urgent need to lay hands on it, she just watched the endlessly shifting strands twine and unwind, and she found herself wishing she knew more about how it all worked--she'd been more of a blunt instrument than a Weaver so far, but...if she just relaxed, didn't try to do anything but let it dance, it all made an intuitive sort of sense.

The longer she watched it, though, the more she began to feel something was...as if...if she tried to focus it disappeared, but when she let go, she could almost see something moving underneath the strands of light, like a Web beneath the Web, made out of something subtler, darker. These strands, which were the same color and luminosity as some of the ones she'd seen in her own part of the Web--the threads that made the Tetrad Thirdborn--reached gently toward her, beckoning. She supposed an Elven Weaver might find them frightening, assuming they'd admit such a thing could exist at all, but to her they were familiar, stretching closer, almost tickling her feet.

She smiled, and followed the threads around her into sleep.

*****

I will kill you. All of you.

I will rip open your throat with my teeth...no, my hands...and watch your blood rain down on the filthy ground of this city until you shrivel and dry out like a dead leaf. I will stand there, watching you die, licking your blood from my fingers and smiling. I will watch your lifeless body burn, breathe in the ashes, draw strength from the memory of your pain.

I will snap every finger you've laid upon me and mine and--

Sharp pain sang through his face, and Nico snarled, snapping back into the room, to the chair he'd been sitting in with his fingernails digging into the arms until the fabric split. His vision was red, and he nearly lunged at the hand that had slapped him, but just in time, he registered violet-black eyes fixed on his, and the bloody loop in his mind faltered and broke.

Distantly he heard a series of small objects clattering to the ground.

He stared up at his Prime. Deven stared back.

"Did you slap me?" Nico asked quietly.

A quirked eyebrow. "You weren't listening to me."

Again, the anger curled up through him like a dragon's foreclaws around his throat. "Do not hit me again."

In response, Deven grabbed him by the head and forced him to look at the room. "Do you see this?"

Nico noticed the overturned lamp, fallen artwork, and stacks of books that he had apparently upset with his mind. The whole room had a strange, ozone-tang to the air, like lightning about to strike. He knew he could start fires the way Cora did...another minute and the whole room might have gone up in flames.

"Now you listen to me," Deven said in a deathly quiet, steely voice, holding his chin so he couldn't look away. "You are going to get control of this, channel it into something useful. Don't give me that 'Elves aren't warriors' crap--Elves don't turn people into soup, either. You're not like the others anymore and it's time you faced up to it. If you keep losing control you're going to wind up chained with a broken neck again, surrounded by bodies. Is that what you want?"

The memory of those days was one of the great horrors of his life, and he shuddered. "No."

The bloodlust was fading, leaving in its place a quaking fear like he'd only rarely known. He felt himself start shaking. His entire body hurt--he'd been clenching his muscles as he sat there seething.

He finally let himself think about what he had done tonight. He hadn't seen the aftermath...thank Theia...but he had felt the rage rise up to claim him, reached through the night, taken hold of those humans and...

Nico put his hands over his face. "This is what the Prophet wanted," he whispered. "For me to become a monster, for all my power to turn to blood and leave me useless to all of you, just an animal to be caged. I used to be this noble creature of light and compassion. I am a ruin of what I was."

Deven knelt in front of his chair. "Perhaps you are," he said, gently drawing Nico's hands from his face and gripping them tightly. "What will you build in the ruins, then?"

"I have nothing to build with."

"Nonsense." One hand slid up to curve around Nico's face, and he leaned into the palm, helpless tears escaping for a moment. They were both silent, the warmth of the fireplace and the warmth of the touch helping ease the ache in Nico's chest.

Finally Deven said, wiping Nico's face with the corner of a throw blanket, "I'm sorry I slapped you. I was afraid to let it go on any longer but I couldn't get through to you."

Nico shook his head. "I am glad you did. If...do not hesitate, if it happens again, to do what you must. Please...promise me you won't let me hurt anyone else."

Their eyes met. "I promise," Deven replied with a nod. "But you must promise me you won't give up. I know you're afraid. But I'm with you now. As long as we're together we'll find a way."

He returned the nod, and the words: "I promise."

A soft smile. "Come on, then...let's get some rest. You're worn out...do you need more blood?"

"No." Nico let himself be drawn up out of the chair and over to the bed, where the Prime set to undressing him, his practiced hands strong and reassuring.

It wasn't until they were tucked into bed, Deven's arms around him and his breath at Nico's ear, that the comfort of skin to skin and the temple-like quiet of the room helped him to truly feel like himself again, whatever that even meant now.

"I don't know what to do," Nico said softly.

"Go to sleep, my love. We'll figure out the next step tomorrow. I have a few ideas...just let me mull them over a bit."

Nico sighed, burrowing closer. *Deven will think of something. You don't have to do this alone. You don't have to do anything alone, now, ever again.* "I love you."

"Is tú mo chuisle," Deven murmured, lightly nipping his ear. "Just rest, and have no fear."

Chapter Four

A low, protracted growl brought Nico out of his reading just in time to catch sight of Stella's cat Pywacket racing into the room and under the bed, Miranda's cat Jean Grey in hot pursuit. A few seconds later Pywacket streaked out from the other side of the bed and careened around the room to hide behind Stella's chair. As soon as Jean Grey barreled after him, however, a jet of ice-cold water hit her squarely in the face.

Nico looked over at Stella, who lowered the squirt gun and rolled her eyes. "Goddamn cat's a menace," she muttered.

Jean Grey, obviously affronted, sat down under the bedside table and started licking herself, ignoring them all. Meanwhile Py climbed up the chair and into Stella's lap, kneading the blanket over the Witch's thighs and purring, Nico suspected purely to spite the other cat.

Nico held out a hand and Jean Grey bolted over to him and began to rub his hand with her head. He picked her up--without being clawed in the face as were most people who tried to do the same--and sat her down on the book in his lap. "All right," he told the cat sternly. "You must be kind to Pywacket, Jean Grey. He is a good cat and you are bringing shame to yourself and your two-leggeds by behaving like a savage."

The cat glared up into his eyes, tail twitching.

"Or to put it as your Queen would," he concluded, "Don't be a dick."

He deposited her back on the floor. She shot him a dirty look but folded herself into a loaf and pretended to sleep, all the while giving Py a periodic side-eye.

Stella giggled. "Do Elves have some kind of animal magic?"

He smiled. "We can all communicate with the natural world, but it's more of a communion than a language. Plants and stones lack a nervous system, so they do not think and feel the way animals do. They communicate in energy. But a particular subset of telepathy allows some of us to speak to animals directly and understand them in return. You can usually spot those with that gift because they are constantly covered in animal hair and they tend to have messy houses."

"Sounds familiar." Stella nudged Py off her lap and smiled, though the expression didn't quite touch her eyes; she looked tired, and her usual sparkle was subdued.

"We don't have to do this tonight," Nico said.

"Yes, we do. I'm with the others--I'm tired of waiting around. I can't do anything else useful. I'm not going to let everyone down with the one thing I can do."

"You have been invaluable to all of us," he insisted, taking her hands. "Don't forget it was your magic that led the others to rescue me. I certainly haven't forgotten."

She met his eyes, tears gathering in hers. "I know. I just...Lark was my best friend, Nico. The only real friend I had outside this place, and...I feel like I've lost my anchor to the world."

He smiled a little. "Believe me, I know how you feel."

There was movement in the doorway, and they both glanced up at once to see the Queen waiting there, unwilling to barge in without leave.

Stella managed a smile for her. "Hey," she said. "Come in."

Miranda bowed slightly and then crossed the threshold. Stella's wards on the room were used to her by now, and Nico watched with his Sight, admiring how the Witch's magic--which according to many Elven elders was primitive and weak compared to their own--melded seamlessly with the Web, recognizing the Queen and parting to admit her exactly as would any Elven protective barrier. Now that Stella could work more directly with the Web her abilities were much more precise and focused, but she had always been powerful, and there was a kind of earthy elegance to her work that was satisfying in a way that rarefied Elven threads of light were not. The fact that she could work with the Web without even being able to see it...who could call that weak?

"Sorry I'm late," Miranda said, joining them around the coffee table. Jean Grey padded over to her chair and took up position sitting Sphinx-like at her mistress's feet. "I had to take a call from my manager."

Stella spread a scarf over the table and started setting out the components of the Speaking Stone spell--there were few, just the Stone itself, a knife, a small bowl, and the little vial of French white dittany that had somehow survived the attack on the shop. Her hand shook a little as she took out the bottle.

"Let me take that," Nico said gently.

"No," the Witch said shortly, then shook her head. "Sorry. I've got it. It's okay."

Miranda took a breath and asked, "What do you need me to do besides bleed?"

"It would be best if you did the talking when it comes time to send the message," Nico told her. "You're the one we need them to trust."

She nodded, unsurprised. "Just tell me when."

"Where are the boys tonight?" Stella asked, perhaps to distract herself as she finished arranging things.

"Thursday is Date Night," Miranda replied. "They're off in town doing whatever it is they do before they do that other thing they do."

The Witch chuckled in spite of herself. "You guys are so weird. I can barely manage my own drama, let alone adding three other people's."

"Right now it's the only part of our lives that isn't a mess," Miranda said.

Nico nodded in agreement. "I have observed many polyamorous relationships in my time, and many have worked beautifully, but up until now I would have agreed with you, Stella. I've had more than one lover at once but never more than one beloved. But then, I never had a mystical soul-bond either, so we are hardly a textbook case."

"Of anything," Miranda added.

"What about you two?" Stella looked from Nico to the Queen. "Does that mean it's your Date Night too?"

Nico felt his ears burning, and Miranda cleared her throat and looked away pointedly.

Stella blushed crimson. "You haven't even broached the subject yet, have you," she said, mortified. "Sorry."

Seeing the look on her face, it was the Queen's turn to laugh, and Nico couldn't help but do the same. "It's all right," Miranda reassured her. "It hasn't really come up--we haven't had a lot of time alone so far." She offered Nico a smile. "I wouldn't be averse to the idea but I didn't want to make assumptions."

He smiled back, and their eyes held for a second before he had to lower his to avoid making things awkward with Stella in the room. "Nor would I, nor did I. But...perhaps that's best left for later...Stella?"

Stella was still pink and trying not to giggle at how girlishly rattled they both suddenly were. "Let's get started," she said. At least she seemed to have lightened somewhat, given something more entertaining to think on for a moment. "Miranda, if you'll get the lights."

Miranda glanced at the light switch, and it flipped; meanwhile Stella lit the central candle on the table. Nico echoed Miranda's motion, concentrating on the wicks of the candles in the wall sconces, and after a beat, they lit as well.

"Nicely done," Miranda told him. "Firestarting takes a lot of effort for me--I'm going to ask Cora for some pointers when they get here for the Solstice. Jacob says she's becoming kind of a badass."

Stella lit a stick of incense, and as the smoke laddered up toward the ceiling, they all fell silent, waiting. They'd elected not to cast a full Circle for something as relatively simple and safe as sending a message; Stella simply uncorked the vial of dittany and poured it into a tiny stone bowl. She held her hand over the bowl, and he sensed her using her own energy to awaken the power of the herb and align it with their purpose. Then, she gave Nico a slight nod.

He recited the incantation to awaken the Speaking Stone. It was fairly straightforward, and as he spoke, Stella gestured for Miranda's hand and picked up the knife. She made a small cut in the Queen's index finger and held her hand over the bowl.

Dark, pomegranate-red blood fell into the bowl drop by drop, and as they all watched, the blood and the dittany swirled slowly around each other, gradually combining.

Stella drew Miranda's finger down into the bowl and dipped it lightly in the mixture. Then she handed the Queen the Stone, pressing her finger into it.

"The dreamer calls to the dreamed," Stella said, her voice clear and calm. "By the blood upon this Stone, hear the words of the Queen of the South, West, Midwest, Mideast, India, and Japan."

She gave Miranda a nod this time, and Miranda nodded back, took a deep breath, and said, "Let the priestesses of Elysium hear my call and heed my warning: Your people are in grave danger. The forces of the Order of the Morningstar have set their sights on the *Moriastelethia*. Help is within your reach; you need only send your location back along this link. We offer shelter and swords in your hour of need."

Nico had to smile at how easily she pronounced the name of the amulet without stumbling. She'd been a little clumsy with the Elven tongue at first, mostly because she didn't know how to adjust to having the whole language in her head out of nowhere and didn't trust herself, but once she got out of her own way, it was as if she'd been born speaking it.

Stella ended the message: "Sundered though we may be we are all children of the Lady of Shadow, Mother of Darkness, the Great Queen of Night. By Her will, so shall it be."

As she spoke, he felt the Stone absorbing their words, and when she fell silent, it began to pulse just as it had when Kalea had called to him from Avilon.

Unlike that night, however, this time it glowed brighter and brighter instead of fading. He'd never sent a call using enhanced blood before, so he wasn't sure if it was behaving normally or not, but the Stone pulsed faster, and brighter, until he and Miranda both had to avert their eyes from the light.

Suddenly it felt like someone had pulled the drain plug from the room. Nico felt energy rushing out of his body, into Miranda's, into the Stone, and *out*. The Queen gasped, panicking at the unexpected drain--she groped after the energy out of instinct, trying to stop it, but before Nico could warn her against it she realized her mistake and jerked backward so hard she literally toppled backward in her chair. The Speaking Stone fell from her hand and Stella snatched it out of the air.

Nico caught Miranda with one hand, though the chair clattered to the ground, sending Jean Grey tearing for the closet in a blur of fur and claws. He had to twist at an awkward angle to avoid dropping the Queen, but he managed to lower her to the floor without injury.

Meanwhile Stella added an extra push to the spell's energy to overcome any errant currents Miranda had created, and the energy whooshed out of the room, the Stone's pulsation hitting a crescendo and then fading out in a matter of seconds.

He looked down at Miranda.

"Did I fuck it up?" she asked, embarrassed.

"Nope," Stella said. "It went. Now we wait."

"Oh, good," Miranda said, and passed out.

Stella looked over at the Queen. "What was that about?"

Nico sighed. "I wish I'd known the energy pull would be so strong--I would have warned her. Such things tend to send her and David both into a panic."

"Why?"

"Because that's what happens when you are Bondbroken," he replied. "The severance causes all the life energy to be sucked out of you forcibly until you are dead. It is an agony unlike any other. David will not admit it but he has nightmares about his own death, and I have never seen such fear on his face. It's easier when they know to expect it, but when it's sudden..."

"God," Stella muttered. "I didn't know...I mean, I did...I was there after it happened. Shit, it should have occurred to me too. It seems like it was so long ago, but for you guys it's just a moment."

"Add to that, the last two times she has done any serious magical work were to save Deven and to save me--both times were traumatic, though at least the last one ended well. She is terrified of what Weaving might do to her and to us, but she keeps trying because she knows she must." He brushed curls from the Queen's face, smiling down at her admiringly. "She is working on a way to approach the Web using music, to get past that fear."

Stella snuffed the central candle and got up, righting the chair and moving it away so they could get the Queen up off the floor. The Witch squeezed Miranda's shoulder, and on impulse leaned down and kissed her forehead. Nico understood. They both knew a great many remarkable people, especially here at the Haven...but there was no one like the Queen. Stella sometimes forgot that her friend, who giggled with her over penis jokes and ate ice cream from the carton, was such a formidable creature.

"I will take her to bed," Nico said, and at Stella's raised eyebrow clarified, "To her own bed to sleep, silly woman." He took the Stone and tucked it in his pocket. "I will see that she keeps this until we get a reply."

Stella looked relieved to have the Stone out of her hands. "Good idea. I think I'm going to take a long hot bath and go to bed early with some of those nice pills Mo gave me. They keep me from dreaming so much."

He rose, leaned down, and kissed her. "Be kind to yourself, lovely one. I shall be here at a thought if you need me."

He wasn't entirely happy leaving her alone, but Stella wasn't the sort to stiff-upper-lip her way through suffering; if she needed company or help she would ask for it. He was thankful for that, as it helped simplify at least one of his relationships. Luckily since they had always been, as the humans said, "friends with benefits" more than a couple, she didn't begrudge him time with the others. From the beginning he'd been attached to at least one other person, even if that person had refused to acknowledge his existence for the first two years of their bond.

He carefully lifted the Queen up off the floor. She murmured something and burrowed into his shoulder. He chuckled.

"Good night, my lady Witch," he told Stella. "Sleep well."

She gave him a knowing grin as he left.

He thought about Misting to the Suite, but given how sensitive she was to Misting he opted just to walk and avoid waking her. She was hardly a burden, though she took up so much energetic space--she, like Deven, was a cosmic event contained within a small body.

The guard at the Suite door bowed and opened it for him; he nodded and carried the slumbering Queen to her bed.

Esther had obviously been in: the fire was dancing, the room uncluttered, the bed turned down. He placed the Speaking Stone on the bedside table and tucked Miranda in, and was sure he'd managed it without waking her until her eyes blinked open.

"Stay," she said blearily. "Just for a little while?"

"Of course," he replied. She moved off to the side and held open the covers so he could climb in next to her and she could resume her position against his shoulder.

He wasn't particularly sleepy, but the power of her weariness was difficult to resist, particularly in combination with the world's most comfortable bed and the lingering scents of all four of them in one of the few places they all felt safe. Miranda herself smelled like whatever botanical concoction she used to keep her hair from running amok, along with the almond-scented body wash she and the Prime both favored, with an undertone of spicy sweetness, like honeyed cinnamon. It was an apt description for her voice as much as her skin.

Plus, falling asleep kept him from focusing too much on how wonderful it felt to have such delicious curves pressed against him--he had always been quite pleased to take lovers of whatever gender, but Elven women had never been anything like the ones he'd encountered here at the Haven. Stella was softer, as the Queen packed a good deal of muscle under her petite frame, but both were damn near irresistible...and he had seen the way she moved with a lover, almost serpentine, hips rolling like the tide. Lucky for the current state of their friendship Miranda was asleep or he might not be able to talk himself out of making an overture and probably embarrassing himself...

A small, strong hand slid up his arm, fingers nimbly sneaking under the collar of his shirt. Her nails scratched lightly over his skin, sending a shiver through him, and a moment later he felt the hot softness of lips on his neck, and had to fight not to groan aloud.

He smiled. "Are you asleep?"

The murmured reply might have been "No," or a laugh, or something else entirely--he couldn't make out any actual words. But as she shifted her body onto his, her hands moving down to work his shirt up over his head, he was disinclined to inquire further...it would be so incredibly easy just to lie back and enjoy it, and his body was definitely on board with that idea...still, if she *was* asleep it would hardly be ethical to let her continue.

To his surprise, she lifted her head and looked down into his face--sleepy, yes, but definitely awake. A tendril of her hair fell down onto his forehead, and another joined it. He reached up and let one twine around his fingers, then touched her face, questioning.

"Is this okay?" she asked, voice a bit husky, making him shiver again.

"Oh yes," he managed. "Very."

Neither spoke again for quite a while.

*****

"Are they doing what I think they're doing?"

Deven looked over at David, simultaneously following David's psychic nudge along the Tetrad bond. Sure enough, he could sense Miranda and Nico were together, and things were getting a bit...unplatonic. "I'll be damned," he said, a little surprised. "I think they may be."

The Prime grinned. "Good for them."

Deven had to laugh at his enthusiasm. "You're incorrigible," he said. "And you have a lousy grasp on the concept of Date Night if this is your idea of romance."

"This from you," David answered with a laugh of his own. "I seem to recall your idea of a romantic evening out was armed combat followed by five or six hours of violent sex with as little conversation as possible."

"Don't forget the alcohol," Dev reminded him. "There was always alcohol."

David shook his head in mock aggravation and gestured for him to follow.

The Mueller Fine Art Museum was small, and not as widely patronized as other museums in town, but it played host to many traveling exhibits from all over the world; Deven had been there once, a year ago, for a showing of Tibetan Buddhist icons. He had no idea what the current exhibit was until he saw a banner stretched across the front of the entrance:

Ink and Faith: The Irish Dominican Order pre 1500 CE.

What the hell...

David saw him balk, but said, "I just want you to see one thing. Five minutes. It'll be worth it."

Deven took a deep breath and followed him along the corridor to the main hall, where instead of paintings and sculptures, there were glass cases in a long row. About two dozen people meandered from one to another, conversing in low voices.

At the far end of the room a fountain lent a peaceful soundtrack. Thankfully they hadn't gone for monastic chanting or anything so cliché.

David led him to the very last case and stood to the side so he could look in.

"I came last week out of curiosity," the Prime said quietly. "I wondered if there was anything remaining from the monastery where you lived. Imagine my surprise when I saw *that.*"

Deven peered down into the case.

His own artwork peered back at him.

It was a single vellum sheet of illuminated Latin--from Psalm 148, honoring God in the natural world. The careful writing was surrounded by intricate drawings of animals, a forest, a river; and inside the large capital P, a white hound leapt from a moonlit scene toward the morning sun.

That exact animal, in a much more practiced and elegant design, had been etched into Dev's skin for well over four hundred years.

The plaque beside the page read, *"Illuminated Biblical Passage, Psalms 148:7-12, circa 1260-1280. Artist unknown. The monastery at St. Alban's (just south of the city now known as Dublin) was one of the first to fall prey to the Inquisitorial hysteria of the era; by 1300 more than 70% of the monks there had been tortured to death or executed for heresy. Few artifacts of St. Alban's remain, but this page survived to be passed down through private collectors until it was donated to the exhibit by an unknown benefactor."*

He stared at it in silence for a long moment, and could sense his lack of reaction was making David uneasy.

"Is...are you all right?" the Prime finally asked. "Was this a bad idea? I just thought you'd want to know something you made lasted as long as you have."

Deven lifted his eyes to David's and smiled a little. "I was sixteen," he said. "It took weeks, bent over squinting in the candlelight." He pointed at a tiny splotch of ink along the bottom border that had been partially hidden with now-flaked gold leaf. "Right there...I fell asleep sitting up and knocked the inkwell over with my arm, but...someone caught it, and it only spilled a few drops."

Kind hazel eyes, shy and serious. "Go to bed, Brother. The Psalms will still be here in the morning."

A hand offered the inkwell. Their fingers touched.

"Thank you, Brother Senchan."

A wave of dizziness broke through Dev's composure, and he actually sagged back a step--David was behind him in an instant, both keeping him upright and shielding them from view. Genuinely alarmed, David took him by the arms and drew him over to a bench by the fountain.

"I'm an idiot," David muttered. "I don't know what I was thinking."

But Deven shook his head, swallowing what was either a sob or a laugh--there was no way to know without letting it out, and he didn't want to startle the humans.

"Senchan," Deven said, the name coming out on a hoarse breath. "Oh my God."

David's obvious worry was almost funny--he never looked worried in public. "What?"

It was definitely a laugh. Deven felt it pushing outward from his chest, and had to ground himself fiercely to stop its hysterical emergence. "The boy," he said. Of course that brought no more recognition than the name itself, so he clarified, "My first."

"The one who ratted you out to the Inquisition?"

"Yes." Deven pushed himself up off the bench and back over to the case, staring at the words and the ornaments, the border of knotwork that had given him hand cramps for days. There were well over a dozen symbols that would have been considered heretical by the Inquisitors, who had been imported from Spain; but at that time, the old ways were still being assimilated by the Church, Pagan festivals clothed in Catholic words. They must not have known he did this page, if they didn't use it as evidence against him.

In the upper right corner of the design he'd drawn a raven...he didn't remember doing that. They were an ill omen to his people, back then. A harbinger of death.

"What happened to him?" David asked softly. "Senchan."

Deven let out a breath he hadn't intended to hold. "I don't know," he replied. "They killed him, but I don't know how. Probably burned. They threw faggots in with the rest of the firewood back then."

It wasn't as if that was news to David, but he still looked stricken at the matter-of-fact way Deven said it. "Come on," David told him, taking his arm. "We should go. I'm sorry I brought you here."

"But you don't understand," Deven said as the Prime pulled him out the museum's front entrance and into the frigid night. "I've been trying to remember his name for years. I couldn't. Do you know what that's like, forgetting someone who for better or worse changed everything? There are great swaths of history I lived through but can't remember a moment of. Some of it I drugged away, but most of it just...fades. After a while you become a ghost to yourself, just a phantom walking the world with nothing to hold you to the surface of the earth but gravity and skin."

David had grown still, and was listening to him with at least a semblance of understanding; he was only half Deven's age, but 350 years was still a long time. Even the youngest vampire understood time differently than a human.

"I forgot my father's name," Deven went on. "It came back to me not long ago, but for years it was lost. My mother's gone, dead most likely now or worse, but her memory still exists in the world because of the Elves. My father, that boy--if I don't remember them they no longer exist. And I couldn't. Until now." He smiled, taking hold of both of David's hands. "Thank you for giving that back to me."

Slowly, David smiled, relieved. He nodded. "You're welcome."

They smiled at each other for a minute before David added, "There's one other thing I wanted to do tonight, if you're amenable...something I've been wanting to do since 1942."

"Oh? What's that?"

David's smile turned mischievous, and he pulled Deven into his arms, spun him around, and kissed him, right there in the middle of the sidewalk in downtown Austin, as cars rushed by and humans hurried to get in out of the cold, and the first few flakes of a rare midwinter snowfall tumbled down from the darkened sky.

*****

Miranda woke slowly, reluctant to let go of sleep but so comfortable and relaxed she didn't want to miss being awake either.

She could sense morning had come and gone, and it was somewhere near noon, but she couldn't feel the sun as strongly as usual this time of day--it must be overcast, even raining. Distantly she could hear a soft hissing sound…snow?

It snowed perhaps once every three or four years in this part of Texas. She remembered how, when she was a kid, she'd wake her mother up at four in the morning and drag her to the window to show her--then she'd put on every piece of outerwear she had and stumble out into the bracing cold to gather up scant handfuls of white and build a ten-inch-tall snowman on the picnic table in the back yard.

Of course, back then she didn't have a bed this comfortable, or a sleeping Elf keeping her warm.

She grinned into the dark, still amazed at her own boldness. Up to now she and Nico hadn't discussed sex, and she still wasn't sure what had possessed her, but…she certainly was glad it had. She'd seen the aftereffects of Elf Tantra repeatedly since David had taken up with him, but aside from a little touching here and there in the midst of whatever was going among the four of them, she hadn't been on the receiving end, as it were.

Now she understood that dopey grin David got sometimes.

Good lord.

She yawned and snuggled deeper into the covers; the arm around her middle tightened slightly. It really was too bad David and Deven were off on their own today…with the weather outside so frightful it would be even more lovely to sleep the afternoon away all tangled up in a pile. She'd been catching echoes of their date off and on since about midnight, which only made her wish they were here even more.

As if by magic--she nearly snorted--when she lifted her eyes, there were two additional bodies in the bed, appearing out of nowhere…and, it seemed, without their clothes.

Miranda couldn't help it; she had to giggle at the look of resigned annoyance on Deven's face when he started awake and realized David had Misted them out of one bed and into another. She tried to smother the laugh in the comforter, but Nico shifted behind her and woke, lifting his head long enough to see they had company and then dropping back on the pillow with a grunt.

After a bit of blanket reconfiguration and a couple of yelps due to misplaced knees and elbows, everyone was under the covers, warm, and settled in.

"So," David murmured into her hair, "Did you two have a nice evening?"

She flicked his ear. "As nice as yours, it sounded like. Just not nearly as loud."

"Don't look at me," Deven said sleepily from his position between her and David. "He's the screamer."

David rolled his eyes. "You weren't complaining."

"How could I? You kept sticking things in my mouth."

The Queen nearly choked on a laugh, and without opening his eyes Nico clapped her firmly on the back a couple of times, which only made her laugh harder.

She loved the look on David's face, watching her silliness--he looked happy, open, and completely at ease. So did Deven, for that matter, at least as much as he could--when they were all together like this, he seemed to shed some of his centuries of weariness.

Deven reached out to her, and she held back a smile; he still sometimes wasn't quite sure how or where to touch her, and she didn't want him to feel self-conscious about it. They'd had a few sexy moments devolve into gales of laughter when, confronted facefirst with the female anatomy, he'd frozen like a deer in headlights. Luckily he was a quick study, and she was good at giving directions. David had taught her that much--his penchant for dirty talk had the useful side effect of teaching her to speak up and make it clear what she wanted. Oddly she'd noticed that even Dev found that a turn-on.

"What's going through that mind of yours?" Deven asked, pulling her closer, laying his head on her shoulder.

"Men are crazy," she murmured. "Straight, gay, bi, whatever the hell you are now..."

"I think of it as gay-plus-one," he replied with a smile in his voice.

"You're really not weirded out by it?" David asked from behind him. She knew he'd been wondering but hadn't been sure how to ask. "You did have a very specific understanding of yourself for over seven centuries."

Dev's answer was wry. "I don't know if you've noticed, my raven, but of everything that's happened in the last few years, suddenly venturing into the Land of the Ladyparts is hardly a cause for alarm."

David snorted quietly at the term. "Seriously?"

A sigh. "It's not as if I've developed an attraction to women in general, after all--just this one." He squeezed her around the middle and kissed her ear. "It's part of the grand glorious destiny that's probably going to get all four of us killed. Just like how you and I never got over each other, and how there just happened to be an Elf of Jonathan's bloodline who could join with us...Persephone owes us a lot of answers and has a lot to answer for, but even I have to admit She's trying Her damnedest to take care of us."

Surprised, she looked over at David, whose expression mirrored hers. It was the closest thing to optimism she'd ever heard from Deven, and she would have attributed it to post-coital glow, but there was a sort of casual sincerity to it she'd come to recognize. The most revealing things Deven ever said about himself always came off as almost an afterthought.

She started to say something, but didn't have a chance.

Thunder struck inside her head.

She immediately put her hands over her ears, crying out in pain, but there was no way to block out sound that wasn't sound and wasn't coming through her sense of hearing--her mind was suddenly full of smoke and screaming.

Her awareness was seized and dragged from the room, across impossible distances--she caught glimpses of stone buildings, trees, and flames.

Her mind grounded hard in a location she had never set foot upon.

A voice she recognized echoed through her, begging: *"Great Queen--please help us. They have come for the Stone. Please. We are--"*

The connection broke as suddenly as it had been formed, and Miranda was left sitting bolt upright in bed with the others all staring at her. She could barely breathe, the fear and chaos were still so intense inside her mind, but she fought for words, for thoughts, for anything.

David took hold of her with his mind and held her fast; Deven and Nico added their own energy, shoring up her shields so she could distance herself from the vision enough to communicate.

"They're under attack," she panted. "The Cloister. I know where it is. We have to go--NOW."

Chapter Five

Lady, help me be brave.

Xara, the Hallowed One, kissed her forehead gently as the alarm bells began to toll throughout the Cloister. "Remember," the priestess said, "She is always with you, and so am I. Now go."

The young vampire was pale with fear and blood loss, but she gathered her courage and looked into Xara's eyes. "I will not fail you," she whispered, and bolted from the room.

Xara set the knife down on her personal altar and closed her eyes, listening: screams, pounding, gunfire. The stench of acrid smoke had begun to fill halls whose sacred stones had, only an hour ago, been filled with soft light and the peaceful drone of evening prayers.

She reached up to her bare neck, touching the skin, ignoring the sudden feeling of loss and vulnerability. She did not need jewelry to mark her as the Hallowed One; it was who she was, in her blood, in her very skin. She would not meet her fate cowering on her knees. She would stand as the Dark Mother's chosen one, and die as she had lived.

Taking up her formal cloak, she dressed, her eyes on the statue of Persephone she had brought from the ruin of Eladra's quarters. Perhaps someone...her own replacement, she hoped...would find it here, and it would find a new home. Perhaps it would be destroyed, as they were being destroyed, and the Shadow World would die as her sisters and brothers were dying now. Still something would be reborn from its ashes...nothing ever truly died, but passed through the lands of the Lady to find a new sunset, a new being.

She did not start at the pounding on her door, or the rough human voices beyond it. She stood before her altar, waiting, whispering a prayer for her people.

Of course the Cloister was not built as a fortress; it was easy for them to break down doors and drag the novices and attendants out into the cold night. They had never been anything but peaceful; the Swords of Elysium had their own strongholds, while the priesthood lived in the serene quiet of the forest. If there was anything left of the Order after all was said and done perhaps the Swords would deign to return and protect their gentler cousins once more. So much had been sundered, so much broken. So much wasted.

Hot, clammy hands closed around her upper arms and hauled her from the room, hammering her with questions and insults, which she ignored. She let them drag her, did not fight or scream; she could hear screaming all around her as the humans murdered their way through the building, but she remained calm, waiting.

They threw her to the ground outside in what had been the back gardens. The night-blooming flowers and berry bushes, which drew in the deer who were their primary everynight food source, had been trampled...such a shame. Shannon had taken such pride in the garden. The angel's trumpets, her favorites, had been smashed under the boots of the men who now stood around Xara in a semicircle, crossbows trained on her heart.

The night stank of smoke and blood. There were flood lights all over the grounds, as the men searched for those in hiding and dragged them out into the brightness, blinded and weeping.

Slowly, she stood, drawing herself up to her full height. *Lady, help me be brave*. She felt the wings of the Goddess wrap around her, lifting her up when her own courage might fail; there was no room for fear in a heart so full of Her peace.

Far to the right she could see a pale, huddled group of women still in their sleeping clothes; they were the Acolytes, priestesses-in-training, who acted as her attendants. When they saw that she had been captured, a cry of horror went up among them, and one of the men struck the first girl to cry with the butt of his weapon. The girl moaned and went down, blood erupting from her skull.

She counted, checked faces: Laila was not among them. Neither, it seemed, was Ashera; she breathed out in relief.

Thank you, Lady. Thank you. Hold them safe. What happens to me does not matter. Keep them safe.

"Where is the Stone?" a cold male voice demanded.

She let her gaze sweep from one end of the semicircle to the other, taking in the blank expressions on most of the humans' faces; so they were cursed, as she had seen in her dream, their free will stolen for the pleasure of the Prophet. The ones in charge, the Shepherds, still maintained some semblance of will, but all the faces before her showed only hatred, disgust. They were here to slaughter unarmed innocents, yet it was she who was an animal?

"I do not have it," she replied, lifting her chin to show her bare throat. "You cannot have it."

One of the men seized a girl from the crowd and dragged her into the circle, holding her by the throat.

"Tell us where it is and we'll let your little whores live," the leader said. "If you keep it from us, you'll watch every single one of them die."

The girl whimpered, her eyes huge with terror, and fitfully struggled against her captor. He flung her down in the dirt and stepped hard on her back, flattening her; as she cried out, he took a stake from his belt and slammed it into her back so hard it pinned her to the ground like a butterfly.

She looked up at Xara, agony in her sweet young face, blood trickling from her mouth. Xara held her eyes, giving her something kind in her last moment, pressing the thought into her mind: *Go to Her, child…She will hold out Her arms and take you in, and there will be no pain, only love. There is only love in Her embrace…only love.*

Great spasms wracked the girl's body, and she fell still, but her face showed nothing but peace.

The leader waited.

Xara met his gaze. "No."

Enraged--though at her refusal or her calm, she couldn't tell--he ordered another girl brought.

Out beyond the men, in the field that bordered the forest, she sensed something…something changing…they needed a little more time, *just a moment more…*

"I will give you what you want," Xara announced, causing the men to freeze.

The leader strode toward her, wrapped one massive hand around her throat. She was not a large woman, never had been, and he towered over her, but she stood fast. "Where is the Darkened Star?" he asked her in a deathly quiet voice.

"Oh, I did not mean the Star," she replied. "I meant the other thing that you want."

He tightened his hand, snarling. "What's that?"

"Death," she gasped. "Blood. You came here to bring death...and death has found you."

A scream.

The leader whirled around just in time to see all hell break loose.

Xara lifted her eyes and watched as dozens of dark figures poured into the field from the edge of the forest, where the fabric of the night seemed to have turned to water. Steel caught the light all around, and the shouts of anger turned to panic.

The humans turned and drew their weapons, but they were already falling; swift and silent, death came over the fields, laying claim to them all.

The human leader barked out orders, his rage a palpable force against her will; he pulled a stake from his own belt and turned on her, and before she could react, she felt it pierce her chest, its shaft forced into her body.

He turned to run--whether toward the battle or away she would never know--but did not make a single step.

A sword flashed.

The human's head parted from his neck and toppled over, his body dropping to the ground in a heap.

Xara sank to her knees, pain enveloping her. She could feel her blood pulsing its way out of her body, but she was still unafraid; she smiled up at the man before her.

A green light shone from his throat, and his eyes seemed to glow though they were black as those of the Lady Herself. Only a few years ago she would have felt fear, or hatred; but now she was Hallowed, and she understood how things must unfold. She knew what Eladra had known, and knew what *he* would know...soon.

She fell over. The ground was hard from weeks of freezing temperatures, but the cold no longer reached her. She held on to her last shreds of life just a moment longer--she wasn't done yet. She had one last task. *Just a moment more...*

Hands took gentle hold of her and turned her over, arms wrapping around her to hold her up.

She stared up at a new face, but another she recognized: The woman whose red hair ran wild, her eyes oak-leaf green and filled with power. It was she who bore the Stone of Awakening; she whom the Goddess had marked as Her own, long ago. It was she whose voice had issued from the Speaking Stone and she to whom Xara had called with it tonight.

Our Queen.

Xara smiled at her, trying to lift her hands in the traditional gesture of honor, but could barely move.

The Queen smiled back and took one of Xara's hands. Xara knew she had no idea what truly lay ahead of her…what she truly was. But that was all right. She was Queen; she would step into her true identity when the time had come…and nothing would ever be the same.

Xara returned her gaze to the prodigal, who was trying to feed energy into her broken body. She summoned a thread of power and denied him.

"Easy," he said. "Let me work."

"No," she whispered.

"Xara, don't be a fool," he told her urgently. "I can heal you."

She lifted her free hand--barely even registering the movement--and closed her fingers over his. "Listen to me," she said.

"Xara--"

"Listen," she ordered, managing to find a touch of her authority.

He fell silent. "Yes, Hallowed One."

Beyond them, the battle was finished. The noise died down, and she could sense the survivors and their saviors gathering, watching.

"Laila has the Star," she whispered. The darkness was closing around her…so sweetly, beckoning. She could feel the Lady drawing close, helping her keep her eyes open just a little longer.

"Laila is gone," he replied just as softly. "They took her."

"…you must find her," she went on. "You must find her." She drew up the last of her strength and reached up to touch his face, finding tears; she held her fingers up into the moonlight, wondering at the wetness, remembering there was a time she had been sure he had no soul and could not weep. "Thank you for coming."

"We got here as fast as we could," he said. "You lost at least eight...I'm sorry we didn't save them all."

She held his eyes. "You are forgiven," she told him. She touched his forehead, lips, and heart, leaving faint smudges of her own blood. "By the...grace...grace of the Dark Mother, whose wings encircle the Night...I charge you...to protect and guide the children of Her Hallowed House...as if they were your own..."

"Xara, don't--"

She continued, ignoring him. "...to keep safe the secrets, as set forth in the Codex, to receive Her knowledge and wisdom and power...to ensure the survival of Her children in the new world to come...from this moment until you draw your last breath and step forever into Her embrace...I name you the Raven's Blade, Guardian of the Mysteries...*Hallowed.*"

The last word rang out, and with it the last of her strength. She went limp, but her eyes held onto the world just long enough to see the survivors of the Cloister who had gathered around her, bloody and frightened but still hearing her final words; and as one, they knelt, and it was done.

*****

Miranda wasn't a hundred percent sure what she'd just heard, but the reaction told her enough: every single surviving member of the Cloister had gone to his or her knees, and Deven had gone stark white.

"God damn it, Xara," he said quietly, lowering the priestess to the ground. He closed her eyes, folded her hands over her chest, and stood, regarding the others silently.

"Some of the humans escaped," he announced to them. "Tell me which way they went."

One of the girls nearest the front cleared her throat and rose. "They left by truck, toward the west, Hallowed One--"

"Don't call me that."

They all stared, confused, but no one argued; no one seemed to know what to do. She could feel Deven's fear--greater than any she remembered ever sensing from him, so intense it was rendering him unable to think straight.

Miranda stood up as well and put her hand on Deven's arm, stepping out in front of him.

"Um...all of you, stand up, please," she said. "We'll worry about who's going to lead you and what Xara's wishes mean once everyone is safe. For now..."

For now they needed someone to take charge, and clearly things weren't going to go the way they traditionally did, so:

Miranda stood tall, hand on Shadowflame's hilt, breathing power into her aura until she knew they could feel it.

"I am your Queen," she said firmly. "Hear me. This place is no longer safe. You have an hour to gather what belongings you can, and then return to this spot to be delivered safely to my Haven. No harm will come to you there. We will work together to find you a safe new home and to restore the Order, but tonight, you will come with us and rest."

She gestured for them to get moving; as one they bowed to her, and ducked away in groups, looking back at the garden with emotions ranging from fear to paralyzing fear.

David appeared from the shadows; he'd made a quick round of the Cloister to make sure the fires were out and the humans were either dead or gone. He took in the scene and asked calmly, "What did I miss?"

"We need to find someone named Laila," Miranda said. "Xara said she has the Star, and apparently some of the humans made off with her and probably a few others. We'll have to track them somehow--can you..."

But Miranda felt someone drawing energy from her, and looked over in time to see Nico's eyes go black, his Signet beginning to glow more brightly.

"West," he murmured. "They went west..."

Miranda felt the Web in her mind's eye, like an itch trying to get her attention, and she found that when she closed her eyes, it was there. She could see Nico in front of her, and moreover could see what he was doing...he was tracking the humans through the Web.

She, David, and a still-shaky Deven watched the Elf as he dove through the strands of light, sorting through afterimages of the battle, back in time, until he caught sight of the truck--there were ghostly figures of humans, hauling a half-dozen vampires into the back. They were well out of sight of the garden or where the Elite had emerged from the portal; they took advantage of the chaos to drive away under cover of the trees, along the only established road to or from the Cloister.

Damn...they were well ahead, and within ten minutes would be clear of the forest and back on paved roads. It would be hard to catch up to them, assuming they could keep track of the truck; Nico needed to know the location to teleport them there, or at least--

At her side, she heard David chuckle, and a second later felt him reach into the vision--he couldn't see the Web at all, but he could follow Nico's mind, and through the Elf could see the truck as it bounced and rattled all over the uneven, perilous road at far too great a speed for safety.

David pulled power from her and Deven, and she sensed him extending through Nico, taking solid hold of the truck and jerking hard--

There was no noise where she was standing, but she still flinched at the "sound" of one of the truck's axles getting stuck on an exposed tree root just at the right angle to rip it from the vehicle.

"We have to hurry," Miranda said. "We might be able to catch up on foot--"

"No need," Nico said, smiling slightly around the massive amount of power he was using. "Allow me."

She stared openmouthed as the Elf sent a thread of energy sideways, drawing the Web open while still holding on to the vision of the truck itself. He fed the portal off of that vision, instead of off a location he'd physically visited, and to her amazement, it worked: with all of their power fueling it that vision was strong enough to act as a homing beacon as if Nico had set foot there a thousand times before.

"Take Dev and go get them," David said. "I'll hold down the Cloister."

Miranda seized Deven's arm and dragged him to the portal, drawing her sword as she stepped through into the darkness.

*****

They slipped through the woods in silence, feet barely making a sound on the exposed dirt of the road, coming up behind the truck unseen.

Miranda bent her mind toward Nico, impressing upon him that he should get the girls out of the back while she and Deven handled the humans.

The Elf nodded and dropped back while she and Deven ducked into the brush to come around the side.

The humans--she counted five, and could sense three more in the truck guarding the girls--were gathered around in the pool of the headlights, trying to get a signal to call for backup. They were arguing; apparently without a Shepherd to give them orders they had no idea what to do, and there was no Morningstar contingency plan for "car trouble."

Next to her in the dark, she felt Deven returning to himself a bit--Xara's announcement had been an enormous shock, but this, at least, he could do without thinking.

She caught his gaze, raised an eyebrow. *You okay?*

He nodded vaguely, tilted his head toward the men. She knew what he was thinking: He could have all five of them down in less than a minute.

She shook her head. There were three more in the truck, and they needed to draw them out, which meant making noise. If they tried to storm the truck the humans might start killing their prisoners. She knew Nico wouldn't go in until he knew it was clear.

As the men continued to argue, she moved out of the underbrush and walked out onto the road, right into the lights.

"Excuse me," she said loudly, "but do you fine gentlemen have a moment to talk about our Lady Persephone and Her plan for you?"

The silence that fell, along with the color draining from the men's faces, was so absolute and so hilarious she burst out laughing.

The best any of them could come up with was, *"Get her!"*

Morningstar trained its soldiers well--the Elite had made short work of them mostly due to the element of surprise, but the few who had managed to get blades in their hands had acquitted themselves nicely. These men weren't as quick on the uptake, but at least two of them were armed and came at her while the other three tried to shoot her with their crossbows.

One by one the crossbows misfired; one of the men saw movement to his right, and turned his head just in time for Deven to cut it off.

Miranda had the first one down immediately, but the second was more of a challenge. He fought back hard, and if she hadn't been expecting him to move so fast she might have hesitated, but this wasn't her first encounter with their mindless soldier-bots, and she already knew their moves.

"You guys need to update your training protocol," she told the man as she spun out of his way. He was getting out of breath; she was not. "You're becoming predictable."

Just as she said that, she heard a gun go off, and felt something impact with her stomach.

Pain coursed through her body--she grunted and stepped back, almost losing pace but holding on by inches, long enough to get her sword through the human's defenses and open his chest. Blood sprayed out, and she was in enough pain that she didn't get out of its way fast enough.

What the hell--

She looked down at the wound, which was bleeding far more profusely than it should have been. Something was wrong with the bullet--what had they done to it? Why wasn't the wound closing?

There were more shots, but she heard them ricochet off the trees and the truck--panic shots, by someone who'd been attacked from behind. She heard more feet pounding up the road. The other three men had emerged from the truck; they were the ones with the guns.

She fought to stay upright, but her vision was swimming. A wooden bullet? Couldn't be--David had said that regular human guns would destroy a wooden projectile as it passed through the barrel...but then the last time he'd seen anyone try it had been during World War II. Had they come up with a new kind of gun?

There was only one thing to do--she took a deep breath and dug her fingers into the wound, crying out in pain but pushing all her will into the movement. Her index finger hit the bullet, and she pushed harder, a wail escaping her lips.

She tried to get her fingers around the thing, but it seemed to squirm out of her reach every time she touched it, and the pain was growing worse with every second--it felt like her blood was on fire, boiling out of her body.

She heard screaming--no, wait, she *was* screaming. The pain engulfed her, and she fell to the ground, trying desperately to dig the bullet out of her body--almost, she almost had it--it was so slippery, she kept missing it--

"Miranda! Stop!"

Someone took hold of her arms and yanked them back, pulling her hands out of her wound. She couldn't understand what she was seeing--was that her? Were those her fingers dripping, was that...*oh God...*

She couldn't stop screaming. Deven and Nico both had her, holding her down on her back while they went for the bullet themselves, but it kept moving, and she writhed against it, *get it out get it out get it out--*

Power flared nearby, and a second later she heard, "Move!"

A hand pressed flat to her wound, and she shrieked in agony as something took hold of the bullet and dragged it out of her, the force of its will undeniable. The little hunk of lead seemed to send spikes into her flesh as it fought against the power that held it, but one by one those spikes ripped away, and after what seemed like an eternity, she felt it burst out of her wound, hit the ground in a splatter of her blood, and explode.

Miranda flailed, mad with pain and fear, but hands had her again and held her more gently this time while Deven's power took the place of David's, and with the rest of the Tetrad's help he poured healing into her ravaged body and closed the wound.

She was sobbing--it still hurt, it still hurt so badly, but at least the thing was out of her. She'd been shot before, it was nothing like this, that thing was *alive*--

"Shhh," David said in her ear. "Sleep, beloved. Just sleep."

The three of them pushed her with loving, careful energy into unconsciousness, and she was more than willing to let go, close her eyes, and leave the aftermath to her boys.

*****

A long, high-pitched shriek of terror and pain--not unlike those the Queen had made only moments ago--split the night air, and Nico winced. The inherited empathy he had to bear from the others told him far more than he wanted to know about the human's final seconds alive.

Another part of him, however, was pleased.

Every few minutes he had to stop and re-ground himself, but he managed to keep the rage at bay this time...mostly. He stood over the bodies of the vampires they had carried out of the truck, his arms crossed, his thoughts dark and poisonous.

Each body had a stake through its chest. They had all been dead when he opened the truck's rear doors.

As soon as Miranda was out David had slowly stood, then walked without speaking to the truck, seizing the one remaining human by the throat and dragging him inside. The doors slammed shut, and a moment later the screaming began. It went on for several minutes. Between screams Nico could hear begging, could hear the stammered answers to questions too quiet to hear.

Now, silence.

The doors flew open. David stood there silhouetted in the doorway, calmly wiping blood from his fingers with what looked like the human's jacket.

The Prime glanced up to his left, and Nico saw a small object detach itself from the top corner of the truck and fly over to his outstretched palm. David stared at it hard...then he said, very quietly, "You are next," and crushed the object with his hand.

Deven looked up from where he still knelt beside Miranda. "Was that a camera?"

David let the pieces of the device fall to the ground. "Yes," he said. He gestured at the truck, the bodies, and them. "This was all a setup--not the attack itself, but them making off with some of the girls. They knew we would come after them. They wanted a chance to try out their new toy."

He stepped down from the truck bed and went on, "Apparently whatever Codex the Prophet has in his possession--assuming it's a real book and not just something he does from memory--includes spells to use against us. They weren't told specifically what the bullet did, just that they were to shoot it into one of us and film what happened."

Dev sighed heavily. "Well, we knew that just making their soldiers stronger and faster couldn't be the whole of their plan."

David nodded. "Fortunately these spells take an enormous amount of power--they could make weapons against ordinary vampires pretty easily, but to fight Signets they needed heavier artillery. That was why they Bondbroke Tanaka--they used that power, somehow. Siphoned it off into whatever ritual created that bullet…and there wasn't just one, more like a couple dozen. This particular fellow wasn't at a high enough pay grade to know all the details, but he told me everything he saw when they were given the gun."

"Would it have killed her?" Nico asked, suddenly feeling cold. If Morningstar could make a bullet that could kill a Signet…if any one of them died…

"I don't know. My guess is that the pain would have made her kill herself--you saw how close she came to disemboweling herself with her bare hands to get the thing out."

They had all felt the Queen's agony reverberating along the bond--Nico and Deven had barely been able to hold any sort of distance from it and nearly got lost, but thankfully David had been far enough away that he could think clearly and react decisively.

"Well, at least we know they didn't get the *Moriastelethia*…wherever it is," Nico said tiredly. He was doing his best to hang onto enough energy to send them all back to Austin, but that wasn't going to last a lot longer. "None of them lived to get it to the Prophet even if one of these women had it, and obviously they didn't. Dev, you said this one was Laila?"

Nico pointed at one of the women, and Deven nodded, frowning slightly.

"We need to get moving," David echoed Nico's worry. "I don't like leaving all of them alone this long, and we still have to get everyone back to the Haven before you collapse, Nico. Let me Mist us back to the Cloister…there's no sense in dragging all of the bodies back too when the sun will be up in a few hours."

But Deven had crouched down beside Laila's body, and was staring at her, his gaze losing its usual sharpness…almost as if he were going into a trance. "Nico," he said softly, "bring me a knife."

The Elf caught David's eye; David clearly didn't know what was going on either, but pulled a pocketknife from his coat and tossed it to Nico.

"Here," Nico said. "What are you--wait, what--"

Deven flipped the knife open and used it to slit the girl's lightweight gown, revealing the smooth, dark expanse of her belly. He held his palm over her, moving it slowly from one side to the other, then paused…and cut into her flesh.

The girl had been dead long enough that the wound did not bleed; he cut a curved line that, Nico realized, followed the faint pale trace of a scar that had not had a chance to fade. Something gleamed in the darkness...and when Deven pressed lightly on her body, that something's edge became visible.

David shook his head in wonder. "She did have it. Xara must have put it in her body for safekeeping...the humans had it and had no idea."

Deven pulled the amulet from the girl's body gingerly, and the second it touched his skin, the dark stone in its setting lit up.

Neither Nico nor David could seem to move, or even breathe...but Deven shook his head and cut a piece of one of the girls' robes to wrap around the amulet and shoved it in his pocket as if he couldn't stand the sight of it.

But then, his gaze returned to Laila, and his expression softened. With reverent hands, he closed her garment, placing her hands on her chest as he had Xara's. He touched her face and murmured something, eyes closing for a moment.

At first Nico wasn't sure what to call what happened, but...something did. Some change in the air, the softest fluttering like a butterfly's wing passing, as if the night itself sighed.

One by one, Deven touched each of the vampires' faces and repeated the words, and Nico felt that same gentle release after each.

That was when he realized what he was sensing: A benediction. How many times had he felt that same kind of whisper-soft energy after one of the Temple priests or priestesses led the evening prayers to Theia? It had been a long time since he'd been anywhere near such a thing--that sense of the sacred had left him when he became a vampire. His whole life he had felt it in Kai's music as well, but not once since Avilon had rejected him.

And now...his heart wanted to cling to the feeling, even for a moment. Every cell in his body longed for that connection to the Goddess...he had forced himself to forget it for so long. If only...

The feeling dissipated. He sighed, eyes burning.

But he didn't have time to dwell on it; he would weaken very soon, and it was time to go. He shoved the memory out of mind again, determined to keep himself together.

Deven wouldn't look him in the face when he was done with his task; he was pale, almost seeming embarrassed at what he had done.

David was staring at Deven as if he'd never seen him before, but he said nothing either; instead he picked Miranda up from the ground. Nico and Deven each lay a hand on his arms, and David had them all back at the Cloister before anything else could happen.

*****

The next couple of days were a blur of pain giving way to exhaustion, and if she'd had the energy Miranda might have been very, very worried about herself.

She remembered waking long enough to feed--repeatedly, a few sips at a time every few hours--and little else.

Any other injury would have been easy work for the Signet bond, and they knew that wood couldn't kill a Thirdborn, but this was something that had been designed to kill Signets...or more specifically the first vampires who had been the Circle's first incarnation. The bond healed physical wounds, but apparently it wasn't created to deal with curses.

It took a full day for her insides to stop hurting; it felt like she'd pulled every muscle in her abdomen and back, like the aftermath of violent food poisoning. If she tried to move too suddenly or too far pain would lance through her body from the bullet's point of entry, even though the wound itself was gone. Internal bleeding, she realized. The thing was still trying to kill her.

The bullet had acted like wood though it had been, based on David's brief observation, a fairly ordinary 38-caliber round. Though the one that hit her had destroyed itself when exposed to air, David had dug two others out of nearby trees and gathered up the shell casings to analyze.

Deven stayed by her the whole time, giving her more healing energy every time she woke moaning in pain.

When she finally woke on the third day, she felt almost like herself again, and with Dev's help managed to take a shower and move over to the couch for a while.

He wrapped a blanket around her and sat down cross-legged at her feet, taking both of her hands. She could sense him looking her over, healing-wise, and after a moment he nodded to himself.

"I think you're out of the woods," he said. "No bleeding this time. How do you feel?"

"Shitty," she croaked. "Situation report?"

He smiled. "All quiet on the southern front. David's at Hunter Development harassing Novotny, Nico is with his mother, the house is full of refugees, and I'm avoiding all of them."

"Oh?" Her throat was scratchy, and she wished fervently she had a--

Deven reached off to the side and held up a can of Coke.

She made grabby hands at it, earning a laugh, and guzzled half the can before saying, "Seven hundred sixty-six years and you haven't come up with a better strategy than hiding?"

"You needed me," he pointed out. "Besides, all the rituals of the Order are in the Codex, and at least a few of them are locked until the Solstice--there must be one to undo what Xara did."

"What did she do, exactly? I mean she basically said you were her successor, right? If you're that dead set against the idea just say no."

"It's not that simple." He reached into his pocket and brought out a cloth bundle; she could see, even through the fabric, that it was giving off light...pulsating. "She passed the Hallowing to me on her dying breath. It's magic...very old magic, as old as the Signets. As long as I don't put this on, it can't be completed, but until I find a way to give it to somebody else without dying..." He looked down at the bundle, frowning, and shoved it back in his pocket. "It shouldn't have worked in the first place - you can't just pass the thing to anyone."

"But everyone knew Eladra meant for you to have it," she said. "Are you sure you should go against her wishes?"

"I don't care about her wishes," he said flatly. "She was out of her mind to think I was some kind of holy being--I never even finished training. And then there's that whole thing where I murdered her in cold blood. That alone should have made the thing reject me."

She understood, of course, how he felt--he'd been abandoned by the God he'd loved to die by the hands of His supposedly holy people, and escaped only to have another unwanted fate thrust on him by Eladra; he'd run away from that, too, but centuries later found himself chosen by another force beyond his control: the Signet. He hadn't chosen that any more than he had chosen to be sent to the monastery or named Eladra's successor...he'd been forced to live after Jonathan went on without him, then forced to bond to her and David, then Nico…and while the Tetrad had so far been a good thing, it still hadn't been what he had asked for.

She remembered David saying, once, that Dev had spent most of his life believing he was little more than a commodity--a prize to barter off to whatever god wanted his worship, a body to buy and sell for drugs or assassination or to rule the West. Of course he would fight tooth and nail not to be pushed into another fate.

But that didn't mean he would succeed.

She didn't argue with him, and in fact her heart broke for him, knowing how futile his anger probably was. If that amulet really was like a Signet, there was no undoing it.

…although how exactly he was meant to wear both at once, she had no idea.

"For now, though, someone needs to be in charge of the Cloister people," she said. "Can you maybe take it on temporarily? They'll cope a lot better if someone they trust is in control."

He gave her an "are you mental?" look. "Why on earth would they trust me? They all know who I am and what I've done. Tradition would make them obey me, but out of fear, not trust. They'll be much happier and much better off once we get this whole thing fixed. Now that you're better I suppose I should go tell them that much--that no, I have no intention of leading them, and in a couple of weeks we'll know what to do. They can take the time until then to figure out who they do want."

"I'm sure it will be just that easy," she told him wryly.

"Anyway," he went on, ignoring her pointedly, "if nothing else, we finally have something over Morningstar: They don't know we have the *Moriastelethia*. But that does mean they'll keep looking for it, so the other Cloisters need to be warned. We managed to salvage most of Xara's records, most of their belongings, and as many relics as we could carry in one trip--as soon as Nico's back up to snuff he's going to Gate us back there to look for more. He's also going to do the same with some of the Elves--take them back to Avilon, see what they can save."

"Good," she said. "Assuming Morningstar doesn't have people hiding there waiting for exactly that."

"He'll have plenty of swords with him, don't worry. And given what he was able to do the other night…" He trailed off.

Miranda thought back, remembered watching the Weaver with her heart in her throat. "Since when could he do all that? I mean, so many things at once, and still manage to transport everyone? I know he's powerful, and that pulling from all of us things can get epic, but that...that was unbelievable."

The pride in his smile made *her* smile. "Elves. Every house should have one."

He pushed himself up off the floor and leaned down to kiss her forehead. "If you think you can do without me now, I'm going to go talk to them...might as well get it over with. If you have any pain at all just call and I'll be here."

She smiled. "I'm okay, really. I probably won't be up and around until tomorrow but nothing hurts. I'm just tired."

Once he'd gone, she burrowed down into the blanket and throw pillows, enjoying the heat of the fire; it was a balm for her worn-out muscles. She drifted in and out of sleep for a while, finally feeling comfortable and safe again.

When she opened her eyes again, it was to a gentle tap on her mind.

"Mmm...glad you're here," she murmured, smiling at her Prime.

David held up a glass of blood. "Fresh from the city, just in time for your 3am feeding."

She stuck her tongue out, and he handed her the glass and stuck another pillow behind her to hold her up.

He wasn't kidding--he must have taken it from a live human himself that very evening. The energy of the blood washed over her with every swallow, and she basked in it as she had the firelight, grateful for the feeling of renewed life that seeped into her veins and soothed the last of the exhaustion into a gentler, easier fatigue.

"Thank you," she said. "I needed that."

He cupped her face in his hand and stared into her eyes for a long moment. "You scared me," he finally said. "I've never seen you in that kind of pain."

"I scared me too."

She started to ask what he'd learned from Novotny, but he lay a finger over her lips. "Later," he said. "Just..."

Miranda nodded, understanding. "Take me to bed."

He picked her up and carried her across the room, where the bed was already turned down and waiting, and took a moment to undress before crawling in beside her and pulling her close. She wrapped herself around him slowly; it still felt like she was moving through water just to put her arms around him.

Safe. I'm safe. No matter what, no matter how many people climb in and out of this bed, you are my shelter.

David smiled at her thought, and kissed her first on the lips, then the forehead, then the nose. *And you are mine. Always.*

He buried his face in her neck, and they clung to each other for a long time.

*****

The two groups of refugees at the Southern Haven had been housed near each other mostly out of necessity; there was only so much room even in such a huge building. This time, the Elite had been forced to double up, but as far as Deven knew nobody minded, or at least nobody complained loudly enough for him to get wind of it. Though David knew which Elite was the Red Shadow spy, Deven had left her in place purely to keep his finger on the pulse of community gossip. With everything changing so rapidly it was important to know if their warriors were happy--and increasingly difficult to find out given how busy everyone was.

He passed by the corridor that led down to the Elven quarters, though he wanted badly to give up on his errand, run down that hallway, and hide in Nico's arms.

He also wanted to see the baby again, but that urge also made him uneasy, and was enough to spur him onward, away from where he knew she and Kalea would be.

Only one hallway further he found the Cloister refugees. This was the first time he'd been down here; he hadn't been lying when he'd said Miranda needed him. He, David, and Nico had been nearly hysterically worried about her for the first day. He'd burned through a lot of healing power keeping her safe…he shuddered to think what would have happened if he hadn't had the gift. Certainly no ordinary vampire could have survived that bullet more than a few minutes, healer-adjacent or not.

He caught sight of one of the Cloister priestesses moving from one room to another, and said, "Wait, please."

She turned, saw him, and actually squeaked, going stark white and dropping to her knees.

Oh, honestly. "Don't do that," he told her, walking up to her and offering his hand to pull her up.

She stared at it like she had no idea what to do, but after a beat took it, and stood.

The members of the Cloister were not normally trained to be servile, but when he saw the cord she wore around her waist he understood: She was an Acolyte, one of the specially chosen junior priestesses whose job was to attend the Hallowed One. She would consider it her sacred duty and honor to cater to his every whim, and while that normally just meant bringing tea and tidying up, she was used to taking care of Xara, not this strange pretender to Xara's throne.

"Can you gather the Acolytes and anyone with a leadership role to meet with me?" he asked, keeping his voice low. If the others heard him out here God only knew how terrified they'd be.

She kept her eyes averted. "Yes, of course, H...um...sir. Where?"

He looked around. He wasn't sure what all was down here. "Is there somewhere you've been gathering for prayers? Anywhere we can all fit comfortably is fine. I'll go where you tell me to go."

Biting her lip, she pointed down the corridor. "There is a room without furniture...we've been using it as a makeshift temple. I will have them there immediately, H...sir."

Sighing, he found the room she'd indicated, which was fortunately empty. It was basically a den, like a half dozen others in the Haven, but instead of sofas and a liquor cabinet it now held cushions, candles, and an altar the Acolytes had set up using regalia and tools they had brought from home.

Part of him balked at the idea of being in such a place. He had spent years as Eladra's Acolyte, learning at her feet and serving her, and hours and hours beyond counting in a Temple meditating, praying, at war with himself all the while.

"I do not believe in your Goddess," he had insisted to her.

"You do not need to believe," she replied with a smile. *"You do not believe in air, or water, or the ground beneath your feet--they simply are. Persephone simply is."*

He stood in front of the altar, chest constricted by what he realized after a moment was longing. For all his confusion, the months he had spent in the Cloister were among the few--the years in the monastery accounting for the rest--parts of his life given over only to peace, to solace. Yes, he had denied Persephone, but he had felt accepted by Her and Her children nonetheless. Eladra had never demanded he believe or have faith; she had simply offered wisdom, and a place free from fear.

And he had thrown it all away. Thrown it back in her face.

Killed her.

Killed them all.

He pulled the Darkened Star from his pocket and practically dropped it on the altar, stepping back, suddenly unable to bear touching it. It was stained with invisible blood that would never wash clean. He had no right to touch it, no right to be here at all. How could Xara do this? Didn't she understand what kind of creature she had chosen to care for her sisters and brothers?

"Are you well, my Lord?"

He couldn't look toward the calm, low voice until he had taken a breath and fought back tears. Finally, he said, "I'm fine. Thank you."

Someone came up beside him. "If you like, I have a box you can place it in that might be more...appropriate."

He nodded vaguely. "Good. Good idea."

He looked up to see a woman in Acolyte's robes--dark-skinned, as Xara and Laila had been, and in fact her features reminded him strongly of Xara's, just younger. She had glorious dreadlocks down to her waist, held back on either side with silver combs, and had Xara's proud bearing.

She moved behind the altar and dug around in a trunk until she produced a carved ebony box much like those Signets were usually kept in between bearers. Her long-fingered hands unwrapped the Darkened Star with reverence, and without reacting to the way the stone was still pulsating, she lay it in the velvet-lined box and closed the lid.

"Are you..."

She smiled at his inability to form a coherent sentence. "My name is Ashera," she said. "I was Xara's senior attendant...and, yes, her sister by blood. We became vampires together, she and I."

"I'm sorry," he said. "I tried to save her--"

"I know," she replied kindly. "I was there."

He looked at the stately, serene woman in front of him, the very embodiment of the priesthood, and said, "She should have passed it to you. I have no business here."

Behind them he heard the other Acolytes entering the room and gathering, hovering, unsure whether to sit or stand or kneel or what.

Ashera started to respond to his words, but he turned away, unable to hold her gaze any longer. "Sit, please," he told the others.

There were fourteen in total: ten women, four men, all but two dressed in the Acolytes' robes. The other two wore more utilitarian-looking clothes; he recognized them as Stewards, another special designation, this one describing the people who took care of the night to night logistics of running the place, just like at a Haven.

Women tended to outnumber men in the Cloisters by three to one, and there were a variety of races represented, just as he expected. Vampires devoted to the Goddess's ancient cult tended to come from all walks of life. The Cloisters were one of the few places he'd found where gender, race, and background were essentially meaningless to the hierarchy. Everyone had an equal share of resources, equal responsibility; the difference was only of kind. Even the Hallowed One had chores. As with the Elves it was communism in its purest sense.

He wondered how they were coping, suddenly dropped here where there were servants and there were no gardens to tend.

Ashera smiled at them as she took a seat, easily and quietly regal. Her presence seemed to reassure the others, as did her pointedly choosing a cushion near him, as if to say, "See? He's not going to eat us...yet."

He fumbled for words for a minute. They didn't look particularly scared, but merely apprehensive, perhaps a little awed. He was used to having power...power he had won with blood. The Signet had chosen him but he had made it clear to all of California that there was a reason. He was used to intimidating people, making them cower. It was his job, what he was good at. This...

"Look," he said, opting, for once, for the bare truth: "We all know Xara made a mistake. I am in no way qualified for nor deserving of the *Moriastelethia*. You all know who I am, what I did to Eladra. She placed her trust in me and I murdered her. Whatever prophetic impulse Xara was following, she was wrong. As soon as I figure out how to undo the Hallowing I'll give it to one of you, you have my word. For now, let's all just be honest with each other--I don't belong here. If you want my orders, for tradition's sake, fine--I nominate Ashera to lead you in my stead until we straighten this out. Follow her as you would have Xara and don't waste a single thought on what I would want."

They were all staring at him. A few brows were furrowing in what looked like confusion.

"What?" he asked.

All eyes turned to Ashera.

She chuckled and stood smoothly. "I am afraid you are mistaken, my Lord," she said. "About yourself, if nothing else. May I show you something?"

Completely nonplussed, he said, "All right."

She returned to the altar, and to the trunk behind it. She withdrew a slender handmade book, and smiled softly down at it before bringing it to him. "Each Hallowed keeps a record of her experiences that he or she then passes to her successor. They continue writing in the same book until it is filled, then start another. It is the closest thing we have to an unbroken line of tradition. The current Hallowed's is private, of course, but Xara let the Acolytes read some of the older volumes to help us learn about the joys and responsibilities of the calling."

He had seen Eladra's journals; they always had purple silk covers. This one was dark brown leather. "Was that Xara's?"

"No, my Lord..." She handed it to him, and he realized it was older...much older. The pages were yellowed with time, the binding brittle; it reminded him strongly of the vellum Psalm David had shown him, though as he opened it, instead of brilliantly-colored illumination it was filled with even, careful script punctuated with diagrams, sketches, and a few illustrations.

Ashera turned to a page near the back and indicated the text with her finger.

He looked down. The date written about 2/3 down the page was July 24, 1204.

The journal's owner had written in archaic French, which he could translate pretty easily, though the writing was faded and took a minute to puzzle out.

They were watching him expectantly, so he took the hint and read it aloud.

"I have received a vision," the author wrote. *"Bleak and full of sorrow it was...I saw the end of all we know, a time of great tribulation. Ancient evil shall devour our world...but in the face of our extinction, the Shadow shall rise."*

He turned the page, and froze.

In the middle of the page, the author had written out a name.

He stared at it.

"Keep reading," Ashera said softly.

He cleared his throat and did as she said - she was right, the only way to understand what he was looking at was to keep going. "Um...*from the blood of those She fashioned with Her own hands...shall come a new Circle, and within it, Her own true children, known forever after as Thirdborn. They shall stand for our people, and fall for our people, and in doing so return our Lady's true power to the world...a new world, blessed in Her blood...a new Order shall rise, regaining its sacred purpose and place within the Shadow World...guided, and guarded, by the Sword of Elysium, whose Earthly name was given to me in this vision, set down here, by my hand, so those in the coming age will know him.*"

His eyes moved down to where the priestess had recorded the name in precise letters...with an additional title he didn't recognize at first until his brain helpfully translated it from old Elvish.

DEVEN BURKE

ILE'LYREN

Deven Burke...The Ghostlight.

He lifted his eyes to meet Ashera's.

"So you see," she said, "It is not a matter of Xara's choice, or even Eladra's. In the time before you were born, you were known to the Goddess....and we have been waiting for you."

Chapter Six

"Next."

The line of Elite stretched around the training hall's entire perimeter; only a quarter of its members were here, as David was taking things in phases. As soon as he was done with his Elite he'd be moving on to other territories. The whole thing was probably going to take months.

Deven sat at his feet, ostensibly helping but really just grateful to dump his frustrations on someone without an agenda in the matter. To David, Persephone was a general more than a deity; She had brought him back from the dead, true, but despite all he'd seen apparently he still didn't harbor any spiritual inclinations.

Thank God.

Dev passed him another chip from the foam-lined case where dozens of them were nestled, each only half a centimeter long and barely a millimeter thick. David popped the chip into the injector, and when the Elite in front of him knelt and bent his head, the Prime quickly pulled the trigger, implanting it in the vampire's skin just behind his ear. The tiny wound healed over almost instantly, and David ran the calibration routine from his tablet.

They were both wearing black latex gloves, which struck Deven as funny given they were operating on vampires, but David was concerned about finger oils getting on the chips. The Prime was even using voice commands on the computer to keep from having to touch the screen.

The whole process took less than a minute, except for the handful of cases where something went wrong; a few of the chips were duds, and on others the routine failed for one reason or another. Those Elite were gathered off to one side, where Mo waited to make a quick incision, pop the failed chip out, and send him or her on their way. They would be called back later once David debugged whatever needed debugging.

"Well that must ruffle at least a few feathers," David noted between injections. "A Cloister full of qualified priesthood, mostly women, and they pick a man who never even finished training to be their great white savior...oh, and who also killed most of their leaders a few years back. They can't all just accept it as Word of God, can they?"

"I'm sure they don't. The Acolytes do--they were close to Xara, and some to Eladra. They know what really goes into it. Just like how the average vampire on the street doesn't really understand what Signets do because they've never actually seen a Signet."

"Next."

It was amusing, or it would have been on another night, to see how some of the Elite reacted to being within hypodermic distance of their leaders. They'd all seen David and Deven, and all of them would have spoken to David in person at least once during their training, but they rarely spent enough time for the awe to wear off. Even an "ordinary" Signet bearer was a creature of legend, so what must they think of this tableau: Deven cross-legged on the floor, occasionally leaning sideways against David's leg, and David pausing now and again to change gloves, taking a moment to run fingers through Dev's hair before pulling on a new glove.

If their expressions were anything to go by, they were surprised. It was hardly a secret that the Tetrad all slept together, but again, it was more of an idea than a fact to most people. Not to mention David tended toward strict professionalism in front of his employees; lately, though, his moods had been a little capricious, and everyone seemed glad he was in a friendly one tonight.

Every now and then Dev recognized one of the California Elite and greeted them personally. Most of his old warriors were still in the West, running out of the satellite garrisons under David's management, but some had relocated here, and there were always a few Elite from the outer territories traveling from place to place. Night to night, things had stayed as they had been before in the areas David had taken over; the same Elite were still in charge, the same power structure remained, just with its commander-in-chief in a different time zone.

After the first of the year David planned to start making the rounds, having in-depth meetings with the lieutenants and Court members, getting to know them better; he wanted to reassure everyone as much as to reassert his authority. Deven imagined he'd be going along as well, to add his presence and make absolutely sure the whole world knew his sword was with the South.

Just thinking about it was exhausting. He couldn't say in all honesty he missed being in charge of the West. He'd never had David's ambition--he was good at leadership, but ruling wasn't his first love; he'd always preferred smaller organizations, more hands-on work, like training warriors, or...

He forcefully cut that thought off before he could finish it.

"How did you leave things?" David asked, part of his attention on the tablet screen as a progress bar turned from red to green and a readout of numbers appeared.

"I told them that for now Ashera would be in charge. I didn't commit to anything else. I took the Star with me, just to pacify them that I was thinking about it."

"But you're not?"

"Of course not! What do I care about prophecies? I care about reality, and the reality is I can't lead these people."

"You mean you won't."

Deven glared at him. "Fine. I won't. Whatever. I changed the subject and told them a little about my idea for the resettlement."

David smiled slightly at the aggravation in his tone but didn't comment on it. "The architect says she has some preliminary drawings for us--for the lower level, that is. I told her about the cliffside structure and she said she'd put something together for that before our meeting using the old Haven plans, and we can go from there."

"Good."

After another couple of injections David gave him a sideways look and said, "Just as a reminder, if it weren't for prophecies, you wouldn't have Nico."

"Don't start."

"I'm just saying."

Deven frowned up at him, and David chuckled, stripped off his glove, kissed a finger, and pressed the finger to Deven's nose. Rolling his eyes, Dev bit him.

David yelped and laughed, and the Elite standing in front of him looked openly astonished.

"Sorry, Elite-309, I can glower at you if you'd prefer," the Prime said.

She blushed. "As you will it, Sire."

Another laugh. "Good answer. On your knees."

"You are in an oddly good mood tonight," Deven pointed out. "Any particular reason?"

"Well," David said, "At the moment I'm playing with my toys, the system is working remarkably well so far, I got word that the Elite in Chicago finally cleared out that nest of Blood Kings, the Morningstar attack in Kenya last night failed miserably, and this morning I had sex with three of the hottest, most amazing people I've known in 350 years of life."

"When you put it that way it sounds fabulous," Deven said, smiling.

"Damn right." He nodded to the woman in front of him, and she rose, bowed, and left, still faintly pink.

Deven continued to study him over the rest of the hour, thinking about the looks David had been getting from Miranda and Nico lately. They all agreed David was...different...since the territories had started falling into his lap, and they all wanted to think it was just stress.

But Miranda had told him privately what David had said about having a plan to run the whole planet, and while such an idea was perfectly in keeping with the David Solomon Deven knew, the fact that David was worried about *himself* gave Dev pause. David had always been reasonably self-aware, especially for a man, and given how often he'd been thrown for an emotional loop since meeting Miranda, he was even more watchful of himself than before. Was there, then, anything to worry about, or was David just internalizing the world's madness?

Either possibility could lead to some unpleasant places.

"You're staring at me," David said mildly, startling Dev out of his thoughts. "There are only five more--surely you can keep your hands off me that long."

"Oh come now," Deven replied, "What was it you used to say when I caught you watching me sleep? You like looking at beautiful things? Well...ditto."

Another chuckle. "Next!"

Deven had tried to reassure Miranda--there were three of them now to keep David balanced and to call him out if he acted like an ass; the important thing was to keep him talking, to make sure he was telling at least one of them what was going on in his mind. Bottling was a good idea for beverages, not so much for people. Both were apt to explode from internal pressure.

Which, of course, was part of why Dev had come here tonight; one of his favorite things about David was his ability to listen almost entirely without judgment and offer advice the same way. Of all the people walking the Earth David had known him the longest, and vice versa. If anyone would understand where he was coming from in all this, it was the Prime.

It was therefore all the more annoying when David said, "You know...that night at the Cloister, when all those Acolytes were kneeling to you, and then later when you were blessing all those poor dead girls...I don't think I've ever seen that look on your face before."

"What look?"

"It's hard to describe. On the one hand you were scared out of your wits, which is another rarity, but on the other...Nico saw it too, maybe he can describe it better. But there was a rightness to it. As long as I've known you, you've been a puzzle to me, and I've put together piece after piece. One of the few I had never found fell into place seeing that, and I realized it wasn't just any piece, but a corner that changed the entire picture. Something about you suddenly made more sense."

"Well you're not making much."

David raised an eyebrow. "Don't give me that. Maybe I lack the language for it, but you know exactly what I mean."

"You don't actually think I should take the Star, do you?"

"I think you should do what you feel called to do. For now, at least I don't think that means leading the Cloister--we've got enough going on. But just like with your little sister, I think you should have a role, even if for now it's a step removed from full involvement. Let Ashera lead, let Kalea find a foster, but be a part of both. You don't have to ditch your life here and start a new one--you can be who you are and this too. Define what that means for yourself."

David smiled at his thoughtful expression and added, "Look around you, my darling--nothing about us is what it was supposed to be. We're making it up as we go along. There's never been a Tetrad, never been a Prime who claimed another Prime's territory, never been an Elven Consort...we have the dubious privilege of being something new. So be a gay-plus-one polyamorous vampire assassin murder pimp priest big brother. Although you might want to find a better word for it--that's a lot to print on a business card."

Deven laughed and snapped the empty case shut; they both discarded their gloves, and David pulled up a graph of the overall results of their efforts, nodding to himself before closing the program. Dev had barely noticed the line dwindling, but the training room was now empty except for Mo, who was placing the defective chips in a separate box.

David stood, stretched, and offered him a hand up, taking the opportunity to pull him close for a kiss. "Allow me, if you will, to distract you from your worries for an hour or two."

Deven regarded him critically for a moment, looking him up and down as if weighing his merits the way he had the first night they'd met. "It will be a sacrifice, but...I suppose I can allow that."

David bowed gallantly. "I am at your disposal, my Lord."

Dev raised an eyebrow and gave him a sly smile. "You're going to regret saying that."

He smiled in return, straightened, and slid an arm around Deven's waist. "You always say that...but I never have."

*****

Miranda missed the early days of her life in the Shadow World when she could go into the city by herself without the clench of worry about who might be lurking out there waiting for her. Even a year ago she'd been more comfortable walking the streets--some naïve, arrogant part of her hadn't truly believed Morningstar was a threat to her as an individual, even though Primes were dropping like flies all over the world and one of her best friends had been murdered in the one place he should have been safe.

She sat in the car for a few minutes, gathering her courage, staring out the Escalade's windows at the human passers-by.

A hand closed on her wrist. "Shall we?"

She looked over at Nico, and it was clear he was struggling as well. That wouldn't do--he'd asked to come with her so *she* could reassure *him,* not the other way around.

It wasn't as if they would be alone, anyway. There was always a team of Elite wherever she went. After years of arguing with David over how many and how close, they'd arrived at a reasonable compromise: her guards kept her in their sights but stayed out of her sight.

"I'd be happy to escort you, my Lady," Harlan said. "Just say the word and I'll put this thing in park."

She smiled. "That's okay, Harlan. I just have the jitters after the other night."

"Honestly, my Lady, at this point if I were you I'd be wearing a Kevlar onesie and a chain mail scarf."

Miranda had to laugh at the mental image, and so did Nico. "Come on," she told the Elf. "Let's be brave together."

It was another frigid night, though there hadn't been another snowfall; the first had turned to ice and rendered Austin extremely hazardous for seventy-two hours, so she hadn't had to make excuses to stay in after she'd recovered from the gunshot. Now, though, she was sick of bagged blood and had serious cabin fever.

She got out of the car and straightened her various outerwear, making doubly sure she could reach Shadowflame without impediment. She peered into every shadow around the car, senses on alert, straining to feel anything dangerous, anything even a touch out of the ordinary.

After a minute Nico said quietly, "We can go back, if you want."

She looked at him and tried for a smile. She wanted to put on her Queen face and be the support he needed, but even if they hadn't had a Signet bond she knew was telling him otherwise, being dishonest to someone so compassionate felt impossible.

"I used to be bulletproof," she said.

He smiled. "I know." He took her hand and tucked it in his arm, started walking. She fell into step with him, thinking they must be a striking pair. He tended to be stared at anyway, both because of his flashing beauty and, well, because of the ears.

"Have you decided about your hair?" she asked, wanting to think about anything but the way her stomach was churning. There were times she almost felt like the bullet was still in her, like a phantom limb. It reminded her of how Deven sometimes rubbed his hands together as if they were still broken, though it had been well over seven centuries.

Nico's eyes lifted up to his hairline. "I don't know…it was so long for so long, and going among the refugees without it I feel like even more of an outsider. But at the same time…I *am* an outsider. As Deven said, I am not like the others anymore and I must learn to accept that. I was never one of the Elves who spent hours braiding and arranging my hair, so at least I do not miss that."

Miranda grinned, thinking of Kai's elaborate braids with their beads and bells. "Another thing I guess your brother got that you didn't."

Nico chuckled. "Yes…Kai was…*is*…the peacock of the family."

There was an uncomfortable pause. Neither of them knew how to talk about Kai, and neither wanted to talk about why.

"Let's stick with present tense," she said. "Sound good?"

"Yes. I would prefer that." He cleared his throat and returned to the subject. "From a strictly practical standpoint it is certainly easier to deal with short. I never realized how much effort went into just keeping it out of the way, and how nice it is not to have your lovers roll over on it every night."

"Elven Kama Sutra, Volume 1: Ow, You're On My Hair." Miranda laughed, and so did he. "There've been times I wanted to hack mine off the way my mom did. It'd save me a fortune in hair care products."

"Don't you dare," he said, smiling. "Imagine Miranda Grey without her trademark red curls."

"I know. My publicist's head would explode. Can't have that."

They took a long, slow route around the downtown area, talking about nothing really, and after a while she started to feel less edgy. A quick detour to a nearby park, a couple of joggers, and dinner was dealt with.

She gave Nico an approving smile as he gently nudged the human woman he'd fed on back toward the flow of pedestrian traffic.

"It's gotten easier," he told the Queen as they watched both of their mortals disappear back into whatever lives they had made for themselves. "Just knowing I don't have to kill them helps a lot. I wish I knew what to expect from the next New Moon."

"Well, it's a week until the Solstice…I'm guessing after that we'll know."

Their errand over, they could go home, but Miranda wasn't quite ready to yet. "Coffee?"

"A beverage made of roasted, ground beans from a tropical--"

"I meant do you want some, you dork!" she laughed, the sound ringing off the mostly-deserted street. People were spending as little time outside as they had to, though there were always a few crazies out running in the frost.

Nico laughed back at her and bowed. "Lead the way."

She liked this, talking and joking with him; she had worried that outside the Tetrad they wouldn't have anything to talk about, and their relationship would depend on sex or need one of the boys as an intermediary. She should have trusted the wisdom of the Signets or Persephone or whatever was driving all of this--even with their manipulation and magic, she knew that if for some reason Nico hadn't fit perfectly into their circuit, he wouldn't be here.

Not that she minded the sex, of course.

She knew Nico wasn't eavesdropping on her thoughts, but he picked up the general theme without realizing it. "So if you had it to do over, would you have gone to bed with Kai?"

Miranda looked at him in surprise. "Of course you knew about that," she said, shaking her head. "You and he would have talked about it."

"You do not have to answer if it's uncomfortable. I am merely curious."

They walked into Slim Shaky's, the blast of the heater almost taking her breath away, and put the conversation on hold for a minute until they'd ordered.

Settled into a table with a mocha and a scone, and he with a chai, she said, "You know…I don't think I would have. At least not yet. If he hadn't been captured, and the Tetrad had still happened…maybe, if we get him back, someday we'll go there. But I'm so glad we got it out in the open regardless."

He seemed to be deciding something, and at length said, "Kai is very fond of you. Perhaps more than he would admit. I hope that you have a chance to revisit the idea--in your own time, of course."

She bit her lip and stared into her cup. "I miss him," she said. "Every time I sit down at the piano I want to play one of the pieces we were working on together, but when I try, I just...I can't keep from crying. I don't want to mourn him. I feel like if I do, I'm giving up on him, and I'm not ready to do that. Not yet."

"Nor am I."

"Would he be upset that you and I..." She crooked her eyebrow at him, and he smiled.

"It might interest you to know," he said with studied nonchalance, blowing on his chai, "that it would not be the first time he and I were both involved with the same person."

"Seriously? At the same time?"

"Indeed. These were all casual affairs, mind you, nothing romantic. If...when...he returns, we will have a lot to discuss, he and I...and you and he, and I. Even if your friendship remains platonic we should talk things over to lessen any chance of hurt feelings."

"No kidding." She tasted her beverage, found it a shade too bitter, and dumped sugar into it.

Nico said, "I had no idea how prevalent sugar cravings were in this realm until I met all of you. By the time Deven's drink is sweet enough for him the spoon stands up in it."

"I know, right? I thought David had the worst sweet tooth in the Shadow World until I saw Dev drink coffee. Apparently he'll do unspeakable things for a peanut butter milkshake."

A speculative grin. "Perhaps I should bring him one home tonight."

Miranda broke her scone in half and offered him a chunk; he took it, eyes sparkling in the coffee shop's amber lamplight. Slim's was a strange Austin hybrid--it had retro lamps and salvaged tables from several different decades and modes of décor, played music from the 80s as well as industrial that sounded to her like a blown vehicle transmission, and hosted art of a dozen different styles from artists all over town. As a 24/7 place it attracted equal numbers of students, writers, and the occasional vampire. She'd even heard her own music over its sound system.

"I have a weird question," she said without really thinking.

He peered at her over his half of the scone. "I, in all likelihood, have a weird answer."

"Have you ever seen anything...I mean, in the Web...the other night, I was looking at it while I was falling asleep, and I saw something...under it."

One eyebrow lifted. "Under it?"

She struggled for words, a little irritated at herself for bringing it up when she had no idea what she was even talking about. "You said that the entire Web is made of the same energy, right?"

"Yes."

"But our part, the threads that connect the four of us and make us Thirdborn...those threads are darker."

"Persephone's touch upon them makes them appear so."

"But what if they don't just *look* different--what if they *are* different? What if we're made of something else now?"

He frowned. "There is nothing else. All matter, all life, is one."

She was definitely screwing it up. "What if it isn't? Or what if...what if there's more to what's there than what we can see?"

A long blink. "I have no idea what you are talking about."

"Okay. How about this. Elves have been Weaving the same way for centuries. Witches use that same energy even though they don't usually See the Web like you do. But what you were taught is the particular vision of the Elves--Theia's children. What if there's a level of the Web that you couldn't see before but could now that Persephone is returning? Like, when She was locked away, that vision was lost to us, but now..."

She trailed off, hoping against hope that he got what she meant.

He continued to frown, but thoughtfully, considering her words. "You have seen this?"

"I think I did. It was there underneath the Web I'd already seen, and it felt like...like it's the thing feeding our bond. Like it's all the same basic reality, but what we've been given has a different flavor, or something, not just on the outside."

Suddenly his eyes went wide. "The Codex," he said. "I have seen several references that I thought they were merely poetic, but may have been intended more literally. Some of the passages I can read refer to something called the *Thiamoriarana*..."

"The Dark Web," she said. "Or Shadow Web? I don't know enough about Old Elvish to get the subtleties."

"I think 'dark' would be closest," he replied. "As with the *Moriastelethia*...the word that refers directly to a shadow is *numbara*, and *moria* itself is darkness as a physical reality, but when *thia* is added in any sense, that darkness becomes the ultimate *source* of darkness, the power of Persephone Herself. She is the *Moria Thia*, and all *numbarai*--all shadows--arise from Her. So *Thiamoriarana* would be a Web belonging to that darkness--Persephone's Web, the Dark Web."

"I think it'll be less of a headache if we go with Dark Web."

"Agreed." Nico set down the scone and sipped his chai. She noticed, without meaning to, that when lost in thought his brow furrowed just as Kai's did, and it was just as attractive. "I will have to look more deeply at the Web later tonight once we are home," he said. "I don't think I could concentrate in this environment, at least not enough to explore something I've never seen."

Miranda sighed, relieved that he didn't think she was insane, or at least was willing to consider she might not be.

"But if you are right..." A spark entered his eyes--she recognized it as the same gleam David got when he figured out the answer to a coding problem. She imagined she had something similar when she got an idea for a song. "Ever since Morningstar...did what they did to me...I have had trouble Weaving. At first it was because I was in such a traumatized state, and so raw. Then the Tetrad was formed and I became Thirdborn, and the problem continued, but I assumed it was all because of the anger."

She frowned at the idea that he could dismiss it so easily. "Some of it probably is, though."

"Oh, of course." He looked surprised at her tone, and she was instantly relieved by his next words. "Deven is absolutely right--my anger must be dealt with. What I mean is that a Weaver with my experience should be better equipped to at least channel that energy into something useful, but time and again I have found it much harder than I expected. The night at the Cloister is the first time I have been successful, and even then, it was more by brute force than the intricacies of the art I spent my life learning."

Now she nodded, understanding. "But if the Dark Web is a real thing, and we can tap into it, part of the problem might have been that you were trying to fit a square peg into a round hole."

"Something like that. The idea is intriguing--if nothing else it gives me an avenue to explore. Thank you, Miranda."

She shrugged, chuckled. "Always glad to provide half a scone and an awkward metaphor."

"It isn't awkward," he pointed out. "If you're right, it's symbolically perfect. The Web the Elves know is Theia's Web, and it is only half of the totality of the universe. Light and dark in balance...it makes sense, and moreover, it feels right."

Miranda nodded. "I think so too."

As they finished their coffee and left the shop to wait by the street light for Harlan, she was still thinking about it, and how much less frightening it was to consider working with something that was, more or less, made for them. The magic of the Elves, and even of Witches like Stella, had always seemed so untouchable; even as strong as she was, she'd felt like she was somehow unworthy of it. But something that came from Persephone...she could reach that. She could touch it without feeling like she was breaking some kind of natural law.

Of course it was possible she'd imagined the whole thing.

That thought, however, rang false to her heart. Between what Nico had seen in the Codex and the gut feeling that she had Seen something real, she found herself willing to suspend disbelief, and just flat out hope it was true. If it was...if they could use it...imagine how much more powerful they would be, using the right tool for the job instead of trying to force light into a place where light didn't belong.

Morningstar wouldn't stand a chance.

*****

"God damn it!"

Deven looked up, surprised. "Did you just--"

Nico nearly threw the Codex on the ground in a fit of temper, but at the last moment managed to rein himself in. "It's not there. It's not there!"

Dev, sitting on the floor wrapped in a blanket near the fire, slurping the milkshake Nico had brought him and intermittently inking over the penciled lines of a possible tattoo design, regarded him calmly. "Fireplace, please."

Nico glanced over at the hearth, and Dev felt him pushing the excess energy that crackled around him into the fire, which leaped up to twice its height. The heat was blistering for a moment, but died down fairly quickly, and better yet, it wasn't the furniture.

"Good." Deven nodded approvingly. He'd just thought of it that evening, and lucky he had--whatever it was Nico was trying to do was obviously not working.

Nico had arrived home from his night out with the Queen excited about something he didn't want to talk about, and Deven hadn't pressed him. Deven had been in an abnormally relaxed mood after his own evening taking out his frustrations on the enthusiastically willing body of their collective Prime; by the time he got back to his own suite he'd actually been humming, which seemed to alarm his door guard. The night got even better when Nico presented him with a milkshake and kissed him madly breathless before planting himself in his usual fireside chair to meditate, or whatever Weaving thing he was doing. Dev could get a closer look if he wanted to, but he didn't want to intrude.

Yet. It had been well over an hour and so far all Nico had done was raise the temperature of the room up to nearly Sub-Saharan.

"It has to be there," Nico muttered. He was sounding more and more agitated by the minute. "She saw it. I have to be able to. It's in the damn book...it must be there."

After a pause, Deven asked, "Can I help?"

Nico put his head in his hands, pulling his hair in frustration. "No. It's me. I'm getting upset and getting in my own way."

Growling, he pushed himself up out of the chair.

Dev watched him, fascinated; he'd never seen Nico quite this agitated before. The Elf looked around the room for a second before grabbing his coat.

"I need a walk," Nico said, thrusting his arms into the coat's sleeves.

"Promise you won't burn down the forest," Deven said.

Letting out an impatient breath, Nico managed a smile. "I promise. I'll be back in a bit, I just need..."

"No explanation required," Dev told him, waving him out. "Do what you need to do."

Nico swept out, taking most of the excess heat with him, and Deven realized how crispy the air had gotten in the room--he could suddenly breathe much more easily.

What on Earth had gotten the Elf in such a twist? At least he was aware of the issue--his own emotional turmoil--and paying attention to it rather than simply acting on his anger. An upside to being several centuries old, Deven supposed, and having spent that time meditating and working magic instead of killing people and suppressing emotion.

Unfortunately now the room was cold. The relatively thin blanket he'd plucked from the chair was wholly inadequate for the task, especially on the heels of an entire large milkshake. Deven got up, stretching; there should be a couple of extras in the trunk at the foot of the bed. He remembered stowing some in there last Spring to keep Esther from packing them away for the summer. He tended to take a chill easily, and if one lacked an Elf or a two-legged furnace like David to keep one warm, extra quilts were a must.

There were two identical trunks, and without thinking he unlatched the one on the right, but as soon as the lid was open, it hit him like a ton of bricks: a wave of scent, registering just as he remembered the blankets were in the other one. The right-hand trunk was…

He wanted to just slam the lid shut and pretend not to notice, but it was too late; his eyes had already fallen on its contents, and it felt like he'd been punched in the stomach. He had to fight to stay on his feet.

Leather, old books, a faint wisp of cigar smoke, whiskey, cologne. An odd assortment of items lived in the trunk, some charred around the edges, some broken but mended or at least held together in a box or bag.

And crammed into a corner, the source of the scent, a pile of cashmere in one of the ugliest shades of brown he'd ever seen.

Swallowing hard, he reached down and lifted it out of the trunk, letting it unfold. It didn't look like much--a gigantic but mostly nondescript cardigan, ugly as homemade sin but incredibly warm and comfortable. He'd stolen it a hundred times to wrap around himself on cold nights just like this one, and been discovered, with a chuckle, wearing it under the covers until its owner climbed in bed and replaced it with his arms.

Oh…oh, love…

He braced himself for the stabbing, consuming agony of loss, but perhaps enough time had finally passed that what he felt instead was sweetness, something so close to the way those arms had felt, that safety.

It hurt…God, it hurt so much. But at least now he didn't want to die from it. He could hold onto it and onto its memories without drowning.

Wiping his eyes, Deven wrapped the sweater around himself and sat back down in front of the fire, letting the tears run how they liked. He thought of the cinder-block memorial on the cliff in California, and the fountain he had designed to replace it once the new buildings went up.

"I hope you like it," he murmured, closing his eyes and resting his head on his knees, the too-long arms of the sweater covering his hands. "It's not very big, but nothing could ever be grand enough to...I think you'll like it."

He wept quietly into the sleeves for a while before finding his voice again. "I miss you...wherever you are I hope you can see what's going on. You'd think it was hilarious. And you'd be mad that you can't join in. I wish you could. I wish you could tell me what to do with some of it. And I wish you could see...don't tell anyone, but...aside from the parts that are scaring me to death...I think I might be happy. I know it won't last, but...there it is. I wouldn't say that out loud, but you deserve to hear it. I know that's what you wanted. But it would be so much better if you were here too. I wish..."

He lowered his head back to his knees with a sniffle, then reached up to the chair to yank a pillow down with him. Curling up in a ball on the floor, pillow under his head and the world's ugliest sweater wrapped nearly twice around him, he closed his eyes and inhaled that scent, the one that had made the world stop running madly out from under him so many times, and exhaled softly, "Wherever you are...remember that I love you."

He woke again for a moment hours later, this time in bed but still in the sweater, with Nico warm against his back, the fire burning low, and the afternoon rising outside. He sighed, contented, and wriggled one hand out of a sleeve to fold his fingers around the sleeping Elf's wrist and seek out his pulse, then drifted back off into sleep, smiling.

Chapter Seven

"Okay…now."

Miranda stepped back into the camera's frame, and watched as her own image began to form on the laptop screen. As many advances as David had made with the tech there was still an odd delay of three or four seconds before whatever the camera recorded was translated into something that made sense.

It really hadn't been that long since she'd seen herself--there had been the video posts on her website, and a series of increasingly clear but still slightly pixelated shots of her in magazines courtesy of the "paparazzi" also known as her husband--but it still threw her for a loop every time she looked into a screen and saw her own face.

Deven watched from his position cross-legged on the bed. She noticed he was looking particularly attractive tonight, in a sleeveless shirt and slightly ratty jeans, barefoot. There was just something about a barefoot guy in jeans. "Not bad."

She held her arms out to her sides. "What about the shirt? I know it's a little more conservative than I usually do on stage."

A wry smile. "Just because nobody can see your cleavage doesn't mean we don't know it's there…and as far as I know velvet can't stop a bullet."

Ah. Of course he saw through her anxiety. "I suppose not. Plus it's itchy."

"You could always cancel," he remarked as if he felt obligated.

"No, I can't. They've been planning this benefit for a year--it's my Foundation, after all." She looked herself over again, adjusting the shirt, knowing it was futile--if she wore this one she might feel less exposed but she'd also be uncomfortable. She'd have to change.

"I think I have something that might help," Deven said. "Wait here."

She started to ask where else she'd go, but he vanished; a moment later he reappeared holding a dark green garment box.

"Merry Early Christmas?" he asked with a shrug. "Or Happy Solstice in Five Days, or something."

"I thought we weren't all doing gifts," she said, frowning. "I didn't shop!"

Another shrug. "Then Happy No Reason. Or Many Glad Returns of Thursday and Thanks for all the Orgasms. Whatever. Just open it."

Miranda giggled and took the box, flopping down on the bed. She slit the tape holding it shut with her thumbnail and lifted off the lid.

"A corset?"

"More or less. Here, let me show you. Stand up and take your shirt and bra off."

Miranda wasn't sure if she should feel awkward or not--he'd certainly seen her breasts by now, but there was something different about a more utilitarian view. Rolling her eyes at herself, she shucked the itchy shirt, then unhooked her bra and dropped both on the floor. Meanwhile Dev took her gift out of the box and held it up.

It was, as it seemed, a corset, but of a slightly shiny, ribbed material that looked incredibly stiff. She gave Deven a dubious eyebrow, but he only smiled and directed her to hold her arms out to her sides.

He reached around to her back, wrapping her in the odd garment, and she realized that the laces were actually ornamental; she would never have guessed they weren't what Faith had always referred to as "girly scaffolding." Instead the sides came together in back in two layers: first, a row of hooks like in a bra; then, a flap over that to conceal them. She couldn't see how it fastened--he was going to have to take it off of her when the time came.

She expected it to be way too tight, but though the fabric held her in--and up--the way she'd anticipate a corset might, she could still breathe quite easily. Still, moving in it took a minute to get used to. It held her posture up straighter than normal.

"What is this made of?" she asked, turning around and running her hands over it. The decorative stitching and lacing was gorgeous, and it had black lace along the bottom edge to make it just a shade fancier without getting in the way.

"Something new I came across," was the reply as he watched her move around in it. "It's a material Army Special Forces is using--they call it Trelvex. Fireproof, knife proof, bulletproof."

She looked at him. "Bulletproof? Seriously?"

A nod. "It won't do much if someone shoots you in the head, but your midsection and sternum are protected--except obviously from a high overhead angle."

She patted the laces with wondering hands. It certainly did feel sturdy. "A tactical corset," she said.

He moved closer again and took her hand, guiding her to a tiny slit in the side where she felt the end of something metal. She got hold of it easily and pulled it out, revealing a curved, hilt-less blade with a loop on the end.

She nodded. "One of your up-close-and-personal blades of last resort."

"Since we're dealing with humans these days being able to slash a throat seems all the more useful."

She replaced the blade. Then something caught her peripheral vision, and she looked over at the monitor again. "Whoa."

Dev followed her gaze. "Oh, that. Now you know why I don't like the whole camera thing."

She could still see herself, but where he was standing between her and the camera, her form was blurry. Instead of Deven's actual shape there was a watery kind of not-light, like a mirage, something similar to the portals Nico built from the Web.

David didn't show up properly on camera either, but he'd improved the tech enough that he at least had a human shape and was almost recognizable as himself. Deven was twice his age, though, and suddenly she remembered all the times she'd looked at him and seen something otherworldly, something rarer even than the inherent strangeness of a vampire.

When she returned her gaze to the actual person in front of her, fighting off a ripple of uneasiness at the way he just...didn't seem to exist, entirely, the way she did...for a second that otherworldliness was intensified, and she thought of what the Priestesses of Elysium had called him, what he'd named his sword, and how none of them believed in coincidence anymore.

"Are you the oldest vampire left alive?" she asked quietly.

"I don't know. Among the Signets, certainly. Even Dzhamgerchinov is younger than I am, though he likes people to believe otherwise. But the bare truth is, even by vampire standards, I should have been dead a long time ago. Don't forget the only reason I'm still here is Elven magic and, well, you."

"How..." She didn't know what she was trying to ask, or if she really wanted to know the answer. Instead she shook off the feeling, the thoughts, and all of it, and brought her attention back to the here and now, for both their sakes. She switched off the monitor and asked, "How do I look?"

Deven smiled, letting his hands rest on her sides. "You just need blood trailing down your neck from a puncture wound and you'll look like the perfect vampire novel heroine."

Miranda laughed. "I'm probably less angular than most of them. Plus I'd hate to stain this contraption. Is it waterproof?"

He grinned just a little wickedly. "Let's find out."

Before she could react, he leaned in and bit her.

Pain--and something that was definitely *not* pain--arced through her body and landed pitilessly between her thighs. She moaned aloud, then blushed at the sound, and pressed against him as hard as she could.

A low chuckle at her ear, and his arms slid around her, one hand drifting down over her hip, the other around her waist. His tongue flicked against her bare skin, stopping the trickle of blood from quite reaching her cleavage, and her knees nearly gave out. Luckily there was no way he'd let her fall; she felt muscles shift and contract and hold her up, his casual strength always something of a surprise even after everything she'd seen...after all, one of the first times they'd met, he'd shielded her from a bomb and pushed a wall off of her.

Remembering that night, and the events leading up to it, she had to laugh a little.

"Ticklish?" he asked. "That's new."

"No…I was just thinking about how our relationship has…evolved…over the years. How much I hated you in the beginning…"

"I certainly did earn it."

"…and now, well…"

"And now." He nipped lightly at her earlobe, then left a meandering line of light yet somehow still scalding kisses along her neck, over her collarbone, and to the upmost edge of the corset.

"Breasts are such an odd thing," he noted almost casually, in amongst kisses. "I'm never entirely sure what to do with them."

Miranda let out a slightly ragged breath. "I think you do fine."

"Of course, I've had some fairly fleshy men, so at least that part I've approximated. Others, not so much. You would think over the centuries I would have encountered a trans man or two, but if I did I was too high to remember."

"Again…you do…just fine…" She let her head fall back, getting caught up in the softness of his lips, gaining just a tiny thrill from something she had tried not to admit, but couldn't seem to help: "I kind of get off on knowing I'm the only woman you've ever touched like this."

He chuckled again. "Do you, now."

"I hope you enjoy it as much as I do. I mean, this part of you obviously does…" She took hold of his belt buckle and tugged on it lightly, which led to him sliding a knee between her legs. She locked on with her thighs partly to keep from toppling over. "But most guys could get hard brushing up against a tree."

"Have you seen the redwoods? They're pretty damn sexy."

Miranda snorted, a decidedly un-sexy noise, but didn't have much time to be embarrassed; Dev kissed her then, slowly, with the kind of care that reminded her of Nico, as if her mouth were some sort of forbidden fruit whose attending damnation he wanted to savor. She was caught between wanting to pin him to the bedpost and wanting to just stand here, winding around each other, unhurried.

"Do you think you'll ever be interested in another?" she asked in his ear.

"Another woman?" A kiss, hands roving languidly down over her hips. "Never say never, I suppose, but I doubt it."

"Not even to compare?"

"There is no comparing you," Deven said, taking hold of her ass and lifting her up off the ground. Her legs wound around him automatically, and next thing she knew her back collided with the bedpost--he must've read her mind.

Neither bothered removing any clothes, only pulling aside and unzipping what was necessary. Miranda reached up over her head to grab hold of the post and use it as leverage, hissing as their bodies collided, that hiss turning into a strangled cry cut off by a mouth clamping on hers.

One of his hands covered hers on the post, the other held onto the small of her back. For a moment the only sounds were harsh breaths and the creak of leather.

Finally, though, he said to her breathlessly, "You, my dear, are a singular event in the world. Persephone Herself couldn't be a more rare and lovely creature."

She groaned. "Say more things like that."

Then she heard, at a distance, the door opening, and grinned up at the ceiling when she recognized both the presence and its wide-eyed reaction to the scene before him.

Miranda generally had bad luck with intimate moments turning into hilarious ones, and true to form, she managed to push sideways gradually until at the height of one undulation of her hips, her back slid off the bedpost and they both toppled over.

Vampire physics being what it was, David was there before she hit the mattress, catching them and steering them onto the bed.

Miranda laughed breathlessly, seized Dev's shoulders and pulled him against her again without missing a beat.

"You two, I swear to God," David murmured, voice touched with something like awe. "What am I going to do with you?"

"Shut up and help me get this off!" Miranda commanded, gesturing without any real coordination at the corset.

If he had questions about the garment or where it had come from, he tabled them for later discussion, and instead lifted her torso up off the bed to lean on his shoulder while he felt around for the hooks. Meanwhile, Miranda busied herself dragging Deven's shirt off over his head, and for a minute or so there was a good deal of frantic unbuttoning and shoving.

Unfortunately all the supernatural coordination in the world didn't help when, in the process of getting her rather snug pants off,

Miranda's hand slipped off the waistband and her knee jerked forward.

Fortunately what she lacked in physical grace she apparently made up for in fortune's favor, as her knee hit him in the stomach, not lower. Still, it earned a loud grunt, and Deven rolled face-first into the pillows, doubled up for a second.

"Are you okay?" she asked, fighting a case of the giggles and losing. When he answered with his middle finger, she inquired politely, "Don't you want to keep going?"

Now they were both laughing, and so was David.

"Sorry love," Deven said breathlessly, uncoiling. "That's a bit of a showstopper."

"She's soft in a lot of delightful places, but her knees aren't one of them," David commented. "Her elbows are even worse. Trust me."

"We were really having fun, too. Sorry, Dev." He rolled his eyes, and Miranda sighed dramatically. "If only there were someone who isn't temporarily incapacitated and could--"

She was on her back before she finished the sentence, giggling over her Prime's shoulder.

*****

The Porphyria Foundation benefit wasn't exactly the kind of crowd Miranda was used to. There were about five hundred people, but instead of t-shirts and jeans these fans were in ball gowns and tuxes. They were some of the richest people in Texas and a few surrounding states, and had shelled out a pretty penny for dinner and a concert.

Many had brought teenage daughters or other young people that fit more in Miranda's usual demographic, but there were plenty who were excited on their own behalf.

The first part of the evening there were speeches and a presentation from one of the primary researchers with the Foundation, as well as another from Dr. Novotny of Hunter Development. Their team was about to enter the second phase of human trials on a topical treatment to help porphyria patients lead more normal lives, and Miranda's fund-raising and her matched donations had pushed the science forward by leaps and bounds.

It was the least she could do given there were actual people suffering from the condition she used as a smokescreen. Porphyria wasn't exactly an epidemic, but like many niche conditions it suffered from lack of attention.

She listened to the presentation from the green room, nervous, but a bit more confident now that she was in the closest thing to a suit of armor she had: Deven's corset, black leather thigh-high boots over skin-tight black pants, and her leather trench coat that let her conceal Shadowflame.

Not to mention the place was crawling with Elite, APD, and of course her favorite personal bodyguard, David Solomon.

He, too, was decked out in vampire badass chic. In the last few weeks he'd left the house a lot less, and when he did he was always fully armed. She knew he worried about their security, given how many Signets had fallen even when surrounded by their best warriors. Now that there were four in their bond it made all of them both exponentially stronger yet perilously vulnerable; if any one of them was killed, that was it, and not just for the Tetrad. There was too much on the line now for any of them to take safety for granted.

Just now he was staring at a wall, or rather through it--she could feel him searching the building with his senses, looking for any sign of danger. All the sensor networks and swords in the world couldn't outreach a combination of empathy, telepathy, precognition, and Sight, boosted by the strength of the four most powerful vampires on Earth.

He sighed. "I don't feel anything particular amiss," he said. "I still need to work on refining the empathic reception--it's hard for me to differentiate among your emotions, mine, the boys', and the crowd's, and then to refine it further still and tell what's just a random bad mood and what's truly a threat. The more I can sense the less I really know, half the time."

She did as he had, and swept the building, just with her empathy; she was used to it, and was able to work a lot faster without involving the other gifts. Having half a dozen extra abilities wasn't as all-powerful-making as it seemed. Most of the time using all of them together brought on debilitating overwhelm. For the most part they tried to work with one or two at a time, maybe three if they were feeling frisky.

"I'm not really getting anything either," she said. "Everyone out in the ballroom is pretty relaxed--there are some seriously unhappy people out there, but it's mostly marital problems, personal stuff...oh, and that closeted gay Senator we keep running into at these things. He's still shagging the gardener, and his wife still knows, but they still won't talk about it."

David shook his head. "Poor bastard. And poor wife."

Miranda shrugged. "She's fucking the pool boy. But regardless neither of them are likely to cause a problem tonight. There are disgruntled employees on the wait staff, nothing extreme. I'm familiar with all of our people and nothing's out of place. Just the usual surface emotions, angst, fun vampire stuff."

She had finally stopped feeling guilty for reading the hearts of her employees after David had the idea to put a clause in their contracts stating they and their quarters were subject to physical search at any time and psychic monitoring and evaluation every moment while on duty. There was a strict confidentiality agreement on both sides--their bosses agreed not to use anything they discovered against them unless it was related to the security of the Shadow World or might contribute to a hostile work environment. But everyone working at the Haven knew Miranda was watching them.

She'd expected some attrition after that, but not a single Elite or servant had quit. With the higher pay in their employ than any other Haven, the considerable benefits package, the prestige, and the state-of-the-art training and security systems, the Elite knew a good thing when they had it.

That was one of the best things about having so much money--she could do right by those who continually risked their lives for her.

"Five minutes, Ms. Grey," the producer said from the doorway.

"Thanks Alicia."

Miranda stood, straightened her outfit, rearranged her hair. "Damn, do you have the set list ready to go? I forgot my notes."

David smiled. "It'll be on the screen by your feet. Don't worry. Just go out there and slay them all."

She leaned down and kissed him. "Be back in an hour."

She nodded to her guards, who flanked her as she left the green room and took the hallway to the stage door. She could hear the emcee announcing her, and the ensuing applause, and took her guitar from the producer who held it out.

A sea of humans in glittering gowns and tuxes got to its feet when she walked out, and she breathed in their affection and excitement, letting it buoy her up past her own anxieties and into the space where nothing mattered but keeping them as happy as they were making her.

"Good evening, everyone! I'm so glad to see all of you here tonight. I hope it's all right that I didn't bring the Empress...the only way to get her in the building was to chainsaw a big hole in the back wall and that seemed like a bad idea. So tonight it's just you, me, and my old friend here." She patted her guitar, eliciting a cheer. "I'd like to start with one I think you'll recognize even without the piano."

She launched into the opening chords of "Bleed," and the cheer grew even louder.

It was only an hour-long set, but it felt so amazing to perform again...just like it had felt the night she'd been arrested and Nico kidnapped. It was getting to the point that every show she did was a shake of a fist in the faces of their enemies, a reminder that they couldn't break her. She wouldn't be driven offstage by cowardly humans any more than she would by a cowardly Prime.

She had just completed her first encore when she saw something moving off to the right of the stage. Though there were waiters moving among the tables the whole time, and there was clapping and singing along in the crowd, something about this particular motion set off a warning bell in her head, and she locked onto it with her empathy while trying to keep her conscious mind on the next song.

Something wasn't right about the woman at the farthest table. She was staring off into space with an odd expression, something that might be dismissed as a glaze from too much wine, but underneath it was a kind of blankness Miranda recognized but couldn't quite name until the woman stood with a dreamlike slowness and took something out of her handbag.

Miranda's hands froze on the strings. Her first thought was of Morningstar's bullets, but the terror that she might have to endure that again was nothing compared to the realization that the woman was turning away from her...toward the crowd.

The first shot went way over the people's heads, but people were staring at Miranda in confusion until someone followed her gaze and saw what was happening.

Screams erupted all over the ballroom, and panic took over; people began to bolt for the doorways, tipping over chairs, and the first gunshots only spurred them on.

One man in the first row of tables went down with blood blossoming on his white shirt. The woman who'd been sitting by him dropped to her knees beside him, wailing, trying to cover his body with hers while another bullet punched into her back. Meanwhile the panic was rising, people scrambling in the cacophony of screaming and glass breaking and gunshots.

Miranda knew there was no way they could all get out through the exits without bottlenecking, which would make it impossible for the Elite or the cops to get in.

Another man fell. Then a teenaged girl.

Miranda took a deep breath.

This was it, then.

Time to go to work.

She stripped off her guitar and dropped it, pushed her coat off her shoulders, and jumped down off the stage, just in time for another human on the other side of the room to pull out a gun and, with the same expressionless face, open fire on the crowd.

Miranda exhaled, holding out her hands, and seized the bullets in midair with her mind. She pushed them hard downward so they all impacted harmlessly with the floor.

Then, she turned her attention to the shooters, taking mental hold of their weapons and jerking them away. She had a sinking feeling that wouldn't be enough, though, and she was right--the minute they were disarmed both humans threw themselves at her, grabbing knives from the tables and coming for her with faces full of pure rage and hatred. Neither looked entirely human anymore, all the more so in their gala finery, the woman's perfect makeup running from sweat and the man's perfectly ordinary features marred with violence.

The woman reached her first. Miranda didn't want to hurt her--she was under a spell as deep as those cast on Morningstar's warriors, but Miranda had no way to know if the woman had volunteered like they did or had been chosen at random. The only way to know more was to take her alive.

It was clear, though, that wasn't going to be an option. The woman attacked her with a steak knife, slicing into Miranda's arm, and stabbed at her again but missed thanks to the corset.

Miranda jumped back and drew Shadowflame. "Lay down your weapon," she commanded, grabbing hold of what parts of the woman she could and *pushing*.

It almost worked--the woman stumbled, a cry escaping her. But the spell on her was strong, and Miranda realized it was still working--there was some kind of connection between her and the person casting it. As long as that link existed he could work his will on the mortal.

There wasn't enough time to figure out how to break it. Not now. She didn't know anything about this kind of magic, her grasp of Weaving was dangerous enough to harm more than it helped, and most pressingly, the woman was still coming at her.

She tried to go for an incapacitating but not fatal wound in the leg, sending the woman to the floor, but it was no use. She just kept getting up, pushing herself forward even though her leg couldn't support her.

Miranda was about to go in for the kill when steel flashed in the dimly lit ballroom and the woman's head tumbled to the ground.

The Elite couldn't get in through the panicking humans, but they didn't really need to. David spun around on the follow-through and The Oncoming Storm rammed into the other human's sternum. The man fell in a heap and didn't move again.

For a second Miranda prayed that was the end of it, but a moment later another human came at her.

"What the hell is happening?" she yelled over at David, who had another to contend with himself. This one, an elderly man armed with another knife, kept driving toward him mindlessly until David snapped his neck. Meanwhile another man, large and bearded and mindless with rage, took a revolver out of his jacket and started shooting...and so did another human...and another.

"The Prophet must be here," David said. "Or watching somehow. I don't know--we need to take away his toys."

"Got it," she replied. "Cover me!"

David nodded and stepped out into the middle of the room, sword raised, drawing the humans' attention. On the far side of the room, the attendees who were trapped trying to get through the doorway saw what was happening and grew even more panicked, pushing and shoving to get out.

Miranda realized their heightened emotional state was making it easier for the Prophet to take them over--they didn't know how to shield in the first place, and fear left them even more wide open.

She stepped back, climbing back onto the stage, trying to ignore the din around her while she gathered up as much power as she could. She reached toward the Haven, where Deven and Nico responded by giving her everything they could; she pulled from David, herself, them, and then reached out to every human mind in the building, gathering them all up in the arms of her power with an iron grip.

She wasn't really sure what she was doing, only that she knew she could. Miranda took one last deep breath and slammed the energy into the Web that surrounded them, pushing it out into every human there, knocking them all unconscious at the same time, even those who'd already been possessed. The shock was enough to overcome the spell and send them to the floor, though she sensed the link itself was still active.

The momentary silence was so complete the room nearly rang with it.

Miranda sank to the stage floor, shaking. Dev and Nico gave her more strength along the bond, and it kept her from passing out, but she still knelt there for a minute, gasping.

With the crowd littering the ground like discarded dolls, the Elite were able to carefully move them aside and get into the room. David was already giving out orders to seal the exits and get Detective Maguire.

"I want these six, and the dead, taken to Hunter for interrogation and autopsy. Make sure the live ones are securely bound and kept in separate cells. When the paramedics get here escort them in but do not let the press within fifty feet of the entrance. I don't give a damn what APD says, 93, *just do it."*

Miranda was freezing, and to her dismay felt herself starting to rock back and forth, unable to disengage from the Web or get her own mind together.

David's voice came again, this time considerably gentler. He crouched down beside her, draping her coat over her shoulders. "Just keep breathing, beloved. It's all over for now. You stopped them."

She stared at the woman she'd killed. Could she have broken the spell? No...she couldn't, not on the fly, and not without knowing more about it. "I tried not to kill her. I really did." She could hear tears in her voice and felt irrationally angry at herself over it. Humans died by the thousands every day. This one was trying to kill her. She'd done what she had to do.

What I have to do.

Miranda sat quietly as the police arrived, along with a fleet of EMTs and, out front, Detective Maguire, who was utterly bewildered at the carnage before him.

Maguire waved away the officers approaching the Pair. "Start taking statements," he said.

He came up the steps to the stage and stood in front of them for a minute without speaking.

"You know," he finally said, voice harsh with what he was seeing, "I've kept my mouth shut about everything up until now, but--"

"Don't start," David said coldly.

"Fine, then, I'll finish!" Maguire practically bellowed, then looked around guiltily as a few officers looked up from their grisly work. "You people say you're protecting us, but every time she sets foot on a stage people die. Is being famous worth all this?" He gestured back toward where the Elite and Novotny had swooped in on the dead and the other attackers and were trying to keep the human authorities from taking over.

"Detective," David began, a note of Oh No You Did Not Just creeping into his voice, but Miranda held up a hand and silence him.

"You're right," she said.

Maguire's eyebrows shot up. "What?"

"It's not worth it," she said. "I'm done. Until we've dealt with Morningstar I'm not performing again."

David looked as surprised as the Detective, but didn't say anything. Maguire just took a deep breath, nodded, and turned back toward the crowd. "How exactly do you plan to deal with all of this?"

The Prime rose slowly, straightening his coat, looking out as if he saw such things every day...which was becoming closer and closer to the truth, Miranda realized with her heart down at her feet.

"All right," he said quietly, beckoning Maguire closer. "We're taking the live shooters--there's a chance we may be able to save them if we can examine them more closely. Your people can have the dead; that will cut down on the questions. As for the survivors…I might be able to influence all of them one at a time to forget what they saw, or at least shield out the memory with a blur or a blackout. We can explain that in a few different ways. But--"

"No," Miranda said.

They both looked at her.

She stood up, breathing slowly, grateful for the added support of the corset to help her stand as tall as she could right now, sheathing Shadowflame and putting her coat the rest of the way on.

"No tricks, no mind games," she said. "Let them say whatever they want. Let it get out however it's going to. What difference does it make now? Let the press invent their own explanation--I'm tired of pussy-footing around precious human sensibilities while trying to save them from their own kind. Besides, after all the spin and all the lies, they're dying anyway."

"We don't know what they saw," Maguire said. "Most probably didn't see you do anything supernatural, but we can't be sure. You're asking for torches and pitchforks, my Lady, or at least another murder rap. And at least a half-dozen high profile investigations surrounding tonight."

Miranda felt a surge of pity for him. "You're a good Detective, Mike," she said, touching his arm. He flinched. She nodded. "But the police can't touch me. You can't touch any of us. This isn't really your war…and if you stay in it you won't just lose your career, you'll die. All of you will. Let us fight. It's what we're here for."

"Ms. Grey," came a voice. The man on the steps said, "Agent Rawlings, FBI. We need to--"

"No," she said firmly. "You may not have my statement. You may not take me down to headquarters. You won't take another step, and if you do, I'll kill you."

She drew back the side of her coat, revealing the sword…still bloodstained.

The Agent paled a shade and froze where he stood.

"My husband, our security personnel, and I have work to do," she informed him calmly. "Now move aside."

"I'm sorry, ma'am, but you're going to have to--"

She took a step. He drew his gun.

Maguire gasped and started to gesture at the Agent to back down, but Miranda silenced him with a glance.

"Put both hands where I can see them!" he ordered.

After years of fighting for her career, of jumping through a thousand hoops to pass for human, of going to great lengths to pacify the authorities and keep her fans in the dark, she really expected giving it all up to be much harder, but in that moment, something dark and heavy settled comfortably around her shoulders along with her coat, and she just smiled softly.

"Humans and their guns," she said. "Tiny little pieces of metal that make you feel like men. Put it away, Agent. You're not going to shoot me. Not after what happened to your grandmother."

His eyes went huge, and he faltered in his stance. "What--"

"Put it away, son," Maguire said. "You're not going to want to file that report."

Finally, he obeyed, and when Miranda caught and held his eyes, he moved dumbly out of the way, visibly shaking.

She nodded to Maguire. "Stay safe, Detective."

David echoed the nod, then stepped to Miranda's right and offered his arm. "My Lady."

She took it, but as they started to walk away she heard Maguire say in a brittle voice, "Miranda..."

She paused. "Yes?"

"If you get my daughter killed, I'm coming after you."

Miranda looked over at him and nodded one more time. "I'll see you then."

Then, surrounded by her guards, they walked out of the human world and, at long last, the Queen stopped looking back.

Chapter Eight

MASS SHOOTING AT MIRANDA GREY BENEFIT CONCERT
11 DEAD, 22 WOUNDED IN ATTACK
WHO WERE THE SHOOTERS? FAMILIES WANT ANSWERS
MASS HALLUCINATIONS? BIZARRE WITNESS ACCOUNTS

Authorities have ruled out a list of foreign and domestic terror groups in last night's shocking attack on a benefit concert put on by Miranda Grey's Porphyria Research Foundation, but are no closer to finding the true mastermind of the shooting.

"We're still in the early stages of the investigation," Detective Mike Maguire, spokesperson for the task force, told the media at a briefing this morning. "No one has stepped up to claim responsibility. Tips are pouring in to our hotline and will take some time to sort through."

Perhaps the biggest mystery of the attack, which left 11 dead and 22 wounded, is what anyone would have to gain from gunning down wealthy donors to a rare disease. A law enforcement source who wished to remain anonymous claimed, "We know they were after Miranda Grey, but we don't know why--and we don't know why they would open fire on the crowd."

Ms. Grey, who took the stage at 9pm and was still performing when the first shots rang out at approximately 9:57, has not made a statement, and her management has not responded to inquiries about her role or her welfare. It is known that Ms. Grey walked out of the Crockett Ballroom surrounded by security personnel shortly after the first responders arrived.

Witnesses and victims of the attack claim that Grey herself, as well as a man several identified as her husband tech billionaire David Solomon, fought back against the shooters and in fact killed several, though evidence has yet to bear that out.

"She had a sword," one victim reported. "I swear to God they both did. I don't understand what happened but I know what I saw. The guy just appeared out of nowhere and cut the shooter's head off."

Another source from APD has verified that the six identified shooters all had valid permits to carry concealed handguns. No other link has been found thus far, though at least eight witnesses have independently corroborated that the shooters appeared to be in some kind of hypnotic or drugged state when they began firing on the other attendees.

Deven responded to David's summons without hesitation, and found the Prime in the hallway outside the music room, leaning against the wall doing something on his phone.

"Good, you're here," David murmured distractedly. A beat went by before he finished what he was doing and gave Dev his full attention. They were all starting to get used to that, with varying degrees of irritation.

"I don't want to leave her," David said quietly, tilting his head toward the door, "but I have to go to Hunter--Novotny's got prelims on the first scans of the possessed. She says she doesn't want company, but..."

"You don't believe her?"

"Usually? Of course I would. She always means what she says. But this time..." For just a moment David shed the years of carefully lab-grown calm and equanimity and was a troubled husband, to Deven's relief. "The last time I saw her like this was just after we met. She's always been scared of falling back into a depression like that--you know how it can swallow you."

"It's been one night," Deven pointed out.

"Yes. But whatever she needs--distraction, an ear--you always know what to do." Again, the worry. "I never know."

"Nonsense," Deven replied. "You know exactly what she needs--you're her Prime, remember?"

"Right now all I know is that she needs her best friend."

Dev nodded. "All right. Go on. I think I might have the very thing."

David kissed his forehead, lips, and nose, and slid his arms around Deven for a long moment, giving Dev another glimpse of the uncertainty that lay behind a lot of his seeming distance lately. There was only so far he could pull away from the entire Tetrad, but it wasn't for lack of trying…though the real reasons behind it, Deven couldn't quite latch onto. What did he gain from trying to be the strongest? What did he stand to lose?

No time to delve into those mysteries now. The Prime let him go, gave him one last kiss, and was gone--David never seemed to walk anywhere anymore if he could just Mist and save that precious minute and a half it took to get somewhere like an Earthling.

Shaking his head, Deven peered into the music room, and saw pretty much what he expected.

The Queen sat with her temple on the closed piano lid. Only a single candle's fitful flicker cast any light over the room. Her performance guitar from the night before lay on a table, and Deven saw it was broken: the neck was cracked, but moreover, there were two bullet holes in its body.

He rolled his eyes at the universe's high-school English-Lit-level grasp of symbolism.

"Hey there," he called gently. She had to know he was there already, of course, and might have overheard his conversation with David in the hallway if she'd been paying attention, but he had a feeling her mind was far from the room.

Her eyes opened partway. "Hi."

He looked around as he approached her. All her other instruments were closed up in their cases instead of on display; the whole room had a funereal feel, radiating in part at least from its mistress, whose weary grief weighed heavy in the air. It wasn't a weeping, railing-at-fate kind of pain, but instead the kind of quiet leaching away of hope that Deven knew all too well.

As long as any of them had known Miranda she had been fiercely devoted to her music, and performing was a huge part of it even though she couldn't tour and promote herself as heavily as other artists. It was a fundamental part of her identity--and she had chosen, of her own free will, to drop it on the ground and draw her sword. That wasn't something she could just get over in a day. She had lost friends, loved ones...now pieces of her life were weathering away from her like cracked stone from a wind-wracked mountain.

Releasing ties to humanity was something every vampire who survived their first decade had to deal with. Even the most normal seeming vampire would eventually have to walk away from what he or she had known in order to live as an immortal. Time wore down all things, but they remained. He knew that better than most.

No, this wouldn't do at all.

She moved over on the bench to let him sit by her, and he put an arm around her waist, letting her turn to rest her head on his shoulder.

She sighed. "Come to tell me it's not forever?"

He considered that. "Is it?"

A pause, then: "I think it might be."

"Well...if you'll recall, you told the Council you'd retire in ten years. They couldn't stop you if they wanted to, of course, but even then you knew there would be a timeline of some kind on your public career."

"I know."

"And assuming you don't end up blamed for what happened at the benefit you can still release albums. You can claim your illness has gotten worse. You never were a huge touring act, and nowadays there are ways to reach your fans that won't even require you to leave the house."

"I know."

He smiled. "But you've been thinking about all of it in endless circles since last night. I wish you'd called me--I would have come sooner, but you seemed to need space."

Her answering smile was wan, but genuine. "I assume David brought you here tonight."

"He's worried."

"I know."

"Well, you don't have to talk about it if you don't want to...in fact I was hoping you could help me."

She raised an eyebrow, clearly not fooled. "Oh? Special weapons practice, sparring, something else diverting?"

"Actually...babysitting."

Now both eyebrows lifted. "...huh?"

"The leaders of the Elven refugees have finally decided to bring Nico in on their meetings, if for no other reason than he has access to the plans for the new settlement. So he and Kalea are busy until well after midnight, leaving Inaliel on her own except for the door guard, who asked Nico personally if they could find someone else to be in charge. Nico batted his eyelashes...among other things...at me and before I knew it I agreed to watch her."

Surprise overrode Miranda's sadness enough to make her sit up and look at him. "Wow, you really said yes to that?"

"It's just for a few hours."

"But you're terrified of her."

He laughed. "In a way, I suppose I am. But you and I both know what happens when we avoid that which we fear."

"It chases us down," she sighed. "Yeah." Now a frown crossed her face and turned into something doubtful. "I don't really like babies, though--"

"You don't have to do anything. She's pretty self-sufficient, and she's my charge anyway. I just need..."

"Moral support?"

"Yes."

Deven had learned over the centuries not to ask for help from others unless there was no other choice. Most people couldn't be counted on; he could only depend on himself. Some of that had worn away after he'd met David, and yet more when Jonathan blew into his life like the West Wind and rendered many of his defenses obsolete. But he was still loath to ask favors, even tiny ones, so when he did, people noticed, and Miranda noticed more than most.

"Okay," she said, nodding purposefully and getting up from the bench. "Long as you don't expect me to do any diapers."

"I wouldn't dream of it."

When they left the music room, Miranda paused to snuff the candle, and then rested her forehead against the door for a second.

He lay a hand on her back, saying nothing, just letting her know he was there.

Finally she sniffed and turned away. He reached down and took her hand.

"Can you repair your guitar?" he asked.

"I'm pretty sure it's toast," she replied. "But that's why you never have just one concert instrument--I had three of that same model, plus several others I had tuned for different songs so I could just switch out during a show. I mean it was more for broken strings than bullet holes, but still, I guess I won't need so many now either way. I still have my original 12-string regardless."

He tried to keep it light. "You could open a music school for displaced Elflings and bored priestesses."

She chuckled. "Now there's a mental image. But you know, if everyone signs off on the plans they're all going to have to get used to each other. Has anyone from either group made overtures toward the other? I'm sure you've been watching."

He smiled--of course he'd been watching. "There've been a few sightings of some of the younger Elves peeking in at the temporary Temple, probably to see if there are any orgies or baby-Elf-drinking going on. And one of the priests of Elysium got turned around in the hallways and ended up in the Elven wing, so they helped him get back to his room. I think given enough time they might start interacting on purpose."

"That would be good. We're all in this together."

"It's always the young ones who get things going. Six-hundred-year-old Elders have done things one way for so long they're scared of anything new, but the young...rather like certain upstart Queens of my acquaintance...always shake things up."

"Have I really shaken anything, though?"

They'd reached Dev's suite, and he nodded to the obviously-relieved door guard and held open the door for Miranda. "You shook me," he pointed out.

She stopped just inside the threshold and hugged him tightly. "Thank you for saying that."

Kalea and Nico had wheeled Inaliel's bed into the suite along with the array of belongings a six-month-old accumulated in a few days' time.

Miranda shot him a look. "How long exactly are you keeping her, again?"

Deven grinned. "Nico volunteered to keep her all night so Kalea could have some time to herself--he'd already asked if I minded. But that was before the others asked Nico to attend their meeting. I thought for a second he'd planned the whole thing but he swears he didn't, and you know Nico, he's a horrendous liar."

"True."

They both leaned over the crib, and Miranda apparently was expecting a sleeping baby, but Inaliel was sitting up quietly, sucking on the ear of her stuffed bear, her tiny bare toes wiggling. When she saw Deven she grinned hugely around the bear, but grew sober again at the sight of Miranda.

Elfling and Queen studied each other. Miranda insisted she didn't know anything about babies, but this was no ordinary baby; Inaliel stared back at her with a degree of awareness many adult humans never reached.

Inaliel's fair face pinched a bit into a frown that was damn near hilarious given it made her look like something that had wandered off the set of *Fraggle Rock*, but she held out a hand and said, *"Vrit!"*

Miranda started. "I forgot she talks!"

"Kalea said she's not quite at sentences yet, but she's definitely mastered demands."

"Okay..." Miranda leaned closer, allowing several of her curls to fall into the crib over the baby's head. "If she pulls it I'm going to punch you."

Inaliel gazed up at the shining strands of red that bounced over her and very carefully reached up to bat at one, apparently fascinated at how it caught the light. The particular red of Miranda's hair was virtually unknown to the Elves, as was curly hair of any sort. Elven hair was uniformly long, silken, and straight as a board, which was why they braided and twisted and adorned it with such abandon. "Fire!" Inaliel exclaimed.

That was new. "Picking up some English, are you?" Deven asked. "I wonder what your kinfolk will think about that."

The baby stuck out her tongue.

Miranda laughed, seeming as surprised by the sound as the baby was--Inaliel clapped her hands and laughed along.

"I should have stopped for some ice cream," the Queen said, stepping back from the crib to sit down on the bed.

"Fridge," Dev said, gesturing. "I had it stocked."

She headed over to the small freezer/fridge where emergency blood, baby food, and ice cream were located. "You think of everything."

Deven, meanwhile, was having a staring contest with the little one now; he wasn't entirely sure what to do with her. Did she need entertaining? Was it better to just leave her in the crib with her toys? But Inaliel knew best, it seemed, and made the universal "up!" gesture with both hands.

He sighed. "All right. You win. You and those ears--your uncle Nico knows how to work his too."

"To somewhat different effect," Miranda said as she deposited two pints of ice cream, two spoons, a bottle of Scotch, and the remote control on the bed and set about pulling down the covers and shucking her shoes. At his raised eyebrow, she replied, "Slumber party."

Deven lifted Inaliel out of the crib; the Elfling immediately wrapped her limbs around him, with one wee hand reaching up to pat his face before it set to poking at his ear. She seemed confused that his ears weren't pointed.

He sank down onto the bed cross-legged next to Miranda. She took a long swig from the Scotch, ignoring Inaliel's curious look.

"I'm your moral support," the Queen told Deven. "This is mine."

Dev shook his head. "At least you have better taste than your husband did when he was strung out over you."

Inaliel's chubby, diapered bottom landed with a *poof!* of baby powder as she slid out of his grasp and onto the bed. She was far sturdier than he'd expected her to be. Elves in general looked a lot more waifish than they actually were, though few were what he'd consider muscular. It was really no wonder Nico had always stood out from his peers--he seemed more of the earth, somehow, even as alien to the Earth as he was. He was rooted in a way other Elves were not.

"Come on," Miranda said. "Let's do this right."

She flopped back into the pillows and grabbed the remote, summoning the television from behind a wall panel.

"What's considered age-appropriate for a six-month old Elf?" the Queen asked around a spoonful of Cherry Garcia.

Deven got under the covers next to her but let Inaliel decide for herself where to sit; the baby sat there a minute weighing her options before laughing gaily, pushing herself up onto all fours, and scooting up next to him in the hollow created by Miranda leaning on his shoulder. She burrowed into the space and gave a satisfied nod.

"I can move her," he said, hoping Miranda wouldn't object.

Miranda pondered the tiny creature who was trying to get hold of either the remote or the Scotch, it wasn't clear. "Can she eat ice cream?"

"Probably not...she won't ever have had dairy. I don't think either of us is prepared to deal with the aftermath of a lactose intolerant baby. Hang on--"

He reached with his mind over to the fridge, and plucked out one of the soy pudding cups Nico had requisitioned for the children. They didn't have much experience with chocolate, but had taken to it like champions.

"Is it an ethical thing?" Miranda asked. "No dairy, no meat, I mean."

"Not exactly. But sort of. Avilon, at least, is in dense forest where there's no grazing land to speak of, so herds would be impractical, and mostly they consider the woodland animals friends. They'd no sooner eat a deer than a dog. And at some point they realized rather than using all the food and water to raise animals, they'd just cut to the chase and eat the food and water themselves. For them sustainability has always been a requirement."

As he spoke he gave the baby a small spoon--just as Kalea had said, she already knew how to feed herself--and also nabbed a towel to serve as a bib in case baby Elves were as coordinated as baby humans in that department.

"It's funny, we're kind of the same way," the Queen observed. "Anyplace there are too many vampires there's not enough to eat without causing trouble. That's part of our job, in theory, making life uncomfortable for those who can't control themselves so they either end up dead or move somewhere else." She frowned again as a thought occurred. "The Order of Elysium kept human servants, did you know that? Was that how they fed?"

Deven nodded. "Partly, depending on how many humans there were available. I think this Cloister supplemented with deer. Traditionally the humans were devotees of Persephone who offered their blood and labor in exchange for room, board, and training in the Order. Some eventually became vampires themselves and others ran their own sort of sub-Order within the Cloister, but they could attend classes and services like we could. But again, the Cloister could only support so many people that way."

Now her expression grew thoughtful as she passed him his own pint and spoon. "Well if they're all going to live together, I wonder what it would take to create a system like that for everyone? I mean the site is close enough to the city that we can bring in blood like you did at the Haven, but it would be way more practical--and safe--if they could work out something with the Elves."

Deven laughed outright. "Fine, you go suggest it to them."

Miranda had to laugh too. "Good point."

Deven pulled the lid off his ice cream, and they settled into the pillows and blankets for what turned out to be a Disney movie, one of the dozen or so he'd actually seen before. Jonathan had had a soft spot for animated films; Deven had introduced him to anime, and they'd had a number of marathons during bad weather, wrapped up in blankets and each other's arms.

"God, what terrible parents," Miranda said about twenty minutes in. "I mean if someone told you fear was your kid's enemy, what kind of asshole--sorry, jerk--would teach the kid to be scared of everything? Seriously, the King was an idiot if he thought depriving her of social interaction and friendship…not to mention her sister…would keep her from losing it."

"Sometimes parents make stupid choices out of love," Deven noted, stealing a bite of her ice cream. "Maybe there was more to the plan once she became an adult but they didn't get that far. I agree it was a bad idea, though. I've never met a shut-in who had a belfry clear of bats."

"And look what happens! It's like when they locked my mom up in the mental hospital to keep her from 'hurting anyone.' It was just to spare themselves shame, is all."

"Oh, I don't know if--"

"Shhhh!" Inaliel said firmly. "Song!"

By the time the last reprise of the main title theme faded, Inaliel had slumped back against him, her empty cup and spoon long since moved off to the bedside table along with the two empty ice cream pints and their spoons. The baby was sound asleep, one hand curled in his shirt and the other touching a strand of the Queen's hair.

Miranda nursed the bottle of Scotch for a while but eventually lapsed into a kind of exhausted silence, and he lay there listening to her breathe as the film ended.

He could feel the wetness through his shirt but didn't comment on it. If she wanted to talk she would.

The screen had been off for about twenty minutes, the fire's light taking the place of its bluish glow, when she said softly, "I'll be okay."

He leaned his cheek on her head. "I know you will."

A moment later Inaliel shifted and murmured something unintelligible but faintly distressed, and her hand tightened on Dev's shirt; she started making fretful noises, and he got a strange mental image of her looking for someone in an empty house...a bad dream, he realized, that he could somehow read.

Inaliel whimpered in her sleep. Deven was about to change positions and try to soothe her, but Miranda's hand touched the baby's head, and with a sigh, the Queen began to sing very softly:

"Just close your eyes
The sun is going down
You'll be all right
No one can hurt you now
Come morning light
You and I'll be safe and sound..."

The baby sighed too, and settled back down, her other hand patting Miranda's shoulder unconsciously.

"Did Kai teach you the lullaby about the moon and stars?" Deven asked softly.

Miranda took a deep breath, her eyes glittering with lingering tears. "I don't think so."

"Take it," he told her, and felt her touching his mind. He let the song float up to his conscious thoughts, and felt her reading it, absorbing it with a combination of telepathy and empathy that had made learning Elvish so easy. By the time she'd gotten the gist, the tears were falling from her eyes, for Kai and for herself, for everything that seemed to be dying without real assurance it would rise again.

She began to hum the lullaby, and Inaliel stirred again, a smile of recognition touching her fair face.

"Eth Luna amasti embra es argena estell..."

This time, when Miranda started singing, he joined her, just barely loud enough to be heard, offering a harmony. She gave him a look of surprise, but kept singing, both of their voices gentle in the darkness, lulling the baby, and eventually themselves, to sleep.

*****

The first lie he told himself was, *This is an act of mercy.*

"Well, Sire, I have to say...my work with you is never boring."

He nodded vaguely at the doctor, then peered into the cell at the woman sagging in the back corner. She stared blankly straight ahead, expression slack. The readout projected on the window claimed her vitals were normal and stable--even her brain activity appeared to function at a regular rate. But something was clearly not right in her head.

"Let her see me," he told Novotny.

The doctor reached over and flipped a switch, turning off the one-way glass.

The effect was as dramatic as it was immediate. The woman, now clad in hospital scrubs instead of her formerly-elegant bloodstained cocktail dress, made an eerie noise like a jaguar shrieking and threw herself forward at the glass. She clawed at the window so hard her fingernails split and bled, but it didn't stop her. Her face became a caricature of humanity, a mask of mindless rage that stretched her generous mouth out to clownlike proportions.

Novotny turned the window back on, blacking it out in both directions. The sound of the woman's body thumping against the glass gradually halted.

"One of the others does the same for humans," Novotny said. "The other is programmed to come after vampires like this one."

"What's the prognosis?"

The doctor made a doubtful noise. "Medically two of them are fine aside from superficial wounds. Mentally...well, that I couldn't say. That's where the Queen and your Healer and Elf are going to have their work cut out for them, assuming they can do anything."

"Of the three remaining shooters...which is most likely to respond to treatment?"

A knowing look crossed Novotny's face, but he considered the data before him and said, "The human-programmed one is a lost cause. These other two have normal brain function but his is essentially a flatline. Assuming it's possible to break the spell over them, that one won't have much left to come back to. I'm not sure what the difference is."

"So we have two under one spell and one under another."

"I'd say it's likely. The data on both of the vampire-programmed victims is nearly identical."

He stared in at the woman for a moment longer. "Then we don't really need this one, do we."

Novotny took a deep breath. "If you'll excuse me, Sire, I need to check on those test results."

"Go ahead."

The doctor left the room, pausing to hit another button on the display, which unlocked the cell door. He didn't look back, but a moment later the cameras on the cell clicked off as well.

David eased the cell door open, eyes on the woman. She heard the movement, saw him, and started to fling herself forward again, but he caught her and pinned her back against the wall firmly, though not roughly. There was no sense in hurting her now.

He stood in front of her for a long moment, holding her consciousness as still as he could; her energy was battering against his, but it was like a mouse trying to beat down a lion. Steely claws had her in their grasp and there was no escape.

"I'm sorry this happened to you," he told her softly. "You won't understand this, but your family believes you died in the shooting. We're working on getting them a body, but don't worry. They won't see you like this. They won't know you killed two people trying to get to us."

She was a beautiful woman, this would-be vampire slayer--she'd also been a good shot, and nearly hit him with one of the cursed bullets before he got her on the ground. All four shooters had been legally armed, but whatever ammo they usually carried had been replaced with the same kind of rounds that had nearly made Miranda disembowel herself. The effect on humans was no different from any other bullet; their poisonous qualities manifested only on contact with vampire blood.

He'd already tried interrogating the fourth shooter, the other one programmed to fire on the crowd. What was Morningstar trying to achieve with this attack? Why there, why then? They couldn't possibly have believed they would kill Miranda, or him; it had to be something else. He also didn't think they seriously cared about

Miranda's career, unless the Prophet had some sadistic interest in making her suffer emotionally. It seemed rather petty, given what was at stake here.

"Your name is Andrea Lofton," he told her as he gently tilted her head to the side. "You come from a wealthy Texas cattle family. You weren't married and had no children, but you were devoted to a number of causes and gave millions to charity. However you got mixed up in this...maybe Morningstar got to you before and convinced you to join up, or maybe they just chose you because you'd have a gun and you never knew what hit you...they took away who you are to fight a war that they're too cowardly to fight for themselves. But the truth remains, regardless: your name is Andrea Lofton."

Even as he spoke the hunger was rising, hell-black and soft, undeniable. It was never far away now, not since the New Moon when he had felt it reaching for him and realized he could take the burden away from those he loved.

He hadn't expected it to come back so quickly. He didn't understand why it had. But it was there, and it beckoned so sweetly, so softly, like a lover's voice in the dark. He began to fixate on that feeling...the taste of death, that final release like no other. The harder he pushed it away the more it overcame his defenses, drained away rational thought.

That was not acceptable. There was too much hanging in the balance to lose even a moment's strength to hunger. Especially not when the solution was so simple: Just kill. There were plenty of humans whose deaths would be of far greater use than their lives. A few mortals for the sake of all of them was logical. It was simple math.

Keeping it secret was less logical. Surely if the math *was* that simple he needn't hide it. But Miranda didn't need to know yet...one death a month was already breaking her heart, though she stood up and did what had to be done with a strength beyond anything even she knew herself capable of.

He was no Weaver, but if the last couple of years had taught him anything it was that a Signet bond was not as infallible as they'd all believed. He had seen how Deven pulled himself back from Nico, and how he'd blocked off the energy and still survived. From that it was easy enough to figure out how to hide one small thing...just a tiny bit of truth they didn't want to know anyway...from the Tetrad without any of them the wiser. They could feel an instability, he knew, but so far they'd attributed it to stress and responsibility. In a way they were right.

The reprieve the others had had before Nico's first New Moon had been short, but in it he'd seen the future of the Tetrad, and that path led to madness for the Weaver and despair for the Queen. Deven would claim he was fine, but he no longer believed that...not now that he had seen who Dev truly was. The elder Prime had used the Red Shadow as a shield, shoving as many deaths as he could between himself and his real identity. He would insist over and over that he was a killer, not a Healer, not fit to bear the *Moriastelethia*.

David was not fooled.

They were not killers. They shouldn't have to be. But they needed the power...*he* needed the power. If they were going to win, if they had a future together at all, it would be at the cost of human life. That much he had already accepted.

Perhaps it was not what Persephone intended. Perhaps, come Solstice night, She would expose his sins to all of the Circle, and they would know the monster they had created behind dark blue eyes that, just now, were fixed, hypnotized, on the possessed woman's throbbing jugular.

"Let her," he murmured, feeling the delicious slide of his teeth, breathing in the human's scent. "I am not ashamed."

He tore into Andrea Lofton's throat and, with a groan that was half relief, half pleasure, took her life into his own.

Chapter Nine

Just before the next midnight, a limousine pulled up along the Haven's circular driveway. A smaller, black van followed it, and its doors opened first, dispersing a half-dozen uniformed guardsmen who stood along the walk from the limo to the broad stone steps leading up to the Haven's doors.

Miranda peered between the curtains and watched one of the guards open the limo door.

First to emerge, as she expected, was the enormous furry head of a black dog.

Vràna jumped nimbly from the car and shook herself. She seemed to have gotten even bigger since the last time Miranda had seen her. Just like always, she wore no leash, but came to attention and waited.

Jacob climbed out next, and he of course had not changed at all. Still bearded, long-haired, with his soft brown eyes full of kindness even as they carried that nobility and, she was well aware, the fierceness of a warrior when needed. Miranda knew a lot more about his past now, and while she'd never doubted his strength or the wisdom of the Signet that had chosen him, now, she understood his wide-reaching reputation as a fair man, an honorable one, but not one to be underestimated.

The Elite bowed to him, and he gave the nod, then turned back to the car and bowed again, offering his hand to the car's remaining occupant.

A slender arm clad in a black velvet glove reached out, fingers lacing in Jacob's.

The woman that emerged from the limo was not the one Miranda was expecting...though perhaps she should have been.

It was still recognizable as Cora, but even the last time they'd met, the newer Queen had been a bit tentative, avoiding eye contact most of the time, still recovering from the scars of her years of torment at Hart's hands. She had not known her own power then, either as a pyrokinetic or as a Queen, and while she had been beautiful and regal in her way, much of her identity was still yet to step out into the night.

Cora straightened, nodding to the guards, and offering Jacob a smile. Her spine was straight, shoulders back; Miranda hadn't realized how tall she was, but she easily topped Jacob--or that might have been the heels.

Miranda had never seen Cora's hair in anything but a fairly ordinary long sweep of dark brown, but now it was in shining layers that framed her face perfectly, allowing her large dark eyes to take center stage. She was impeccably made up and dressed, complete with a very vampire-like long black coat that had a vaguely Victorian style about it. Her Signet shone at the base of her long neck, and now she wore it the way they all did, like she had been born to it.

Most amazingly of all, just around the edges of her elbow-length gloves, Miranda caught sight of the shapes of flames--not drawn of fire, but in ink, as if they were licking up her arms.

Tattoos.

Miranda heard a quiet whistle to her left, and finally noticed Deven standing next to her, his eyebrows lifted in surprise. "Well now," he murmured. "Look who's awake."

Cora took Jacob's arm and the Pair, flanked by their guards and the Nighthound, took the steps to the front doors.

"How does she do that?" Miranda murmured. "I'd kill to look that elegant without even trying."

Deven chuckled and rolled his eyes. "Honestly, Miranda, where do you think *she* learned it from?"

Miranda moved back from the window and returned to the entrance where David was waiting for her; she slid her arm into his just as the double doors began to open. Deven took up position behind the official Pair of the South, joining Nico, and together the Tetrad stood in the doorway to greet their first set of honored guests.

Cora smiled warmly at Miranda as the visiting Pair bowed, and they bowed back.

"Welcome once again to our Haven, Lord Prime, Lady Queen," David said. "It is an honor and a privilege, as always, to open our home to you."

"As we are honored and privileged to receive your welcome," Jacob replied formally. That bit done with, he laughed and held out a hand, grasping David's, while Cora stepped away enough to hug Miranda tightly.

"You look fantastic," Miranda said. "I barely recognized you."

Cora grinned. "I barely recognize myself, some nights--and yet I absolutely do." She offered the same hug to Deven, and another to Nico; this was the first time she and the Elf had met in person.

"You are even lovelier in reality than you are in the Web," Nico told the Queen. "It's an honor."

Cora looked from Consort to Prime, one eyebrow quirking as she took in the obvious differences between Deven now and Deven...before. "It is a great pleasure to at last meet the one who brought our Deven back to us."

"I was hardly the only one," Nico said, but he was smiling, as was Deven, who took his hand and kissed it.

Once everyone had greeted each other, including Deven dropping to accept a full body embrace--which was nearly a tackle--from Vràna, they walked the Pair to their guest suite.

"Things are a bit crowded around here these days," David told them. "There are hot and cold running Elves down that hallway--" He gestured as they passed--"and the Cloister's inhabitants down the other. But we have managed to keep the visiting dignitary suites open. You'll remember this one, I imagine."

It was in fact the same set of rooms the Pair had been installed in for the Council summit, which was also the same one where Jacob had stayed during the Magnificent Bastard Parade those fateful days when he had met Cora. It seemed decades ago, now, though not even a full ten years had passed.

That was before they'd defeated Marja Ovaska...back when she still hated Deven...before Kat had left, before Faith had died, before David had died...before they had become Thirdborn...while Jonathan was still alive, before the wedding...

Miranda wondered, shaking herself out of the reverie, if Deven and Nico would ever do something similar--follow some Elvish marriage custom, perhaps. Dev still wore his wedding ring, and she couldn't really imagine them getting married in the traditional human sense as he and Jonathan had. That was something that had belonged to Dev and Jonathan, one of those things Nico would never want to infringe upon...but surely Elves had their own way of sanctifying a commitment like theirs.

There was a light nudge on her mind, and she started. She'd been zoning out while conversation went on around her, and Dev had noticed. Thankfully no one else seemed to have.

"When are we expecting our seventh and eighth?" Jacob asked as Cora directed their Elite to deposit the Pair's luggage on the bed.

"Tomorrow just after sunset," was David's answer.

Jacob looked like he wanted to ask another question, and Miranda had her suspicions what it might be, but the usual protocol was to leave the Pair to get settled and then all meet up for drinks in an hour or so, so he refrained from further inquiries for the moment. The Tetrad left the Pair to it and headed to the study.

"Have you spoken to Olivia?" Miranda asked, sitting down next to David on one of the big leather couches. A servant brought a tray of glasses--dinner--and soon they were all four nursing some of the extra-large batch of donated blood brought in for the weekend.

David sighed. "Not in a few days."

"Are you still worried?"

"Yes and no." He already had his phone out, she saw with irritation. It was impossible to have a conversation with him these days that involved any eye contact. If she hadn't known how busy he was she would have sworn he was avoiding them all on a disturbingly regular basis. But as usual, nothing felt amiss in the bond, just preoccupied.

"Care to elaborate?" Deven asked wryly.

"Hold on."

Now Deven sighed. Miranda knew he was as annoyed with David's behavior as she was, perhaps more. "I hope you're planning to at least be present in conversation with our guests," he said. "They did fly all the way here from Europe, after all--they might like to actually see your entire face for a minute."

"That's why I'm running a systems check now," David said shortly. It wasn't quite a snap, but close enough. "To get it out of the way. In case you hadn't noticed I do have a lot going on right now."

"I have noticed," was the reply. "And I've also noticed that you refuse to let any of us help you even though we have a considerable pool of skills available."

"Since when do you want to get involved?" David asked, still not looking up. "You never liked any of the night to night logistics of running a territory. You wanted the fun parts, not the responsibility."

Deven sat forward, and Miranda and Nico both sat back at the unexpected anger that crackled suddenly in the air between the Primes. *"Excuse me?"*

Miranda knew that tone.

Luckily so did David.

And, luckily for the sake of their collective evening, David knew when he had made a mistake.

He took a deep breath and put away his phone.

Miranda noticed that David didn't apologize, but Deven didn't seem to expect him to. Just the acknowledgment that he'd overstepped was enough.

Deven might have--for the time being--left leadership behind, but every once in a while he reminded them all that he was still very much a Prime, and that he hadn't just been David's lover, he'd been David's commander. Certain tones of voice and mannerisms, Miranda had noticed, still brought David to heel before the younger vampire even realized what he was doing.

Nico cleared his throat. "You're worried about Olivia, David?"

Blue eyes flicked over to the Elf. There was gratitude there. "Um...worried isn't really the word." He picked up his glass again with one hand and twined the other's fingers with Miranda's. She squeezed them gently. "Obviously the Signets know what they're doing. They always have. And they're getting along, just..." He trailed off as if unsure how to describe the situation.

"Sometimes it's not instantaneous," Deven pointed out, pretending their tense moment hadn't even occurred. "Look at Jacob and Cora. It took them months to do more than hold hands."

"It's not that. According to Olivia they're sleeping together. They're just butting heads a bit more than I would like."

"Is Avi trying to take charge?" Miranda asked. "That doesn't really seem like him, but then, she's the first female Prime. Centuries of tradition and gender roles are hard to overcome."

Deven shook his head. "I doubt it's anything to do with Avi trying to assert control. Look at their life experience: Avi is a powerful vampire and a skilled warrior, but he's always been subordinate to someone else. He went from the Mossad to the Israeli Elite, to the Red Shadow, then to your Elite. He can make his own decisions but he's used to framing that within a set of orders. Olivia was never a full Second since Jeremy was usurped, and she has been out of the Elite for quite a while--she's used to independence, and she's been Prime on her own for a couple of years. Neither would have the slightest idea how to create a partnership."

"That's what I've observed," David agreed. "Granted I've only seen her side, but it seems like they like each other a lot on a personal level but are having trouble ruling together. He definitely wants an active role, but it's hard for them to figure out exactly what that is--I suppose that's where tradition butts in. We all know what Primes are *supposed* to do and what Consorts--up until recently only Queens--are *supposed* to do. But they have the chance to completely redefine those roles however they want. The issue is how."

"Maybe this weekend will be good for them in that respect," Miranda mused. "They haven't had much opportunity to observe other pairs from the perspective of equals. We all have different ways of defining what Prime and Consort mean. That aspect of their relationship will affect the rest--you can't fully compartmentalize something that goes as deep as your soul."

Nods all around.

Not long after, Cora and Jacob joined them, and Miranda got a better look at the Queen's forearms without her gloves. Rather than a solid design, the tattoos were almost a combination of flames and vines, winding around her wrists and up to her elbows in a pattern that were intriguingly reminiscent of Nico's.

"They're only two months old," Cora told them, holding out her arms so they could admire the artwork. "Jacob was not terribly enthusiastic about the idea, but I think he changed his mind once they were done."

Jacob smiled at his Queen. Miranda loved how he looked at her--with adoration, of course, but also with pride that was neither paternalistic nor proprietary. He obviously loved watching Cora come into her own, and was excited to see what fruit her blossoming would bear.

"Well it's your skin, of course," the Prime said with a laugh. "And I've learned that whenever you get the bit between your teeth about something, there's no dissuading you, but I admit I wasn't expecting them to be so...attractive."

Miranda studied the tattoos and said, "I love how the color changes as they get closer to your hands." She looked up at Jacob. "Are you and I the only two people in the room without any tattoos?"

Jacob and Cora exchanged a look, and Jacob said, "I'm afraid you're on your own, my Lady. I have a couple of rather old ones from my days as a fighter, and Cora persuaded me to have a small design done that coordinates with hers."

Deven raised an eyebrow. "Do we dare speculate where it is?"

The Prime laughed. "It's on my chest, don't worry."

Dev looked Miranda up and down and told her, "That means you're next. If you need suggestions I have a few ideas for you."

Miranda felt herself blushing. "I bet you do."

He seemed to realize how it had sounded, and she noticed his ears went just the slightest bit pink as well, which made Nico stifle a laugh--Jacob too.

"I didn't mean it that way," Deven insisted, as the stifled laughter turned into actual laughter at his sheepishness. "Tell her, Nico."

The Elf grinned. "He's been doing sketches--I've seen them. Nothing salacious, I assure you, though I fear it doesn't matter--you know how those two are about tattoos. If you ever have any done you'll never have a peaceful day's sleep again."

"Those two?" David gave Nico a sardonic look. "Good evening, my dear Kettle, this is the Pot calling."

Nico blinked. "I don't know what that means."

"Never mind," Deven said, feigning weariness with their behavior. "Cora, light something on fire for us, would you?"

Miranda started to point out the obvious about being in a room full of wood furniture, but Cora just smiled and held out her hand, palm up. Miranda heard a faint, familiar noise she realized was like a stricken match, and a small flame appeared in the Queen's hand, floating just a scant half-inch above her skin.

They all stared at it in sudden, dumbfounded silence.

Cora, clearly amused by their expressions, continued to smile as she stared at the little flame, and it grew taller, dancing in the study's warm air. Just like her tattoos, it was blue at the base--a slightly different color than regular fire, Miranda noticed, a little more on the purple side. It faded into more traditional blue, then into yellow-white as it rose. While the fire was bright, it had a strange sort of quality to it that made it easy on their eyes--almost as if the flame was born of darkness as much as they were.

Cora passed her other hand through it, and opened that palm, the flame transferring from one hand to the other. "I wear the gloves to remind me not to play with fire in public," the Queen explained. "Humans find it rather distressing."

"So do vampires," Jacob pointed out. "Let's not forget all the Elite you've spooked walking around with that going on."

"You said you found a teacher," Miranda said. "How long did it take you to learn to do that?"

"Only a few weeks--my yoga training had enabled me to ground and center very quickly, which is the first step to controlling any gift, as you know. The hardest task was learning not to fear the fire. To view it as my friend, almost as I do Vràna. A companion, a guardian, an ally."

"I've lit a few candles," Miranda admitted, "but I don't think I have enough of it to do much more. I'm kind of relieved to be honest. Fire and empathy seem like a potentially destructive mix."

"Fire *is* destruction," Cora said, her eyes dancing with the flame in her hands. "But then everything is, in its way." She closed her fingers around the flame, shrinking it until it vanished. There was no puff of smoke or smell of a snuffed candle; it simply ceased to be. Cora picked up her wine glass as if nothing extraordinary had happened. "We are all creators and destroyers, darkness and light, life and death. Still, it is probably best that we don't all have the full force of all everyone's gifts. Controlling one is labor enough." She looked at Miranda with a hint of mischief. "I can give you some tips, if you like, while we are here. Even without a large dose of the gift it is rather useful."

"I'd love that." Miranda and Cora clinked wine glasses and grinned at each other.

Conversation continued in an easy, companionable flow; though they all spoke at least occasionally over the phone and internet, it was rare for any Pair to have their allies face to face and just have a chance to spend time together. Miranda felt that sense of rightness again, albeit with a feeling of absence where the rest of the Circle would be soon.

This is how we're meant to be. Family.

She watched, amused, as Vràna gradually snuck closer and closer to Nico until her head slid ninja-like under his hand, and he was rubbing her ears before he knew what had happened. One of the dog's huge paws hoisted off the ground and came to rest on the Elf's shin, as if she were hugging his leg. She'd probably have her head in his lap in the next few minutes if he didn't notice.

Jacob inclined his head toward the tableau. "Have you ever thought of getting your Consort a Nighthound, Dev? You found Vràna for Cora, after all."

"What would you think of that, Nico?" Dev asked, watching the Elf fondly.

Nico smiled down at the dog, who looked up at him with her tongue lolling out in a canine grin. "I never thought about it."

"A guardian like Vràna would help you feel safer walking around the city without us," Miranda pointed out.

Jacob was nodding. "She was a godsend for Cora, especially in the beginning, wasn't she, my Lady?"

Cora, too, nodded. "I cannot imagine how I would ever have come out of my shell without her, and not only because her size and strength cow most possible threats with any survival instinct. Her presence is grounding--I do not think she is aware of it, but I have leaned on her energy more than once in a moment of panic."

Nico's eyebrows lifted. "You're saying she does a sort of intuitive magic? That tracks with what I've heard from the creature-speakers among my people, as well as Stella's tales of familiars." He looked at the rest of the Tetrad a little sheepishly. "Assuming of course that my bondmates would not object to another animal's continuous presence, the idea is intriguing."

"It's got to be better than that damn cat," David said. Miranda punched his arm, but he just shrugged. "I love you dearly, my Queen, but that beast is what would happen if a wolverine shagged a cactus. I'll bet you a hot fudge sundae the boys agree with me on that."

Miranda looked at the others, who pretended not to hear for a moment before Nico said, "Well…she shredded the arms of two of our chairs."

"And my thigh," Deven added. "For just a second I thought she was going to let me pet her, then she went berserk and clawsploded all over me."

Miranda burst out laughing at the word "clawsploded," and she wasn't the only one. "Fine, get a dog," she managed between cackles. "When she eats all your precious leather goods don't come crying to me."

As the discussion drifted to Jacob and David's Friesians, Miranda caught the way Deven was watching Nico, and when Dev glanced up at her, his lips quirked in a half-smile, and she knew at least one of them might receive an unexpected Christmas gift. She smiled back.

So now there would be a baby *and* a puppy in their lives. Things were getting almost disturbingly domestic in the Haven these days.

She half expected some emergency to crash their evening, but amazingly, things remained quiet out in the world, and eventually the party started to break up; Jacob and David headed to the stable for their traditional late-night ride.

"Have you learned anything from those poor humans at your concert?" Cora asked a while later.

Miranda hadn't been expecting the question, but said, "A little. All but two of them have died, and Novotny thinks there might be hope for those last two. I'm going to see them on Monday night after all this Solstice stuff is done. I'm hoping with our combined gifts we can figure out a way to break the spell over them. I was able to disrupt the Prophet's control long enough to knock them out, but it wasn't broken."

Cora looked thoughtful. "It is too bad we cannot get our hands on a copy of Morningstar's Codex. If we could see the spells themselves we could learn a lot about how to counter them."

"And how to save the person inside such a possession, if there's anything left to save," Nico said. They all knew who he meant.

"It really is a shame all the Morningstar soldiers are brainwashed--and that they're all human." Deven shook his head in frustration. "I would love dearly to get an operative in there. At the very least I hope unlocking the rest of our Codex will give us some more ammunition, perhaps a scrying spell or something to get a look at their plans. This whole thing where we have zero intel on what they're up to is driving me mad."

"You and all of us," Miranda replied. "The Prophet must be wetting himself with glee knowing how powerless we are right now. We can defend ourselves, and we can counterattack, but we can't get a step ahead if we have no idea what the steps are."

"Let him laugh," Nico said quietly, a low current of anger in his words like rolling thunder. "He will have little to laugh about when I get him out of my brother and have him at my mercy."

There was a moment of silence, no one entirely sure what to say that wouldn't make Nico feel worse, but again Cora took the lead. "I don't suppose I could convince you to play for us, Miranda?"

"Play music?" The Queen blinked at the Queen--Cora had a particular skill, it seemed, in catching her off guard. "Oh, I don't know, I haven't..."

"Haven't touched an instrument since that night," Deven finished for her, frowning. "All the more reason you should."

"I'd have to go--"

As she should have expected, she didn't have the sentence out before Deven disappeared, and by the time she finished rolling her eyes, he had reappeared with her guitar--her "real" one, not one of the performance instruments like the one that had been shot. This was her oldest, the model that had been custom designed for her, and all her others were based on it. It was the one David had given her to replace the one burned in her apartment, and in its way it was like her own inanimate sort of Nighthound.

Miranda sighed, sat up, and took the guitar, giving Deven a dirty look he pointedly ignored.

Well, if they wanted her to play, she was going to do it comfortable; she pushed off her boots and crossed her legs on the couch, guitar in her lap. Taking a cue from her, Cora smiled and took off her own shoes, shifting off onto the floor onto a cushion, Vràna peeling herself off of Nico to join her mistress on the floor.

Meanwhile Nico nestled into the corner of the sofa with Deven leaning on him as Miranda started picking out a few chords, gradually drawing them into a melody with no real destination in mind.

She wanted to keep the quiet, relaxed mood of the evening without veering too far into up-tempo or down into depressing, so she stuck with a couple of her less angst-ridden singles--that being of course a relative concept--and some of her old favorites, like Mazzy Star and Katie Melua, some early Tori.

She hated to admit it, but putting her fingers on the strings was an immense relief; tension in her heart she had ignored for days began to dissipate, and rather than losing herself to sorrowful thoughts about her career, she just enjoyed the music and the company.

She had a sneaking suspicion that was Cora's intent from the beginning. Miranda shook her head a little, smiling behind her hair. Queens.

"I search your profile for a translation
I study the conversation like a map
'cause I know there is strength
In the differences between us
And I know there is comfort
Where we overlap..."

Eventually, Miranda became aware of something moving out in the hallway besides the usual breathing and shifting of the door guards. A youthful but timid presence drew closer, and another behind it. The person's energy was shimmery and light, with a moonlit edge around it.

Elves, she realized. A couple of the younger refugees must have overheard her singing as they passed by, and decided to investigate.

Miranda reached out into the hallway and mentally tapped the guards, impressing upon them to leave their post for a little while and do a circuit of the other end of the wing, getting them out of the way and leaving the hallway empty of scary vampire types. If anything threatening got this close the Signets in the room would certainly know it.

Once the guards were gone, the Elves emerged from whatever they'd been hiding behind and came almost up to the door, just barely leaning close enough to see in the crack between the door and the hinges. Miranda lowered her eyes and kept playing, but added a tiny bit of volume to her voice and to the strings so they could hear better.

Not long after, a third presence appeared, and a couple of songs later, another from a different direction. This one stayed farther away at first, and Miranda realized with no little surprise that it was one of the vampires from the Cloister, keeping his distance so not to scare the Elves. He was just as fascinated with them as he was with Miranda's singing.

Smiling to herself, she pushed the tiniest bit of empathy into the song, not to push them to do anything, but to make sure they knew they were all safe here, and everyone was welcome. She carefully extended a thread of energy, then another, loosely weaving them into a connection among everyone there, just a little touch, nothing intrusive.

The three Elves noticed the vampire, but didn't run off; in fact she sensed something, maybe a smile, maybe a blush; some sort of tiny overture that persuaded the vampire to move just a little closer, though not all the way to the door.

Such a small step, but so important--Miranda held back her enthusiasm, not wanting to overpower the shy progress out in the hallway, and just kept playing, letting the music do the work it was meant to do.

She looked over and saw Cora was meditating cross-legged with Vràna's head in her lap, a soft smile on the Queen's face, the dog sound asleep. Across from them, the boys were also asleep, or Nico was--she caught Deven drifting in and out, finally settling on drowsy but awake, sometimes lending a quiet harmony to whatever she was singing the way he'd done when they babysat Inaliel.

She made a mental note to flick his ear for never mentioning that he could sing. He had, in fact, a lovely tenor, one she could easily imagine singing in Gaelic, perhaps in the middle of a stone circle, or perhaps in a church...somewhere that music echoed with sacred resonance, or somewhere old gods walked and forest spirits waltzed beneath the stars. Miranda loved how they sounded together, even as softly as he had joined in, and added to her mental note to offer whatever favors she had to to persuade him to really sing for her, and with her, and soon.

Miranda herself was happy to keep singing as long as she had a voice, and far from feeling sad at the loss of her public career, she found herself feeling a rare sort of contentment that came from doing something she'd been born to do, for people who needed to hear it.

After an hour or so, she wound the music down. It wasn't until she ended the last song that she sensed her guests leaving--hopefully smiling at each other tentatively as they slipped back down their respective hallways.

"Come a little bit closer
Hear what I have to say
Just like children sleepin'
We could dream this night away..."

It might not change much, or it might make all the difference in the world; she could only have faith in the music, her own power, and the shared joy and sorrow of lives that seemed so radically different but weren't, really, at least not in the ways that mattered.

"Because I'm still in love with you
I want to see you dance again
Because I'm still in love with you
On this harvest moon..."

Chapter Ten

The fourth Pair's arrival the following night got off to a slightly different start.

Miranda was halfway through getting dressed when something started to niggle at her intuition. Not an alarm, just yet, but...something.

She paused with her hands on her zipper and looked over at David, who saw the look on her face and looked down at his phone. "They're on schedule," he said. He started to say something else, probably to ask the driver his status, but:

"Star-One, this is Elite-214, requesting permission to reroute to 49."

David glanced at Miranda. "On what grounds?"

"There's a vehicle a quarter-mile back that I think might be tailing us. Prime Daniels agrees an evasive might be wise."

"Permission granted, 214. Do you have a lock on the vehicle?"

"Sending now."

David had already reached his desk and opened his laptop, bringing up the sensor grid, which now had a variety of other systems overlapping it including APD's traffic cameras. Miranda wasn't sure what kind of information the driver had on the other car, but whatever it was, David was already feeding it into another window, and in seconds both the Haven car and the one he was tracking had appeared on the map.

"Elite-214, you're definitely being followed," he said, still sounding calm, though Miranda could feel tension climbing up the back of her mind from his. "The car's listed as stolen and has been on you since you left the airport. Forget 49--reroute to Rendezvous 3 and await further instructions."

"As you will it, Lord Prime."

Next he called Olivia. "Guess what."

A sigh. *"I figured. Where are we going?"*

"A warehouse on the East Side--not far from your old place. You'll pull into the building. It's already under guard, but stay in the car for now."

Miranda finished arming herself quickly. "Too much to ask that all this go smoothly, I suppose."

"I told you we should have had them come in to our airstrip. After this no more commercial flights for any of us."

Miranda made an irritated noise. "We've been over this, baby, Liv couldn't leave until Prime Natalegawa went home, and that earthquake screwed up his flight schedule. It was the only way to get them here in time for tomorrow night. Besides, that's why we have all those backup plans you dream up in the shower."

Deven, Nico, Jacob, and Cora met them in the hallway, all looking concerned. "Rendezvous 3?"
Dev asked.

Miranda nodded. "With a detour to Indonesia for David to bitch at the earthquake."

Jacob chuckled. "Even you can't control tectonic plates, my Lord--at least not so far. Maybe give it a year."

"We're not all going," David said firmly. "We're much too big and irresistible a target all together--which is probably part of their plan. Jacob, you and Cora wait here. Dev and Nico, you stay back too, and be ready to gate everyone out at my word."

Miranda expected a disagreement, but Dev caught her eye and said, "I've been to the location--I can Mist there in a heartbeat. David's right, as of now all we know is there's a car following. There's no need to jump the--"

"Star-One, this is Elite-214, we are taking heavy fire! I repeat, we are--"

Silence.

David looked nothing so much as tired. "Lieutenant Xiu and flanking teams, move in and escort the limo away from Rendezvous 3 toward the dummy dropoff point. We're en route. You know the plan."

"Yes, Sire. As you will it."

The Prime glanced at Nico. "You're with me."

The Elf nodded and took the Prime's hand; a moment later, they disappeared.

"Well," Miranda said into the suddenly echoing silence, "We might as well have a drink."

"Is there any point to asking what exactly the plan is?" Jacob ventured a few minutes later as they all resumed their spots in the study from the night before. "Why a dummy location instead of the warehouse?"

"Because the car will be empty when Morningstar catches up to it," Miranda replied, handing Cora her glass of wine. "The boys Misted into the car, and Nico will gate them back out. Ari's too new to have his Misting down yet and Olivia really doesn't either, so it's easier to use the Web."

Jacob blinked at her. "You're telling me David can Mist into a moving car."

"It's one of our limos," she explained. "He's been in it a thousand times. All he has to do is triangulate exactly where it is at the exact second they land there, and that's Nico's other job, to track the car through the Web and let David use his Sight."

"And they've done this before?"

"Not exactly. Something sort of like it, when we rescued the Order. But it should work."

"Won't there be pretty nasty side effects? Migraines at the very least?"

"Undoubtedly," Deven said, and he at least looked a tiny bit anxious...and a little angry, though Miranda doubted anyone else would notice. "They shouldn't have tried it without practice--even as strong as Nico is he's not omnipotent. He was out of commission for a day after the Cloister, and he was in a lot of pain from overextending his gift. But of course, if Our Lord commandeth..." The last sentence was laced with sarcasm and accompanied by an equally sarcastic grand, sweeping gesture from Deven.

"It was an emergency," Miranda said, hoping to defuse his aggravation. "You know David wouldn't put Nico in danger if he didn't think--"

"He didn't think," Deven said shortly. "And he didn't ask. He had a resource and he used it. There were half a dozen other possible ways to get the Pair out of jeopardy. And if Nico comes to harm because of his recklessness, the Prime and I are going to have words."

Just then, luckily, Miranda felt the familiar change in the air--she looked up to see part of the wall turn to liquid, and a blast of cold air hit the study a few seconds later.

Jacob jumped back from his chair out of reflex, and Vràna barked a warning, barely listening to her mistress's attempts to calm her. The gateway opened, and with a blinding flash of what Miranda thought were probably headlights, two figures tumbled through, landing facefirst on the floor with a grunt and the clatter of weaponry.

The other two shapes in the portal stepped out calmly, resolving into Nico and David, who were used to the ride--it was far less bumpy and nausea-inducing than Misting, but still quite a trip for the uninitiated.

Nico turned and banished the portal with a gesture, then took a deep breath and sank into the nearest empty chair, looking sick.

Deven was at his side instantly and wrapped him in a blanket. He already had a glass of blood poured for the Elf, and held Nico's shaking hand while he sipped it, the Prime kneeling at his feet, his expression a rarity: Worry, undisguised.

David, none the worse for the trip, offered Olivia a hand to help her up, and another to Avi. The Pair got to their feet shakily, untangling coats and weapons. Miranda noticed a pair of suitcases up against the wall; Nico had apparently thought of everything.

"Welcome to our Haven," David said, laughing.

Olivia was clearly happy to see David, and gave him a hug right away, but Avi seemed a bit unsure where to put himself. He was, technically, the equal of everyone here now, but as Deven had said, he was used to serving, not ruling.

"It's so good to see you," David told Olivia, squeezing her around the middle and lifting her up slightly off the floor. She laughed and stepped back, tilting her head slightly toward her Consort, earning a look of "Oh come on now" from the Prime, who promptly offered Avi his hand.

"And good to meet you on equal terms at last," David said. Avi shook his hand firmly, though Miranda could tell Avi was under no illusions as to how equal the terms were. He was brand new to his Signet, one of the first male Consorts, and David was...well, David, the Prime who now ruled half the planet.

"I'm honored to be here," Avi said, trying perhaps a bit too hard to be comfortable in such company. Miranda wondered if he'd be so awestruck if he knew David went through a half-dozen pints of Ben & Jerry's a week and sang Taylor Swift off-key in the shower.

Meanwhile, Nico had finished his glass and was standing again, though he did lean a bit heavily on Dev's arm as they came closer for a real introduction.

Dev's attention was on his Consort at first, making sure Nico was steady, but as soon as his gaze turned to Avi, Avi's eyes went wide, and he knelt.

There was a moment of surprised silence. Miranda saw David about to say something--probably something sarcastic, knowing him --but Deven took the Prime's arm and pulled him back calmly out of the way so he could step out in front of Avi.

She had never seen Deven actually in the presence of one of his operatives, and almost the second they were within a few feet of each other she understood: there was a subtle current of energy, one that hardly anyone would notice, between the Alpha and his agent. Miranda knew that joining the Red Shadow was a binding oath, but it had never occurred to her there was actual *magic* at work.

Now, she could feel it: Deven had created this spell himself, centuries ago. Not even the Signet's call could fully break it. As long as it lay over Avi he would be divided in loyalty, whether he realized it or not, though she suspected he did by the way he waited, silently, head bowed.

The Prime held out a hand. "Your right hand, 1.3 Alizarin."

Avi wordlessly lifted his head and did as he was told. He wasn't cowering, didn't really seem *afraid*, per se, but he was still beholden to the spell upon him, and was duty and honor-bound to kneel to his master until the spell was broken.

Deven took out a knife and drew a line down Avi's palm; he touched one finger to the blood that rose in the blade's wake and drew a waning crescent Moon on Avi's forehead. The blood disappeared almost as soon as it touched skin.

The Alpha's words were quiet, but clear, and touched with a power Miranda had never felt before, a part of the Prime's life that had, until now, been mostly a mystery.

"I hold your oath to me fulfilled. I release you from my service and name you subject to the will of no blood but your own and that of the Signet at your throat. Your designation among the Red Shadow is no more. Rise as Avishai Shavit, Consort of the Eastern United States, and look your equal in the eye."

Slowly, Avi met Deven's gaze and held it as he stood up. Miranda felt the thread of power retracting, then disappearing altogether, and finally, Deven gave the slight bow that was customary from one Signet to another.

Avi returned the bow, let out the breath he'd been holding, and blinked a few times before smiling. "Thank you, my Lord...Lord Prime."

Deven nodded once. "Now then. I'd like you both to formally meet my Consort, Nicolanai Araceith--Nico, Prime Olivia Daniels of the Northeastern United States and her Consort, Avishai Shavit."

Nico shook both of their hands and smiled. He was still pale, and didn't look like he'd last much longer without lying down, but he stood as straight as he could. "An honor."

"The honor is ours," Olivia said warmly. "But as much as I'd like to visit with you, Nico, I think you might need a nap first. Don't worry, we'll be here when you're rested."

Nico looked a little embarrassed. "I fear you are correct, my Lady Prime--building a gateway so quickly took a lot out of me even with the Tetrad behind me. I will be much better company after an hour or two of sleep."

Deven shot David a cold look. "It was a risk that you didn't need to take," he said.

David raised an eyebrow. "He's an adult, Deven--he can make his own decisions."

"Only if you let him."

"I will be fine," Nico said firmly. "Let's go, Dev...I lack the energy for an argument at present." He offered Olivia and Avi a smile and let Deven lead him out of the study.

David shook his head. "He's got to stop underestimating Nico--trying to shelter him from danger isn't going to stop danger from coming for him."

"Can you blame him?" Miranda asked, tugging him down onto the sofa while everyone else got re-settled. "After what happened to Jonathan--not to mention what happened to Nico himself--it makes sense he'd be a little overprotective. Plus...as strong as Nico is, he's not invulnerable. None of us is." She met her husband's eyes. "Not even you."

She didn't know how to interpret David's expression, but she didn't like it, nor did she like the mixture of anger and something perilously close to fear she felt in him at that moment. He was afraid of being weak...why? None of them had to go it alone anymore; as long as they were together they were strong. What did he need to prove, and to whom?

Before things could get even more uncomfortable, though, Olivia cleared her throat. "So what do we have to look forward to tomorrow night? Do we have to sacrifice a chicken or anything weird like that?"

Miranda grinned. "As far as I know all we really do is show up--Stella said it's really simple--the important thing is who's there, and when, and the magic of the Signets and the Codex does most of the work. Nico might be able to tell us more after his nap."

She looked at Jacob and Cora, and added, "One thing she did tell me is that anything that happens once we're in the Circle is strictly by our consent; nobody's going to be forced to make any oaths or promise anything they're not okay with. Whatever Persephone wants from you if you say no there won't be any brimstone."

"Just the end of the world," Jacob pointed out. "And for those of us who don't take up Her mantel, the guilt of knowing we refused to help. But Cora has said repeatedly that it won't be like that, and I trust my Queen's judgment."

Cora smiled at him and touched his arm. "I am certain, my love. Persephone does not want the worship of anyone who does not offer it freely. She will help us protect our world regardless. This war, the cost that might come due, is too great for such pettiness on Her part."

"Do you think She's really a Goddess?" Olivia asked.

The Queen frowned a little. "I am not sure *what* to call such a being. And I am not sure it matters, in the end. I believe that our God is true, and I know that Persephone does not demand us to call Her our God, and that is enough for me...for now. Ask me again tomorrow night and my answer may be very different. But the being I have met in my dreams...yes, I trust Her, as I would any ally."

Olivia nodded, thoughtful. "I've never been a devout anything, to be honest. I don't have a problem with anybody's religion as long as it's not hurting anyone. I'm not really looking for a deity. But an ally...that, we could definitely use."

"Are you sure Stella will be all right?" Cora asked after a moment of everyone drinking and thinking. "It seems odd to ask a human to undertake such an enormous task when there are vampire priestesses of Persephone aplenty in this very house."

It hadn't really occurred to Miranda to wonder, and she said guiltily, "I hadn't even thought to ask." She ran her hand back through her hair, thinking of her friend, who she'd barely seen since Lark's death. "Maybe..."

"Do you really think at this point Stella would let anyone else do it?" David asked. "She did the Drawing Down, she lost her safety and her best friend, her lover was tortured...all because of Morningstar. She's not going to back down until she knows they're defeated any more than any of us would. And asking her to step aside would be an insult to everything she's been through and learned."

He had a point. "I know she can do it, and I know she wants to. And she said it's not the same as the Drawing Down--that nearly killed her. We have to trust her. It's pretty clear she's the one who's supposed to do this...I just hope when the time comes, when she really needs us, we can do half as much for her as she has for us."

******

Stella had a feeling she was being watched.

Even after living in the Haven all this time, wandering around it during daylight was surreal. It was never a hundred percent silent--there were day guards, though they numbered less than half the full post-sundown roster. There were vampires monitoring the network somewhere, and humans came and went to tend the grounds and do other contracted work that couldn't be managed at night.

On lonely days, unable to sleep even with the meds Mo had given her in plentiful supply, she used the override code on her windows and peered out at the sunlight, watching the gardeners.

She could have gone out to say hello, but there were too many questions that she didn't want to answer, even if she *could*.

Now, of course, the building was teeming with newcomers, and not all of them were nocturnal--the Elven refugees glided from room to room in their section of the Haven all throughout the day, but they didn't interact with, or even make eye contact with, the guards or anyone who wasn't an Elf. The one time she'd ventured down there they had all but run screaming from the sight of her.

She couldn't entirely blame them, though what they expected her to do, she wasn't sure. All most of them knew of the human race was murder and torture--the few who'd been living before they'd sealed themselves off in Avilon remembered the Inquisition, and that was enough of humanity for a thousand years.

And while she knew at least a handful...and probably far more than any wanted to admit...were madly curious about the Order of Elysium, and weren't nearly as snotty as their elders, Stella didn't much feel like being looked at like a plague rat, so she avoided that hallway altogether. She did hope eventually that Deven would at least let her meet the baby, or maybe even Nico's mother. Kalea sounded a lot like Stella's grandma.

The afternoon of the Solstice she was too nervous to sit still. She was finishing up the ritual room until sunrise, and after that she just couldn't imagine sleeping, so she stayed up, drank coffee, and tried not to think too much about what they were asking of her tonight.

She and Nico had spent weeks translating the ritual and its diagrams from the Codex--it wasn't complicated, but the last thing she wanted to do was draw out the symbols wrong and summon...well, whatever the unpleasant alternative was to a vampire goddess. Cupid? A unicorn?

There was nothing for her to do but pass the time. Her only real friends here were all spending the day together, reveling in that connection that no human could hope to understand. What must it be like to be bound to someone, let alone three people, the way they were? From what she'd seen it seemed beautiful and terrible...so it probably wasn't that much different from any other love.

After walking her usual solitary circuit around the building, she passed by the guest quarters where she knew the Pair of Eastern Europe and the Pair of the Eastern US were asleep. She would meet them tonight, of course; no one had thought to introduce her beforehand. That was all right. She wasn't in a hurry to deal with any more Big Important Vampires.

The closer she got to the guest wing, however, the more she felt that sensation of eyes on her. It wasn't unfamiliar, around here, since she was used to being the only human surrounded by creatures who, well, ate humans. She'd never felt any sort of malice, though, merely curiosity from the guards and other vampires who caught sight of her; Miranda had assured her they were well fed on all the human blood they needed, and they knew very well that if anyone lay a hand on her they would lose far more than a job. Stella had never felt unsafe here, despite her father's dire warnings.

Today the eyes were curious, but there was something else, too…something like awe? She wasn't sure what to make of it. The Elves by and large had little experience with humans, but surely the Order of Elysium ate something besides deer and bumblebee blood out there in the forest. Humans couldn't be that much of a rarity to them.

She started to turn back, but a flicker of light in her peripheral vision caught her attention, and she realized where she was: the Cloister's hallway, only a few doors down from the temple they'd built in one of the larger rooms.

The Order was nocturnal, as far as she knew, and would be asleep right now like any vampires, so it was unlikely there'd be anyone in there at this hour. Surely given her history with Persephone, and her place here, the vampires wouldn't object to her looking in, if she didn't interrupt anything? Would it offend them to see her there as if she was one of their own?

To hell with it. She'd sacrificed plenty on Persephone's altar already; if they had a problem with her being there they could take it up with Her.

Still, she moved as quietly as possible to the partway-open door, listening hard, hoping she'd hear if someone was inside before she walked in and caused a scurry.

The room was the size of one of the big studies where the Tetrad liked to drink and hang out, but the usual couches and liquor cabinet were gone. In their place were a lot of floor cushions, trunks and tables salvaged from the Cloister, and a wooden altar draped in velvet at the end of the room.

Stella felt the change in the air as soon as her feet crossed the threshold; it wasn't warded like her room was, nor was it shielded to contain magic, but it had the sense of spiritual presence that built up in sacred groves, churches, and permanent ritual circles the world over. Anywhere people congregated to offer their love to the Divine in whatever guise they were drawn to, their combined reverence and joy would saturate the very wood, the carpet, the stones. She could feel the energy of quiet night time services, almost hear the chanting; the scent of some incense she almost recognized but couldn't quite pin down still hung lightly in the air.

She exhaled slowly, then breathed in, finally able to fill her lungs without feeling like she was choking for the first time since the night Lark had died. She'd spent a lot of time weeping and sleeping, but not much time really feeling the vast chasm of loneliness that had been opening in her wider and wider the whole time she'd lived here and now threatened to swallow her whole.

She stood in front of the altar for a moment, looking at the objects the vampires of Elysium had deemed holy: A statue of Persephone remarkably like the one on Stella's own altar; a bowl of pomegranates, with one split open, its jewel-red seeds scattered over the altar cloth; offerings of flowers and what she devoutly hoped was wine in beautifully worked decanters; and a carved wooden box whose contents she suspected she knew.

Before she could stop herself she reached out and touched the lid, flipping the hasp open and lifting it just enough to see the Darkened Star resting inside.

She'd been told it was pulsating with light, the way Signets did when they chose their bearers, but she hadn't been able to imagine what that would look like--labradorite wasn't a gemstone like ruby or emerald that would let clear light through. Indeed, the smooth stone didn't flash, it sort of shimmered in waves over its surface. Striations in its minerals were illuminated in pulses of quicksilver, violet, and blue.

It was also a lot flatter than the Signets, she noticed. She'd been up close and personal with Nico's, and it was about half an inch thick from front to back, but the Star was perhaps half that.

Feeling bold, she picked it up and turned it over. For all that it looked a lot like a Signet on the surface, up close it was more of a flat disc, and it had odd little metal bits on the back whose purpose she couldn't divine.

She placed the Star back in its nest and closed the box, and just in time, too--that feeling of being stared at had returned.

Stella wheeled toward the door, suddenly angry that anyone would gawk at her here, of all places, and not respect the temple at least--

A young woman had appeared in the doorway, and when Stella caught her eyes, she immediately dropped to her knees at the Witch's feet.

"What the--get up!" Stella hissed, blushing furiously. "What are you doing?"

The girl lifted her head, and she too was red.

That's not all she was.

"You're human," Stella said as she realized it. "Who..."

"My name is Siobhan, Honored Priestess," the girl said. "I am leader of the Blood-Bound of this Cloister. Forgive me for intruding on your meditations on this of all days."

Stella took a beat to process that. "You know who I am?"

The girl nodded. "Of course. The entire Cloister knows who you are. That is why I have come, to offer you our gratitude and any assistance you need."

"Gratitude...for what?"

Again, Siobhan looked a bit confused at Stella's confusion. "You are the mortal priestess chosen to help bring the Goddess back to us. Because of you, after hundreds of years sundered from Her, the vampires of Elysium will be able to stand in Her presence again, face to face as they once did. And someday we Blood-Bound will too, if we take the Dark Gift."

"I don't...I don't think I understand. What does Blood-Bound mean?"

Siobhan rose gracefully and smiled. "We are the human children of Persephone who live in the Cloister. Our sacred duty is to offer our blood to the vampires of the Order, and in return we are brought into the fold in all ways but one. Only those who have died can stand before Her. Mortals are limited to visions, dreams, the rite of Drawing Down. For some of us that is enough, but for some..."

It hadn't really occurred to Stella to wonder what this might all mean to the Order. She'd heard the Elves could make direct contact with Theia--in fact that was one of the things that had hurt Nico so much when he became a vampire, losing that sense of Her Presence that the Elves all felt every moment of the day. And Theia had never been taken away from Her children; Persephone had.

"Ever since the Awakening we have all been dreaming of Her," Siobhan said softly, her eyes on the altar. "My whole life I longed to see Her, to be held in Her arms. The vampires' dreams are more vivid, ours more symbolic, but we know it is She who comes. Imagine...imagine it, Honored Priestess. Imagine the beauty and terror of what you are giving back to the Order...back to the entire Shadow World. The Order will grow again, once others realize they can join us and be initiated. And one day I may be held in Her arms for real, not just in a dream...because of you, and the Circle."

Stella found her eyes burning. The enormity of it hadn't touched her, in all this. She'd been too focused on the immediate, on Morningstar, the war. The thought that she was doing something bigger, more beautiful, had never occurred to her...even though she, too, had wished she could reach out to the Goddess with her clumsy human hands and find more there than visions and energy.

She might find more than that tonight. This wasn't just some conference call with another Signet, it was...it was holy.

Siobhan seemed to sense her overwhelm, and brought her a glass of water. "Sit," she said gently, steering Stella to one of the cushions. "This temple is as much yours as it is ours. You will always be welcome here."

She tried to thank the girl, but nothing came out; instead she just took the water and stared into the glass.

"This ritual," she finally said in a hoarse whisper, "...it might kill me. The power needed to build a bridge from Her to here...it's not as simple as I've made it out to be, to the others. And I haven't let myself think about it, not since my friend died. I've just thought about getting it done, about beating Morningstar and getting back at them no matter the cost. But now...I'm scared. I'm afraid I won't be able to do what has to be done."

Siobhan nodded. She sat down on the floor cross-legged at Stella's feet. "If you need power, you need only reach for the Order. Not a single one of us, mortal or otherwise, would deny you. We know what's at stake even if the Signets don't."

Stella nodded, too, and whispered, "Thank you."

The girl looked at her keenly, and after a moment said, "If one day you decide you need a place to stay, you would be welcome among us no matter where we settle. You are one of us...Stella. You are one of us."

Stella was crying now, and didn't try to stop; she took the hands that Siobhan offered her and stayed there in the temple for a long time, feeling the touch of hope and strength she had been missing since what was left of her life had gone down in a hail of bullets.

And for a while, it felt like the hands that held hers did so in token of greater Hands that she hoped would be there to catch her if she fell tonight, and she closed her eyes and whispered the only prayer she could come up with:

Lady, help me be brave.

*****

Midnight, the Winter Solstice.

They crossed the threshold into the ritual room one by one, letting the wards on the chamber recognize and admit them.

Stella was already inside, lighting the last few candles and ensuring all was ready. Miranda entered first among the vampires and caught the Witch's eye; she tried to give a reassuring smile, but Stella's expression was all business, both nervous and focused. Still, she felt Stella reach out and give her an energetic squeeze of sorts, and Miranda returned it, wishing she could just go over and hug her friend as long as Stella needed to be held, take her away from all of this insanity, and give her something like a normal life...or whatever life she wanted.

David, Deven, and Nico followed, Nico joining Stella at the altar and conferring with her quietly while everyone else came in.

Cora paused, looking down. "What about Vràna? Should she wait--"

But the dog had her own ideas, and stepped primly over the threshold as if she were perfectly aware of the shields around the room and the importance of the evening's events. The Nighthound walked through as slowly as the others had, then padded over to a corner of the room outside the Circle where she'd be out of the way but nearby.

As the dog sat down, she looked over at Nico, who gave her a nod; Vràna returned it, and sat Sphinxlike, watching, taking everything in.

Cora smiled and shook her head, and Miranda caught her eye--Nico definitely needed a Nighthound of his own.

When everyone had come in, Stella closed the door behind them, and Miranda sensed her closing the gap in the shields that had acted as a doorway.

The Witch wore a simple black robe, much like those the Order of Elysium wore...no, *just* like one, the Queen realized. The embroidery around the hem was identical, as was the cord around her waist. Stella must have met members of the Order, and they gifted her with their ritual wear...that had to be a mark of high respect for them. And it seemed that the outfit was helping Stella feel more confident as she returned to the altar, her head high, spine unbent, the same way the other priestesses walked.

"All right," Stella said quietly, her voice carrying easily. "If you'll all look down at the symbols on the floor, you'll see the four sets of two circles on the outside Circle's circumference. That's where you guys stand."

The altar was in the center of the complicated set of nesting circles, hexagrams, and other geometric figures that had what looked like Elvish Runes inscribed among them. Stella and Nico had painted the entire thing on the floor in white paint, and it was as beautiful as it was baffling. There was definitely an astronomical alignment of some kind, but Miranda didn't know enough about the stars and planets to even guess at its purpose. Still, it was clear what those eight circles were for--each set of two was close together, and each set marked a "corner" of the Circle that surrounded the entire diagram.

"How do we know who goes where?" Olivia asked. "Is it Elemental? South is Fire, right? That would be Cora?"

Nico smiled. "It's far simpler than that, actually."

"It's geographical," David concluded. "Not the four Elements, more like the four corners of the Earth."

"Well, of the Western hemisphere, if you want to be precise," Deven noted. "None of us are Asian or African. The original Circle was made up of eight white vampires from Greece, after all."

"Maybe we can talk about the ethnocentrism of our forevampires later?" Jacob asked, sounding far more nervous than Miranda would have expected.

Stella said, firmly, "Places please."

Miranda took up position beside David in the South; Jacob and Cora moved to the East; Olivia and Avi took North; and Deven and Nico took West. Looking more closely at the diagram, Miranda could see a smaller Circle set into it, also with eight places more closely spaced; and there was an even smaller one with four spaces.

Stella stood at the altar, carefully opening the Codex to a page marked with a long black ribbon. She took a deep breath and told them, "I'm not exactly sure how this will work--there may be a gateway to walk through, you might be transported someplace, She might even just show up here. The text is vague on that point, but it says you'll know it when you see it. So be ready for anything I guess."

Nods all around.

The Witch took a moment, breathing deeply, eyes closing as she gathered her power around her.

Miranda wasn't sure what to do, but she felt David's fingers lace in hers, and she held on tightly. The last time something like this had happened, he'd gotten back his memories of death and his first meeting with Persephone. It hadn't been dangerous for them, but it had been its own kind of trauma having to relive it all and then realize that the only way the Pair could move forward together was as Thirdborn. What would this mean?

Stella picked up a knife and a silver goblet. "I need a few drops of blood from each of you," she said. "It's not binding--it's to make sure the gateway recognizes you, kind of like the wards on the room."

She moved from Pair to Pair, quickly and efficiently nicking their fingers and collecting a couple of dark ruby drops from each. They'd all had introductions earlier before she'd started casting the Circle, so at least everyone was familiar with each other. Stella had long ago lost the awe that most people had in the presence of Signets, but still, being surrounded by them like this had to be a bit strange, in her Sight if nothing else. What did she See when she looked at all of them together?

Miranda took her hand and held it a second before letting her take the Queen's blood. She met Stella's eyes and smiled, trying to put as much love and appreciation into that one look as she could, and to her surprise there was the faint shine of tears in Stella's eyes as she gripped Miranda's wrist with one hand and cut her with the other.

Stella had another smile for Nico, who leaned forward and touched his forehead to hers. Miranda saw Stella's lip quiver just the tiniest bit...but in a mere second the expression was covered up, and Stella was back to work, returning to the altar and setting the cup down next to a cast iron cauldron.

She lit a match and dropped it into the cauldron, igniting whatever was waiting inside; flames leapt up and banished the shadows from the room.

"Everyone let your eyes fix on the flames," Stella said. "Stare into them until the fire dies--concentrate on the light, don't look away. Once I do the incantation things might get weird, like you're Misting only worse, so it's best to stay focused on the fire so you don't fall over or throw up on the Goddess or anything."

David chuckled next to her, and Miranda smiled too, but they both did as they were told, and Miranda let her vision fill with the leaping flames, pretending for a moment she was Cora and the fire was her friend and companion. The light was blindingly bright but didn't hurt her eyes the way man-made light did; it would burn at a touch but not at a distance like the sun. She watched it dance, and twist, and somewhere outside her immediate attention she heard Stella begin to speak.

Miranda knew the incantation was in ancient Elvish, and didn't even try to translate it--none of them spoke it well enough to pass it among them psychically the way they had modern Elvish, so only about half of it would make sense to her without serious study anyway. It sounded like music, though, especially with the energy of the room beginning to rise along with it, and Stella had a lovely, if untrained, singing voice that wound through the language with practiced ease.

Miranda felt the room begin to change, the air heating, folding on itself, and she smelled burning blood--Stella must have poured theirs into the fire. The smell of blood became overpowering, and it must have been even more intense up by the altar, as Stella faltered in her intonation for a second before taking a shaky breath and resuming.

Somewhere within her, Miranda could feel the Dark Web rising, and she opened herself to it. She could feel David's power twining through hers, and Nico and Dev's reaching toward them; as their energy sought each other's, the other two Pairs were drawn in, a slow current of energy moving around the Circle from one to another, focusing in the Signets themselves. She could feel the stone at her throat growing hotter and hotter, and knew it must be brightening--they all were, all changing color to red, then to white, as power flooded through them, Signet to Signet to Signet over and over, becoming a whirlpool, spinning, spinning...

Miranda could feel the power filling the Circle, and she understood then what it was doing: the Circle was a generator, creating a vortex that bound all eight of them and could, with the right push in the right direction, destroy...create...decimate... renew...creation and destruction were a part of what they were, what they had been made for, and it was all right here, in the strands of the Dark Web that connected them all and twisted and braided until the power had grown so high, so fast, there was no containing it, no way to--

She didn't know what signal she was waiting for, or how she knew it was time, but there was a soft sound within the Circle...a gasp? ...and Miranda felt everyone release the power at the same time. It flooded the Circle and filled it, and she felt it flowing out, as if the altar was a drain and everything they had, everything they were made of rushed out, out, *out*--

The fire went out.

Miranda felt reality warp around her, and yes, it felt something like Misting, but that was like comparing a kitchen tap to a roaring waterfall. She didn't know if her body was moving, but it felt like her soul was sucked out of her body...like dying...she fought against it at first, and felt the others doing the same, fighting to live, to get free.

But within a heartbeat the panic evaporated as darkness, soft and beguiling, washed through her. The fear of death faded into nothingness, and she knew this place she was in was beyond death, beyond fear.

Shadows moved around her and through her, lifting her up. She was safe...so safe. She didn't know where the others were, but she knew they were with her somehow, all of them holding each other even though they had to take this part of the journey alone.

She felt the ground beneath her feet.

The darkness gradually subsided like water, leaving her aware of herself standing up, and aware of the fact that she was definitely not still in the Haven.

Instead, there was a forest at night, surrounding a clearing at whose edge she had arrived. The sky held no Moon, but she could see by the light of the millions of stars moving overhead. She stared up at them for a moment watching them shimmer and turn; every few breaths the sky would ripple like someone had stuck a finger in it.

Finally, she looked down at the clearing. None of the others were here, but Miranda knew they were safe; for now, the only thing to do was go forward.

She could see things moving in the trees...not animals, but pale watery lights, vaguely human-shaped. They drifted among the trees in a dream of peace, and she could sense that peace, a kind of relief, the sense of a burden set down, of walking free.

The dead. She was seeing the dead.

Did they stay here forever? She wondered. Or was this quiet, peaceful place with its soft breeze and endless starlight only a temporary reprieve? Did they remember themselves? Or anything?

She watched them for a long moment, feeling a little of that relief herself. If this was it, if that's what death was, it didn't seem so bad. It was getting there that was the horror, the grief. Leaving everything behind, being afraid, being in pain...none of that remained here.

Miranda walked into the clearing, unsure what else to do, and felt eyes upon her. It must be strange for the souls in the forest to see her here; or maybe they'd been expecting her.

Something moved off to her right, and she turned toward it, her hand automatically reaching for the hilt of her sword. To her surprise it was there. She hadn't come into the Circle armed; none of them had. But looking down at herself she was dressed as she would be any night as Queen, in black and a long coat and all her weapons, Signet glowing red.

She saw the mist that moved along the ground begin to swirl around itself, and a faint light seemed to kindle within it. More mist and shadows flowed into the spiral, and it slowly grew taller, much like the power they'd raised in the Circle but gentler, without any of that urgency.

The column of shadow began to take form, and solidified into a woman, her features emerging slowly from the darkness. She stood tall and proud beneath the starlight. Hair the color of old wine flowed down her back, and she wore a gown made of shadows and spider's webs, threads of the Dark Web itself, strands of dreams and nightmares woven into her cloak.

A deep red light shone at her throat, and the setting of an amulet formed around it.

Last to take shape were her eyes: they were black and fathomless, with neither pupil nor iris, as black as eternity, full of stars like the sky.

She smiled.

In that smile, Miranda felt a wave of love so endless she almost couldn't bear it; she found herself kneeling, overcome, hands pressing into the cool, damp grass that wasn't grass.

A hand touched her head. Again, that love washed through her, along with strength more vast and beautiful than anything she'd ever felt.

"Rise, child," Persephone said.

Miranda looked up into those eyes and tried to say something...anything. She couldn't. All she could do was stand.

"I know You," Miranda finally managed in a hoarse whisper. "I dreamed You."

"You did indeed."

Her voice was a resonant contralto, full of contradictions like everything else about Her: It was hollow, kissed with the cold wind over a graveyard, but also vibrantly alive with the rush of an owl's wings and the cautious steps of deer into a moonlit meadow.

And, beyond her, there were ravens.

There were ravens in the trees, watching Miranda through glittering black eyes. There were ravens in Her gown, sometimes only shapes and sometimes taking flight.

Standing in front of a Being like this, any questions the Queen might have had seemed completely pointless. She found herself laughing.

"I don't know what to say," Miranda told Her helplessly. "I had all these questions, things I had to know. None of it matters."

"It matters," was the answer. "And you have a chance to ask them all. Tonight there is only one question that matters, and it is one I must ask you."

"Wait..." Something came to her, something she wasn't sure she'd get an answer for but felt compelled to ask before it slipped her mind. She looked over at the forest, where those glowing spirits still dwelt. "Is...is Faith in there? And Jonathan?"

The question felt like it came out of nowhere, but Persephone was unsurprised. "No," She replied. "As you sensed, this place is not forever. It is a resting-place, where those who have passed over the Bridge can abide with Me for a time. But they must all move on eventually."

Miranda let out a long breath, eyes burning. "So Faith was here...and she was okay?"

"Yes."

"Where is she now?"

A smile. "That is not for Me to tell you, child."

"Does everyone come here? Even humans?"

"This place is for My children," She said. "Human, immortal, it matters not. But there are other places...other paths."

"Other gods?"

"Yes, and no. There are thousands of Us...and only One. Just as there are many strands but only one Web. We arise from the Web, from all that is, has been, or ever will be. And We wear many faces for Our children, out of love for them. We want to know you, and love you, as much as you want to know Us. Only your choices and actions keep you away."

"Or Morningstar."

"Yes. Long I was imprisoned, yet now I am free. The sacrifice made on this night will echo off all the worlds, and change everything. It begins with all of you, the brightest stars in My night, the greatest of My lineage." She looked at Miranda with pride, and reached out to touch her face. "You will reshape the Shadow World, and through it the Day World, and your hands shall be Mine. But first you must make a choice."

Miranda felt the night around her shifting again, and between one breath and the next, they were no longer alone in the clearing.

The rest of the Circle appeared from the darkness, all standing in the same places they had been back in the Haven. Jacob and Cora were clinging to each other, wide-eyed and pale; Olivia and Avi were both smiling. Deven looked like he'd been crying, as did Nico, but Nico's face held only joy.

Miranda felt David's hand in hers again, and she grabbed sideways to put her arms around him. He stood silent, strong, steady; she looked up at his face, and he looked relaxed but purposeful. She could feel a calm surety radiating from her Prime.

Persephone stood in the center of the Circle, looking at each of them as if they were the rarest and most precious treasure in the Universe. "You have come to Me tonight seeking knowledge and power. You have it now. Everything you need to know about the fight ahead of you...everything I can tell you...is in the Codex. The first Circle, your forbears, wrote down the Mysteries both for what would become the Order of Elysium and for you. When Morningstar imprisoned Me, your Mysteries were obscured, as they could not be performed without the Touch of My power. Now you will have that power. And each of you will have the ability to return to Me, here, to this room and this Forest of Spirits, whenever you have need of Me for counsel or comfort."

She lifted Her hand, and a cut appeared in Her wrist; dark blood trickled from it, and where it hit the ground, Miranda watched vines of energy growing out of the grass...strands of the Dark Web, born from Her blood.

"All of this must come with a price," She went on. "I ask not for your worship; if you revere me as My children have for centuries it is by your own will, by the call of your soul. I ask not for your obedience; you will have choices to make that I cannot make for you. I ask for something much simpler, and yet much, much more grave: Your lives. Each of you must offer your blood, and take Mine in return, and in so doing become more than any of your kind has ever been. Even those of you already Thirdborn must do this, for though you were transformed through My lineage, it is My blood alone that can truly remake you."

She paused, and Her eyes swept them all again, reading their uncertainty. With a nod, She said, "You fear the cost is too high...you fear the death-lust already visited upon four of you. But these are the terms: Life and death exist in balance, and that overall balance must be maintained. For each of you to live and wield My power, a life must be paid at each turn of the Moon. How that happens is up to you. But the power I offer is not a trifling thing. It is the power of darkness and death--Mine is a path of fire, children. To serve Me is to burn."

Now She smiled softly. "But you should know, your debt for the next month has been paid--a sacrifice was offered on your behalf during the ritual."

"What do you mean, paid?" David asked, shocked. "Who could have paid it?"

Persephone looked out over Miranda's shoulder, and Miranda and the others all followed Her gaze to the trees.

Miranda's heart shuddered in her chest with realization as one of the ghostly figures in the forest moved out from the trees. As it drifted closer, it took on a shape, and Miranda found herself crying, shaking her head.

"No...no. Stella..."

The ghost smiled at her. Her voice was calm, peaceful, but had that same wry edge it always had, even here. "It's okay, Miranda. I knew what I signed up for."

Miranda turned back to Persephone. "You can't do this!" she cried. "She can't be dead--You can send her back! She deserves better than to die for us like this!"

"I offered her a chance to return," She replied, sounding for a moment as wry as Stella. "She refused."

"As a vampire," Stella said. "And hell no."

"You could change your mind," Miranda insisted. "We would take care of you. It doesn't have to be...Stella, please, don't do this. Don't go."

"Oh, Miranda..."

Stella came forward and put her arms around Miranda, and for a second, they were warm and solid, not those of a disembodied spirit, but of a real, living friend.

"Knowing all of you has been amazing," she said into Miranda's hair. "I wouldn't trade it for a hundred years. I know you're going to blame yourself, but that's not what I want. I made my own choice, and I need you to honor it...honor me...by doing what you're here to do."

Finally Miranda nodded, barely able to speak. "You have my word."

Stella turned to Nico, who was also crying, but didn't try to dissuade her. He only put his arms around the Witch, and they held each other for a long time.

"I will always love you," Nico whispered. "In every world and for all time."

"You too," she said. "Don't worry...I'm going to be fine. Better than fine."

Stella looked at Deven next and said only, "You know what you have to do now, right?"

Deven sighed. "I do."

"Okay, good." Stella smiled at all of them. "It's time for me to go now. Miranda...take care of my dad, okay? He won't understand. But tell him the truth. I had work to do, and it took me away, but it was important. And big. And he'd better not start drinking again or I'll haunt his ass."

Miranda laughed through her tears and nodded. "I will."

Before any of them could say more, Stella turned away, and was gone. A moment later Miranda saw the light that had made up her image reappear in the trees, joining the other spirits at rest.

They all turned back to Persephone, who was still waiting, blood still running from Her arm.

"It is time," She said. "Time for your own choice. Will you walk My path, risking all and serving all, though the price is high and the future uncertain? Will you take one another's hands and My own, and dedicate yourselves to the Shadow World in a way that no Signet has in a thousand years? Or will you go your own way, alone?"

Miranda glanced back at the trees, wondering if Stella was watching them, or if she trusted her friends to do the right thing. She could feel the weight of all those souls who had passed through this place just since she'd become a vampire...all the people, human and vampire, who had died in her Elite, or by Morningstar's hand, and all those who stood to fall if she didn't do what, in her heart, she knew she had been born to do.

The Queen was the first to step forward, the first to kneel, and seven others followed her lead.

Chapter Eleven

Miranda came to on the floor of the ritual room, barely able to make sense of where she was before she forced herself up onto her knees and turned toward the altar, frantic.

It was Nico who first reached Stella. He was first to get up and go to her, to lift her body from where she had fallen across the altar as the last of her blood ran into the cauldron. She had slit both of her wrists and stood there bleeding to death as they made the journey across the Bridge that had been forged from her blood.

The Elf lowered her to the floor, tears streaming from his eyes, and tenderly straightened out her robe and her hair, folded her hands over her chest, and closed her sightless eyes.

He leaned his forehead to hers, shaking. Miranda could feel waves of grief over him, and she struggled to her feet to join them, dropping back to her knees on Stella's other side to hold him, and the Witch, and weep.

A moment later she felt David's arms around them, and Deven's. She could feel the added love and strength of the others, but they kept their distance. They hadn't known Stella, not like the Tetrad had.

"I have to call her father," Miranda whispered. "What am I going to tell him? Oh, God, what will I say?"

"The truth," David said softly. "What she told you to say."

"She died for us...why does everyone we love have to die for us?" She wept even harder into her friend's lifeless shoulder, bent over double with the pain.

Behind her, she heard a quiet noise of discomfort--not quite a moan, but nearly, and it broke through her grief. Miranda lifted her head. "Cora?"

The Queen looked embarrassed at interrupting. "I'm fine, my Lady. Just...a little dizzy."

In truth, none of the others looked like they felt well, and Miranda realized why just a beat later than she should have.

"You all need to get to bed," she said. "You're about to change...hopefully you can go to sleep and not feel it. It wasn't that bad for me, and Dev and Nico missed out entirely, thank God, but you'll need rest if nothing else."

They looked at each other in alarm. "Change...oh, God, David, I forgot all about that," Olivia said. "I saw it happen to you. It was awful." She looked genuinely frightened. "My first crossover I was totally unconscious."

"We can get you drugs," David said. "I'll have Mo come to your suites and see if he can medicate all of you. It didn't work for Nico because of his Elven blood, but for you it should. Like Miranda said, get to bed. I'll have extra blood sent as well."

Miranda lowered her eyes back to Stella's face as she listened to the others leaving. Just before they left, though, she heard Deven speak up. "Cora...before you go...can I ask you something?"

"Of course."

"You didn't hesitate to take Persephone's offer. What did she say to you two that made up your minds?"

Unable to deny her own curiosity Miranda looked up again in time to see Cora and Jacob exchange the strangest look she'd ever seen on either.

"Um...well..." Jacob began, but the Queen finished for him.

"It was not Persephone who persuaded us," she said.

Deven's eyebrows shot up. "Oh?"

Jacob nodded, looking at his Queen. "No, She...She didn't come alone."

"So you met Someone Else as well?"

Now, Jacob actually laughed, and there were tears in his eyes now that had nothing to do with pain, fear, or worry. He looked at

Cora again, drew her close. "No, it was Someone we already knew."

He didn't elaborate, and Deven didn't ask him to. Jacob and Cora were still hanging on to each other as they left.

Left alone, the Tetrad gathered around Stella again. "What should we do with her?" Deven asked softly. "It's too late in the morning to take her anywhere and we can't have the police come here."

Just then there was a knock at the door, and she looked over to see two women standing in the doorway, both dressed in robes like Stella's; Mo stood just behind them.

"Ashera," Deven said. "Siobhan."

"I am sorry, Hallowed One," Ashera said, "but we were hoping we could take Stella to the temple and dress her properly--she'll be safe there, and the others wish to pay their respects. We have a traditional blessing for those who have gone ahead…then Mo can take her to the infirmary. We've brought something to carry her on."

Miranda noticed that Dev didn't object to the title she gave him. He met Miranda's eyes. "Is that all right with you?"

She nodded.

Ashera, Siobhan--who turned out to be one of the human Order members--and several others came in with a stretcher Miranda recognized from the clinic. Mo came in first to do a quick examination "for the record," as he said. Human authorities cared about things like time and cause of death, and Detective Maguire certainly would.

Mo was as efficient as always, but she could see the sadness on his face as well. He'd been as fond of Stella as everyone in the Haven. It already felt like a light had gone out somewhere much more profound than this one room.

Miranda looked at the altar, at all the blood staining the cloths that covered it. She thought of Stella's room…and Pywacket…and everything the Witch had left behind. She thought of the phone call waiting for her.

She was crying again, and David drew her close. "Come on," he said gently. "They'll take care of her. Let's go make the call and get it over with…waiting won't make it easier."

"I'll go with them," Nico said. "I'll stay with her."

"I have something I have to do," Deven said. "Then I'll go wherever you need me."

Miranda nodded. "Come to our suite," she said. "If Nico doesn't need you I will."

She leaned on David, letting him be her support as he led her out of the room; behind them, the priestesses of Elysium were cleaning up the altar and seeing to Stella, who they carried between them with reverence, like a Queen.

*****

"Do you want to live, Deven?"

Nico's face held an emotion he would never forget: Astonishment, spilling into fear…fear of him.

"What are you?" Nico whispered.

Confused, he looked down at himself.

A memory flashed: Miranda staring at the monitor, where the camera had captured only a blurry light instead of his actual shape.

Out beyond the clearing, the forest was filled with light…the same light that poured out of him now, as if he had no skin, no edges, just the watery glow of spirit barely held within the confines of a body. He held up one hand, able to see the outline of his fingers, but also right through them, to Nico who stood a few feet away.

He lifted his gaze to Persephone. He remembered Her now--She had come to him many times during those two years he'd suffered after Jonathan died. She had come to his dreams, held him, offered a shoulder when She could not give him the one thing he wanted above all else.

Death. He had wanted death.

It seemed he'd had it all along.

"Am I dead?" he asked. Even his voice was different here, as if the wind blew right through it as it did through him.

"In a way," She replied, moving in a slow circle around him. "You know the truth, Deven. You have lived longer than any human-born creature should. Were it not for the intervention of your Tetrad you would have died, of course, but for a long time now you have been losing what held you to the Earthly plane. Nicolanai's matrix of energy and the Signet bond are all that hold

you there now. They bought you time...but that time is limited. Even a power that great cannot defeat time."

"But if I die so will they."

"That depends."

He Misted to the temple, giving him a moment before the others arrived with Stella's body. There was no time to think about that, no time to let himself feel; he had to hurry, before the spell of those moments in the Forest of Spirits wore off and he had time to doubt.

"Do you want to live, Deven?"

He stared at Her. "What kind of question is that?"

"The one that matters, at present." She came to stand in front of him again. Her gown whispered over the ground, and in Her footsteps the grass died, withered, and sprouted again, all in the space of seconds. "You have a choice."

He laughed coldly, bitterly at the words. "No I don't. I never have. If I die, the entire Tetrad comes with me, and the war is lost before we even truly join the battle. That's not a choice. That's extortion. Whoring myself out like always, just sucking a different dick."

If She was offended by his words She gave no indication. "What if I told you that you could die, right now, walk into the Forest of Spirits and leave all the suffering of the world behind, knowing with no doubt whatsoever that those you love would survive without you?"

He stared at her without speaking, and She went on. "I am offering you peace," She said. "A new life, perhaps, when you are ready--but for now at least, the rest you have craved for centuries. The others will live on, still bound to each other. They will grieve you, but they will not die from your loss. They will have as much help as I can give them to win the war. I give you My word that their chances will not suffer because of your death. And you know, as well as I, that they would wish you only love and peace knowing what you have been through in your life."

The box was just where Ashera had placed it on the altar.

"What's the catch?" he whispered, refusing to look at Nico. "This can't be for free."

She lifted an eyebrow. "If you choose death there is no price. Only the rest you have earned a hundred times over in your life. It is living that carries a price. You cannot remain as you are now--even with magic and bonds you will not last much longer, and even

I cannot predict how long that might be. So if you return to the world of form, you will have to be changed, just as the others of the Circle who are not already Thirdborn must change. But you, child, must become something else...something new."

At that, the light at Her throat flared, and the stone She wore--whatever it was--appeared to be something else. Labradorite. "Hallowed," he said. "It would mean something different for me than it did for the others."

"It would. In taking up the Darkened Star you would become a being half of your world and half this one; anchored to the Earth by love and flesh but anchored to Me also. That balance would hold you to your life indefinitely. Serve Me, lead My children as you were called to do, and live, perhaps forever."

"Forever..." He closed his eyes in pain at the prospect. He had seen enough of forever, lived long enough. Endless nights passed in his mind, the planet turning and turning and turning, standing so still, so still while everything turned to dust in his hands.

But to walk into the Forest...to close his eyes forever, to let it all go, lay down his sword once and for all...oh, his heart cried out for it, just to reach a little further, to step out of his body and let it crumble in the dirt.

But...

His fingers trembled as he fumbled the box open and took the Star from inside. He'd never really looked at it closely, but now he saw it--it wasn't a pendant, at least, not on its own. It was a flat disc like the Stone of Awakening that Miranda wore, but with a stone cabochon instead of just metal. He turned it over and saw the same little hooks the Stone had. Xara must have worn it mounted to a setting, and they'd removed the setting after it spoke for him.

The first Circle had been made up of the first Signets, and one of them had founded the Order of Elysium. She had worn this, but her Signet had passed to someone else on her death, and the Darkened Star must have stayed with the Order.

Now, he looked at Nico.

The Elf's eyes were full of tears, and they spilled over and ran silver down his face as he looked at his Prime, nodding, his voice a rough whisper. "It's okay, i'lyren. *I wouldn't ask you to stay for me. You can go. It's all right to go."*

Nico...oh, Nico, my love, I...

The words didn't come in a voice anymore, they were only energy, emotion, drifting across the clearing, touching Nico as he watched his beloved fade into the shadows.

But...

He could feel himself dissolving, sweet darkness gently lifting his cells apart.

Nico...

Wait. WAIT!

He held onto himself by mere inches. He couldn't let go yet. He needed time, there was so much to say. He wanted to hold Nico again, kiss him, feel those arms around him the way a disembodied soul could not.

And Miranda--he had to tell her goodbye. She had to know how much she had meant to him, how she had saved him over and over again just by being her. How much he admired and loved her. And David--there would never be enough time to say everything he wanted to say to David.

He would have to leave behind those nights in their suite, all four of them together, waking up just long enough to listen to everyone breathe, to feel their heartbeats all around him. He would have to leave behind Nico's mouth on his, the shuddering desire that overtook him when they lay joined together in the dark, the heat of Nico's breath at his throat. Hours by the fire talking about magic, literature, anything. David's hands, dear God those hands, and the sound of Miranda's voice as she gave new life to old songs.

The God of his humanity had abandoned him so long ago, but in a way he had made this life his new god; the taste of blood, the sweetness of long languid kisses, a quiet laugh in a firelit room. Reaching over to touch the stone in Nico's Signet with one finger and watching its light, and the light in Nico's eyes, dance.

He had told Jonathan, that night he'd found the sweater, that he was happy. He knew it was true even as he'd said the words, though just knowing that frightened him with its hugeness. He didn't know how to be happy. Didn't know how to love without constantly being afraid that love would be ripped from his hands. He didn't know how to live without wanting to die.

But he wanted to learn.

"No," he whispered. He could hear the words now. "Nico--Nico, take my hand."

"Are you sure--"

"I don't want to go. I want to stay here with you. With them. I want this, I want you. Help me."

He felt the Elf's joy as he felt his tears--for real, against his skin as the Elf's arms closed around him. Nico held onto him almost too tightly for a moment, shaking, almost sobbing. They clung to each other tightly...so tightly. He felt Nico's muscles and bones, his clothes, his breath...and he felt his own.

Not only that, but he felt Her pride as She watched him make the choice.

The Darkened Star snapped onto the back of his Signet with almost no pressure. It was as if it had been waiting for the chance to do exactly that.

He could still remember the feeling of being chosen as Prime, and the feeling of bonding to Jonathan--that surge of power, the tidal wave of strength and bliss as connections that had always existed within him flew open and filled, empty places now overfull.

That feeling was nothing to this. Now, not only was he bound to those who wore the Signets that linked to his, but to She who had made them all, whose love and strength were just beyond the edge of his vision, waiting, that darkness flooding everything he was or had ever been, cleansing the sorrow of his old life away and leaving behind something new, someone made up of every moment of his past but not bound by any of it.

In the darkness of his closed eyes he could See now what Miranda Saw, the Dark Web, reaching out all around in endless strands crossed and crisscrossed from one end of creation to the other. The rush of wings battered him from all sides, and he opened his arms to it, feeling those wings touch every inch of his skin, feather and bone merging with his.

He wasn't sure when exactly he hit the ground, but he knew that Ashera and the others found him on the floor in front of the altar, surrounded by a vortex of power that gradually sank into the ground and ebbed into the Web from whence it had come. He listened without moving as she calmly directed the others to place Stella on a draped table they had prepared as soon as they realized the Witch had died.

A moment later he felt warm hands on his shoulders. "My Lord...can you hear me?"

He managed a nod. Everything was swimming around him; he didn't dare open his eyes yet.

Still, he knew the presence that appeared at the door as well as he knew his own soul. "Deven!"

Nico knelt beside him and, with Ashera's help, uncurled him and helped him sit up. The solidity of their bodies and their energy was reassuring, and he let them move him about like a doll until he was reasonably upright.

"Are you all right?" Nico asked softly in his ear. "I felt...it. What do you need?"

Deven took a long, deep breath, feeling the strange new power in his skin settle around him like wings folding over his back. He wouldn't be entirely surprised if that was a literal description now.

"I think I'm okay," he said. Thankfully his voice sounded exactly like it should, if a little shaky. "But I might need a nap."

Nico laughed weakly. "I wouldn't say no to one either."

Ashera was smiling at him, and she reached up to touch his face. "Welcome, Hallowed One," she said.

He smiled back. "The hand of the Raven Mother be upon you," he said automatically.

Her smile grew. "Can we help you up, my Lord?"

He nodded, and she and Nico helped him to his feet. He could feel the others staring, clustered around Stella, and when he turned to them, they knelt as one.

Deven sighed. "Rise," he said. "And from now on, no kneeling, not to me or anyone else. You're the children of the Goddess--you kneel to no one but Her." By way of demonstration, he bowed to them the way the Signets bowed to each other.

They echoed the motion in silence.

Another deep breath--it was still hard to think, but he managed to frame a request. "Ashera, if you would, gather the Hallowed diaries for me--I have studying to catch up on."

"Of course, Hallowed One."

He saw Nico smile to himself, and asked, "What?"

The Elf chuckled. "I was all set to feel guilty about being the reason you wanted to stay, but...that wasn't the only reason. I can see it now, as I should have all along."

Deven took his hands and kissed him. Then he looked over at where Stella lay; the others were waiting, and he knew what they were waiting for.

"Go to the others," he said to Nico. "Get some rest--tell Miranda I'll be there soon. Right now, though…" He took a step back, kissing Nico's hands, then brushed himself off, standing up straight.

"Tell the Queen I have work to do," he said.

*****

"I know," said a hoarse voice over the phone. *"I already know."*

Miranda fought not to break down weeping again, even though she had steeled herself for the rage she knew was coming…only to have it not come, to have this instead. "What?"

David was already holding her, the two on the couch, his arms around her solid and real in the real world, not some dreamtime forest where those they loved just…walked away…into the dark. This was the world where everyone was left behind, and it was the world she had to live in, fight in, and somehow find the words to apologize.

Maguire could barely speak, but she heard him say, *"She came to see me. My baby girl. She came to see me in my sleep and told me she had to go away."*

She lost the fight. Tears spilled from her eyes and she gasped around the sharp pain in her chest. "I'm sorry, Mike…I didn't know she was going to do this. I would never have let her. I should have…I'm sorry."

"She said…she said if I blamed you she'd never forgive me," Maguire managed. *"But I can't help it. My girl is gone, and if it weren't for you--"*

"She'd still be here," Miranda nodded. "I know. I know. It is our fault. She never should have set foot in our world. But she did, and she saved us--you'll never even know how many times or in how many ways."

Across the room, Nico came in the door bearing a small crate of books including the Codex; the others looked like handmade diaries of some sort. He saw what the Pair was doing and closed his eyes a moment, took a deep breath, and set the crate down on David's desk for the time being. Then he came to join them on the couch, leaning sideways into David's shoulder, one hand resting comfortingly on Miranda's leg.

"I don't know what to do," Miranda said into the phone. "It's too late for us to leave the house--you're welcome to come here now if you want, or wait until sunset. She's...she's safe, Mo's taking care of her. Whatever you need, just..."

They were both crying again, too hard to talk for a moment. Eventually David took the phone from her and--with surprising gentleness, given his usually professional demeanor with the Detective--arranged for Maguire to come for Stella at nightfall, when he could also take any of her possessions he wanted to have right away. Packing up the rest of her things could be done later.

"Nonsense," David was saying. She watched him pace the room slowly. "You make whatever arrangements made you need, Mike, but you're not paying a penny. I owe you that much at the very, very least."

Miranda took a slow, shaky breath. She had done as much as she had promised--she'd told Maguire what happened, without spin, without sugar coating anything--and it was a relief to let David do what he did best, handle the logistics. Even death was something he could manage if there was a plan, steps, a to-do list.

Nico pulled her close. She felt wrung out, her tears at least momentarily spent, and nestled into his shoulder.

"Is Deven okay?" she asked.

He chuckled, a bemused sort of sound. "Yes, I think so."

"What is it?"

A long pause, while both of them watched David for a moment. Then Nico said, "In the Forest of Spirits...She offered him death. She said he could go, without hurting any of us, or losing us the war. He could find peace, forget all the pain."

Miranda sat up and stared at him. "But...he's still here."

Nico smiled. This time his laugh, though quiet, was genuine, born out of joy even through the sorrow of the night. "I know," he said. "He stayed."

They stared at each other. "And he's going to lead the Order," she said.

A nod. "It was the price of living. Not only did he stay here, with us, of his own will...he chose to take up the Darkened Star in return for that life."

"My God," she whispered. "I don't...I don't know what to do with that."

Another smile. "Neither do I...except to be happy."

She nodded, as across the room David ended the call with Maguire and came back to them, sinking heavily into the couch.

Miranda was about to tell Nico to relay the news to David, but then she saw her husband's face, and forgot all about it. She scooted closer and put her arms around David, who burrowed into her shoulder and cried silently for a while, Queen on one side of him, Elf moving to the other.

It took a while, but they all found a state of quiet, just holding onto each other. She could smell the sunrise beginning outside the windows, and she had nearly gathered the strength to ask David what the plan was with Maguire, when the suite door opened again.

"Glad you're here," she said, looking up as Deven came in. "I think..."

The words died on her lips. She blinked once, then again, and just...stared.

"Oh," Nico said, glancing from her to his Prime and back. "I meant to mention that."

David, too, was staring. "What the hell..."

Dev's eyebrows shot up. "What?"

Miranda stuttered for a second, then, "Your...um, your hair."

"For starters," David added.

Deven frowned, lifted his gaze, grabbed a strand of hair with his fingers and tugged it down into view.

It was white.

"Oh," he said. "Um...okay."

"And your arms," she said.

He looked down; he'd pushed up the sleeves of his shirt doing whatever he'd been doing, and apparently hadn't noticed anything amiss.

"Whoa!" He immediately pulled the shirt off, and now all four of them were gaping.

Deven's skin was flawless, unmarked, centuries of tattoos just...erased.

Except for one.

Inside his right wrist, wrapping around his forearm, was an entirely new tattoo, this one of a raven in the same stylized kind of design as the one on David's back.

Miranda had no idea how to react to any of it, but she didn't really have time--just then the skin of her own right arm began to burn unbearably, and she half-screamed, batting at it as blood blossomed all over her wrist.

Beside her, Nico sucked in a pained breath, and David did the same, all of them gripped by what she knew was the same pain--one David and Nico had felt before, but that was brand new to her.

She watched in morbid fascination as lines began to appear on her arm, healing up in black almost as quickly as they showed up in blood. In less than two minutes, her wrist bore the same tattoo as Deven's, and David's, and Nico's, and she suspected the other four members of the Circle's. The lines healed instantly, the blood fading as if it had never run.

Nico still had the Elven clan markings he'd always had, and a quick check showed David's back was the same.

"Well," Deven said, "She's certainly got a literal grasp of the idea of a blank slate."

David gave him a look that was a combination of astonishment and the particular brand of aggravation that he only ever felt toward Deven. "You are way, way too calm about this!"

"I hadn't had a chance to tell David about your...arrangement with Persephone," Nico said. "Miranda knows."

"Oh." Understanding dawned, and Deven looked a little sheepish. "Well...I'm not sure quite how to..."

Nico sighed. "Persephone offered him a choice between life and death--if he chose life he had to change. Whatever the hell he was, he wasn't going to last much longer. She had to turn him into something new."

"Thank you, love," Deven said with a wry smile. "Also apparently I'm in charge of the Order now."

David met Deven's gaze. "Does that mean if you had died we would have survived?"

"Yes," Deven said, the smile fading. "She gave me Her word that whatever I chose, you would survive, and the war would not be lost because of me."

"But you stayed anyway."

They held each other's eyes. "I did."

"Why?"

Now, the smile returned, just a little. This time it wasn't wry or edged with anything but sincerity. "Because I love you," Deven said. "I love Nico. And I love Miranda. And I love the life we're building here, whatever it leads to. For the first time in centuries I want to know what's next. I want to be here for the world we create. So I chose to stay."

David's eyes were bright again, and Miranda's were burning, but this time not from grief. "As an Elf," David said, laughing a little.

Now Dev's expression turned quizzical. "I'm not an Elf."

"Oh?" David tilted his head to the side. "Tell that to your ears."

Eyes widening, Deven reached up and touched his ears, which immediately turned scarlet.

"Son of a bitch," he said.

Miranda couldn't help it--he was so dumbstruck she burst out laughing through her tears. "Come on," she said, pushing herself up off the couch and dragging the boys with her. "Let's go to bed--we all need a long sleep, to begin with. The world will make more sense when we're not all exhausted."

The Tetrad began its usual rituals of settling in for the morning: showers, dress or undress, climbing into the bed to claim a spot in the tangle. Miranda was first in, and listened with her eyes closed to the others getting ready for bed, letting the familiar warmth and affection of their voices and activities soothe her battered heart.

"I don't get it," Deven muttered, and she had the sense he was still poking at his ears as he said it. "Why this?"

Nico had sat down on the edge of the bed, and she heard the love in his voice, as well as the gratitude. "You belong now," he said. "Your whole life you never felt like you were one thing or another. Not enough Elf to be an Elf, not human either. But now you belong."

"How can you say that? The Elves don't accept you, why would they accept me?"

"I didn't mean you belong with them," Nico replied softly. "I meant with me. What I am…I was the only one. I was something new, and alone. I'm not anymore. There are two of us now. Our own clan."

Miranda opened her eyes to see Deven put his arms around Nico, who leaned his cheek against the Prime's chest, smiling, eyes closed.

David returned from his shower and climbed in beside Miranda; he was still staring at Deven, and there was doubt in his eyes. Even with everything they'd seen and everything that had happened tonight, he still didn't know how to process this--he had known Dev for decades, more intimately than any of them, and this new Deven, though he seemed the same, was...not.

She could feel it too, more and more each moment, and even stronger once Dev got close enough to get in bed. She'd always sensed that otherness about him, but this wasn't that; it was at once deeply familiar and totally alien. It was as if he smelled differently, but didn't; as if his voice had changed, but hadn't; there was a quality to his energy now that had been there before but had been drawn out, put down roots, and unfurled its branches all around.

Dev pulled the covers up around him, but when he moved closer to David, David stiffened.

Alarmed, Deven looked from one of them to the other, seeing their confusion. "I'm still me," he said. "I promise...some parts are new, but...I'm still me. Like you said, David, I can be who I am and this too."

"But what exactly is 'this'?" David asked. "Nico says you're sort of part vampire, part divine energy...what do we call that? Are you some kind of angel, a demigod, or an actual ghost?"

"He's Deven," Nico told him. "That's what matters."

But David shook his head. Miranda understood--Dev might still be Dev, but David was also still David, and he needed to make sense of things, to find the logic in an utterly illogical situation.

Nico looked at David for a moment, but then his face cleared as he understood it too. "I think perhaps we need a new word," he said, placing a hand on David's arm. "Hold on a moment." He got up, went over to the box of books on the desk, and fetched the Codex and one of the oldest-looking diaries. "This one's the one that has your name in it, right?"

Deven frowned. "Yes, why?"

Nico sat cross-legged on the bed. "Can you find the page? I'd like to see exactly how they refer to you, and maybe we can combine that with something from the Codex, maybe a descriptor or title for members of the old Circle. If you're something new, well, we should call you something new. Right, David?"

The Prime already looked less panicky and nodded, peering down at the Codex with Nico. "Good idea."

Deven smiled slightly. "Yes, of course." He paged through the diary for a moment. "Here it is," he said. "This entry…trials, tribulations, and right there, is my…um…"

Miranda followed his finger as he read along the page, and she stared at where he stopped. "Deven Burke," she read. "This priestess from centuries ago knew your married name?"

Deven nodded, but that wasn't what he was staring at. Just under his name was a title, which he'd said was ancient Elvish for "The Ghostlight."

She didn't know the language as well as he or Nico, but she knew very well that's not what it said now.

"What is that?" she asked.

Nico leaned over the Codex, his mouth dropping open as he stared at the diary.

"It says Deven Burke…*Morianaela…ile'Kaiatala*." He swallowed hard and said, "Morianaela is basically Dark Elf…like we both are, now. And ile'Kaiatala…"

He lifted his eyes to meet Deven's. "The Kaiatala," he repeated. "The Raven's Blade."

******

It was a lovely face, even if it wasn't the one he really wanted.

He stared into the mirror, admiring its bone structure, its immortal youth. Certainly an upgrade from the one he'd been born with--that one, he'd been all too glad to rip from his skull in anticipation of something a bit more…refined.

"You made us ugly," he murmured. "I will make us beautiful, as we are meant to be."

"My Lord," came a timid voice, "Everything is in place."

"Good," he said, catching a glimpse of the groveling, stinking human in the doorway over his shoulder in the mirror. "I am coming."

The first human scurried away, but a moment later there was a knock. This time, at least, he wasn't annoyed. "Collier."

"Yes, my Lord, I believe I have found a suitable vampire for your purposes, if…if you are certain this is still the course you wish to take."

"Of course it is." He turned from the mirror to look at the Shepherd who served, at the moment, as his second-in-command. The last one had survived a week; Collier had served him for over a month without earning a messy screaming death. Promising.

"This is a useful enough body," he said, "And God knows I've enjoyed myself in it, but it won't do for the long term unless it can tolerate blood. Elves...simpering creatures...I have enjoyed ruining this one, but I'm not quite done. It won't truly be comfortable until It has fangs."

Collier bowed. "Of course, my Lord. I will arrange for my candidate to arrive whenever you desire."

"It will be a few days," he said. "Tonight there's enough work to do...let's get on with things, shall we?"

He swung a cloak around his shoulders and followed Collier out of the room, down the hall toward the temple where he knew a slender, ivory-skinned figure was bound naked to the altar, gagged for the moment until he was ready to hear her screams. She, too, was tall and lithe like this body, dark haired...but pale eyed...just like he wanted...just like *she* would want.

Yes, my beloved, my beautiful creature...you will enjoy this flesh I have found you. What fun we will have together, using these once-pure bodies, turning these idiot light-bearers into rutting, murdering monsters. Just imagine.

He had taken such pleasure in using this body to torture, to destroy. He had made sport of the Elves they'd captured from Avilon until little of them remained but viscera and demented shrieking. He had defiled every age and gender of human he could find, both for the sheer hedonistic revelry and the spite of it, knowing how Elvenkind would recoil knowing the pretty, magical sack of meat he had stolen had raped and killed and eaten flesh. Those fools who had banded together with Persephone's children to bury his kind in the Earth forever...he had spent long centuries dreaming of ways to make them pay.

The best part was seeing those who knew the Elf he was wearing...seeing their faces, having to stare up at someone they had loved now tearing them apart or debasing them so utterly they might as well be dead.

It was unbearably arousing, their fear.

After tonight you will feel it too, my beloved. Let us join hands now and make this world our plaything once more.

Smiling, he stepped out into the temple. The she-Elf he'd chosen--fourth in a line of attempts, but this one he knew would be strong enough--was spread-eagled on the altar, her humiliation as wondrous as her terror.

Not much longer. In an hour the eyes looking up at his would be ones he knew. Oh, how he had missed the days they both wore skin!

On the altar lay also the Signet his soldiers had brought him, charged with the power of a dead Pair--one still lived, in body, but her mind and life were in truth far fled. The spell he had crafted took the power of a Bondbreaking and fixed that power into the remaining stone, where it could be tapped...but only for a while, and only for one use. He'd had to waste one already, and it galled him.

This time he was ready. This time he knew how to make sure it worked. A few refinements on the ritual, and that dead Pair would rise again, in a way, their mutated power going to those who deserved it.

One by one...two by two...we will rise...and THEY...they will all...fall...down.

Part Two
The Raven's Son

Chapter Twelve

"We all come from the Goddess
And to Her we shall return
Like a drop of rain
Flowing to the ocean..."

Nico's voice echoed quietly in the room that seemed so much bigger now, so much less alive. He had already taken down the wards over the doors and windows, and the energy of the suite had started to fade from the minute it was no longer magically sealed.

He had woken in the middle of the day unable to lay still, and when even the slow pull of Deven's slumber hadn't helped him rest, he slipped carefully out of bed and made his way here.

He'd found Pywacket sitting in Stella's favorite chair, eyes hopeful when the door opened.

Nico had lifted the cat into his lap and curled up in the chair for a while, trying to help the cat understand that his human wasn't coming back.

"Don't worry," he told Py. "We'll keep you safe and in kibble and neck scratches for the rest of your life. I'll miss her too...but we can hold on to each other."

Pywacket looked up into his eyes, searching, and finally went to sleep on his lap, while he stared around the room, trying to accept the truth himself.

After a while of crying into Py's furry neck, Nico got up and tried to get his thoughts in order. No one had declared Stella's room his job, but he couldn't bear the thought of the housekeeping staff or strangers being the ones to decide what became of all the Witch's belongings. At the very least he wanted to take care of the things on her altar.

Maguire had come and gone, taking with him a few remembrances and, of course, Stella's body, to whatever fate his particular brand of human deemed appropriate. Nico knew Stella would want to be given back to the Earth, but most humans favored being pumped full of chemicals and locked in a box underground for reasons Nico couldn't quite grasp. Still, it would matter less to Stella what became of her flesh and more whether her father could find peace with her death.

Nico sighed. He'd been standing in the middle of the room for several minutes, turning in a circle--counterclockwise, he noticed, Stella's laughing voice in his mind asking if he was trying to banish her wardrobe.

He smiled a little. He would miss her so much--and the way she made him laugh, even in his darkest nights. She had been so much more alive than most of the immortals he'd known; perhaps it was knowing that her light was a fleeting one, meant to burn brightly for a little while rather than cast a dim glow for centuries. For all their talk of light few Elves were half so bright as their Stella.

"Couldn't sleep?" he heard, and turned toward the doorway to greet the Queen. There was no denying she gave off plenty of her own light...even though just now it was darkened by sadness, seeing what he saw, mourning as he mourned.

Nico shook his head. "You either?"

She shook her head back. "I thought you might want a hand."

"I don't know how to do this," he said. "Few of my people are solitary, so when they die--are killed, more like, since we do not die of age or illness--their possessions already have a home. Unless we have a trade or art that requires a lot of tools we tend not to have many belongings anyway."

"You lived alone," Miranda said, coming into the room, looking up at the doorframe as she did, acknowledging that the wards were gone.

He smiled. "I never thought the world would be troubled overmuch by my passing."

"Oh, Nico." She put her arms around him, and he leaned on her strength. "I hope you know better than that now."

"I do."

"Good." She kissed his forehead--standing on tiptoe to do so--and sighed. "Let's get to work--we'll feel better if we're not just standing here upset."

They started with the closet; Stella's wardrobe had been rather eclectic and showed a good deal of contempt for the czars of human fashion, but there were a few pieces of outerwear that made Miranda's eyes light up…and a set of cartoon cat pajamas that made her eyes glisten for a moment.

"I'm keeping these," she said with a sniffle, depositing them in the "keep" pile they'd started, next to which was a box for items to donate to a local women's shelter. "She loaned them to me once…after finding me half-dead in the street."

At his quizzical look she related the story of her stay with the Witch, dwelling on the entertaining parts, few as they were. They spent the next couple of hours trading anecdotes about Stella, laughing at the memories, sometimes pausing to wipe away tears as they filled boxes.

"She was the first human I ever met," Nico said, chuckling at the memory of running into the Witch that morning outside, and of how fascinating he found her from moment one.

"You lucked out," Miranda told him. "You got to start with one of the best."

Nico wrapped items from the altar in the cloth draped over it as well as in a couple of t-shirts he couldn't bear to part with.

"I never saw her wear those," Miranda observed.

"She only wore them to bed," he replied, and her chuckle made him blush a little.

The sun was well set by the time they decided to finish up for the night. Nico took a moment to gather up Pywacket's accoutrements to take to the suite that he and Deven now shared.

The cat gave him another searching look before jumping up on his shoulder.

"You can come back here if you need to while we're still working on it," he told the cat. "But you need to be with those who will care for you, not haunting a room alone. There's a big fireplace and a lot of pillows for you to shred if you so choose."

They reached the suite and settled Py in, leaving his litter box in the bathroom under the vanity counter and making sure he had food and water in his dishes. The cat walked around the room for a while, sniffing, before seeming to sigh and resign himself to the situation; he hopped up on Dev's chair by the fire and set to licking himself with determination.

Miranda was about to say something--probably that she had somewhere to be now that it was night--but there was a knock at the door.

"There you are," Deven said, giving Nico a warm smile. Yet again, Nico nearly started at the change in his appearance. Miranda, he noticed, did something of a double-take.

Dev noticed too, and smiled. "It's only been two days," he said. "It's all right if you're not used to me yet. I'm not either."

"But you can't really see you," Miranda pointed out.

"Trust me," he replied, "the inside is a strange picture too right now. But Nico, if you have a moment, there's something I'd like to show you...you too, my Lady, if you're free."

Miranda and Nico exchanged a look, and she shrugged. "I'm headed into town with David in a couple of hours, but I'm good for now. Lead the way."

He led them out of the Signet wing of the Haven, past the guest suites where he devoutly hoped the two visiting Pairs were still asleep--they'd been getting occasional echoes of pain and confusion from both suites, but nothing alarming, and nothing to suggest the Pairs weren't coping with the transition. David had dropped in on Olivia and Avi yesterday just long enough to ascertain that they were all right, didn't need anything, and would send up a flare, whatever that meant, if something went wrong. David had said that Olivia looked like "death warmed over," which Nico took to mean "terrible," but he'd also said she was adamant that they could handle it.

Deven veered left at the Elite wing and headed for one of the indoor training areas--there were a few inside the main building but the big training gallery and the main sparring suites had to be reached by either daring the frigid air or the underground emergency tunnels. Fortunately they stayed in the building, and Dev halted at one of the smaller rooms where Nico was pretty sure one-on-one combat lessons were held.

"I had intended to wait until after the first of the year," Deven said as he ushered them inside, "But, well...I didn't."

Nico and Miranda both drew up short when they saw what awaited them inside.

Puppies.

There were four long-limbed, long-haired, floppy-eared young dogs rolling around on the floor, nipping at each other's feet, a squirmy mass of gigantic paws and tongues.

Miranda actually squealed like a little girl before remembering herself and reassuming her Queenly dignity.

Even so, she was no match for the dignity of the older dog sitting nearby--a full-grown adult, near as Nico could tell, as regal as Vràna but even larger, with calm, intelligent eyes.

There was also a woman, though she was the last thing to register.

"Queen Miranda of the Southern United States and my Consort Nicolanai Araceith, I would like to introduce Madame Camille Lucerne, one of the oldest and most renowned breeders and trainers of Nighthounds in the entire Shadow World."

The woman, who had flawless coal-dark skin and the bearing of a Queen herself, bowed to them. "A great honor as always to stand in the presence of Signets."

"I contacted Madame Lucerne to see if she would have any upcoming litters to look at, and as luck would have it, she has these beauties without buyers."

"No buyers?" Miranda asked. "I thought Nighthounds were on waiting lists years long."

"They were," Lucerne said, raising an eyebrow. "But half of my clientele have been murdered in the last year."

The Queen blinked at her. "Jesus."

Lucerne, amused, added, "Do not worry, my Lady, my business still thrives. Signets have always been my best customers, but there are plenty of vampires out there with a newfound paranoia. I've had offers pouring in, but this litter was already spoken for."

"Nighthounds are usually bought and paid for before they're born," Deven explained to Nico. "A trainer as skilled as Madame Lucerne will tailor the pup's training program to the particular needs of her future owner. Once they hit six months they're ready to go home, assuming they bond properly with their owners."

"Bond?" Miranda asked.

"Nothing as showy as a Signet bond," Lucerne said. "My instincts are usually impeccable when it comes to matching a Hound with a vampire, but sometimes things go awry."

"But if these have all been spoken for, how could any of them bond with me?" Nico asked.

"They may not," Lucerne replied. "But since these little ones have nowhere to go, I thought it best to at least try a meeting."

"Wait, what will happen to the ones you can't sell?" Miranda asked warily.

Lucerne saw the look on her face and smiled broadly. "Even abandoned, a Signet-trained Hound is a priceless creature. They will all find homes. But as my lord Deven is one of my oldest customers, I jumped at the chance to give him first pick."

Nico watched the puppies tumble, wondering how trained they could be at such a tender age; he had no idea whatsoever how to train a dog, but Deven clearly did, so he could probably help. Still...they were adorable, but...

"Shall we begin?" Lucerne asked. At Dev's nod she stepped out in front of the dogs and merely held her hand out, palm down, at her side.

The puppies instantly froze and, as if she'd flipped a switch, snapped to attention, forming a line next to the adult Hound.

"Nighthounds are the distant cousins of human-bred dogs called Scottish Deerhounds and Irish Wolfhounds. They are larger than either, which is saying something, and smarter than any breed in the world." As she spoke, Lucerne rotated her hand, and the puppies all stood, their attention riveted to the woman. "They can keep pace with a horse, jump fifteen feet, and survive injuries that would kill most other canines. They also outlive other breeds, an average of 35 years. The oldest I have ever encountered was 43 when she died. For centuries the Nighthounds have been our protectors, our companions, and our steadfast friends."

Nico found himself enchanted with the pups; their intelligence was clear and keen, even so young, and they were eager to please their leader. He watched each in turn as Lucerne showed off some of their training.

"Now, these pups have all the skills they need for a basic companion Hound," Lucerne said. "They also have more specialized learning based on who had ordered them. The two females in particular I think might interest you--in the middle, there. Both were meant for Signets in similar Havens to your own, situated in a rural environment but spending a good deal of time in an urban setting."

Lucerne met Deven's gaze and added, "Two, there, was purchased by Prime Tanaka for his Queen. She never got to meet her."

"They don't have names?" Miranda asked.

"That is for their masters to decide," Lucerne replied. "In some cases, the potential owner meets them as soon as a few days after birth, and gives them a name then. As I said, Mameha didn't have a chance to name little Two."

Nico knelt in front of the pups. "How will I know if one wants to bond to me?"

Deven was smiling. "Well, for a normal vampire I'd say just see who can't resist you, but given your particular talents...ground yourself a little, and then hold out your hand the way Lucerne did. Then in your mind, invite them to come meet you."

Nico glanced at Lucerne, who nodded slightly and made a small gesture that apparently meant "at ease." The pups visibly relaxed, tongues lolling out. All four were looking at Nico now, since he was on their level.

He did as Deven had said and dropped his attention into his center, taking a few deep breaths. He closed his eyes and imagined he could speak Dog.

"Simplify," Deven said, crouching down next to him. "They're young, remember. Use feelings more than words."

Nico nodded and tried to frame a thought that conveyed the same as a dog tilting his head to one side. *Friend?*

He held out his hand, eyes closed.

A moment later, something furry bumped up against his palm.

Nico opened his eyes, grinning into the pair of blue eyes inches from his own. The puppy stared into his eyes for a second, then let out an excited yap and practically bounced up and down.

Then, she tackled him.

Nico fell back into Deven and into a fit of laughter, suddenly covered with wriggling Nighthound--even at a few months old she was taller than he sitting down.

Lucerne cleared her throat, and the puppy slurped her tongue across Nico's face then jumped back and sat primly, still giving him a canine grin.

Nico saw the medallion on her collar: A two.

"Normally I'd recommend several training sessions with myself, you, and the pup," Lucerne said, "But Prime Deven can show you everything you need to know without my being stuck here in Texas."

"They're in good hands," Deven said. "Your reputation is secure."

A laugh. "I have no doubt," she said. Lucerne made a clicking sound, and the three other puppies bounded over to her and sat while she attached leashes to each of their collars.

The older dog, who had barely moved the entire time, got smoothly to her feet, clearly not needing something as pedestrian as a leash. She was even larger than Nico had thought--she would dwarf Vràna, and would have even given Osiris a run for his money.

Nico was vaguely aware that Lucerne and her pack left, but he was too busy letting the Nighthound--*his* Nighthound--sniff him all over and pin him to the ground. He couldn't seem to stop laughing at her, particularly at how her back end and front end were apparently operated by two different brains.

He looked up to see Deven and Miranda both watching him. Both looked a mixture of grateful, elated, and taken aback at his behavior.

"What?" he asked.

Miranda shook her head. She was smiling, but did he see the faintest mist in her eyes? "I've never seen you laugh so much," she said. "It's amazing."

Deven's expression held so much affection Nico felt himself turning pink. He returned his attention to the dog, who had paused in her licking and snuffling while he spoke to the others, but went back to it with gusto when she had his attention again.

Experimentally, he imagined he could tap on her mind, and thought, *That's enough.*

She grew still, sat.

Deven raised an eyebrow. "You might not need my help after all."

Nico leaned his forehead against the Hound's. She let out a little *rowf* and licked his nose.

"What do you think you'll call her?" Miranda asked. "You don't have to figure it out right this second, but, any ideas?"

"I know exactly what to call her," Nico said. "Her name is Astela."

Miranda smiled. "Elvish for starlight...so, Stella."

Nico slid his arms around the pup. "Damn right," he said, sighing. Then he murmured to Astela, "I hope you like cats."

*****

Hours later and miles away, Miranda stood peering into the mirrored room where one of the possessed humans from the shooting still lived.

She frowned. "This is the last one?"

Novotny cleared his throat and glanced down at his clipboard, an odd, almost dissembling maneuver that made her eyebrow quirk. "Yes, my Lady. We had to euthanize one, and there was the one that attacked the Prime..."

Miranda nodded, glancing over at David. He stood cross-armed, frowning at the human who couldn't see them and was therefore calm for the moment.

"What?" she asked.

David's brow furrowed a little more. "I don't like the idea of you getting up close and personal with that thing, especially not mind-to-mind. What little I saw was more than scary--it was dangerous. She's big black hole that could suck you into her."

"She's not a thing," Miranda reminded him sternly. "She's a person in there somewhere. That's what I want to know--if we can get her back. And the only way to know that is to take a calculated risk. I'll have you anchoring me, and the boys back at the Haven. Besides, since when do you doubt me?"

He blinked. "I don't doubt you."

"Then let's get to work."

Not satisfied, but resigned, he nodded and gestured to Novotny to open the door.

For his part, the doctor didn't look terribly enthusiastic about their prospects either, but he did as he was told and had one of his assistants carry a chair into the room for the Queen.

She had been holding her shields up as hard as she could against the woman until she was ready to get started, but kept them up a while longer, giving herself a chance to evaluate her subject with normal sight alone.

David joined her, staying on his feet and in the corner. They had already agreed that if the human attempted to lay a hand on

Miranda he was going to snap the human's neck without a parting glance...but it didn't seem that would be necessary for the moment.

The human was pretty securely zip-tied to a chair of her own. She wore hospital scrubs, and had plain white socks on her feet against the chill of the tile floor.

Based on their descriptions of the possessed victims' behavior Miranda had partly expected a zombie-like creature with filthy matted hair and dirty clothes, but Novotny's people would have none of that nonsense, especially since the woman was docile as a lamb if there were no vampires in the room. The woman's long hair was scrupulously clean and tied back from her face, and if it weren't for her vacant stare, she'd be the picture of blooming health.

"Why isn't she attacking?" Miranda asked.

"She's sedated," Novotny replied. He was already preparing a syringe. "This will bring her out of it in a few minutes." He gently lifted the sleeve of the human's shirt and injected her with whatever it was.

"Does she eat? Sleep?"

"We can feed her by hand, and she swallows," Novotny replied. "She's the only one whose programming didn't override basic survival instinct, it seems. She passes out when she's too tired to stay awake. The last survivor--the one programmed to kill humans--was impossible to tend, and I had requested Mo's help, but before he could send someone, the victim died."

Miranda realized she was stalling and mentally smacked herself. "Okay. I'm going to start before she's completely conscious so I can watch the programming kick in. David, are you ready?"

"As I will be."

She grounded herself as completely as possible, reaching out to anchor firmly in David's strength; she could feel Nico and Deven back at home, ready to help if she needed them. She couldn't imagine this one human woman would test her power that deeply, but then again, the whole reason she wanted backup was for things she *couldn't* imagine.

"What's her name?" Miranda asked, sinking into the level of attention that she needed to access the deeper echelons of her empathy.

"Luisa Munoz."

"Luisa," Miranda murmured, pulling her legs up into the chair and letting her palms rest on her knees. She stared at the human for a moment longer, then closed her eyes.

Very, very carefully, she parted the first layer of her own shields and reached through the gap, keeping most of her protections up but extending a touch of energy to tap lightly around the woman's aura. There wasn't much response, but that was fine--she just wanted to get a feel for Luisa Munoz as a person.

The woman was painfully normal, or she had been. She was in her mid 50s, a nurse who worked in her husband's cosmetic surgery practice. They were extremely successful, and like many of the wealthy who had attended Miranda's benefit that night, involved in a number of charities. Luisa had brought her granddaughter to the concert; thinking over the list of survivors Miranda knew the girl had escaped physically unhurt but probably traumatized for life at seeing her *Abuela* feral and bloody, trying to attack her musical idol.

Miranda had already informed the Porphyria Foundation that they were to reach out to the survivors and offer them any aid required on Miranda's behalf, whether it was medical care or a lifetime of therapy. Everyone there had suffered because of a war they should never have known existed.

The surface sweep told Miranda about the woman's life...a life that was over with unless she could help. Luckily whatever spell was on them didn't do anything to shield them against prodding and poking; Luisa was an open book, either because the Prophet was too stupid to know what the Queen was capable of, or too arrogant to believe she could break the spell.

There was a third option, of course...that there was no breaking it, and the Prophet simply didn't care what she found out, because there was nothing she could do. But Miranda wasn't ready to entertain that notion just yet.

She braced herself and reached out with a stronger "hand" this time, looking for an easy access point to the woman's internal world. She could sense that the woman was starting to wake up from her sedation; aside from her energy shifting, Miranda could feel...smell? Hear? It was hard to describe how a vampire sensed someone's muscles tensing, the slightest uptick in adrenaline beginning to seep into the body. Heightened states of emotion all smelled bright and acrid. Fear had a particular tang like vinegar.

The woman began to twitch. Miranda waited.

Between one breath and the next, Luisa's eyes flew open, and she saw what was in front of her. With nearly vampiric reflexes the human threw herself forward against her bonds, letting out a shriek of rage that made Miranda's ears ring--it was an animal noise, beyond coherent thought, primal.

The human's placid, pretty features, which practically embodied "nurse" or some other kind of caregiver, twisted into a mask of hatred, and she kept throwing herself forward, her chair starting to inch across the floor with repeated loud creaks and clatters.

David started forward almost undetectably, but Miranda held up her hand to stop him, and he froze. "She's fine," she said sternly. "Leave her be."

Miranda wanted to see her this way for a minute; she needed to know what she was up against. She dove into the cracks in the woman's psyche, leaving only enough space in her own shielding to reach out with her empathy.

Instantly her mind was overloaded with pain, anger, and hate. She wanted to *strike out, to drag her nails down the creature's face, to tear into her skin, keep clawing, clawing, clawing until she hit bone, scratch her nails into the bone, leave gouges, keep clawing,* KILL IT KILL IT KILL IT KILL IT--

"Miranda!"

She jerked back at David's sharp voice, but waved him away again. "I'm fine! Stay back until I call you, damn it!"

"The hell you are--look at your leg!"

She glanced down and saw her thigh was a bloody mess of long, parallel scratches--and so were her fingernails. "Well, shit," she said irritably. "Still, I'm fine. If it happens again bring me out."

"Miranda, I'm not going to let you--"

"You do not get to *let* me do anything," she snapped. *"Back off."*

She could hear the spell on the human speaking through her own voice, but she was still in control--she could sense what it was doing, wrapping tar-like sticky tentacles of energy around her the way it had the human's mind. Once they took hold, they sent in tiny suckers, like a parasitic vine, and began to feed on her energy, using it for fuel for the spell. If it got a deep enough hold in something as powerful as a Queen, it could turn her into a monster, ride her, until she was a burnt-out husk, the way this human was destined to be.

It was not, however, sentient--it had only one operating instruction and one goal, to consume and drive its host to kill. It could be programmed to seek out different kinds of creatures to attack, but it could only be programmed once; if it did get hold of Miranda, she'd start killing her own kind.

It was terrifying in both its simplicity and its evil. There was no positive use for this spell. To create a compulsion this strong took something that was darker than the Dark Web itself--not just darkness, but darkness merged with malice.

And it would not let go.

Miranda watched the sickening strands trying to wind around her own legs as it tried to crawl from Luisa to her, and she felt David's rising panic at what had to be a gruesome sight.

She took a deep breath.

"It's okay, baby," she said calmly. "I think I know what to do."

Her sudden stillness in the face of the monster shocked him into obedience, and he energetically "stepped" back where he'd been about to grab hold of her and try and pull her away from it.

Miranda kept breathing slowly, evenly, ignoring the creature for the moment, drawing power into herself from the Dark Web, which emerged in her mind with barely even a thought this time. She had a sense it would be there all the time now, for she had access to something now that neither the Prophet nor his disgusting blood magic had anticipated.

The Porphyria benefit had been before the Solstice, and based on the Prophet's obvious intentions this human and the spell on her should have been dead days ago. It had not been designed or cast to counter the new power in Miranda's blood.

Next time the Prophet would doubtless be ready, but this time...oh, this time, he and his toys didn't stand a chance.

The Queen reached out to the Web, taking hold of the silver-black strands that wove through her body and her world, and pulled on them, gently, for there was no need for force, no violence. When her hands touched the threads she could feel them vibrating...she could feel music, the same melodies she had worked with when she had decided to teach herself to work with the Dark Web.

She knew this Song...she *was* this Song.

Miranda looked down at the pathetic, slimy thing writhing around her and still gripping the human woman. It was so tiny now, where before it had frightened her.

But why should she be afraid? It was barely a moment's dissonance, a few jangling notes out of tune--

AND I AM THE SYMPHONY--

Power sang through her body, out through her hands, and her entire being filled with music, her vision with blood, her heart with wrath. She took hold of the spell and flooded it with power, and it began to dissolve, falling apart molecule by molecule. She burned its sticky fingers from around her legs, scorched its body, and then put her hands on the tentacles that held onto Luisa Munoz, watching them burn...loving how they burned.

Something behind her was niggling at her consciousness, something else she needed to see, but she knew she wouldn't last much longer channeling so much energy--the part of her that was still Miranda knew she had to hurry. She didn't know enough about what she was doing for fine control; right now she just needed to get the job done.

She finished burning out the spell and tried to "turn down" the energy as much as she could to avoid hurting the human even more. She had grown so used to using her empathy as a weapon she sometimes forgot it had another use.

Miranda put her physical, flesh-and-blood hands on Luisa Munoz's shoulders, and stared into her eyes, reaching for her...for the real Luisa, praying she was still in there and that the monster hadn't cleaned out her body.

She called to the woman, mentally, searching, hoping...there had to be hope. She sought Luisa's soul in corner after corner of her mind, refusing to give up...*please, please be alive...please come back...it's safe now, Luisa, you're safe. The monster is gone.*

You can go home, Luisa. You can see your grandbabies again, see your husband, your daughter. You can feel the warm sun and the cold wind. You can eat chocolate and listen to the Hamilton *soundtrack...everything you love, Luisa, it's all still here, waiting for you. You're safe now. You can come back. Come back.*

Come back.

And for just a moment, she felt her...felt Luisa, the soft flutter of a human life, a butterfly's wing against her cheek, kissing her in gratitude, in peace.

"Miranda," David said softly, "She's gone."

"No," Miranda whispered. "Not yet. I've almost got her."

"Beloved...she stopped breathing."

Miranda's eyes flew open, and she saw the flatline on the heart monitor, the woman's open, dilated eyes.

She was smiling.

"No, no..." Exhaustion, overwhelm, and grief hit Miranda at the same instant, and she burst into tears, slipping onto her knees in front of Luisa's chair, where the human's head hung over her, her muscles slack now against the zip ties.

"A moment please, Doctor," she heard David say, followed by the sound of the door opening and closing.

His arms wrapped around her as he knelt behind her, the sides of his long coat draping over her as they often did. She wept into Luisa's lap, thinking how close she had been...so close, and Luisa could have gone home to her family, so close...

"You need to disconnect," David told her in her ear. "You're still hyperextended...you need to shield yourself again before you burn out completely. You've done all you could for her. You set her free. She doesn't have to die a prisoner in her own body."

He was right, and she knew he was, but it still felt like a failure, and she knew why.

Kai.

If she couldn't free a human from a simple possession, how could she hope to free Kai from what the Prophet had done to him? Now she knew it was possible he was still in there, still alive, trapped beneath the filthy beast that had stolen his skin. He might be aware of everything, or he might be asleep, but either way he was trapped, and she couldn't save him.

"Of course you can," David told her, pulling her back against him, resting his chin on her head. "Look how close you came this time...your *first* time. None of us has ever dealt with this kind of magic before, but you stepped up and killed it without hesitation. Imagine what you'll be able to do now that you know what you're dealing with and can study it, practice, and plan."

Her breath shuddered, but she listened, and clung to him, letting the words sink in. She had...what had she done? She had...

"You did what you do," he said, kissing her. "You sang, and you changed the world. And you've barely even begun."

She closed her eyes a moment and gathered her shields back around her where they belonged, letting them settle, feeling her edges, his edges. She was worn out but her mind had already begun to turn, taking the last few minutes and holding them in her palm, examining what she'd seen the way David would examine a troublesome line of code. She could already see places she could do it better next time, a better approach, a smarter way to anchor herself to her boys. More precision, less force. She had learned that from him, too--that she could combine intuition and intellect and come up with something stronger than either alone.

"That's my Queen," he murmured, holding her tightly. "Now…let's let Novotny take care of Luisa. May I take care of you?"

She smiled at the wording, remembering how she'd snapped at him. She leaned back and turned so she could see his face. "Blood," she said. "Home. Shower. You. Now."

He bowed his head in assent, lifted her up off the floor, and would probably have carried her to the car, but she refused; many things had changed since her first night as Queen, but this had not. She would walk on her own two feet as long as she had the strength to stand.

She made it almost all the way to the car, which, she reflected as she passed out, wasn't bad, all things considered.

*****

The study adjacent to the Haven library was the perfect place to settle in on a stormy late night and pore over books of ancient magical lore. It had large, sturdy tables, comfortable chairs, and cushions perfect for sitting by the fireplace to read or, if one was a gangly young dog, flop down and nap.

At the moment one of the tables also featured two half-dressed vampires in a state of breathless euphoria.

Nico chuckled up at the ceiling and panted, between the tremors still running through his body, "When I said…we should explore that passage more in depth…not what I meant."

Deven had attempted not to collapse directly on top of Nico and had partly succeeded. His head had landed on Nico's shoulder, one arm flung over the Elf's middle, the rest of his limbs both on and off the table.

"Are you complaining?" Dev croaked, wincing at the strain in his voice. Surely they hadn't been *that* loud?

"Not at all." Nico grinned at him. "But as the corner of the Codex is stabbing me in the hip right now, I am reminded that there are beds all over this building and you in particular can Mist anywhere in seconds."

"Sorry," Deven told him, shifting off and trying to right himself by grabbing the far end of the table. He lifted his other hand and trailed his fingers down the Elf's exposed torso, earning a weak shudder. "My mind was on something far more urgent."

One body part at a time they gradually untangled and slid off the table, gathering their hastily shucked clothing and righting the stacks of books they'd knocked over. Nothing damaged, thank Goddess--he would have hated having to explain that to the Cloister.

Nico winced a bit as he got back into his chair and tried to reassume his work. Deven did the same, leaving them where they'd been half an hour ago, on opposite sides of the table, each absorbed in his own pursuits.

"That was your fault anyway," Deven pointed out with a smile. "You're the one who couldn't stop staring at me."

"No, you're the one who's so insanely damned beautiful," Nico replied mildly, eyes sparkling. Their hands touched when Nico passed him one of the Hallowed Diaries that had ended up on the floor, and for a moment they just held each other's gazes.

"Not to mention I now have a whole new way to send you writhing into orbit," Nico added, opening the Codex again and lowering his eyes to its pages. "You always had the advantage over me in that regard, but now, an ear for an ear."

Deven felt the ears in question growing warm at the thought. They'd always been sensitive, but now...good Lord. Just thinking about Nico's tongue--

Nico pretended not to notice him shifting in his seat. "So much to learn," Nico noted, running his fingers along the lines of the Codex, pausing to slowly follow a hand-drawn spiral adornment with his index finger.

"You bastard."

Nico laughed. "The fact that you have any energy at all after that is a little scary."

Deven opened the diary he'd been paging through before they'd pounced on each other and stared sightlessly at the words for a moment. "I don't really know what to do with it all, to be honest."

He'd spent the last two days trying to get used to a body that was the same one he'd always known but still something else entirely; it felt like each cell had been copied exactly out of some new material. Everything still worked exactly like it should--his muscles responded with the same speed and agility they had before, and he had the same grace and coordination he'd gained from centuries of fight-training. Holding a pen or an Elf, every movement was what he remembered, but...

He stared down at one hand, flexing and bending the fingers a few times. Just the same. But...

"Was any of that...different?" he finally asked, almost afraid for the answer.

Nico looked up at him. "Yes and no."

"I need more than that."

The Elf smiled softly. "Don't be afraid," he said. "You're still you, my love. Those are still your hands--they've taken life, and given life, and given so much to me. The way you touched me is the same. The weight of your body is the same. You shiver the same, grip my shoulders the same. You even moan the same words in Gaelic."

"Then what's different?"

"It's hard to say," Nico replied, lifting one eyebrow mischievously. "I'm afraid I'll need more data."

Deven put his head in his hands, frustrated. "I'm serious, Nico."

"So am I. That was the first time since the Solstice, after all. We've both been too tired for much else, which is why I was so surprised when you jumped on me."

"I think it was a mutual jumping."

"Fair enough." Nico reached over and took one hand, drawing it away from his face, ensuring Deven was looking at him. "You have changed, yes. But you are still you. The only analogy I can come up with at the moment is..." His eyes lit up a bit as it came to him. "In the Temple in Avilon there were four statues of Theia representing the seasons. They were carved centuries ago and have inspired our people with their beauty all those years. But once a year they were thoroughly scrubbed and polished. Layers of incense smoke and candle soot were removed, and they gleamed like new. Like you."

Deven considered that, eyes moving down to their joined hands. "Still me but I've had a bath."

"In a manner of speaking. You feel like you've been polished, renewed. And yes, it's strange--look at how long you had to accumulate those layers of sadness and the dirt of living. They must have weighed a ton."

"They did." He moved his gaze up his left forearm, to where there had been tattoos for decades but was now nothing…or, not nothing…a blank canvas.

Nico's arm wasn't blank; it had the long, scrolling lines of the tattoos that curved along the entire side of his body.

In his mind's eye he saw lines forming on his own arm, an echo of Nico's. Not exactly the same pattern but complementary.

Nico saw his expression and grinned. "There you go."

Deven let out a breath he hadn't meant to hold and nodded. "Thank you."

Again, their eyes met, moonlight for moonlight. Nico sent a pulse of love and understanding along their bond, and this time Deven's sigh was much more relaxed. It was so like Nico to know what to say, and how to say it, to get through Deven's centuries of issues and strike to the heart of him.

He'd always had that talent. To think there had ever been a time Deven had denied loving him.

"Back to work?" Nico asked.

Deven smiled and nodded. "You were about to tell me about the Gate spell, I think."

Nico smiled sweetly back and turned the Codex around to face him. "Yes, of course. As I said, the first Circle along with their allies spread across the globe to create the Signet system and bring the Shadow World to order. The Circle was devoted to each other, however--some were lovers, all were close friends, and did not wish to be parted. There were no airplanes or internet back then…but they had this."

Deven scrutinized the diagram and its attached set of instructions. The diagram had always been there but until the Solstice, everything around the image had been basically the Elvish equivalent of *lorem ipsum*, so they'd had no idea what the diagram was for. "A permanent portal."

"Exactly. They created these in their Havens, keyed so that only those who were part of the Circle could use them. We can do the same--one end anchored here, one at the new Cloister or the new Elven settlement. Then you can divide your time between the Tetrad and the Cloister, and I can visit my mother whenever I want, in a matter of minutes. Also, if you look at this second diagram, I can build one that serves as a permanent endpoint for *any* Gate spell. I'd still have to create the portal each time but it could be anchored in that terminus, which would make it more stable and less draining for me."

Deven nodded again, pleased. "That does solve a lot of potential problems. And if you can get it up and running before we have to relocate the Elves it will make moving them far less traumatic."

"Exactly. It'll take me a while to learn the spell well enough to try it. It's based on the one I use already, but uses the Dark Web, and I haven't worked with that enough to be confident in my anchoring. But I can do it."

"That's fantastic. Definitely add that to the report."

The Circle was planning to meet for official Codex-related business the next night once Miranda had rested from her work with the possessed human tonight and the other two Pairs were feeling well recovered from their transition. Nico had volunteered to do the first read-through of the whole Codex now that it was decoded, and had been making a long list of important items to impart to the others--like the real history of the first Morningstar war, more information on the key players, and more about the Circle's members.

There was one in particular Deven knew had surprised Nico: the Hallowed he had mentioned--the woman who founded the Order of Elysium--as well as her Consort, who had founded the Swords of Elysium, were both what the Codex called Dark Elves.

"They were like us," Nico had said in a half-whisper. "Long before the Elves were massacred by humanity, they and the vampires were still allies. Some of Theia's children felt called to Another's touch and became vampires themselves. Back then they weren't considered abominations, just different. There was even a Dark Temple in one of the earliest Sanctuaries."

"What happened to them all?" Deven had asked. "Why aren't there any left in the Order?"

"Once Persephone was imprisoned, Her influence grew weak over Her children. Vampires forgot the Order, their Creatrix, everything. When the Inquisition came around some of the human heretic-hunters hired vampires to help wipe out Elven clans. As the Elves fled to the Sanctuaries and sealed them away, any trace of the Dark Elves was driven out. Most would have been murdered by the Inquisition just like the other Elves. Perhaps a few survived in the Cloisters for a while. Beyond that, I do not know."

"You mean your Enclave might have known about Dark Elves the entire time and excommunicated you anyway, without even telling you there had been others?" Anger, hot and fierce, ignited in Deven's chest, thinking of the grief Nico had suffered because of his supposed people.

"I imagine they didn't want me to know," Nico had replied, eyes bright. "I represented something that terrified them…and if the Codex is right they knew there would be a time when Dark Elves would appear once more. My coming meant more than just an immediate threat, it meant everything they knew was about to change forever."

"As opposed to the change Morningstar brought by destroying Avilon." Disgusted, Deven had pushed his chair back from the table, wishing he could get his hands around the necks of the hidebound, frightened Elves who had treated Nico with such revulsion.

"Dev," Nico told him with a warm, if sad, smile, "It's done and there's no undoing it."

"That's fine," he all but snarled. "There's plenty I'd like to do now. They think *you're* scary? I'll give them something to be scared of."

Now, the Elf actually chuckled, the smile turning loving, an odd response to a threat of violence, unless of course one was soul-bound to a vampire. "I fear you may be picking up some of my anger issues," Nico told him.

Deven breathed out slowly, grounding, acknowledging that the Elf might be right…but he'd never been the kind to let emotions control him before, and he certainly wasn't going to be now. If there was one thing he knew how to do it was regain a shaken calm.

At that point, Nico had decided to change the subject, and though his original idea for doing so was to discuss the Gate spell, one look led to another, and well, here they were.

The story about the Circle did give him one idea, however, that might solve a different problem. When he had trained with the Swords of Elysium long ago, they had only been nominally connected to the Order, and had no religious allegiance. But the Hallowed was at least technically the boss of them too.

What had once been sundered could be reconciled. He had essentially shut down the Red Shadow not long after Jonathan's death, letting most Agents finish their missions and then go into inactive status while a few stayed on call. He had no need for the money the Shadow generated, and trying to train spies while running the Order and working with the Circle was more than even he could manage at once, but...if he disbanded the Shadow and offered Agents a chance to join the Swords of Elysium, brought the Swords back into the Order, and returned them to their original purpose as warriors for Persephone...he could do what he had always loved--teaching--and also offer protection to the Elves, who would be living close by and needed all the security they could get.

"You look excited about something," Nico observed.

Deven grinned. "Plotting and scheming," he said.

"To overthrow a tyrannical government? Or topple a drug cartel?"

A laugh. "Not this time. Not anymore. More along the lines of creating a new Elite for my Haven-turned-monastery."

Nico didn't look surprised at all. "Once a Prime, always a Prime," he noted, reaching over to take Deven's hand again and kissing the back of it. "Whatever it takes to make your eyes light up like that, as often as possible...I am all for it."

"In that case I have an even better idea," Deven said, and gripping Nico's hand tighter, hauled him up on the table again, and into another kiss.

"Wait just a minute," Nico panted, pulling his mouth away for just a second. "We do have work to do--"

"You're quite right. And I don't think this table can take any more punishment. Hold on."

Deven imagined that the room echoed behind them with Nico's laughter and the sound of book pages flapping in an imaginary wind as they vanished into thin air. He also imagined Astela, still on her cushion, rolling her big dark eyes and resigning herself to an hour or more forgotten in the study, until a hand came out of nowhere and dragged her along into the Mist.

Chapter Thirteen

In her sleep, while her body lay safe and surrounded by her lovers and a surprising number of animals, Miranda's mind wandered along a familiar path under the stars, her gaze searching the edge of the darkened wood for something...someone.

She knew not to expect Luisa here. Luisa had been Catholic, and Persephone had intimated there was somewhere else for her...and if Cora and Jacob's reactions were anything to go by, Someone Else there for her as well. Miranda wished her peace...however long peace lasted where she was. Was it different for them? Was there an eternal Heaven for those who believed in it? Was *all* of it real?

She didn't have to wrestle with such possibilities, however, in this place. She only had to keep walking, and keep looking.

Faith had walked here once. So had Jonathan. They had taken this path and eventually stepped off, into the trees, into the sweet shadows. Their deaths had been horrifying, but at least at the end of all that pain, there was this, only quiet and the sense of belonging that called to her as well. This was where her soul was meant to go, one night, whether tomorrow or in a thousand years. Even the last Queen standing would walk here.

In the dream she knew she had to keep looking, though she wasn't thinking about for whom. She wasn't afraid, or anxious; she wasn't in a hurry. She had all day to linger here, to enjoy the beauty of the opalescent starlight shining on her skin, the wind through the trees that was so much like the music she knew. She wasn't looking for the Raven Mother, that much she knew--she didn't have to *look* for Her, only call, or be called.

It wasn't until she followed the path around a long, downward-sloping curve that she saw something...someone...huddled at the edge of the trees, curled up amid the roots of a great black oak.

She started to run.

It was a far greater distance than she'd thought. She ran for what felt like forever, until her legs burned and her lungs were full of knives. When she finally veered off the path and dropped to her knees beside the tree, she reached out to the figure...curled up on himself, shuddering, so cold and afraid and alone...

...and he was gone.

All that remained in his place was a single piece of sheet music.

Miranda picked it up with trembling hands. She recognized the elegant, fine handwriting, the precise arrangements of notes; this was Elvish staff paper, as much a work of art as what it could produce.

She stared at the sheet, trying to make sense of it. It was nonsense--the handwriting was his but it said nothing.

She thought of the Codex. Was this, too, encoded? Or was her dreaming mind scrambling the letters?

"What are you trying to tell me?" she whispered. "I'm here, I'm listening."

She held onto the sheet with both hands, concentrating, trying to reach through it and through the dream to the mind that had left it here. He had to be there; this gift, in this place, had to mean *something*.

Slowly, as she stared at the notes, one of them seemed to tremble on its line. She kept reaching, hoping...

The single note quivered once more...then the one next to it followed suit, and the one after that. Of course--if it was a message it wasn't in words. A Bard would reach out to her in their common language.

Miranda hummed the notes, following the melody that started simply but grew more and more complex with every measure. At first nothing extraordinary happened, but once she'd reached the end of the page, the first note trembled again, and taking the hint she started over.

She recognized it. It was one of the songs Kai had taught her from his homeland, a hymn to Autumn whose arrangement he'd been updating for the Harvest. One of Kai's favorite pastimes was bringing old, dusty Elvish songs from past centuries and modernizing them, which was why he'd been so drawn to her work in the beginning. He'd scandalized the Elders by bringing in a lot more percussion to sacred music, and wanted to learn more about human harmonies to further unsettle the old and delight the young. He especially liked the songs with darker edges. This one...she thought back, trying to remember the lyrics, and one in particular leaped out in her mind:

Follow the raven's flight...

What was the next one? Follow the raven's flight...far and far from home, into the falling night...no, not "falling" night..."hungry" night. Was that it? No--she remembered now:

Follow the raven's flight
Far and far from the warmth of home
Into the hungry teeth of night
As it falls--

Miranda nodded, satisfied with her translation but not with the meaning--what was she supposed to learn from that?

She looked at the sheet of paper again, and to her surprise the lyrics now appeared in front of her where the music had a moment ago; they were written in a familiar hand that made her heart ache with its swoops and swirls, but before she could lose focus, a line slashed through one of the words, then another, editorial marks suddenly showing up and changing the entire verse:

Follow the ~~raven's~~ flight of the Raven's Son
Far and far from the warmth of home
He is ~~Into the~~ hungry ~~teeth of night~~
As ~~it~~ he falls
The Hunger calls
The Hunger calls

As soon as her eyes hit the end of the last line, a memory shuddered into her, the sound of her husband's voice, hollow and young and afraid:

"I was so hungry."

Miranda gasped herself awake, sitting bolt upright, trying to grasp a sheet of paper that didn't exist. In the second it took to realize there were only three people in the bed, she was out of it, bare feet on the floor and headed for the door.

She heard the boys stirring behind her, making irritable noises at her sudden absence; she'd been on the edge of the bed when she woke, a vacancy beside her, so while she'd shaken the bed she hadn't woken either Dev or Nico entirely.

Miranda grabbed the doorknob and started to charge out of the suite, but drew up short with another gasp.

David, on the other side, had his hand on the doorknob as well, and was pushing as she pulled.

He gave a quiet yelp and jumped back. "Jesus, Miranda!"

She stepped back too, staring at him as if she'd never seen him, trying to make sense of what was racing through her body and the accusations she had no idea how to make even if she knew what they were.

"Where have you been?" she managed, wincing at how shrill she sounded.

His eyebrows shot up. "In the Batcave," he said. "I couldn't sleep."

She looked him up and down. "You're wearing city clothes."

A blink. "This is what I had on before bed--it was the first thing I grabbed."

That was true. Same long-sleeved shirt, same pants. No coat, which surely he would have worn if he'd gone into town in this freezing weather.

Now, he said patiently, "It's noon, Miranda. Where would I have gone?"

That was also true.

She shook her head, moving back out of the way to let him in. Reality was starting to reassert itself, and the utter absurdity of what she was even *contemplating* contemplating was hitting her as the dream wore off.

David watched her as he walked past, worry on his face, but was he worried about her losing her mind, or her knowing something? And what would he have had to call Novotny for in the daytime?

What was she even thinking? That he would lie to her, to all of them? That he *could?* One of the most valuable parts of being Signet bound was that it all but destroyed the possibility of dishonesty between partners; they were simply too closely linked to each other's minds.

But Deven had blocked Nico out...

"Are you all right?" he asked, half-sitting on the back of the couch. They were both speaking quietly to avoid waking the others, but Deven was muttering and shifting toward wakefulness.

"I..." She tried to force her mind back to sense, out of paranoia and into the facts; she had absolutely no reason to distrust him, even assuming he could block them all out enough to have some hidden agenda, except for a dream about Kai that had been far from conclusive.

She decided to go for the truth, or most of it, while she tried to figure the rest out. "I had a dream," she said. "A dream about Kai--he told me you were in trouble. That someone had you."

The confusion in his face turned to concern, and this was definitely for her. "You're really shaken up," he said, coming forward to put his arms around her. "I'm sorry, beloved. You don't usually react when I get up in the middle of the day."

She clung to him, trying to shove away her fears--baseless fears. They had to be. The whole thing was insane. What could he be up to, anyway? What could possibly be worth lying for? He was one of the most honorable men she'd ever known.

"We're going to find Kai," he said, voice rumbling against her ear. "And I'm here...like I always will be."

She nodded. "I know...I'm sorry for freaking out, I just..."

"With your precog I'm surprised all of your dreams don't send you into a fit," he said, a smile in his voice this time. "Let's go back to bed, my Queen."

Miranda nodded again and let go of him so he could take his clothes back off; she was starting to feel foolish, on top of everything else, the longer she was awake.

And she probably would have dismissed the whole thing as the random firings of her overburdened mind if her eyes hadn't caught one tiny thing, a single anomaly in the life of a vampire who had taken dinner from a glass last night and had not spilled a drop:

There was a bloodstain on his sleeve.

*****

Nico perched on the edge of the table next to where Dev stood while the others assembled in the study, settling into the plush sofa and chairs, none looking much the worse for wear even after their ordeal the past few days.

Jacob and Cora seemed to be holding each other's hands even more tightly than usual, but after plenty of rest and blood looked completely recovered; Olivia and Avi were much the same, and if anything Avi was more comfortable here among them than before, either because he had realized he was welcome or because after the trial-by-fire of becoming Thirdborn, what did he have to feel inferior about?

Miranda sat down next to David but, Nico noticed, didn't immediately snuggle in against him. She was a little stiff for a second, but took a breath and sat back, drawing her legs up and crossing them. David squeezed her knee and she smiled at him, and there was nothing worrisome in their faces, but...something didn't feel quite right with the Queen.

There'd be time to ask later, he supposed. They might have had a fight, though echoes of it would probably have made it to Nico at some point. She might just be in a bad mood. She was hardly obligated to share every detail of her inner world.

Once everyone was seated and wine and other "adult beverages," as the Queen called them, had been poured, Deven took the lead with the meeting.

"First of all, let's start with what we already knew about the Firstborn. Jacob, you start."

The Prime looked around, smiling faintly at having been "called on" like in school, and cleared his throat. "Well, there never was a lot, just the usual bedtime stories--that somewhere sleeping in the Earth were the first vampires, so old they had no sires. Mindless killing machines, monsters, with no conscience or remorse. Some people said there were thousands of them, some said a dozen. Some said they were leaderless. Some said they had a king. All anyone really agreed on was that they probably weren't real."

Deven nodded. "Anyone else hear differently?"

"I heard they were buried in Russia," Avi spoke up a bit reluctantly. "That Dzhamgerchinov knew where they were and kept them secret so he could raise them if he liked. I always thought it was nonsense, but some do believe it."

Deven chuckled. "The old bastard probably started that rumor. It sounds like something he'd do."

Everyone blinked at him. "Wait," David said. "You actually *know* Dzhamgerchinov? Personally?"

Deven lifted an eyebrow. "Of course I do. Not well, and not as anything like an ally. He doesn't do allies. But I was hardly going to let him off without an introduction."

The focus of the meeting momentarily fell by the way as wild curiosity overtook everyone's intentions. "So...what's he like?" Jacob asked.

"Like? He's an asshole. A lot of what you've heard about him is true--he's brutal, violent, looks like a boulder covered in hair. One thing he's not is an idiot--he manages the stories that circulate about him very carefully. He threatened me with disembowelment, I threatened him with rumors that he liked to wear show-pony livery while being fucked with a giant leather dildo. We had an understanding."

More blinks. Deven saw their faces and laughed outright.

"The point being," he went on, still laughing, "while it's entirely possible the Firstborn were buried under his territory, he had no idea where they'd be and wouldn't have wanted to. He liked using the imagery of the myth for his own gain but he would never have let anything that unpredictable near his Haven."

They all looked like they wanted to ask more questions, but at least for the moment everyone let Dev get back on topic:

"The going story is that Persephone created the Firstborn to win a competition with Theia over who could better manage humanity's uncontrollable breeding. The Codex has a slightly different version. In it the goddesses were asked for help by a third deity--the one that had created humans in the first place. The Codex is notably disinterested in the identity of that deity; all we know is they wanted to see which of the sisters could come up with a better solution. They apparently found Persephone's idea appalling, as you might imagine."

"The Firstborn," David said with a nod. "She created them, and whoever this deity was said no thank you."

But Dev shook his head. "Not them. Him. To begin with there was only one Firstborn--a prototype, let's say. Seph made him out of pure darkness."

"I thought She is pure darkness," Cora said.

Another slow shake of Deven's head. "No. That's the distinction we all need to grasp about Her, just as with Theia. They are, neither of them, *pure* anything. They're yin and yang, each containing a touch of the other. How can we know light exists?

Only by comparing it to darkness. The night contains light of all kinds, and the day contains shadow. They're both meaningless without each other. So it was with the Firstborn--Her mistake was to create him without any light at all. No Moon, no stars, only the abyss--like a black hole, swallowing everything, never satisfied. The Codex called him the Hungry One, or simply the Hunger."

Miranda started. "The what?"

"In Elysian Elvish--the Elvish in the Codex--it's--"

Miranda said it at the same time: *"Agnilath."*

Deven glanced at her, nodded. "There are about a dozen other names for him, but the takeaway is that he was the very first of the Firstborn. When the deity who'd asked for help basically told Her to fuck off, She decided to try again, thinking it was the power that was too great and that weakening the Hungry One would make him manageable. So She split him in half."

"This is starting to sound awfully familiar," Jacob said with dismay. "Let me guess--She made him a Queen."

"Agdilan," Deven confirmed. "That was pretty egregious failure too, so, Persephone decided to start over. But She didn't destroy them, not yet. She thought the basic design was sound, and that by further weakening the darkness in them She would hit the right concentration. It was Theia who pointed out Her mistake."

"All of this is making Persephone look like kind of an idiot," Olivia pointed out dubiously.

"Perhaps. I think it's closer to the truth to say She was young and inexperienced--creating things wasn't Her area. But if it's any consolation, Theia was screwing up just as badly. She started with the other extreme--all light. But Her creatures were just as useless because they did nothing but shine--blinding everything around them, leaving no room for thought or will, just purity. Still, Theia was the first one to get the hint, and being the nicer sister shared it with Seph. They had to borrow from each other's toolboxes if they were going to get anywhere."

Now, Nico took up the story. "At this point, Persephone took the Firstborn and buried them--She should have destroyed them completely, but She couldn't bring Herself to. She felt pity for them, grotesque beasts that they were--they were Her offspring, and She wasn't ready to give up on them. Once they were locked away She set to work on the Secondborn, and taking Theia's advice, tempered their darkness with moonlight and starlight, as well as with a touch of humanity. She made them out of humans to ground their power in the mortal world, and from that they gained compassion and a need for family. They were still made to kill, and that purpose would drive their hunger, but She made sure they had reason and intelligence and self-control. And She kept one important aspect of the Firstborn: Duality. The Secondborn too would be split down the center, with the power and temperament of each balancing the other. They sired more vampires, but the next generation had less of a hunger for death--only for the power in blood. So while many still killed, many chose not to, and the Secondborn were given the authority to rule them and keep them from killing too many at once in one place. But in Her devotion to Her new children, Persephone neglected the old, and years later, they escaped their prison."

"That's how the first war started," Deven said. "Agnilath and Agdilan vowed to kill Persephone before She could kill them. In the meantime they started slaughtering everything in their path, human and animal, and destroying the Earth in every way they could think of. And worse yet, the Firstborn were after Theia too--in fact their ultimate goal was to murder all the gods and rule creation themselves."

"How would that even be possible if Firstborn themselves weren't gods?" Jacob demanded. Clearly the whole story was straining credibility to his ears, and Nico didn't blame him his doubt.

"Apparently they could have become gods," Nico replied, causing Jacob's eyebrows to shoot up almost into his hairline. "There is something called the Godspell--in the Codex it's called the *Dialora*, but there's no further description, no indication that such a thing still exists or even really ever did. But it was their endgame. Whatever it is, if they use it, they become deities, or at least as powerful as deities...again, the Codex isn't clear. What's important is that they didn't find it."

"What they did figure out was that they could use the blood of their victims--their lives, and their death-energy--to do magic." Deven tapped his Signet. "And these."

"And the Prophet knew how to do it," Miranda said softly. "The Prophet knows."

"Agnilath," David said into the silence that followed.

"We still don't know exactly how the Hungry One was freed," Deven said at length. "We know that Morningstar raised him using a ritual like the Awakening. Based on what I've read in the Hallowed Diaries, there's always been the threat that he would return. But the rituals needed--this Codex of Morningstar's we've heard about--I don't know where it came from, or who found it."

"How did the war end?" Miranda asked.

Nico and Dev exchanged a look. "Cataclysm," Deven said. "At this point in history there were around fifty Primes, even though the human population was still pretty low; there was already a lot of bickering going on, threats of war. But the Hungry Ones started capturing them, two by two--not killing them like they are now, but saving them up for one very, very powerful ritual. Because Persephone had spun Her own being into the Signets, they could be used against Her. Agnilath murdered so many Signets at once that it essentially broke Persephone's power--just long enough for the Firstborn to take Her prisoner and banish her to someplace called the Outer Dark, which isn't really even a place, just...nothingness."

"There was only one thing to do," Nico added. "The strongest of the remaining Signets, the Circle--the first She had made, a close-knit group of eight--came together one last time, and in essence repeated the ritual Agnilath had performed, sacrificing themselves in order to destroy the Firstborn. The Hungry Ones fell to dust, their souls--or whatever passes for souls in such filthy creatures--were scattered and buried deep. The entire Circle was vaporized...except for their Signets, which remained whole and were found to be indestructible. They, like all other Signets, passed from bearer to bearer, while empires rose and fell. The Order of Elysium became all but extinct, and the book of magic written down by the first Hallowed, one of the Circle, was passed from Hallowed to Hallowed, copied over and over, even the parts none of them could read. There were prophecies, of course, that one day it would all begin again--that the Raven Mother would return, but so would the Hungry Ones, and there would be another war, this time to decide the fate of everyone--even the Goddess Herself."

This time the silence went on for a while, each of the others absently touching their own Signets, trying to wrap their minds around what they had just learned. Nico had intended to tell them about the Gate spell and other discoveries from the Codex, but in truth it might have to wait for another time.

He knew that they would need time to consider the full import of the story on their own lives, on their own possible fates. If it had taken the destruction of the Circle to defeat the Firstborn before...what chance did they have now?

A very good one, he had already realized. After all, the first Circle had been working without Persephone's help or true power; he could only imagine how traumatic it had been for them to lose their connection to Her, yet they had given everything they had left to ensure the survival of Her children and, in doing so, of the entire planet.

"Is he raising the others?" Cora asked softly. "He must plan to, or at least his Queen. And if only an immortal body could contain him..."

"He probably used an Elf for her too," Deven realized.

Nico felt his stomach lurch with nausea--any one of the captured Elves, including Deven's mother, could have been taken over by one of those monsters by now. And only the luck of being close enough to the forest to hide had saved Kalea from a similar fate.

"But he hasn't been stockpiling Primes," David said, sitting forward suddenly. "He's been killing them for comparatively minor magic--creating what amounts to a zombie army. There are far fewer Signets than there were back then. So we can conclude that his intention isn't to attack Persephone the same way as before."

"Then what is he planning?" Olivia wanted to know. "What does he want this time?"

"What he didn't have last time." All eyes turned to Miranda. "It's obvious. Why did he banish Her instead of annihilating Her? Because he couldn't kill Her. Even a creature made of pure darkness with godlike power can't kill a god. But my guess is something can."

"Another god," Nico finished. "This time he's not throwing away his shot on a wound...he's going for Her throat. He wants the Godspell."

*****

The second limo pulled away from the Haven drive, and the Tetrad watched its taillights gradually fade down the long road to the edge of the property where the exterior gate and guard towers stood.

No one had wanted to leave. The embraces were long and reluctantly released; smiles turned into tears. In the space of a few days the Circle had become even more of a family, and putting a continent between them was more painful than anyone expected.

"I'll start working on the permanent Gate spell tonight," Nico said, determination fixing the thought in his mind. "We can have them among all of our Havens and visit any night we wish."

"What do you need for the spell?" David asked.

"A room we can dedicate to the purpose, ideally. Something small, perhaps one of the studies we never use. We'll clear out all the furniture and each wall can hold its own Gate."

"One to California," Deven said, counting out on his fingers, "One to New York, one to Prague."

"And one for the blank terminus. That one only I will be able to use because it will require a spell each time, but I can set up the other three to be activated by Signets, so even the others can come and go when they like."

"So Jacob could get to New York by coming here," David mused, nodding. "We'll be Grand Central Station. I like it."

While they were talking, the Haven Town Car pulled up. "Were you going into town?" Nico asked David.

"Yes, but I didn't call for a car," he replied.

"I did," Miranda spoke up. Everyone looked at her. She was still behaving a little oddly--preoccupied, even subdued. "Meeting."

"You didn't mention one," David said.

She shrugged. "It's kind of last-minute--my PR firm needs to talk to me, and I figure after what I've put them through lately if they want to meet, I'll meet. I don't think I'll be out late...do you want a ride?"

David smiled. "That's all right, I've got transport."

To illustrate, he vanished, and Miranda rolled her eyes, but her smile wasn't quite as good-natured as it normally was when amused by her Prime's quirks.

"Are you all right?" Nico asked the Queen, laying a hand on her arm. "You've been...you don't seem quite yourself tonight, or last night."

She gave him a long, searching look, and for just a second he saw anguish in her face, but she covered it up quickly. "I'm okay...for now. There's something..." She took a deep breath and squared off her shoulders. "It might be nothing. I'll tell you both all about it when I get home, if there's anything to tell. Just...give me until then, okay?"

"Of course," he said, impulsively hugging her. She held onto him tightly for a moment before letting go and all but diving into the open car door.

Nico looked at Deven, who shook his head. "I don't know what to make of it either. But I can feel it...something isn't right...something we've all missed."

"Do you have any idea what?"

The Prime frowned. "I'm not sure. I have...not an idea, exactly, but a feeling, or not even that. Just...I don't know."

It wasn't like Deven to be lost for words, and it was clearly bothering him, but since neither he nor Miranda seemed to know what to say or what to think about it, Nico decided not to push. Sometimes even just a few hours could give someone the time and space to make sense of a problem; there was no need to force it.

"Well, I'm going to get to work on the Gate spell," Nico said. "What's your night looking like?"

"Cloister," Deven said with a smile. "I'm trying to get to know the Acolytes better, so I asked them to meet with me a few at a time just to talk. Ashera and Siobhan will both be there to help make it less weird."

"What sort of thing will you talk about?"

"Well, their histories, why they joined, that sort of thing--and any ideas they have for ways to make things work better now that they've been uprooted. They know their community and their customs far better than I do, so, I want to know what they need."

Nico grinned at him--despite all his protestations and stubbornness Deven was taking to the role of Hallowed like a hawk to the air--and Deven made a face at him, then stood on tiptoe to give him a kiss.

"Have a good meeting, then, and I will see you later on," Nico said, holding him tightly, comforted by the way his now-white hair tickled Nico's chin. So many changes...but the important things stayed the same, as did a lot of the little comforts that he'd taken for granted.

Nico started to follow Dev back inside, but paused just at the door, looking down the road that all the cars had taken. A slow ripple of foreboding moved through him, thinking of the Queen's face just before she left. He was tempted to go into the Web and follow her, to at least reassure himself she wasn't in danger, but such an intrusion was a gross invasion of a loved one's privacy, and he had to have trust that the Queen would say she needed help and not try to take on the world alone.

The problem was he didn't really believe it.

*****

After years of working for vampires, perhaps it shouldn't have surprised Novotny to turn on the light in his office and find one waiting for him, but he still started and dropped his briefcase.

They stared at each other for a long moment.

Finally, the doctor took a deep breath and bowed. "My Lady."

She watched him without speaking for a few more seconds; in a vain attempt to hide his discomfort he bent and picked up the case and, standing, straightened his glasses. Under her unwavering gaze, he came into the office and closed the door, walking around her--cautiously, as if, should she attack him, he had any prayer of defending himself or escaping--to his chair.

She turned as he walked, keeping her eyes on him as he did on her, until he stood waiting for permission to sit. Finally, she nodded, and took the opposite chair. As soon as she sat, so did he.

"You know why I'm here," Miranda said. She kept her tone steely, without any of the personable warmth she normally graced him with. Right now, for all she knew, he was her enemy. At the very least he was lying to her, and regardless of whose orders that was under, she wasn't going to trust a word out of his mouth without reading him with her empathy as he spoke.

"I suppose I do." Novotny removed his glasses and cleaned them, time-honored activity of an intelligent person trying to buy time. "I confess I didn't think this would last as long as it has; if nothing else it's a fascinating study into the nature of the Signet bonds."

She leaned forward, elbows on the arms of the chair. "I suppose he swore you to secrecy."

"On my very life," Novotny confirmed, though he didn't seem terribly worried. "And I'm sure you could make just as credible a threat...although I imagine at your hands I would meet my end much more humanely and quickly."

She considered that, then said, "You have a point. He does know how to draw out physical agony to the fullest extent possible--he could turn your ribcage to shards inside your chest without breaking your skin. But do you really think I don't know how to hurt you?"

She pinned him with her stare, letting him see just the edge of the anger under her shields. "Do you think I wouldn't lock you inside your own mind for the rest of your life and make you relive your worst moment over and over? Or take your greatest day...the birth of your son, perhaps...and mutate it in your memory, turning the joy into fear, or shame? I could twist your heart around so hard you'll never feel a moment's peace again."

As she spoke she nudged his mind, seeking out his instinctive fear and dialing it up, without trying to hide she was doing so, to the point of terror. "I could even make you so afraid your heart would give out. Isn't that one of the worst fates a human can face, to die alone and afraid?"

She let the fear slide back down to a sensible level, leaving him panting and sweating, his eyes huge and white like a panicked horse's.

After letting him sit with that a second, she said, "Now...let's not get ahead of ourselves. We're not enemies, are we? I know that whatever's going on, you don't like it any more than I do. So I'm going to stop waving my dick around, and you're going to tell me what's happening to my husband."

They talked for nearly an hour.

Chapter Fourteen

"Good evening, Hallowed One," the guard at the door said, bowing.

It took Deven a beat to realize the greeting hadn't come from one of the Acolytes--it had come from one of the Haven Elite. He paused and looked at the man.

The guard looked down, suddenly self-conscious. Deven recognized him from the most recent round of Elite trials but didn't know his name. "Are you a member of the Order?" he asked.

The guard cleared his throat, apparently shocked at his own temerity in using the title in his greeting. "No, my Lord, I...I've been posted here all week, and..."

Deven nodded, smiling. "Why don't you come in?"

"Oh, no, Sire, I couldn't leave my post--"

"Of course you can. You have my permission. Come on."

Eyes widening, the guard nodded. "Thank you, my Lord."

That was hardly the last surprise of the evening; upon entering the temple, Deven saw there were at least twice as many people there as expected--he'd meant only to talk with a few Acolytes, but it looked like everyone in the Order was here...and they weren't the only ones. There were at least three other Elite, one of the servants...

...and one of the Elves.

Deven looked them all over without letting his gaze linger on anyone, especially the latter--the last thing he wanted to do was spook the poor girl, who already looked like she was about to come out of her skin sitting in a room full of vampires and humans.

Instead, he joined Ashera and Siobhan at the front of the room by the altar and, after bowing slightly to the crowd to indicate they should sit, turned to Ashera.

"What's going on?" he asked quietly. "I thought this was a small meet-and-greet thing."

Ashera looked a bit sheepish. "I apologize, Hallowed One, but...they all wanted to be here...everyone is wondering..."

"Wondering what?"

"How to reach Her," Siobhan finished, her young face determined, touched with a very mortal immediacy.

"Oh." Of course...they all knew where he'd been, to Whom he had spoken.

He turned to them.

He knew what they'd been hoping--that he could take them there, right now, tonight. That longing he could see on their faces was so raw and aching, a need he'd felt himself for most of his life but pushed away. Wandering the world knowing there could be so much more, that that empty place could be filled, was a pain all its own.

That yearning...it made him ache as well. There had to be something he could do for them now.

He tried to think back to Eladra...she had been denied direct contact with Persephone as well, but she had performed rituals that at least brought Her energy into the world for the others to experience. Drawing Down the Moon, Aspecting...it had always been an important part of the Order. He had no idea whatsoever how to do it, but perhaps he didn't have to know; perhaps he only had to be willing.

He took a deep breath and touched his Signet, letting his fingers close around the Darkened Star. He didn't know what to say or ask, hadn't had time to learn the liturgy or the prep work. Eladra had spent at least a full night in meditation before a ritual to invoke the Goddess, but she'd been working blind. He might not have her training or experience but he wasn't going to let them down.

First he addressed the Blood-Bound: "You all understand that only those who have died can have direct contact with the Raven Mother. That much hasn't changed."

The humans looked at each other and nodded, unsurprised. It had always been a condition of joining the Order as a human that their devotion to Persephone involved far more faith than experience; historically after years of service and study they would be given the choice to fully initiate, at which point they'd be allowed to join in the vampire-only rituals where the Hallowed performed an Aspecting and drew the power and presence of the Goddess into the temple through her body.

"Shall we leave the temple, then, Hallowed One?" Siobhan asked, though it was clearly the last thing any of them wanted to do.

He looked at her, seeing her pain, feeling it echoed in everyone in the room. The Order had served Her for centuries with no promise She would return, and that included the Blood-Bound as much as the immortals.

"No," he said. "I want all of you to stay."

Deven nodded to himself and faced them with the absolute certainty that, at this one moment, he knew exactly what he was doing.

He took a deep breath and said, "The Blood-Bound are held separate for a reason--to ensure they understand what it means to surrender their humanity and leave the daywalking world behind forever to enter into the service of the Lady. And the ability to enter into Her presence at will, while awake, is a privilege reserved for the Circle. For centuries members of the Order have communed with Her in meditation, in dreams--and through invocation rituals performed by the Hallowed or the High Priestess of their particular Cloister. In the past those experiences have been by their nature limited because She was so far beyond our reach, but that's no longer true."

He found himself smiling at the way their eyes lit up with hope, and went on. "Tonight is a celebration. A new era among our kind has begun, you might even say a new Order, and you here in this room are its first initiates. Together we will shape the future of Elysium on Earth. And the truth is, I have no idea what it will mean for you; I barely even know what it means for me. I ask your patience going forward as I learn to serve you, and Her. But tonight...tonight I want to give you all a gift."

Deven waved a hand, drawing up the touch of pyrokinetic power that everyone in the Circle had inherited from Cora, and the candle sconces on the walls all burst to light. There were gasps--it occurred to him that most of the people here weren't used to the weird variety of powers the Circle had. Another gesture and the electric lights went out.

He didn't stop to consider how embarrassing it would be if his plan didn't work; the truth was, he knew it would, because he could already feel the energy building in the back of his mind, rising up along the Dark Web, lapping like water around him. He could feel something else...approval, much the same as he'd sense from one of the Tetrad, but from somewhere beyond them, beyond anything, yet bound as intimately to his every cell as Nico was.

She was listening. It shouldn't have surprised him...but again, he had spent most of his life calling into a void that never answered. Now, it seemed, he didn't even have to call.

He closed his eyes and opened his shields to Her, extending himself down through the Web, reaching out to take the offered Hand.

Silver-black surrounded him, and he considered it for a moment, part of him trying to balk. What She was asking him to do required an act of trust he would have laughed at before.

But he had already surrendered to Her in asking to live. There was work to do, and this was part of it. The time to hesitate had come and gone. And when he remembered all those eyes on him, all that hope and longing, it wasn't nearly as terrifying as he thought it would be to just...*let...go.*

He could, again, feel Her pride, and Her love, as She surged into his body, flooding through him like the sea, pouring out into the room and into every heart and mind before him. He could sense Her speaking, not to him but to each of them at the same time, dozens of conversations, embraces, touches, blessings, love, healing...all of it at once, Her energy weaving its way through them all, bringing renewal and strength to even the most jaded heart...his own.

He understood, then, why to take this role he had to be "something new." No single person could channel this much Divine energy without either dying or going mad, but whatever he was now, this was what he'd been remade for. She had taken a broken heart and mended it with veins of silver, leaving it empty but ready to fill until overflowing, to reach through him to Her children...not every night, but when the Moon was dark...yes.

She imparted knowledge to him as She embraced the others in the temple: This would drain him, dramatically, and he would have to replenish himself with the power of death. He at least would have to kill every month even though the others could divide up the sacrifice in whatever way they needed to as long as it totaled eight lives. His need would be unavoidable...and he would need help in satisfying it.

He had no idea how long the communion lasted. It might have been five minutes and it might have been five hours. By the time he felt the rush of power beginning to wane, his awareness of himself as an individual creature was all but gone, and he had no way to know how weak he was until he felt his skin enclosing him again and, seconds later, his knees hitting the floor.

Hands took his arms and lowered him, as they had lifted him up only a few nights ago; he could neither speak nor move on his own, and would probably have been terrified at his own helplessness if he'd had the capacity.

He had no way to communicate what he needed. Neither limbs nor lips responded to his will. He could only lay there barely conscious, able only to keep breathing.

"I am here, Hallowed One," came a soft voice. "I am here for you."

Someone got his mouth open, and a moment later he tasted blood. Suddenly hunger overwhelmed him, what tiny bit of strength he still had staggering forward to seize the throat before him and tear into it, the need so powerful there was no room for thought or reason. There was no fighting it. There was only blood.

He drank until he felt the life in his hands shuddering, heartbeat matching heartbeat and slowing even more, and he couldn't stop. The body against his didn't struggle; in fact it seemed completely relaxed, unafraid, and the first sensation to break through the hunger was the feeling of a gentle hand on his face, stroking his cheek, accepting.

Death erupted from her and into him, filling him up until every iota of lost strength was replenished and thensome. He'd killed on the hunt before, long ago, but it was nothing like this. This had not been murder, it had been sacrifice, willingly given out of love and devotion.

The hand fell away from his face.

Silence descended.

The first sound was his own breath, panting; the next was the sound of a crackling fire. Smells came next: blood, of course, and smoke, candle wax, incense...

Deven opened his eyes, expecting to see the entire congregation gaping at him in fear or disgust, but this was not the temple. Where was he?

"Easy," someone said. "Move slowly."

Ashera. He swallowed, still tasting blood, his mouth dry; before he could try to frame a plea, he felt a cup at his lips. Water.

It was quiet and dark aside from the fireplace, and only he, Ashera, and two other Acolytes were there. He couldn't come up with their names, but it didn't matter just now; they were here to tend to him as Acolytes had done for their High Priests and Hallowed for centuries.

He was on the floor, and pieces of the room came together: A bedroom, most likely adjacent to the temple room. At some point they'd brought him in here.

"What..." His voice was hoarse.

"You fell," Ashera said simply. "As soon as She departed, you collapsed. We knew what to do."

Yes, they would have; Xara would have been exhausted after an invocation ritual too, though probably not to this extent. He thought far, far back to his own days in the Cloister; the Acolytes had done the same for Eladra, taking her somewhere dark and peaceful, making sure she fed and rested while the rest of the Cloister spent the night celebrating.

Fed...

Deven looked around, confused--he had killed, he knew he had, but whom--

He remembered the voice even as his eyes fell on the body beside him.

"Siobhan," he said softly. "Oh, no."

Ashera touched the human's too-still face; her eyes were already closed, her hands folded on her belly. Her expression wasn't the slack blankness he was used to seeing on the dead. She looked completely serene.

"She said she had offered herself," Ashera told him, staring down at the woman, smiling a little. "She said she was ready."

"Ready--"

He barely got the word out before Siobhan's body shuddered, and she gasped, a cry escaping her. Her eyes flew open, and her arms flew out, madly groping for something to hold onto.

Deven stared, bewildered. Ashera let Siobhan grab hold of her and held her close, murmuring to her gently, telling her she was safe.

Siobhan's wide, wild eyes fixed on Deven, and he recognized the look. Siobhan worked a hand free of Ashera's arms and reached out to him, panicking as her body reacted to dying and waking in the space of minutes…just a pale imitation of what she was about to face.

He took her hand. "Be at peace, child," he told her, staying as calm as he could though his heart and mind were racing. "She's still with you. Close your eyes. Breathe."

She did as she was told, and slowly got herself under control. He gripped her hand tightly, and Ashera held onto her, and gradually her shaking and gasping stopped.

"Remember the Affirmation," Ashera said to her. "Say it with me."

Siobhan whispered harshly, but the words came. "The Raven Mother brought me forth…She dwells within me, as me, all around me. Her hands are my hands, Her voice is my voice, Her heart is my heart. The Raven Mother brought me forth…"

Deven remembered those words. They were given to every novice who came to the Order to use as a mantra; some Cloisters also had beads they held while repeating it, like a rosary. Over time there were dozens more prayers added to their repertoire, along with chants, songs, and poetry, but there was always the Affirmation to return to. Hearing the words made his eyes burn with memory…and with something like joy, like coming home.

He leaned his forehead against Siobhan's and spoke along with her for a moment, his free hand taking Ashera's. He could feel the transformation beginning in Siobhan's body; would she sleep, he wondered, or suffer? He'd never been privy to the mysteries of the Blood-Bound…but now they were his mysteries too.

Hang the mysteries; he wasn't going to let her hurt if he could help it. "Sleep, little one," he told her softly. "Rest in Her arms while you change and come back to us when you're ready."

Her fear was fading, and so was her consciousness; before long, as he'd hoped, she was out.

Ashera gestured to the other two Acolytes, who came and picked Siobhan up and carried her over to the bed.

Deven's head was spinning. He wasn't drained like before, but he was still physically exhausted as if he'd been fighting for his life.

"Are you well, Hallowed One?" Ashera asked.

He nodded. It wasn't really a lie; he would be fine. "How are the others?"

She smiled. "Rejoicing," she said. "I wish you could have seen them all, when She had gone and we were all waking up. I have never seen such happiness in so many people at once. Some wept, some laughed. Some needed solitude but most have started a party in the temple."

"What about the Elf?"

"Dalhenna," Ashera said, nodding. "She went back to her people but plans to return. They are hard to read at the best of times but I believe whatever she was seeking, she found it."

"There will be more," he said, knowing it was true. "And the Enclave will be outraged."

Ashera chuckled. "I invite them to express their outrage however they see fit."

He couldn't help but laugh at the wryness in her voice. He was seized with an intense wave of gratitude for her, and the other Acolytes whose names he didn't even know…yet.

"I can only do this once a month, at the New Moon," he said. "I hope they won't all be too disappointed."

"Disappointed?" This time her laugh was bright. "My Lord, you need not worry. Just the thought of being able to feel that again, even once in my life, would sustain me through the worst day I've ever endured."

He smiled and very slowly and carefully--with her help--stood up. "I need to go to bed," he said, "But I think I'll sleep better with my Consort beside me. Besides, I need to tell the others what I've discovered tonight."

"Of course, Hallowed One. Do you need assistance walking?"

There had been a time…well, a very long time…when he would rather have crawled over broken glass than admit needing help, but tonight, he actually thought about it before saying, "No, I've got it. But thank you, Ashera. You honor me."

"It is we who are honored." She bowed.

As he was about to leave, he heard a whisper from the bed. "Hallowed One…"

Deven went to where they had bundled Siobhan up in the blankets, surprised she was awake. "Yes?"

Her eyes were already glazed with fever and pain, but also with determination. "Will you bless me?"

Smiling, he leaned down and kissed her forehead, lips, and throat. "May the Raven Mother, whose wings encircle creation, whose blood sustains all that dwells in the darkness, be with you tonight and always, Siobhan."

She smiled back, sighed, and closed her eyes.

Moving slowly but with gradually increasing strength, Deven left the room, closing the door quietly behind him. He could hear music coming from the temple, along with singing and laughing. The atmosphere throughout the Cloister's wing of the Haven was one of unreserved celebration.

I did that.

"Ha!" he muttered, startling one of the wing guards he passed, who stared at him--everyone seemed to stare these days, though whether it was the hair and ears or the fact that he probably looked like absolute hell startling them, he couldn't say at the moment.

And now he was talking to himself.

"Ego check," he said to the guard, who pretended to understand the way people often humored the mad.

He was in a watery sort of bliss-bubble himself--nothing ostentatious, just a feeling of satisfaction and, dare he think it, contentment, that he didn't bother questioning. There would be time to go back over the night's events with the rest of the Tetrad and discuss their implications after he'd slept for about twenty hours.

But the farther he got from the Cloister, the more something began to bother him...nothing concrete at first, but...something... something wasn't right, he could feel it. Now that the emotions of the revelers were no longer interfering, he could sense something gravely amiss, and he remembered what he'd said to Nico earlier that very night, when Miranda left the Haven...

Then a panicked, desperate voice broke through his daze and into his mind, and despite his exhaustion, he was running before its origin even registered.

"HELP ME!"

*****

Building a permanent Gate, it turned out, wasn't all that much harder than building the regular kind...twenty times in a row...standing on one foot...while building a house of cards...that were on fire.

The first attempt was a total failure, but Nico figured out his error pretty quickly. One thing he'd always appreciated about Weaving was that he could step back, look at what he'd made, and examine it like a physical thing. In this case he was essentially creating a strand that linked two other locations in the Web, and when that strand was activated by a Signet, it would allow someone to cross the intervening space. But every strand in the Web had to be counterbalanced, anchored, and supplied with energy from somewhere; some spells required siphoning off energy from surrounding threads, and some required the energy of the Weaver.

This one would power itself using the Signets and their bearers; that would help ensure no one else could use it. Nico couldn't imagine anyone of ill intent getting into the Haven undetected, but Miranda had told him about her early days here and how David's enemies had infiltrated the Elite, and even with security an order of magnitude tighter than it had been then Nico wasn't about to risk the other Havens or the future Elven settlement and Cloister on the assumption that any system was foolproof.

Right now he was working to establish the Gate to California, since it was the only location of the three he planned to create that he'd already set foot in. Before he could build Gates to the others he would have to physically visit them and find a place to create the Gate's other end somewhere in the New York and Prague Havens, which would require discussion with the rest of the Circle.

This one he could manage by himself since he had studied the plans for the new structure. He'd considered building the terminus at the cliff base, which would make moving the Elves easier, but he had to think long-term, and that meant a location accessible for a vampire day or night. It made more sense to use someplace in the Cloister since that was where Dev would go most often. So he found a room on the site blueprints that was earmarked for storage, right down the hall from the Hallowed One's private residence.

Right now that room was only a foundation since the focus had been on the cliff base and getting the Elves to their new home as quickly as possible. The Cloister vampires were perfectly comfortable here in the Haven for now.

Nico spent several hours experimenting with the Gate strand, shoring it up in different ways, using the Codex spell as a starting point; whoever had designed it had been a powerful mage, but not an Elven Weaver, so he was able to fine-tune it in ways they could not. But the process was frustrating and tiring, and after the fourth failed attempt at opening the Gate, he decided to stop for the night.

He sat down on the floor for a while with pencil and sketch pad and drew out the variations he'd tried, making notes about their advantages and detriments, both for his own memory and so he could show them to David later. The Prime would almost certainly have useful suggestions. He understood enough about Weaving, mostly due to his understanding of circuitry, that they could sit down and brainstorm productively--perhaps even tonight, if David was back from town yet.

Yawning, he dropped his pencil and stretched. Right on cue, Astela bounced up from the pillow he'd brought for her and came over, bumping her head against his, demanding attention.

He laughed and spent a while scratching her neck, rubbing her ears, and her belly while she yipped happily and wriggled in his arms.

She didn't speak, of course, but he could sense her emotions, and she his. She had a puppy's boundless excitement for everything, but beneath that he could already tell she was going to make a marvelous companion--she was whip-smart and attentive, and when he wanted her to be still and serious, she came to attention like a seasoned soldier, shedding her youth in seconds.

"You're named after a remarkable woman," Nico told Astela. "I wish you could have met her. Cats were her first love, but she adored all animals and always wanted to stop and meet the dogs we saw in town." He felt his heart squeeze, thinking of Stella, the loss still so new he didn't know what to do with it. He'd spent most of his life in the same company, day in and day out, with little changing; and here in a couple of years he had loved and lost more than in three hundred. "I wish you could have met her...I wish she was here."

Astela scooted closer, tilting her head in a way that was unmistakably an offer of her shoulder. Nico smiled through his sadness and put his arms around the dog.

"You are remarkable too," he said. "Be proud of your name, little star."

She *grrrrrrfed* in his ear, earning a smile.

"Let's go see if our Lord and Master is home," Nico said, gathering his notes and standing. "Maybe he'll have an hour to give me."

He locked the door to the soon-to-be-Gate room, and Astela fell into step beside him down the hall to the Signet suite. His head was pounding from overexerting his gifts; hopefully there wouldn't be any emergencies that demanded magic in the next couple of hours, and he would be fine. He'd be even better if he could convince David to snuggle up with him in the bed, poring over his notes and talking about magical technology, the Prime's scent and solidity a balm for even the most frazzled nerves.

Luck wasn't with him; the suite was empty, and he was too tired to extend his senses through the Haven to see if David was even back from town. Still, the couch was nearly as comfortable as the bed, and no one would mind if he waited here and had a catnap. Miranda would roll her eyes at finding him on the couch rather than the bed, but in his mind, this was still the Pair's space, and he would only take the bed when invited. He'd observed enough polyamorous relationships to know that boundaries were all-important.

He'd just started to doze off when he heard the door open and shut, and he could sense it was David. He smiled to himself, keeping his eyes closed so he could listen to the familiar footfalls, the sound of a coat being taken off and hung up…

…but something didn't seem quite right. David was moving strangely, almost gracelessly, which wasn't like him. He seemed to be off-balance.

Nico opened his eyes, but didn't have time to form a visual impression of the room before a mouth had latched onto his, hungry and wanting.

He kissed back even though he was far too weary for any real passion, then said, "As much as I hate to deny such a delightful welcome, I'm afraid I'm too tired."

David didn't seem to hear him…no, something was off, beginning with how forcefully David's tongue thrust into his mouth, and how tightly the Prime's fingers gripped his arms.

Nico started to pull back and ask what was wrong, but could only grunt in surprise as he was hauled off the couch and onto the floor. His back hit the rug and knocked the breath out of him, and he couldn't get it back--David had him pinned to the floor so solidly he could barely move.

The hands on Nico's body were possessive and rough, with none of the finely-honed skill the Prime had always displayed in his touch. Kisses turned into bites, David's teeth pressing harder and harder into Nico's lower lip until it hurt--then bled.

"What's gotten into you?" Nico demanded, wrenching his head to the side to get a breath. "I said I was too tired--"

"I didn't ask," David snapped. As Nico watched, his confusion turning into genuine alarm, David's eyes began to blacken.

David seized him by the shoulders and flipped him onto his stomach--again, the impact with the floor was painful, but not nearly as painful as when David bit his neck hard, latching on with both sets of his fangs, holding Nico underneath him like a falcon with its talons in a mouse.

Nico heard a low, animal growl at his ear, and there was nothing he recognized as his lover in that sound. Fear gripped his belly and he started to struggle, instinct taking over where logic could find no purchase in the situation.

"Let go!" Nico panted. "Whatever you're doing, stop it, right now, damn it!"

The growl came again, this time turning into a hiss. David finally spoke again, but it was a cold, hollow whisper that sent Nico into a near panic. *"You're mine."*

David latched back onto Nico's throat, drinking forcefully, the pain as terrifying as the feeling of the Prime's body holding him down, arousal hard against Nico's hip that finally made the Elf understand what was happening. The idea of fighting David off physically was laughable, and Nico groped for the power to paralyze or knock him out, something, anything, *oh Goddess please don't let this happen no no no--*

With one free hand, David took hold of Nico's belt and tore it downward, and in among the primal, mindless need to take what he wanted, there was also a rage there, a compulsion to destroy, to kill, to drain the Elf until he shriveled, to bathe in the sweetness of his death no matter what the cost.

Blindly panicked, Nico did the only thing he could do--he called with every ounce of strength he still had, reaching down the bond and every connection he could touch, all but screaming into the Web:

"HELP ME!"

He felt the room's suddenly-cold air on his bare back and the searing pain of another bite on his neck seconds before something heavy slammed into them sideways, knocking David off of him and rolling with the Prime into the bed. Nico heard wood splintering, but didn't look back to see what had happened until he had scrambled away toward the fireplace, blood running down from his throat and making him slip as he tried to get up.

The sounds he heard were terrifying--it was like two wild animals tearing into each other, snarling and growling, nothing human in it at all. He caught a flash of white in the tumble of limbs, then a cry of exertion as David flew back across the room again, this time into the coffee table.

Deven rolled to his feet, eyes black as hellfire, blood soaking his shirt where the Prime's teeth must have gotten past his defenses.

There was no talking. Deven didn't try to reason with him or figure out what was going on--there was only one thing that mattered, and it wasn't David's welfare.

David flung himself at Deven, the naked animosity in his face so alien Nico shrank back from it even though he was already ten feet away.

Nico pushed himself back behind the arm of the couch, shaking so hard he could barely feel his fingers gripping the upholstery. He tried to come up with the power to help, to push the balance toward Deven, but he could tell Dev was worn out too, and didn't have the force of whatever madness had seized their Prime to tip the scales in their favor. Deven had never lost a fight, he said, but it looked like he might now--

This time David threw himself into Deven so hard they both went over, and David had his hands at Deven's throat, trying to break his neck. Deven twisted in his grasp and got an elbow into David's sternum, managing to break his grip long enough to get some air, but David was already on him again, snapping his teeth into Dev's shoulder and tearing backwards.

Nico saw something small and furry race across the room toward them, and he yelled in fear at the Nighthound, scared she was about to try and join in the fight; but Astela was smarter than he could have hoped, and bounded past them, a blur of motion darting to Nico's side where she took up position in front of him, hackles up, teeth bared in a surprisingly ferocious display for such a young animal.

"Good girl," he whispered. "Stay with me."

Nico had no weapons training, no energy, not even enough to call for help again. Deven was losing. Whatever had happened to David he no longer seemed to care that killing either of them meant his own death, and his Queen's--

"Deven, MOVE!"

Dev reacted from instinct at the voice, pitching himself sideways and out of the line of fire. Something whistled through the air and struck David hard in the back; he howled in pain and spun toward it, trying to get hold of the hilted stake…a hilt Nico recognized with such gratitude he nearly wept.

David, unrecognizable from the blood all over his face and the seething violence in his eyes, faced his Queen, who stared at him calmly, framed in the light beyond the doorway, stone cold fury in every inch of her body and her black, black eyes.

She didn't bother with explanations, quips, or questions, any more than Deven had. She waited until she had David's attention and he came at her as he had the others, a killing light in his eyes. She didn't draw Shadowflame, didn't throw another stake, didn't move aside.

But she was absolutely armed to the teeth.

Nico saw behind her shield just before she dropped it: A well of power drawn up from the Dark Web, churning around her, crackling like the air before a lightning strike. She raised both hands and clapped them together in front of her, and the power around her *ignited*.

With a surge of unbelievable heat, the Queen's power rushed forward, engulfing the Prime, obscuring them both in a light that was also darkness--the flames were black, silver, tongues of shadow that burned.

David screamed.

Nico had never heard a sound like it and hoped to all the gods he never would again--it was a sound of fear, and agony, and outrage, and it was both David's and something else's, an energy Nico could suddenly sense--something wrapped around the Prime's mind, something with slimy tentacles and poisoned teeth that had been slowly and quietly curling itself through him, driving him to kill more and more, to feed…

Now, the creature that wasn't a creature--for it had a form of consciousness but wasn't sentient, only programmed to take over its host and use it until it died--screamed alone as Miranda moved forward and sent more energy into it, more fire. The creature was burning, the stench nauseating even though there was nothing physical to burn. It kept screaming--and it was David screaming, but not his screams.

She continued to burn the thing long after it stopped moving, long after its shrieking faded into sobs and then into silence. The Queen had her own rage to contend with.

Finally, she seemed satisfied that it was well and truly dead, and with one last burst of energy the creature fell to ash and disappeared.

All that was left was a shuddering, whimpering figure curled up in a ball, and Miranda dropped to her knees beside him, her eyes returning to their usual green but her lovely face still set and determined.

Breathing hard, she waited a moment--grounding, Nico realized--before reaching with one hand toward her Prime and touching his shoulder.

He flinched and, seized with sudden panic, tried to get away from her, but he was simply too weak to go far, and collapsed onto the floor and curled back up on himself.

Miranda reached out again, this time taking hold of his shoulder before he could pull away, and Nico felt her hitting him with another wave of energy, this one knocking him unconscious.

Once that was done, she seemed to deflate. She put her face in her hands and leaned on her knees for a minute, shaking as hard as they all were.

Nico forced himself to move and crawled out from behind the couch; he made it to the Queen's side and fell against her before he could stop the motion. She didn't fall over. She was like a mountain, there, rooted in the Web and as strong as the Earth itself.

And she was crying. Nico got his arms around her, unable to give her anything more.

A few seconds later Deven joined them and touched his forehead to hers. Nobody spoke.

For several long minutes the only sounds were the fireplace and their ragged breathing gradually slowing down to normal. Nico felt

Astela sit down next to him, sphinxlike, keeping watch as if she were three times her size.

"I got here as fast as I could," Miranda whispered. "I couldn't Mist that far and still call up enough power to kill it."

"What...what was it?" Nico asked.

"The same thing that possessed the people at the benefit," she said, voice shaking. "It must have gotten hold of him when he killed one of the other survivors."

Deven took a breath, swallowed. "He's been killing since the last New Moon, hasn't he--after that night he took the compulsion from us."

"Longer," she said. "Novotny told me it's been going on for months. Only one or two at a time until that night. It's why the need never got as strong as it should have after we all bonded--it wasn't because of the magic. And since the benefit...it's been every night. Even in the daytime. He Misted to Hunter and killed there."

"And we had no idea," Nico said. "How is that possible?"

"Because of me," Deven answered softly. "He learned how to block us out because I did it to you. And you know David...he would have studied it, figured out how to fine-tune the process."

"But how could something like that, designed to possess humans, be strong enough to do this to a Prime?" Nico asked.

"It wasn't designed for humans," Miranda said, sitting back. "The Prophet sent it for us."

They stared at her.

"I felt it when I killed the first one...they were still connected to him, like he was monitoring them somehow. I didn't think anything of it at the time--you told me yourself that doing any kind of magic, especially with blood, binds you to the spell. But when I saw this one, the way it had him, I could see *him* on the other side. He used the humans at the benefit to snare one of us, knowing we would examine what he'd done."

"But why? To kill us?"

"Maybe. Maybe not. I don't know."

"I do," came a rough whisper.

They all looked over to where David lay, no longer unconscious but with his eyes half-open, glazed with pain and with tears. Screaming had turned his voice into a choked, hoarse sound that was nothing like what they knew. He barely even seemed to know where he was, but he was pushing as much meager strength as he had into the words, determined to speak them.

"He wants me," David said. "Kai isn't enough for him. He wants me." His eyes lost focus, then sharpened again, this time on Miranda. "And she wants you."

Chapter Fifteen

"I warned you, child."

Her voice, stern yet still somehow kind, echoed in his mind as the bedroom began to take shape around him.

Oh, how he wanted it all to have been a nightmare...to wake up in the puppy-pile of slumbering bodies with a hand around his wrist, breath against his neck, a chest pressed against his back. The sounds of breathing and murmuring to dreams in the dark, even the occasional snore--not that he'd ever tell--and the quiet certainty that was their unusual, but lovely, reality.

But that was not what awaited him this time...perhaps not ever again. It was tempting to feign amnesia, even just for a moment, but he had done enough lying...especially to himself.

She was sitting up cross-legged on the bed beside him, just watching, her face that seemingly unreadable expression that was, to him at least, still an open book. It was the product of too many emotions in too short a time.

For just a few seconds he took in the beauty of her face in silence, loving every inch of her, wishing he could just say so and go back to sleep.

She looked tired...and he knew why. There was no pretending.

He could feel his eyes burning, and he tried to find words to explain what had no explanation. Perhaps the only way to begin was with the bare truth.

"I fucked up," he whispered, what there was of his voice breaking.

Whatever hardness was in her face melted, and she let out a long breath before stretching out beside him and pulling his head to her shoulder. "Yeah," she said. "You did."

He held onto her desperately, thankful for her strength--and for what felt like forgiveness, even though he hadn't earned it. It took all he had not to sob into her chest, and not only because of the last few hours; aside from guilt and fear and exhaustion, the biggest thing he felt was *relief*.

She knew. They all knew. He could stop lying. God, why had he ever started?

"I'm such a fool," he said. "I knew I wasn't strong enough."

"Strong enough for what?" she asked, winding her hand through his hair. God, was he still bloody, even in their bed? Or had she cleaned him up? And what about--

"Oh God--Nico--"

He struggled to sit up, but she held him down with dismaying ease. He felt like he had burned every scrap of energy he had...and if he'd been fighting Deven, even with the elder Prime off his game, it was no wonder David was a wreck. "He's not here. They're in their own suite for the time being. I thought it was best."

"Is he all right?"

"That's not a fair question."

He shook his head. "No. It's not. I can't..."

"What do you mean when you say you weren't strong enough?" she asked again, refusing to be deterred.

He took a deep breath. "You're not a killer. None of you are. You shouldn't have to do it. I thought I could handle it for all of us...to take the burden from you."

She was quiet for a minute before saying, "There's something I think you're forgetting in all this, baby."

He waited.

Her brow furrowed. "You don't get to make that decision for me, or for any of us. Persephone gave all of us that choice and you took it away--for loving reasons, yes, but without our consent. Then you blocked us all from finding out the truth. That thing would never have gotten past us if you hadn't let it. You treated our combined strength and love like it was an afterthought, when it could have stopped this before it started. And look what you did to yourself--and to us."

Closing his eyes, he said, "I ruined everything."

She sighed, but didn't immediately reply, and that pause said it all. Shame to a depth he didn't even know could exist washed over him, and he could barely breathe beneath its drowning weight.

Shame wasn't the only problem, however…now that he was fully awake and able to look at the memories of the past few days…and longer than that, going back at least as far as the last New Moon…realizing how little control he'd really had over what was happening…he had told himself over and over he was doing this for them, the thought obsessive, letting the spell feed on his fear of losing all of this…and how close had he come to losing them anyway? Was there even a "them" to lose anymore?

"He had me," David said, eyes still shut tightly. "He had his claws in me from miles away and I didn't even know. He might still--how would I know? How can I know anything I'm thinking is my own? The fact that I thought I should hide anything from you tells me how little control I had even before that thing got me."

"Calm down," she said, tapping on his forehead. "You're starting to panic."

"Of course I am!" he exclaimed, sitting up abruptly and wresting himself from her embrace. It felt obscene, just then, for her to touch him, for him to be anywhere near this bed, this room, these people he had professed to love. Again, he found he couldn't breathe, and his heart was pounding thunderously in his throat. "I've had a monster in my head…in my *mind*, Miranda, the one thing that's made me who I am. And I let it in. I practically gift-wrapped myself. How can I trust anything I think? Or say to any of you? How…how can I…"

"David…" Her concern rose as steadily as his hysteria did. "You need to calm down or you're going to start breaking things."

"I already have. How can I ever look Nico in the eye knowing what I almost did to him? It doesn't matter if I was in control or not--I might not be next time either. And what difference does it make who was steering if it's still this body trying to rape him? I can't--"

Across the room he heard something small shatter, then another similar noise; a bulb in one of the lamps popped a second later. Miranda put her hands on his arms, but he couldn't hear what she was saying; the fear of what he could do, of what could turn into…or had already…

Pain sang sharply through his face. The impact sent a shockwave through his spinning thoughts, knocking them off kilter and disrupting the loop they'd gotten into.

Dizzy, panting, he looked up.

Deven stared at him calmly, his face imperious and impassive, lavender eyes icy. "You will pull yourself together, boy, or I will break your neck."

That voice always, always had the desired effect. He froze, dropped his gaze, and fought to control his breathing.

Miranda took his hands and nudged her way into his shielding--when he noticed what she was doing he let her in without hesitation. She sent waves of calming energy into him, soothing the fear that was driving him mad. When he was calm enough, she started exploring, running her psychic "fingers" through him and looking for anomalies. He'd seen her do it before to new Elite recruits to find outside allegiances and anything that might compromise their loyalty.

And now she had to do it to him.

"I don't see anything lingering," she said. "Although...wait."

His heart dropped again as her face clouded.

"Dev, would you come in here?" she asked. "I need a second opinion."

"I'm not sure how much I can help," Deven replied, climbing onto the bed and mirroring her cross-legged posture. "If you're relying on a Weaving level of Sight I might miss something."

"I won't."

They all looked up. David's stomach, heart, and conscience all clenched so hard he felt nauseated.

Nico, arms crossed, stood in the doorway. He looked as exhausted as the others and even worse; there were the remnants of ragged bite wounds on his neck and shoulder that should already have vanished if he'd fed...which meant he hadn't. Either he'd been asleep or old trauma had already resurfaced and he'd lost his appetite.

"You're awake," Deven said to Nico, worried. "I didn't expect you to move until at least nightfall."

A shrug. "I want to know what's happening."

David wanted more than anything to beg his forgiveness, to swear on any god or blood or Elven curse that he would never so much as touch him again, but he couldn't speak, only watch the Elf move closer, wary, refusing to meet David's gaze. Nico joined them on the bed but kept his distance and kept his arms crossed over his chest, a shield.

"What are we looking at?"

Miranda shook her head. "I'm not sure. I need a more experienced eye to tell me if this is anything or just paranoia. If it's something, and I get too close poking at it, it could trigger something nasty."

"All right."

Nico started to extend his energy, but balked, a shudder running through him.

Miranda put her hand on his shoulder. "You saw me kill it," she said. "You know it's gone."

But Nico gave another voice to the chorus of fear in David's head: "Do I? What if you're right and there's still something there?"

"Then you can help me burn it too."

Nico still looked like he wanted to cut off his own hands rather than touch David's aura. After a tense moment, Miranda told him softly, "Nico...it's David. Don't you think he's worth the risk?"

Finally, Nico lifted his eyes to meet David's. The fear there was wrenching, and David wanted desperately to look away...to curl up so tightly on himself he disappeared rather than exist as a creature who could hurt someone so loving and kind. But he would not look away; he wouldn't hide anymore. The only way to repair even an iota of the damage he'd done was to look it in the eye and tell the truth.

He was in such a horrifyingly vulnerable state that he couldn't stop more tears from trailing down his face, but he tried with everything he had left to hold Nico's eyes and tell him, without words, that Miranda was right, that they could get through this somehow.

The only thing he could say was, "Please help me."

The Elf drew a shaky breath and nodded. After a moment's hesitation Nico reached up and wiped a tear from David's face; the Prime leaned into the touch involuntarily. "I will," Nico said.

David no longer had the strength to keep his shields up anyway; he let them drop, knowing that nothing could pass through the three miracles in human shape that surrounded him. They might not be safe with him...but he was safe with them. He had to believe that.

Nico reached out again, tentatively, but when he found the same energy he knew so well waiting for him, he visibly relaxed and echoed Miranda's careful probing, comparing the landscape he had learned inside and out with the current reality.

"All right," Nico said. "Show me, my Lady."

David didn't have the Sight unless they brought him along into theirs, so he had no idea what they were looking at when they looked into the Web; to an outsider it would look like they were just sitting there staring into space, or more accurately at his sternum.

He felt Deven's eyes but couldn't meet them.

"Were you aware of what you were doing?" Deven asked suddenly.

David swallowed and tried to articulate it. "Yes. And no. Mostly I felt like me...except when I fed. Every time, it got worse. I felt the hunger all the time, and it kept getting stronger and stronger. The stronger it got the less control I had over it...even before the benefit."

"How many of those victims did you kill?"

David had heard Deven interrogate enough people to recognize the tone. Unlike most of those unfortunate souls David had no intention of trying to beg or dissemble his way out of it. Even if he'd been idiot enough to try he knew it wouldn't work. Holy being or not Dev was a predator, and he could smell blood a mile away.

"All of them. Except Luisa. Any one of them could have been the one that infected me with that thing. Everything after that starts to blur...it was just one human then another, as many as Novotny could bring me. I tried...at least mostly...to be discreet."

"Where did they all come from?"

"The list we made with Maguire...most of them anyway. A few were random on the street. I barely even remember those. They could have been anyone. But when I was here...home...I could hold it together. I could pretend someone else was doing it."

"Until tonight."

David nodded. Nico was listening keenly even as he sorted through the strands of the Web. For his benefit David went on, quietly, praying the right words would come. "I don't remember going to town or coming back. I remember feeding. And feeding. I don't know how many...and I was still hungry, and just...angry. I don't know why I was so angry. Everything went red...and I could see what I was doing, but it was like I was watching myself, unable to stop, unable to do anything but watch."

"That was the spell," Miranda murmured. "Ratcheting up underlying anger and fear to an obsessive fever pitch. It did the same thing to the humans, only a lot faster because they're so much weaker. It worked more slowly on you…the way it was designed to."

"You said the Prophet wants you," Deven prodded. "How do you know?"

David blinked. The truth was he didn't know. He couldn't remember what had driven him to say that as he lay on the floor. "I'm not sure."

"I think I might know," Nico said. "You're right, Miranda…I see it."

"What is it?" David asked, his pulse skyrocketing again, the panic squeezing his throat. "Is it another spell? What is it?"

"Calm down," Deven said shortly. "Ground. You owe us that, don't you?"

The word were as sharp as a slap; he obeyed again out of instinct.

"Can you break it?" Miranda asked Nico.

The Elf was silent for most of a minute. "I can."

"I'll anchor you, then, if--"

"No."

All three of them looked at Nico. The Elf's jaw was set, and when he looked into David's face, his dark violet eyes were hard. They stared at each other again for a long minute.

"You hurt me," Nico said coldly. It was like a stake of ice to the heart.

"I know. I'm sorry, Nico, I--"

The Elf shook his head. "I don't want an apology. I want to know you won't ever do anything so stupid again. I want to know that you trust us--that you understand we are stronger together, and that you have neither the obligation nor the right to act on our behalf."

"I do. Tell me how I can prove myself and I will."

Nico considered him, weighing, evaluating. "I want you to do something for me…and you're not going to like it on any level."

"Anything." He put the full force of emotion behind the word.

Finally, Nico nodded. "I want you to save my brother."

"How?" Miranda asked.

Nico was still looking into David's eyes. Still weighing. Was there hope there that they could ever reclaim what David had destroyed?

Did it even matter anymore, if this was what Nico wanted of him? Whatever it was, he'd do it or die trying.

"By giving the Prophet what he wants," Nico said. "You."

*****

"Out of the question."

"Miranda, I don't think you realize--"

"That you want payback? That you're willing to use guilt to coerce someone you supposedly love to walk into the lion's den when he can barely stand? What the hell is wrong with you?"

"We may never have an opportunity like this again. If this works we can stop this whole thing before anything else happens, before anyone else has to die. Isn't that our purpose here?"

"Our purpose is to work as a team. Not to..."

David let the argument drift out of his mind; he no longer had the energy to follow it. He sat on the couch, mostly dressed with his coat in his lap, fingers refusing to cooperate as he tried to fasten a com around his wrist.

He was weak. His entire body shook on the inside as if he'd worn every muscle to a frayed string and they were popping one by one. He could barely concentrate...and he was hungry...so hungry.

For the first time in his life as a vampire that hunger scared him. If he started feeding, could he stop anymore? Was Nico right...was there still a beast crouching inside his head waiting for the taste of death to lunge forward and destroy what was left of him?

The creature that the Prophet had so cleverly installed in him had been more than a devil on his shoulder; it had been a carrier for something far worse. If indeed Agnilath wanted David's body as his host, he would need a way to catch the Prime. With so much security and so much strength, trying to overpower David from the outside was a tricky proposition that stood to waste a lot of time and magic. Better to go from the inside...to distract his lovers with violence and fear and then yank the leash, dragging David to him.

It was efficient, smart, played to David's weaknesses. Rather brilliant, all things considered.

Worst of all Agnilath could activate it at any second, as soon as he realized his creature was dead and they were onto him. The longer the Tetrad waited to act on their knowledge the less leverage they had.

"He needs rest," Miranda insisted. "We can lock him up and let him sleep a day. Agnilath won't try to draw him out while the sun's up unless he wants a roasted host. It's a risk, but we risk far more by letting David go while he's this vulnerable. Look at him, Nico!"

David let the sounds flow out again, instead focusing on the sound of his own breath, trying to stay grounded. He had no idea what it was safe to think; they were working on the assumption that the connection would be triggered by feeding, based on how it was attached to him, but they could be wrong. He of all people understood now how a blind eye could cost them all their sight.

A shadow moved before him, and quietly, Deven knelt at his feet, taking his hands and silently finishing the work of clasping the com.

"Your hands are shaking," Deven said softly. "I've never seen them shake before."

"I'll be fine," David replied, just as softly. "I can do this, Dev. There's no more time to lose."

Their eyes met. For a moment it was as if the moment fell away, and with it the decades of pain and loss between them, leaving only those first years they'd spent wound so tightly around each other. No Signet bond, no wedding rings, no promises; only love.

"I can make this right," David told him. "I won't fail you."

Deven touched his face, holding his eyes, searching...then shook his head as if clearing it of fog and turned toward the others. "No," he said sharply.

Miranda and Nico both went silent and stared at him.

"This is ludicrous," Deven said. "I know it's a good plan. I know what's at stake. But it's too big a gamble when the gamble is David's sanity, let alone his life. Miranda's right, Nico--look at him. He can barely dress himself right now much less head for the fight of his life. We're reacting, not acting, and it's going to lead us all to disaster. What happens if our timing is off, and the Prophet gets what he wants? Do we kill David, and ourselves, to stop him?"

"We don't have to," Nico said, looking away. "I can remake the bond, if I need to. I've been studying it. I can make sure we'll survive, if..."

"Don't you dare," Miranda said.

Nico looked over at her, clearly surprised at the quiet menace in her voice.

"If we go through with this and it goes south, don't even think about breaking him off of me. If the alternative is living bound to you, if you're the one who gets him killed...I will gladly go down with my Prime."

Nico had gone pale, but said, in a whisper, "As you will it."

"That's enough...from both of you." Deven stood, squeezing David's hand before turning to the others. "I'm not letting him take a step out of this room until we've talked this over more. Once he's had a little rest David could piss out a better plan than this one. After the last twenty-four hours I don't think--"

Once again, David didn't hear the rest...but this time he didn't tune them out. Instead, he forced himself to his feet and Misted out of the Haven before they could stop him.

Chapter Sixteen

The first thing to do was feed.

The second he came out of the Mist he knew it was the last one he had in him; whether he could control his hunger or not there was no other choice.

Wavering on his feet, David stepped back out of sight, letting his senses come into focus to listen for a human passing by. Even exhausted, a hunter's instincts never wavered. He only had to wait a few minutes.

Hyde Park, a neighborhood not far from UT campus, was a bustling hip community with lots of pedestrian traffic. He'd aimed for a street just on the edge of the area where by now the population would be sparser and someone could vanish without causing a scene. He'd always loved hunting here...lots of healthy young humans, full of vigor and excitement, still young enough to dream of changing the world before it changed them.

It was a strange thing, sometimes, to walk among humans, watching them carry out their short, hurried lives without any idea what might happen to them while they rushed from one place to another. This one might be on her way to break up with a boyfriend; that one might be pondering astrophysics or the latest idiot politician's idiot gaffes. Any of them could carry in their minds a cure for some devastating disease, or a novel that would shift the entire culture.

Before long a young male caught his eye; alone, no dog, distracted by whatever he was listening to on his phone. Fit, but not strong enough to pose a real challenge even to a vampire half-dead on his feet.

The problem, of course, with feeding around here was that most of the young tended to be decent people, or at least had enough potential to work through their silly seasons and grow up to be decent people. If he had to kill, he was better off among the rich.

Luck, or something, favored him for a change. As the boy grew closer David managed an empathic sweep, and realized right away he'd struck gold. This one was a serial rapist--not that he'd ever call himself that, of course. That was what women were for, right? All the other men he interacted with online agreed. Men had to wake up and realize they'd been fooled into trying to please what was, essentially, a brainless toy.

Well, at least if David was going down, he'd take this piece of shit with him.

David was in command of his faculties--at least as far as he knew at the moment--and would in most cases have eased the human's passing if for no other reason than to keep him quiet.

After the week he'd had, however, he was disinclined to be so generous.

He dragged the human away from the street, into a side yard among the overgrown shrubbery of people who had better things to do with money than hire gardeners.

The human died struggling violently, terrified, trying to scream but unable to make a sound. David had never really learned much of Miranda's empathic offensive strategy but it was easy enough to create a private hell for the waste of skin whose death brought back the Prime's strength. The rage that had consumed him while the creature had control was hardly gone, and letting it drive was a delicious feeling, even as it was terrifying.

For all their pretense of sophistication, they were vampires, after all.

How does it feel, boy? How does it feel to be used up and thrown away? To be afraid, but unable to fight a force bigger and stronger than you? How does it feel to be treated like garbage? That's what you are, you pathetic child. Die in the gutter the way you deserve.

He let the body fall to the ground in a heap and leaned back against the fence, breathing hard, smiling. There it was again--that feeling of rightness, and righteousness. Such an easy high if you were willing to commit murder.

David relished the boy's death flooding through his veins, soothing the itching glass-shard hunger and giving him strength. He drew the power through his body, letting it straighten his spine, lift his hanging head, gather his hands into fists. It healed him almost fully; if he were to find another, just one more, just one...all he needed was one more and he'd be at a hundred percent, then nothing the Prophet could do would...

He never completed the thought. Something reached out over the miles and seized his mind where he'd deliberately left it vulnerable. Even as he realized he knew that presence, had felt it in every step from the moment the spell had activated, his will caved before it.

Come and get me, you bastard.

David's body was restored, but underneath the fury and death, his heart felt hollowed out and raw, and sad...so sad. Whether things went as they were supposed to or not, he had a sense--prophetic, perhaps, or just a tiny flash of sanity in a life gone abruptly insane--that some part of him was not going to survive the night.

And so he waited, five minutes into ten, eyes closed, listening for footsteps. He knew Miranda was trying to find him, but the power that gripped him from the inside was blocking her. He couldn't have called for help if he'd wanted to.

He didn't hear footsteps. Instead he heard gunshots.

By the time he realized what kind of bullets were hitting his body, he was already screaming.

*****

"They have him," Miranda whispered, half-sobbing. "Oh, God, they have him. They're hurting him...we have to hurry."

Dev and Nico were both pale, faces tight with strain, as they tried to do what Miranda couldn't and keep David's suffering separate from themselves. But she knew what those bullets felt like...she could feel them as if they were still in her own body...and they were doing it to David, who was still so hurt...he never should have left...

For a moment she wasn't sure she could go on; it had hit so suddenly, as had the realization that she couldn't reach her husband, couldn't comfort him, couldn't even say she was coming. Whatever the Prophet was doing to him, he was alone. That was the worst part, he shouldn't be alone--

"Miranda." Deven tapped her cheek firmly--not a slap, but enough to get her attention. "You can do this. We can do this. Together. I'm not going to let him die--trust me if you trust anything."

He held onto her and kept her attention, breathing with her for a few seconds to steady her before steering her toward the car. "We can do this," he said again. "You are Queen. You can do this."

She nodded. "I can. I can. I am...okay. I can. Let's go."

*****

"At last...we've been waiting for you to arrive."

The four guards who had dragged him into the building and down dozens of stairs to what had to be two or three levels belowground hauled him up to his knees. He could feel blood pouring out of the bullet wounds, as the bullets themselves kept squirming through his flesh, inching their way toward organs, one already rubbing up against a lung...the pain was beyond agony, it was enough to drive anyone insane. He had tortured people to this point over the course of hours, not minutes, and by then they were nearly incoherent, nothing but drool and piss begging to tell every secret they'd ever heard.

Justice for them, he supposed. No more than he deserved by now.

A hand seized his hair and pulled his head up. The blurry world around him was thrown into sharp relief.

"Kai," he whispered hoarsely.

"Don't insult me, boy," the Prophet snapped. "You know my name. Say it."

He fought for a breath against the bullet that had just pierced his lung. "Agnilath."

"Good boy." The Prophet looked at the guards. "Get him on the table."

They all but slung him onto a broad stone slab, and with a few efficient knife swipes, one of them cut through his clothes while another fastened heavy chains to his wrists and ankles as well as another to his neck. A third guard removed his wedding ring, Signet, and wrist com.

The human held the com up to the Prophet, who snorted; the guard produced a hammer, set the com on the stone, and smashed it.

It was hard to tell what Agnilath was actually doing, but it sounded like he was changing clothes off to one side of the room. "This chamber is magically shielded," he said. "Your helpmates won't be able to track your bond in here, and as long as that little toy of yours is out of commission and your phone is dealt with--" David heard another smash, and winced in spite of everything-- "we shouldn't have any aggravating interruptions."

The room was freezing, even without substantial blood loss. His teeth began to chatter; right about then he realized he was naked.

"Well you're a mess," Agnilath said, drawing closer to the table. "I can't have that gorgeous body looking like a carved-up side of beef when I come into you. Would you mind, my love?"

"Of course."

David recognized the face that peered down at him even though he'd never seen it before. Those heathered lavender eyes, the ears, that chin...unmistakable...but not *real.*

Kai had been beautiful; Agnilath was not. Neither was this creature, this parody of an Elf, serene features twisted into a kind of viciousness that was still vacant of any soul, anything approaching humanity. Neither one truly inhabited the body they had stolen; they moved them around like puppets, used them for pleasure and cruelty, but the flesh wasn't theirs.

He understood, then, watching the way they moved, almost naturally but still the slightest bit stilted. As long as they were borrowing bodies they were on borrowed time; their lives, like those of any living thing, could only last as long as the skin that contained them. But both wanted to be gods...wanted true immortality...and for that they needed bodies that could transform with them, something they could fully own.

Why was that him? Why should it be Miranda? While it made sense to him somewhere deep down, it had no logic. Why were their bodies any better than that of a three-hundred-year-old Elven Bard?

"Oh, beloved," Agdilan murmured, "He's exquisite. I can't wait to see you in him."

"Nor can I," Agnilath replied, taking a moment to bite her earlobe. "Especially once you have yours. Imagine it, my darling...in a few hours you can put this one through his paces."

"Mmm." She reached over David's bare skin and held her hands out, palm down; a second later he cried out in pain as he felt the bullets inside his body begin to reverse course, burrowing upward instead of downward. The flesh had closed behind them as his body tried to heal itself, but all that accomplished was making their exit twice as agonizing. He bit down on screams over and over as, one by one, the bullets emerged from his skin, popping out and then rolling harmlessly off onto the floor in a rivulet of his blood.

After the bullets were removed, she ran her fingers over his muscles, the intimacy in the touch making his skin crawl.

"You will be a perfect being," she murmured to him, leaning down to say it in his ear. "When he comes inside you, taking your flesh, your old life will fall away, and you will be what you were meant to be all along. Don't fight it, beautiful one...this is fate, long foretold. We've been waiting for you for so long."

Another pair of hands joined hers, and the two Firstborn touched him all over, caressing, gauging his reaction. Luckily for what remained of his pride, the disgust he felt at what they were doing was more than enough to deny them the pleasure of watching him get hard in his humiliation.

It was so like what they'd done to Nico...except without the surgery...keeping him weak, stripping his defenses, debasing him as thoroughly as they could. It was what they loved...he'd thought that the motive for torturing Nico was to figure out if an Elf's body could hold a Firstborn, but this was the truth. They wanted to do this because they *enjoyed* it. They existed to destroy, but even more, to blaspheme...to take the creations of their Mother, Persephone, and defile them. He didn't want to imagine what the ritual to take over a body was like.

The thought of what they'd done to Nico, and to Kai, and even to Deven's mother now, brought the first flush of something other than pain and fear. Not only had they gotten their filth all over the Elves, they fully intended to do the same to Miranda...

Like hell you will.

Agnilath was smiling, though, watching his face. "Look," he said. "He thinks he can fight this."

Agdilan chuckled. "Poor thing. I do like his spirit."

"You didn't have much chance to see him in action…too bad, really. He's truly the finest example of vampire kind ever to exist, with the possible exception of his woman. Look at this craftsmanship…the one I'm wearing has such dexterous hands, but imagine *these*. Such games we'll have."

"I've seen her," Agdilan answered with a nod. "She's magnificent. What a goddess we will make of her, my love. The old whore and all her ravens could not do better. And with the power she already commands the Godspell is as good as ours."

"That's enough talk of such things," Agnilath said. "We can work on the search once we're finished here tonight."

She smiled in a way David supposed was meant to be flirtatious, and moved aside, leaving Agnilath standing over David's naked body, looking possessively from head to foot and back again.

"I'd like to feed you before we move forward, just so I can be sure you'll survive, but it's more important to keep you docile for the time being. You see…" He picked up something heavy--a book, David realized, as thick and worn as the Codex. "What I've been doing with my bodies so far is really only a partial transfer. Each time I've gotten closer to taking full possession, but they've all given out on me in the middle of the transition. I even tried having this one turned into a vampire once I'd taken it over, to buy myself some time."

David stared up at that face, wishing he could get past the mask and speak to Kai, even for a second. "I'm sorry," he said weakly, trying to push the thought inward. "I'm sorry."

"Don't bother. There's no coming back from where he's at…or at least that's what I thought. I have to say, your little bitch surprised me. No one's ever pulled out one of my hungry ghosts before. If she'd had more time she might even have saved that pointless human life. Such a waste of power! But that's the problem, you see; even as a vampire this body is too frail for me. Elves, simpering little twits that they are, are strong, but they're not made of our kind. What I needed was something close to the source…something touched by, transformed by, the old whore Herself, that had Her energy and Her power in its veins. You…well,

I just had to wait until I was sure She'd touched you all…because then, if I can claim one of you…"

"You can have us all," David affirmed, only able to summon harsh, ragged whispers. "All of our power, through the two of us."

"It won't take long once I have you."

A moment of pure, golden relief: Agnilath didn't know Nico could split the bond, or at least that he could do it quickly enough to stop the Firstborn taking over the entire Circle.

Not much longer now…surely not much longer. *Wait for it. Wait for it. You can do this.*

"I can make this right," he told Deven.

But even Deven hadn't believed him.

"How do you want him, my love?" Agdilan asked. "I'll have the men get him into position."

Agnilath smiled, this one pure and cruel. "What would you rather watch? You had to miss out on the last one, so it's lady's choice."

"I want to be able to watch his face," she said silkily, running her hand down David's chest. "And your face, when the moment hits…those ridiculous purple eyes going blank while these lovely blue ones become yours. Both at once."

"Very well." Agnilath gestured to the soldiers, who moved forward again and started shifting the chains around, jerking David's arm and leg over until he was flat on his stomach.

He heard clanking; there were wheels attached to the chains, like a rack, but these were designed to move his limbs. After so much blood loss he couldn't break them, and even at his best they would have been a challenge.

It wasn't until they locked into place, leaving him bound on his knees, and the neck chain was hauled downward so hard his face struck the stone altar violently enough to fracture his cheekbone, that cold fear gripped him.

The Firstborn had both gone silent; the only sound was his panting breath as panic raced through his body with the realization of what exactly was about to happen. He felt something hot and wet being dribbled on his head--blood, though whose he couldn't guess. Meanwhile, Agdilan began to read something from their Codex. The language was like nothing he knew, had no antecedent he could attach to it with his mind whirling like it was.

There was a knock--hesitant, faint.

The Prophet was standing by the altar, his hands on the knot that held his black robe closed. He hissed to the guard, "What did I say about interruptions? Take care of that!"

The guard nodded, looking petrified, and darted to the door. After a moment of scuffling and a faint cry of pain, he returned, and said very quietly, "My Lord…it seems there's a disturbance at the perimeter. Nothing serious, someone asking for…"

"For *what?"*

The guard shrank back, stuttering, but got himself together enough to say, "For you, my Lord, they asked for you…by name. They wanted to know if…"

Agnilath seized the man by his neck and shook him. "Out with it, you sniveling animal, what did they want?"

Every word stammered, the man answered, "She…wanted to know if…you had time…to hear about…"

David closed his eyes and smiled. *Thank you.*

"…our lady Persephone…and Her plan for you."

Taking a deep breath, David summoned all the strength he could to "tap" mentally on the com implanted behind his ear…the real one…and he spoke as clearly as he could:

"This is Prime David Solomon, Star-One, issuing order Sigma Four-Two. All Elite converge on this signal and *fire at will."*

Within ten seconds, somewhere high above, he suddenly heard distant, soft popping sounds…rushing feet…shouting…

He saw the rage on Agnilath's face and couldn't stop himself from laughing.

"My Lord, the entire building is being overrun!" one of the guards yelled over the growing din. "They came from everywhere--and they have *guns!"*

Agdilan, already near panic, seized the Prophet's arm. "What do we do? There's no way out of this building--"

Agnilath struck her, sending her staggering into the wall. "Get back to the book!" he snarled.

He reached down and took David by the hair, forcing David's eyes to meet his. "We'll just have to hurry, then," he said with a cold, cruel smile.

The giddy relief David had felt turned back into ice. Out of pure animal instinct he started to struggle against the chains, against the hand on his jaw that then slammed his head back down to the stone surface, sending pain and stars through vision that greyed in and out.

"I know the atmosphere isn't ideal," the Prophet said, "but try to enjoy it...it's the last thing you'll ever get to feel."

******

The Elite cleared a path for her, and Miranda shoved her way through the battle into the building where they'd tracked the Prime. He was several levels underground, and between her and him were several hundred human soldiers--the first wave of which was armed with those poisoned bullets.

Historically vampires had little need for guns. What use was a bullet against their kind?

But while Morningstar's soldiers may have been brainwashed, cursed, and suicidal...they were still mortal.

Swords had their place. But not here, not tonight.

Only the outermost sentries had the magicked bullets, though, and once inside the building there was far less need to be careful. She ordered her Elite to switch to close-quarters tactics and charged ahead.

"Should we keep them alive?" one of her lieutenants had asked dubiously. "In case they can be set free?"

The look she leveled on him gave her answer, but just to be clear, she said, "No quarter."

It didn't take long to see, even as distracted as she was with her singular goal, that there was no other way it could have played out. The people that the Prophet had cursed at the benefit had been under a different spell designed for a different purpose. The one used on these poor bastards was irreversible, at least, not by any power she possessed. Whomever they had been was dead already; their bodies were just shells holding their master's orders.

Perhaps later she could pretend she'd cared; at the moment it was convenient. All they were to her right now was an obstacle between her and her Prime.

As she rounded a corner to the stairwell, something hit her--a wave of power, the same crawling oily evil that had made up the creatures she'd burned away. This was ten times stronger, and it was growing...reaching...

Suddenly fear stronger than she could fight grabbed her around the throat, as did a horrible pain in her lower body...she cried out in terror, her body reacting as if she had gone back in time to that alley, that night so long ago, dear God was someone using empathy on her or--

No. No no no--

Miranda's vision went red with rage, and she drove herself past the horror, past the pain; she had her sword out before she even reached the stairs and jumped down over the rail, falling down the stairwell to bypass the teams of Elite grappling with the remaining humans.

Her feet hit the ground, as did four others, and she barely had time to register that Nico and Deven were with her before another blast of power hit them, nearly knocking them down. It was building--and when it reached the peak, it would be too late--

The three of them threw themselves at the heavy double doors at the end of the hall, where several Elite were already trying to break it down. The bodies of the door guards littered the hallway.

"Fight him!" she cried. "David, we're here! Fight!"

He was so tired, and so hurt...the fear, the humiliation, guilt...they all assaulted her as the Prophet assaulted him, and there was no time--

"Miranda!"

She didn't know where the voice was coming from, but she knew it. "Cora?"

"Reach for me, my Lady! Reach for all of us!" The distant Queen's mental voice was strong, firm...and *angry*.

Yes.

Miranda opened herself to the Circle, drawing in their strength on her breath, filling her lungs with Cora's fire...

...and she exhaled through her fingers...

...the door didn't just catch fire, it *exploded.* Every inch of it burst into flame and turned to ash in less than two seconds, the whole thing falling under her outstretched hand.

The Queen didn't give herself time to digest what she saw when she entered the room.

All she saw were targets.

She saw the Prophet's face...and his expression of pure bliss, of triumph, would haunt her nightmares for the rest of her days, as she knew she had to be too late, that--

But when his body jerked forward, it wasn't to finish his ritual.

A wooden stake burst through his sternum, slammed so hard into his back it threw him off David's bound, bleeding body and onto the floor, a mindless animal scream filling the air as the power of the ritual was broken before it could be completed.

Agnilath's face was a rictus of hatred and violence. He scrabbled forward, naked and grotesque, gripping the stake and trying to pull it, finally getting his bloodstained fingers around it.

But before he could, Nico stomped hard on his shoulder, forcing him back down onto the stake and impaling him over again.

Whatever the Prophet was, he needed a body. The one he wanted had been denied him and the one he was in shuddered hard, then lay still.

On the other side of the room, Agdilan screamed in grief and fury and tried to fight her way free of Deven.

Deven was staring at the woman, seeing his mother somewhere in that ghastly face, perhaps...but only a moment of regret touched his face before he let her go.

She started to lunge at Miranda, but Deven reached into his coat and pulled out something Miranda would never have expected him to carry, no matter how they'd armed the Elite tonight:

A 9mm.

A single shot to the head, and the monster fell.

Silence.

"Clear the room," Deven said quietly.

The Elite all backed out, eyes averted, leaving the Tetrad alone.

Miranda wasted no time on the fallen bodies. She dropped her sword, pulled off her coat, and slung it over David.

He whimpered but didn't move.

She could hear Nico sobbing softly, though whether it was over David or Kai, she didn't know or care; all she could see, all she knew, was her beloved's torn flesh, the chains binding him in obscene angles, the degradation of it beyond anything she could process. She fumbled with the chains, trying to break them with brute strength; a second later the first wrist manacle went slack as Deven got to the winches that controlled them and released one after another.

Dev joined her and together they lowered David onto the altar, removing the shackles, the neck chain. They carefully stretched out his limbs, their own hands shaking.

She heard Dev call on his com for blankets and blood, but all she saw was David's face. He looked so young…so sad.

He moaned softly and his eyes fluttered against the incongruously peaceful candlelight, but if he was conscious it was half at best, caught in some kind of feverish horror he could still see.

"Is it him?" Nico asked from the floor where he had Kai's head in his lap. "Were we too late?"

"Of course it's him," Miranda snapped, finding enough of her voice to croak at him. "He's fine."

"You can't be sure--"

"Go to hell!" she cried, wanting nothing more than to claw the Elf's eyes out.

"Miranda," Deven said gently, "Easy. He just wants you to be safe, is all."

"You can go to hell too!" she sobbed. "Look what happened…look what we did to him, Deven. *Look what we did.*"

"I know…I know. But he's safe now. They're gone."

"No…"

None of them recognized the voice, and they all started, even Miranda through the haze of her grief; she covered David's body with hers and went into defensive mode, ready to attack anyone who came at her.

But it was the woman on the floor who'd spoken. The one with the bullet in her head.

"They're not gone," she whispered. "Please…"

Deven knelt by her. "What is this?" He slid a finger into the Elf's mouth and cursed.

"Vampire," he said, looking up at Miranda. "Bastards must have turned them--it's lucky Nico had that stake."

He stared down at the woman who had once been his mother. "What do you mean they aren't gone?"

"They can…come back." Her strength was starting to return as her body pushed the bullet out of her skull. "They'll be trapped…between worlds…for a while, but they can find another way in. And once they've been inside you…they can find you…take you. We'll never be free."

She reached out and grasped Deven's arm, her eyes pleading. "Kill me," she whispered, weeping. "Please...my son...if you ever loved me, if you love the world you know...don't let her have me again. If you knew...the things she did...I cannot live with that, not in this...this thing...I am now. Please...have mercy on me."

"Mercy is for the Hallowed," Deven said coldly. "Not for assassins, and not for your son."

"Please...and have mercy on him too...kill him now, before it's too late. Before *he* comes back, before the one you loved is nothing but a beast. Kill him...kill me...please..."

He stood, and for a second Miranda thought he was going to spare her, but he only wanted enough space to draw Ghostlight.

"Farewell Mother," he said. "May you rest at peace in Theia's arms...if She'll have you."

He swung the sword, and she plead no more.

Miranda returned her attention to David, and Deven and Nico both joined her, helping ease the Prime toward the edge of the table, pushing as much healing energy into him as they could.

The Elite found two clean blankets, and she and the boys wrapped David in one and then spread out the other under him to use as a litter. As they worked, Miranda caught Nico's eye and said, "If you so much as *hint* that we should--"

Nico's eyes widened, then filled with tears. "No, no...never. I swear to you, Miranda, I will never let that thing near him again...I will keep him safe no matter what it costs. I swear it."

Miranda gestured for the Elite to come and help get David out to the car; as she straightened, numb inside, she saw his Signet and wedding ring on the lectern where the Prophet's book had been. The book itself was on the floor where Agdilan had dropped it.

She wanted so badly to fall apart, to go to her knees screaming, but she didn't. As she had the night of the benefit, she slowly straightened her spine, squared off her shoulders, and reached up to touch her Signet for reassurance.

Her Elite were watching. There was clean-up to do here. The work did not, would not ever stop for them. It was who they were.

It was who she was.

She picked up David's Signet and ring and tucked them safely in her pocket. "Lieutenant," she said, "I want this book in containment and delivered to Hunter. Have them put it in the vault for now--no one goes near it until I give the okay. Then have this building processed and burned, standard scene protocol. Contact APD and AFD and ensure they keep the area clear. All data routed through the Prime's server, copies sent to Hunter for full analysis. Have at least six of the dead humans sent to Hunter for full autopsy."

"As you will it, my Lady." He bowed and darted away, already relaying her orders.

"Harlan," she said into her com, "I need you at the front entrance."

"Already there, my Lady."

She gestured for two of the other Elite to come and help them carry the Prime. "No one is to touch him," she ordered. "For your own safety keep your hands on the blanket. He's badly injured and may react on instinct at physical contact."

Both Elite nodded, their faces and actions professional even though she could feel their worry. She knew that by the time any of them had gotten in the room it was difficult to tell exactly what had happened, which would save David that much humiliation later on; word would doubtless get out, but for now at least all anyone knew for sure was that he was hurt and unconscious. That in itself was a rare and frightening event, but at least it wasn't unheard of.

She held on to her sense of determined purpose long enough to get to the exit. Harlan was in the SUV, and had laid the far back seat down, so Miranda climbed in first and pulled David's shoulders until she was cross-legged with his head in her lap.

The boys got in the middle seat. Neither seemed able to look at her, or even each other. They were all in shock.

"Back to the Haven, my Lady?" Harlan asked, voice tight.

"Yes. Thank you."

As the SUV pulled away from the building and sped along the Austin streets toward home, the Queen stroked her husband's hair, closed her eyes against tears, and began to sing.

*****

"Strange how hard it rains now
Rows and rows of big dark clouds
But I'm still alive underneath this shroud
Rain..."

She sang to him for hours, and then all day, waiting.

As the afternoon waned, and nothing changed, her vigil became a fearful one...they had no way to know how much damage the ritual had done until he woke. Apart from the violation he'd suffered-- which was trauma enough--who knew what that spell did to its victim? Did it destroy the soul inside the body? Send it into hiding? Was there anything left of the man they knew?

And if there wasn't...what then?

And if there *was*...what then?

The sun had dipped below the horizon, but only her sense of smell told her that--it also told her it was raining. The world outside was near freezing, and the whole city would probably be covered in ice.

It felt the same inside the Haven. Everything was held frozen, suspended between one reality and the next. Across the globe there were two other Havens in the same holding pattern...waiting...

Miranda sang.

She didn't know what else to do.

Deven joined her after dusk. He tried to convince her to sleep.

She shook her head. There would be time for rest. She had a watch to keep.

A little while later, she looked up to see Nico hovering uncertainly at the door. He looked as awful as she felt, and she knew he hadn't slept either. The sorrow and guilt in his face and in his energy...an aura usually so alive and comforting...made it impossible to be angry at him, even if she'd wanted to be.

But they were in this together. She knew that much. There was no place for blame in this room, not now--they all had to hold onto each other if they were going to make it through.

She held out her hand.

Tears slipped down his face as he came forward and took it. He and Deven sat with her on the bed. Miranda sang, and sometimes Deven added a harmony. Nico stared, and cried.

The Weaver was wearing an elegantly tooled leather cuff that she recognized--the Elite must have found it somewhere in the building. It had a design of Elvish musical notation that she knew was one of Kai's first official compositions as a Bard. The cuff was a traditional gift for a graduate of the Bardic House.

She had spent all the tears she had for the time being, but sorrow nearly choked out her voice until she let the song she was wandering through turn into the one Nico was wearing.

Finally, perhaps an hour later, she felt something change.

She didn't let herself react until she finished the verse she was singing, and looked down, almost afraid of what she might see.

Dark eyelashes lifted. Deep blue eyes touched, and held, hers.

She didn't speak, but stretched out alongside him, gingerly taking his hand. The boys stayed sitting up, keeping their distance.

"Hey," she said in a whisper, squeezing his fingers. After a pause she asked, "Do you know where you are?"

He drew a shaky breath, licked lips long dry from sleep and said softly back, "Home."

She nodded. "Yeah. You're home. Safe."

"Safe. With you."

Miranda touched his face with her free hand, smiled a little. "Yes."

He shut his eyes tightly for a second, and when they opened again there were tears in them. "Nico?"

The Elf's breath hitched in surprise. "Yes...I'm here."

He leaned down where David could see him.

"I'm sorry...about Kai. I tried...I tried to push him out. To fight back. But..."

Nico nodded, his own tears falling on David and Miranda's joined hands. He leaned down farther until his forehead touched David's. "I know, my love. I know. But he's at peace now. Perhaps we will see him in the Forest of Spirits."

"I tried," David whispered again, lip trembling. "But it hurt so much. I'm sorry...I'm sorry..."

Miranda pulled his face to her shoulder and held onto him as he broke down, still murmuring "I'm sorry" over and over. She held him close and reached for Nico and Deven along the bond, drawing their energy in around her and, by extension, around David, though at first neither touched him directly. The Elves lay down with her, Nico snuggled up against her back, Deven on David's other side with fingers very lightly touching the Prime's wrist, but it wasn't until David himself reached out to them with desperate hands that they gave themselves to him as well...and the Tetrad wept, while the sky above the Haven seemed to do the same.

Chapter Seventeen

"Such a shame we don't have time for the niceties...I know the Elf enjoyed it much more than you will..."

The abyss crawled over him, eating away every inch of who he was, like acid, burning inside, those sticky, slimy tentacles of black energy twisting and driving deeper, white-hot pain destroying thought and reason, leaving only the emptiness...there was nothing behind that mask of evil, nothing but a void, no soul and no joy and nothing but being torn in two, torn apart, feeling himself devoured one cell at a time. The blackness seeped into his skin like sweat, the way a cool rain should but a chemical burn, lye, as if his brain was bubbling and turning to *oh god stop, please, I can't end this way, make him stop, help me...*

"Fight him! We're here! Fight!"

There was nothing to fight with, but he tried. He reached for everything left of himself, everything that mattered, everything that the acid and the driving, driving, driving agony couldn't shatter into dust.

Perhaps it made no difference. Perhaps it bought him half a second. But something was enough. Something made the door explode, the stake ram home, that blackness that was a heartbeat from searing the world away miss, by inches, thrown clear, *it's over*.

But it wasn't over. It would never be over. The Elf woman had said as much. And the door had been opened...yes, slammed shut just in time, but still...*he* had been inside, touched everything, left his stink and his fingerprints. Everything was filthy, bruised...marked.

He woke shaking. Even with the warmth of blankets and bodies around him, the fireplace burning low, he was freezing.

Nausea turned his stomach into a stormy sea. He managed to get free of the others, out of the bed, and into the bathroom before what little blood he'd had came back in a rush.

Cold…the bathroom tiles were cold against his forehead, like the stone had been cold, but everything else had been burning hot, flesh tearing over and over again…

One hand managed to reach up and flush the toilet, but he stayed on the floor for a long time, trembling too hard to concentrate on getting up.

The stone of his Signet clinked faintly against the tile. How was the stone even alight anymore? How could anything fashioned by a loving Creatrix bear to contact his skin?

Why were the others there, in the bed--how could they not feel it? How could they stand being bound to something so diseased…so…

Disgusting. You can still feel him, can't you…that power, and how at the end…you wanted it, didn't you, that oblivion. You wanted to give up and let him have you. Is that why you didn't fight harder? It started to feel good, didn't it, and such an attractive idea, to let it all go, to just…cease.

There was no way to know how long he lay there curled up in a ball on the floor, trapped in the hell of just breathing, remembering…but if the others found him in here they'd see it, they'd know…

Too late.

"David," came a soft, gentle voice, "Look at me."

I can't. I can't look you in the face. I can't.

As he had only…God, had it been days? A thousand years? Minutes?...before, Deven knelt beside him. He was wearing the forest green Elven lounging robe Nico had given him for Yule…with his white hair, and his ears, there was no way anyone would think he was anything other than an Elf now. Even his energy had changed subtly in the last few days, and just now it was nothing but loving, wanting only to heal.

David shrank back. "Don't touch me."

"I won't. Not without your permission."

"Go back to bed…I'm fine."

A lifted eyebrow. "The hell you are."

"It doesn't matter. There's nothing you can do."

"Perhaps not. But I know Someone who can. Come with me."

The thought of walking through the Haven…of the Elite seeing him like this, this…broken thing…no. Never. He'd die here first.

"Oh come on now," Deven said with a smile. "Since when do you walk anywhere?"

He shut his eyes, and felt the room shifting around them; curious how Deven's Mist felt completely different from his own, or Miranda's. There had been a time he might have wanted to learn more, to study the phenomenon and see if it held true across Signets.

The ritual room where the Circle had met on the Solstice, where Stella had died, materialized around them. For a moment he feared there would still be blood everywhere, but of course the Cloister had cleaned and magically cleansed the room. The altar items Stella had left had been polished and arranged just as she'd had them. There was even a seven-day novena candle burning.

They were kneeling in the middle of the diagram that Stella and Nico had so carefully painted on the floor. There was still power there…even in his exhausted, weakened, broken state he could feel it.

"Close your eyes," Deven told him. "You're safe here."

"Everyone keeps saying that," he muttered.

"And it's true every time."

"Not anymore. Nowhere is safe…not even with you."

"You're safe here."

The words came with the light scent of jasmine on a night breeze, and he lifted his head.

Almost instantly he felt something inside his chest unclench. All around them, the Forest of Spirits spread out to the farthest horizons, and he could hear the quiet rustle of movement among the trees, the distant call of an owl.

"I don't think I can walk," he whispered.

Deven touched his face…and here, right now, he didn't shrink back from the touch. "You don't need to, my darling. Look up."

Fear returned. What would She say? She had warned him the night of the Solstice that the path he was on was walking straight toward tragedy. She had not given him orders, not forbade him to kill, but She had warned him the consequences would be dire.

Surely what he was feeling now was a just reward for his foolishness.

A hand touched the top of his head...larger, longer-fingered than Deven's. Dev moved back and bowed his head.

"My child," he heard Her say softly. "I am so sorry."

How he wanted to hate Her...She had made them, all of them. She had brought the Circle together and set them on their path.

But he had made his own choices. And if not for Her he wouldn't have any of what had come before...so much love in his life, and so much rightness. He would have died a human in obscurity and never known such happiness was possible...even if it was all over with...She had given him so much.

"Can You help me?" he asked.

She did as Deven had, and knelt beside him. He started to protest at the idea of Her on Her knees in the dirt, but She gave him a look of faint amusement coupled with affection that reminded him so much of Miranda he almost, almost smiled.

She opened Her arms to him, and he fled into them with a cry.

He felt great dark wings encircling him, Her love a fortress, wrapping him in power beyond any he could comprehend. No one here would judge him, no one would see; as Deven had said, he was safe here.

Finally he felt like he could let everything fall, throw down his shield...he wept for what felt like hours, giving Her all the shame and rage and helplessness, the guilt...so many mistakes, and such a high price paid for them.

"I can give you a choice," She said after a while. "There is only so much even I can do to your part of the Web without completely unmaking you. I can take away the memory of what happened...of Agnilath's presence in your mind, of his violation of your body. But to do so is to risk taking away part of who you are. You would lose something of yourself forever, be diminished...but your dreams would be peaceful, your memory untroubled by what you have endured."

He swallowed hard. He wanted that...too much. "Or?"

"Or I can set a seal upon you, one that would block any attempt on his part to enter you again. It is true that they are not gone forever...Agnilath could return, and he would find you no matter where you hid. The vengeance he would exact before consuming you forever would be terrible. But I can place such protection upon you that even he could not breach it...ever. You and you alone would have the power to undo it. You would still remember everything, but you would know you are safe from it happening again."

He closed his eyes, leaning against Her, feeling so tired...imagining what it would be like to live with this...to live broken, perhaps forever, to force the others to deal with the wreck of who he'd been...

"You will heal," She told him, stroking his hair. "And you will become even stronger. As long as you avoid the mistakes you have already made...let your beloveds in, let them help you, keep reaching out instead of shutting down...it will be painful, and may take a long time, but it will be worth it in the end."

"I'm immortal," he sighed. "Time, I have."

After a long moment, he lifted his head and met Her eyes. "Door number two, please," he said, trying to sound certain but mostly just managing resigned. "Best not to meddle too much with a mind this brilliant."

She smiled and kissed his forehead. "Then sleep," She told him. "When you wake it will be done."

He didn't think he could possibly fall asleep, but he needn't have worried; the night around them lapped at his mind softly, drawing him down into the dark--a darkness that was dreamless and quiet, warm, and loving.

"Remember that you are loved," She told him just as he drifted off. "And remember that I am proud of you, my storm...and remember that you are not alone."

*****

Funny how winning a war felt so much like losing one.

On the outside life went on and there was much to celebrate. With the threat of Morningstar gone--and the surviving Primes had reported that attacks on them and their territories had ceased that very night--the Shadow World could breathe again, and districts all over the world had reopened. The Elite had their hands full with all the rabble-rousing those first few weeks.

Meanwhile word was trickling in that new converts had swamped the existing Cloisters of the Order of Elysium; free now to touch the lives of Her children again Persephone wasted no time letting them all know She was back.

And perhaps most surprisingly, Kalea and the rest of the Enclave heard from the far-flung remaining Elven sanctuaries, which were all still safe and sound; offers came in for the refugee Elves of Avilon to leave Austin and relocate to the other sanctuaries...but with a handful of exceptions, the Elves stayed.

The ones who departed were all of the older generation who'd been the most stubborn about the new settlement, which meant that New Avilon would be almost entirely populated with younger Elves who were ready for a new world no longer so disconnected from Earth.

Where the Haven of the West had once stood there would be something new that was, at the same time, ancient: a partnership between the Order of Elysium and the Elves, with the vampires under Deven's leadership standing guard over the forest.

Nico finished building the Gate from Austin to California, then set to work on the others connecting the Havens, though now there wasn't as much urgency to get them made. The Circle members didn't need to hurry to each other's homes; if they used the Gates now it was to spend time together in peace.

Peace.

Nico knew it wouldn't last, and that the Shadow World had gotten off lightly, for now. They had averted the cataclysm that had ended the first Circle's existence and had stopped a global war before it could spill over into the mortal world...for now. He knew, with both the certainty of a Consort and the fatalism that seemed to dog his steps nowadays, that it wasn't over, that Agnilath would return...it was just a question of how long they could avoid it.

The Morningstar Codex was safely locked away at Hunter Development while Novotny ran tests on it to be sure it couldn't exert any sort of influence on humans or vampires around it. They all expected the book to have some kind of magical traps and protections on it...but so far it was turning out to be just a book, which made Nico worry even more. They knew nothing about this Codex--who had found it? Who had begun the rituals that brought Agnilath back? Was there another one out there that could fall into malevolent hands?

Deven turned the Red Shadow's operatives to a new purpose and had them investigating Morningstar's origins; they were undercover and listening everywhere, trying to figure out where the story had begun. So far it had been frustratingly fruitless; no one could even say for sure what had happened to the remaining Morningstar soldiers. With the exception of the building where Agnilath and Agdilan had been living, which was combed for evidence and then razed, Morningstar had vanished.

No, it wasn't over. They had a respite...one hard-earned and desperately needed.

Outside the Haven life returned to normal. Inside, well, life went on.

Nothing was the same. For just a little while, the Tetrad had been happy in their unusual life together, even with the world going mad outside their doors. Now where there had been laughter there was silence; where there had been passionate lovemaking there were flashbacks and nightmares and, eventually, withdrawal. There were no blocks on the bond, but there was constant strain and worry.

Nico found himself hesitating outside yet another door, unsure whether to knock or flee. This time, however, he knew there would be no dancing in the firelight, no tumbling into bed--if for no other reason than this wasn't Deven's suite, it was the Batcave.

He steeled himself and knocked.

"Come in."

The sight before him should have been comforting in its normalcy. The Prime of the Southern United States and assorted other territories was in his place at the desk, all the computer systems of the Haven and communications with the rest of the planet around him chirping and beeping happily. He wore his reading glasses and a t-shirt bearing the logo of someone named Doctor Strange; his Signet shone atop the shirt, its ornate setting a perfect contradiction and yet perfectly fitting. He was barefoot, legs crossed in the chair. It was so normal, on the surface, that it broke Nico's heart.

"Yes?" David asked without looking up.

"If you're busy," Nico began, but David shook his head.

"No more than usual. What do you need?"

There was no getting used to the lifelessness in his voice. He was perfectly functional; he had gone back to governing his own and all the other vacant territories as before without missing a beat. He spent long nights walking around Austin reminding the Shadow

World that its leader was still very much in power, and now with the additional legends surrounding the Tetrad--whatever had happened, they had defeated the Firstborn and saved vampire kind--he was as terrifying as he was reassuring to his people.

The shield Persephone had built around him was flawless, made of the magical equivalent of steel; Nico had marveled at it from a distance, watching the energy of the Tetrad bond flowing in and out of it unobstructed though absolutely nothing else got in or out without David's consent. He was a fortress, surrounded by high stone walls...and no one saw behind them.

No one.

"Nothing," Nico said. "I'm just checking up on you. No one's seen you for days, except Miranda."

"Then perhaps you should talk to her."

"I want to talk to you."

David pushed the mouse away from his hand, removed his glasses, and swiveled the chair toward him. He cleaned the lenses on his shirt and asked, "What do you want to talk about?"

Nico stammered, suddenly caught off guard by the coldness in his stare. "I...I just want to know if you're okay, I guess. If I can do anything to help you."

"Am I okay. Well, let's see. I have to have a babysitter when I feed to make sure I don't murder any more innocents. Deven's taken over the New Moon killing for all of us and I'm mostly living off bagged blood because I'm too afraid of myself to hunt like an adult. Every time I try to have sex I end up screaming. I never know if my emotions are real or not. My wife thinks I need a therapist, but oddly enough qualified professionals for this sort of thing are thin on the ground. One of my lovers looks enough like my nightmares that I can barely look at him without having a panic attack. I'm shielded against anything like this happening again but the problem is it *already happened.* So to sum up I am barely holding it together and the only thing that keeps my mind from flying into pieces is work. What else do you need to know?"

Nico looked away. "I'm sorry."

"Fine. Anything else?"

The Elf shook his head, ashamed that he had even asked; coming here had been selfish, a mistake. He was trying to reassure himself that David didn't hate him or blame him, but it didn't really matter--Nico blamed himself. He had driven David to surrender to

Agnilath, and by the time he realized what he was doing it was too late.

"I'll go," Nico said softly. "I'm sorry to bother you."

He backed toward the door and had almost escaped when he heard, "Nico."

Holding back tears, he stopped.

There was a pause before David said, "You didn't hesitate."

"To what?"

David wasn't looking at him, but sat head bowed, eyes closed. "You sent me there to save Kai. But when you walked into that room you didn't hesitate for a second--you killed him knowing you were killing your brother too. Why?"

"Why?" Helpless, not understanding the question, Nico said through his tears, "He was hurting you. Kai would never do...anything like that. Even if he had come back he wouldn't have been able to live with himself. But that wasn't even why, it...it's awful, I know, but...at that moment, I didn't care who it was. I would have used that stake even if Kai had been there himself, because...it's you. *You.* Nothing else mattered right then. It didn't matter if I could save Kai. I had to save you."

Silence. Neither could seem to look at the other.

A breath later, David cleared his throat softly and took a deep breath. Nico could feel him struggling, shield or no shield. He reached up to the keyboard again, and brought up some kind of schematic on the big screen.

Nico took that as his cue to leave, but to his amazement David said, "I could...since you're here, I could use your help with something...if you have time."

Nico froze, hope and fear both racing for his heart, shoving each other out of the way to get there first. "Um...of course."

He moved closer, and David gestured, drawing one of the other chairs over behind the desk...a foot or so away, but nearby. Nico wiped his eyes and sat down, heart hammering.

"This is something new I'm trying for the sensor grid, a way to make the entire system more organic--some AI adjustments that will help extend the grid over larger areas. But I'm...I'm running into trouble at a certain distance."

Nico nodded and fixed his attention on the screen, refusing to think about anything but what was in front of him...and beside him. "Let's see what we can do, then."

*****

"One thing I shall certainly miss about this place is central heat," Kalea said as she finished changing Inaliel and set the baby on the floor. "Perhaps Nicolanai can come up with some magical alternative for us."

"Or you could get electricity," Deven pointed out from his seat at the fire in what had been Nico's room. "It would be easy to run it down to you."

Inaliel had, in the last week or so, apparently decided crawling was for puppies; according to Kalea one evening she had simply put her hands on a chair, pulled herself up, and was now waddling around the room quite freely. She was still clumsy and had trouble coordinating all her limbs, but that didn't stop her from toddling after Pywacket, Jean Grey, and Astela with giggly abandon.

Kalea chuckled, watching her drop onto her diapered bottom with a grunt and reach for the stuffed otter Deven had given her. "Somehow even with all we have adjusted to of late I doubt what remains of the Enclave would be able to go that far. Perhaps I can convince them to have it run into one of the common buildings so when we gather in the worst weather it can be in greater comfort. We shall see."

"Well if you can't convince them, no one can."

Inaliel pushed herself back onto her feet and carried her otter over to Deven; she gestured "up!" but before he could help her he had to help the otter. Deven smiled and set the toy on the arm of the chair, then lifted the baby onto his lap. She sat facing him, grinning and pointing at his ears.

"I know, I know," he said. "Better?"

A decisive nod.

Kalea had gone to the bathroom to wash her hands, but when she came back she said, "I wanted to tell you I'm sorry about Aila. Not only that she is gone, but that you had to kill her, and that she never had a chance to know you."

Deven had steadfastly avoided thinking about that too much, but now, he smiled a little and kept his eyes on the baby. "Thank you, Kalea. I still wonder if..."

"If your Queen might have been able to save her? Perhaps. But would she have been saved? I sincerely doubt she would have had the strength to live as a vampire. And as you said, your own

Goddess offered to strip the memory of a few moments of Agnilath from your Prime. Imagine being forced to live with weeks of it...knowing everything that had been done in your body while you were helpless to stop it."

Deven knew who she was really thinking about...those tears would never have been for Elendala. "I'm sorry about Kai."

Kalea nodded and wiped her eyes. "As am I. But I am glad, at least, that he is no longer prisoner, and that he is free...and perhaps we will meet again, in time."

Inaliel turned and wriggled into the crook of Deven's arm, wrapping herself around him and clinging like the world's most adorable barnacle, sighing happily as she patted his shoulder. But after a minute, something seemed to occur to her; she sat back, looking at him keenly.

"Aila," she said carefully.

Deven's heart skipped--did she know? "That's your mother's name," he said quietly to her.

She nodded. "Gone?"

He looked helplessly at Kalea, who nodded. "Yes, Inaliel...we talked about it, remember? She was badly hurt, and could not be healed. She died."

Another nod. "Better now?"

"Yes," Deven said. "The Goddess is holding her now, safe, and healed."

"Goddess!" Inaliel's eyes lit up. "Bird lady!"

Deven looked at Kalea again. "Bird lady?"

This time, though, Kalea looked bewildered. "I have no idea."

"Does Theia appear with birds as well?" Deven asked. "I don't remember."

"No," Kalea said. "At least not with any one kind. What bird lady are you talking about, Inaliel?"

The child frowned as if they were both idiots and said, "Black birds."

Deven's eyebrows shot up, and he guessed Kalea's did too. "Wait...are you talking about a Lady in a black dress, with red hair? At night?"

She nodded. "Pretty bird lady."

"And when did you see this Lady?" Kalea inquired.

Inaliel frowned again. "Before," she finally said. "Before now. Hurt," she said, trying to explain something she didn't have the words for. "Lady held me. Safe."

Understanding--as well as wonder--dawned on Kalea's face. "She may be talking about a past life," she said. "Sometimes the young remember moments of old incarnations--they usually forget as they grow."

Deven had way more questions than he knew the baby could answer--why would an Elf have gone to Persephone after death? Did Elven souls incarnate across racial boundaries? Could Inaliel have been a Witch once, or a vampire? Was that why she'd been born here and now, into this particular family?

But Inaliel had already lost interest in the conversation, and got down from Deven's lap to chase after Jean Grey, who despite her standoffish and irritable temperament seemed to find her way to wherever Inaliel was with surprising regularity.

"You know, that would make sense," Kalea mused, sitting down in the other chair and offering Deven a glass of wine. "When she was born, Aila--Elendala--wanted to give her a human name, one she'd heard in a dream while she was pregnant. But she was too afraid of what others would think, so she asked your grandmother for help coming up with something similar."

Deven watched the child pick up the cat around the middle and half-drag her to a pillow; Jean Grey went limp, looking resigned, but Deven could hear her purring across the room. "Inaliel would translate as…one who knows, or maybe one who believes?"

"More or less. The name was something we don't really have--a belief in something unknowable, without any empirical evidence. She said it's how humans relate to their gods, most of the time, because they cannot see and touch them as can we. Their Sight is so weak and their ability to connect to the Divine so faint that they have to rely on this blind form of trust that often leads them to despair. It sounded terrible to your grandmother, so they settled on something more in keeping with our own tradition."

"Wait…" Deven sat forward, gripping his wine glass with suddenly cold fingers. "What was the name she wanted to use?"

He heard the baby laugh merrily and looked over in time to see her roll onto her back, the cat licking her forehead fiercely. Inaliel turned her head and met Deven's stare, and to his absolute astonishment, she *winked*.

"I think it was--"

"Faith," Deven said softly. "It was Faith."

*****

No matter the weather, the season, or the situation, there was one place she knew she could always find her husband in Austin...much to her dismay.

The world was coated in crystalline ice, everything gleaming like glass in the street lights. The storms that had brought in all the sleet and frozen the whole city into silence had calmed, leaving the avenues empty, businesses closed, even on a Friday night.

She would never have asked Harlan to drive in such dangerous conditions--the roads to and from the Haven were especially icy this week. The whole Haven, or most of it, was living on their backup blood supply and going a bit stir-crazy unable to leave the house. Elite patrols had been reduced to skeleton crews, and they were staying in town during the day rather than trying to travel to and from the city.

Miranda pulled her coat tight around her and walked out onto the roof of the Winchester building, treading carefully and analyzing each step to avoid slipping. She had opted not to Mist directly to the ledge, lest she appear on an icy patch and tumble off into the freezing air to break her neck on the sidewalk below.

She caught sight of the dark silhouette and sighed. She'd known he was here, but had hoped that for once her senses were misfiring and he was actually back home in a warm, dry room with sane things like blankets and books.

Taking a deep breath to strengthen her resolve, she stepped up onto the ledge and stood next to him for a minute without either speaking.

The city was breathtaking tonight--everything so quiet and peaceful, shining, still. Every great now and then a police cruiser or other car would pick its slow way along Congress and its headlights would burst into dancing color in the prisms of ice covering everything. The winter had been harsh in Central Texas, but she could feel deep in her bones that here in late February the worst was over. Spring would be here in a few weeks and the world would erupt in wildflowers that her kind could never see.

"It's late," she said after a moment. "Come home to bed. The boys are already there warming it up."

He nodded. "I know."

He was a closed book, her Prime, to everyone but her. "They don't have to stay," she said carefully. "They just wanted to see you for a bit."

"It's all right. I want them to stay."

"Okay. Come on, then--it's freezing."

There was the tiniest flicker of a smile. "You mean you're freezing."

"Well, obviously. But you are too, I can tell."

His breath puffed out in a cloud. "Thank you."

"For what? Telling you you're cold? Someone has to."

"No...that's not what I meant. I know things aren't..."

Miranda sighed and resisted the urge to reach for his hand. "It's okay, baby. You're doing the best you can, and you're doing better. We're going to be all right...all of us."

"Are you sure?"

"Absolutely. We're the goddamn Tetrad. We can do anything."

Again, the flicker. "I admire your faith."

"I don't need faith. I know it's true."

Another pause before he said, "I love you."

"I love you too. But I'd love you more if I could feel my nipples."

It had been far too long since she'd heard him laugh, and the sound made her feel warm from the inside out for the first time in weeks.

"All right, all right," he said, turning away from the view and toward her. "You win."

He hopped down off the ledge, and to her surprise, held out a hand to help her down. She was wearing gloves but she could still feel how cold his fingers were; she held onto them and stepped down, taking his hand in both of hers and rubbing it to thaw it out.

"I'm all right," he said, squeezing her fingers.

"Liar," she muttered, intent on her task.

Again, a shock; he touched her face, lifting her chin, and leaned down to kiss her forehead. It wasn't the first time he'd touched her, but such simple gestures of affection had become rare enough that she craved them, constantly afraid that the easy intimacy of their life together was lost forever.

"All right, I'm lying," he said into her hair. "I'm not really all right. But I will be."

"How do you know?"

This time the smile was real, though it was weary, and touched with sadness. "I don't know. But I have faith."

"In Persephone?"

He shook his head slowly. "No. Faith in you, my Queen. Always in you."

She smiled back. "Good answer."

"Let's go home."

Still holding her hand, he led her away from the frosty night and into the Mist.

Made in the USA
Columbia, SC
18 October 2020

23058439R00190